**NOW THAT OUR FRIENDS ARE GONE, HOWEVER, AND THE HOUSE IS QUIET, I FEEL A STRANGE LETHARGY OF SPIRIT CREEPING UPON ME. I TRY NOT TO THINK OF THE VISION I HAD AS WE STOOD ON THE COLD HILLSIDE BENEATH CASTLE DRACULA, BUT IT WILL NOT LET ME ALONE.**

I felt that a tall shape was watching us; a solid, black shadow, simply *watching* yet exuding such an intense, brooding malevolence that it pushed all the breath and reason out of me! Whichever way I looked, it was always behind and to one side of me – yet if I turned, there was never anything there.

I will say nothing to the others. They were all satisfied that the journey was beneficial. But I cannot rid myself of a persistent suspicion, like the most horrible insidious anxiety, that we were dreadfully mistaken to go there again. That it was the worst thing we could possibly have done.

# DRACULA THE UNDEAD

## Freda Warrington

This first world hardcover edition published 2009
in Great Britain and in the USA by
SEVERN HOUSE PUBLISHERS LTD of
9–15 High Street, Sutton, Surrey, England, SM1 1DF,
by arrangement with Harlequin Books.
First published 1997 in the UK only in mass market format.

British Library Cataloguing in Publication Data

Warrington, Freda, 1956-
  Dracula the undead.
  1. Dracula, Count (Fictitious character)--Fiction.
  2. Vampires--Fiction. 3. Graphic novels.
  I. Title
  823.9'14-dc22


ISBN-13: 978-0-7278-6817-6    (cased)

*All Severn House titles are printed on acid-free paper.*


Printed and bound in Great Britain by
MPG Books Ltd., Bodmin, Cornwall.

b18856970

This book is dedicated to the memory of Dee Ann Farey,
talented artist and much-missed friend,
and to her sons, her family, and her husband, Nic Farey,
with love and fond reflection.

'How eagerly is the Devil welcomed under a beautiful form or a fascinating presence, a silvery tongue or a gilded offer of assistance; yet he is the same as would be loathed if presented to the gaze as the incarnation of filth, ugliness, wickedness or fraud.'

*J. Charles Wall*

# Note

'Seven years ago we all went through the flames; and the happiness of some of us since then is, we think, well worth the pain we endured. It is an added joy to Mina and to me that our boy's birthday is the same day as that on which Quincey Morris died. His mother holds, I know, the secret belief that some of our brave friend's spirit has passed into him. His bundle of names links all our little band of men together; but we call him Quincey.

'In the summer of this year we made a journey to Transylvania, and went over the old ground which was, and is, to us so full of vivid and terrible memories. It was almost impossible to believe that the things which we had seen with our own eyes and heard with our own ears were living truths. Every trace of all that had been was blotted out. The castle stood as before, reared high above a waste of desolation.

'When we got home we were talking of the old time – which we could all look back on without despair, for Godalming and Seward are both happily married. I took the papers from the safe where they have been ever since our return so long ago. We were struck with the fact, that in all the mass of material of which the record is composed, there is hardly one authentic document; nothing but a mass of type-writing, except the later notebooks of Mina and Seward and myself, and Van Helsing's memorandum. We could hardly ask anyone, even did we wish to, to accept these as proofs of so wild a story. Van Helsing summed it all up as he said, with our boy on his knee:-

' "We want no proofs; we ask none to believe us! This boy will some day know what a brave and gallant woman his mother is. Already he knows her sweetness and loving care; later on he will understand how some men so loved her, that they did dare much for her sake."

Jonathan Harker'
From *Dracula* by Bram Stoker

# Note

Some of the documents in the following account passed into our hands only a considerable time after the events they describe. Nevertheless, in my type-written transcription, I have incorporated them in as close an approximation of chronological order as possible. In this way, we were able to piece together what had happened, and thus understand – too late, it is true – the manner in which, so soon after my husband wrote his postscript to our dreadful adventures, the disaster gathered and swept over us anew.

Mina Harker

# Chapter One

**22 June**

Van Helsing has proposed a journey to Transylvania. The very idea has given me such a shock that I have come into my study to turn the prospect over in my mind; to see if setting down my thoughts in my journal will help me to reach a decision.

It is nearly seven years since we made our last trip and destroyed the monster, Count Dracula. There is something significant, almost magical about the figure seven; it seems an anniversary of great meaning, coinciding as it does with the new century. It is like the crossing of a symbolic bridge. Quite irrational, yet very potent, so Van Helsing says. At least, that is how he explains the sudden dwelling of our thoughts, in recent months, on the events of seven years ago.

As I sit in my study, contemplating the garden through the tangle of pink climbing roses that droops across the window, I cannot help reflecting upon our happiness since Mina and I came to live in Exeter, in the house of my dear late friend Mr Hawkins, who was as much a father and mentor as a kind employer to me. We miss him still, and it feels wholly right that we have made his home our own. It was what he wished. Mina and I have had every reason for contentment (excepting only the frequent illnesses of our boy). Why, then, is it, that of late I have been plagued by memories and nightmares of Dracula?

Mina, I know, thinks that I have never been my old self since my ordeal at Castle Dracula. I have been happy; I thought the ghosts would slumber for ever. But several times in past months I have woken, sweating and trembling, from some oppressive dream of a smothering darkness, of dust-laden cobwebs and malevolent scarlet eyes.

Van Helsing says that it is a natural working of the mind, to submerge bad memories for a time, then to be ambushed by their sudden return to the surface. There is a lingering terror that the monster is not truly gone; that time has deceived one's memory. The good professor's solution is drastic. 'A journey back over the old ground will serve a dual purpose,' he said. 'First, to reassure ourselves that the evil was, indeed, utterly destroyed, to drive out sick imaginings with healthy reality. Second, to perform a Christian rite at the spot, to bless it and thus ensure – for the sake of that country and of Dracula himself, as much as our own – that the haunts of the monster are cleansed and his wretched soul truly at peace. To that end, all those of our little band who survived must go; that is, Mina and Jonathan, Lord Godalming, Dr Seward, and myself.'

I confess, I do not want to go. The thought fills me with panic. But Mina is in accord with Van Helsing, even though it will mean her being separated from Quincey for several weeks. If she thinks it is important enough to leave the boy, then I cannot argue.

Well, I have made my decision. We must go; I must face my fears. Yet I have the gravest reservations. At the very thought of Transylvania, a darkness presses on my eyes and my heart tries to lift out of my chest in cold terror. A brandy. God help me hide these fears from Mina!

Memo: Must ask Joseph to cut away these roses from the window. They are overblown, they obscure the view and their thorns scratch at the window. If they are not pruned, I believe they will choke the whole house.

14 July, Buda-Pesth

My darling Quincey,

Did you receive our letter of yesterday? That was written on the train from Vienna, but we are now arrived in Buda-Pesth and the city is beautiful. Cities, I should say, since the River Danube divides the two parts. We showed you on the map before we left, do you remember? Papa and I have been strolling around some magnificent buildings of every imaginable style. I wish you were with us. There are delightful fountains everywhere, which you would love. One day, when you are older and stronger, you will travel with us, I promise.

We are staying here for two days, before travelling south and east to see the mountains of Transylvania. Then it will be time to begin our journey home. Pleasant as it is to travel, it will be so much more exciting to see you again!

I hope you are feeling stronger and eating well. The fresh summer air is good for you, so get plenty of it – only take care not to overtire yourself, or catch a chill. Be good for Mrs Seward and Nurse. Papa and your uncles Arthur, John and Abraham send love and kisses – as do I. I shall write again tomorrow – until then,

Your loving,
Mama

## MINA HARKER'S JOURNAL

### 18 July

How strange it feels to retrace the steps that Jonathan first took more than seven years ago, and in which I followed – in such dire circumstances, but with such loyal friends! – a few months after. By train to Munich, onwards to Vienna and Buda-Pesth. As well as Jonathan and myself, all our party is here; Abraham Van Helsing, Dr Seward,.Lord Godalming. All, that is, except brave Quincey Morris, who gave his life to save us. He is with us in spirit, I know.

We have time to look round this time, and Buda-Pesth is delightful, an eclectic mix of Gothic, baroque and classical architecture, with water burgeoning everwhere in the form of fountains, springs and hot baths. We are staying two nights with a friend of Van Helsing, Professor André Kovacs of Pesth University. In a way I wish we could forge on with our journey, tiring as it would be, rather than interrupt it for social calls. Not that I feel unsocial, but I dearly wish this journey to be over as soon as possible. The past, and the thought of going back over the ground where the events took place, cast a shadow over my heart. However often I tell myself that it is all over and there is nothing to fear, I cannot shake it off!

I am sitting in an airy room with a most lovely view across the Danube. Professor Kovacs, a bachelor, is a delightful man, tall and energetic, with a fine intellect. His features are rather strong and heavy but his ready smile and brown eyes reveal a kind soul. He has the most wonderful head of thick silver-grey hair! He lives in this house with his widowed brother Emil, and niece, Elena. The brother I like less, though I know one should not go by first impressions. He is courteous enough, but seems always to be frowning and displeased by everything. He is an artist. Perhaps we should excuse his disagreeable demeanour as artistic temperament! At any rate, his daughter, Elena, seems unspoiled by it. She is eighteen and a most charming girl, quiet, demure and self-effacing. A little lacking in spirit, if anything.

They have another guest, a cheerful, blond young man named Miklos. He is one of the Professor's students and paying court, I gather, to Elena. Professor Kovacs treats him like a son.

4

We have not explained the reason for which we are making this journey to Transylvania. I believe Van Helsing has told them we are simply enjoying a tour. I do hate to tell untruths, and that would have been another reason to travel with speed and privacy. Still, I must not let the others think I am ungrateful for this warm Hungarian hospitality!

They are calling us now for dinner. I will continue this as soon as I may.

### 19 July

We have had a change of plan. It will inconvenience us hardly at all, except that we will be unable to talk freely amongst ourselves about certain matters as we travel – but perhaps that is just as well. It will make the journey seem less burdensome.

Last night at dinner, Emil was speaking of his intention to go to Transylvania with his daughter to paint a series of landscapes. Professor Kovacs was making a joke of this. 'The peasants of Transylvania come to Buda-Pesth to find work,' he said, 'while all the artists of Buda-Pesth flock to Transylvania to paint!'

Van Helsing laughed. 'Is this considered a fair exchange?'

Emil told us that he knows a family of Szekely farmers with whom he has twice before spent the summer in order to paint. Their farm, he said, is on the edge of a village beyond Bistritz and near to the Borgo Pass. As he spoke, Jonathan looked at me, and there passed between us a sort of mutual agreement that we would say nothing. It was Van Helsing, however, who at once exclaimed, 'But that is our destination; I mean, to explore the Carpathians from the Borgo Pass!'

Emil replied at once, 'Then we shall travel together. Elena and I can leave with you, we have no special time at which to arrive; the family are always glad to receive us. Indeed, you shall stay with us at the farm!'

'But this is excellent!' said Van Helsing. 'It will make easier

5

our expedition, if we have not to travel from Bistritz into the mountains in one day.'

I said, 'As long as it will put the farmers to no trouble.' I was taken with Emil's outburst of friendliness and thought I had probably mistaken his sullen demeanour after all.

'No trouble,' said he. 'They delight in visitors. The kindness of Transylvanians to strangers is legendary.'

'Indeed,' I said. 'It will be only for a short time, anyway, two or three nights at most.'

So it is all decided. Emil and his daughter will join our party, and we shall convey them with their easels and paints to the farm, and there leave them when we depart again for home. Ah, how I anticipate that time! I miss our son so much. I must stop now and write to him. Jonathan and I are preparing for bed. We left Van Helsing alone with Professor Kovacs, no doubt to talk late into the night and catch up on several years' wisdom. Kovacs is an historian with an interest in folklore . . . I wish – oh, unworthy thought – that I could eavesdrop upon their conversation! Sometimes I think Van Helsing a little indiscreet, and it would surprise me not at all if he told his friend about our experience with Count Dracula.

### 21 July

I am writing on the train to Bistritz, which seems interminably slow although the landscape through which we pass is picturesque. We spent last night in Klausenburgh, from whence I wrote to tell Quincey of the spires, cupolas, red-tiled mansions and storks' nests. And of our strange hotel; a double door led through a vaulted passageway to a shrub-filled courtyard, from which a staircase curved up to the timber galleries which ran along the rows of bedrooms. The rooms were clean enough, but inferior, Jonathan said, to the hotel in which he stayed last time. He wanted to stay at a different place so that no one from last time should recognize him. The people here are kind, but so curious and superstitious! I can understand him wanting to avoid their attentions. I did not mind, but the tall courtyard with its shadowed galleries was very eerie. Once as I crossed it, I glimpsed in an alcove a tiny gypsy woman, brown and gnarled within layer upon layer of filthy clothes, a twist of black hair upon her head. She made a sign against the evil eye at me and said something in Roumanian, which I half understood. 'His blood and yours,' or something of that sort. I cannot explain it, but her feral look and her words sent a violent shiver through me. Yet when I pulled at Jonathan's sleeve to point her out, she had vanished! Whether she was a spirit, or had simply slipped away, I could not say. To think of it makes me shudder. I was very glad to leave that place!

I have talked a little to Elena on the journey. She is shy, but warming to me as we become acquainted. Her English is excellent, and her German puts mine to shame – and my Hungarian, of course, is non-existent, so why she should be in awe of me I do not know! She asked what I was writing, and I told her that I always keep up a journal, however uneventful our domestic life may sometimes be (I thank God for those quiet times, I must confess).

I suppose I am a creature of routine. Besides, I was determined that the end of those dreadful events would not mark the end of my diary-keeping. There is Quincey's capricious health to provide drama enough, and Jonathan's work at Hawkins & Harker, of course.

I am missing Quincey terribly, though I know he is safe in the care of Mrs Seward, Mary and his nurse. I have written to him every day since we left England. He reads well and is quite the young man, as I have been telling Elena! I have always encouraged him to read. At least he will have rich compensation in life for being less vigorous than his fellows.

But let me not dwell on that now. Very strange, as I said, that this journey should feel so familiar yet so different. The season is warm and lush, and we make our way without the urgency that so oppressed us before. This time we have leisure to enjoy the tranquil green slopes of central Transylvania. There are long gradual climbs, where brown and white sheep graze on the grassy hillsides that appear to sweep up to the very sky. We passed a tall flour mill where horses and donkeys stood with their muzzles in nosebags, waiting for their loads to be milled. We also see many wagons drawn by oxen and buffalo, as the train makes its way past dense beech woods and along fertile valleys where red-roofed villages and ochre churches nestle. The buildings are quite beautiful, with decorative plasterwork under the eaves, pillars and wrought-iron balconies. The shepherds – who wear ankle-length fleece coats and have ferocious-looking white dogs with spiked collars – hold an honoured place here, so Emil tells us. I notice so much that I failed to see last time! I reflected then, I recall, what a pleasure it would be to fill our minds and memories with all the wonders of this beautiful wild country. Jonathan seems at peace, but sometimes he is quiet, and lines gather in his dear face. Then I know he is remembering. Dr Seward, too, often looks sombre, but Van Helsing is hearty, reminding us that the past is over, that we triumphed and must therefore retrace our steps with light hearts.

All the same, the nearer we go to Castle Dracula, the more nervous I feel. Yet I am strangely excited, too, for I know there is nothing there now to harm us. I must be cheerful, at all events. Jonathan broods enough for both of us, and it is my duty to be strong for him.

We are arriving at Bistritz. Once we are at our hotel, Dr Seward and Lord Godalming will go to procure a carriage and horses to convey us to Emil's friends in the foothills of the Carpathians. That will make the last stage of our journey far less arduous, and possible to complete, we hope, in a day. That eases my anxiety considerably, most of all for Dr Van Helsing who, for all his lion-like spirit, is not a young man and tires easily.

## 22 July

Today we travelled from Bistritz to the farm, with Jonathan, Dr Seward and Lord Godalming taking it in turns to drive. We wound our way through hilly farmland, the great spruce-covered folds of the mountains drawing ever closer, and beyond them the bare peaks wreathed with cloud on the horizon. The villages have long rows of single-storey dwellings built of wood and stone or brick, wrought-iron gates leading to tidy yards with conical hayricks constructed around poles. All seems fecund, with fruit trees everywhere; apple and plum, pear, apricot and cherry.

The farm, at the far end of the village, was concealed by a stand of birch trees, their leaves and silver trunks glittering softly. Then the trees parted and we saw the magnificent arched gateway that led to the farmyard. The moment Lord Godalming checked the horses, a crowd came surging out to meet us; women and girls in striped aprons, full skirts and sheepskin bodices, men in homespun trousers and tunics with cowhide boots. Some of them took charge of our carriage, others ushered us into the yard. Here were more hayricks, vines trailing over trellis, pigs rooting, geese and hens in coops, with their chicks running free. The house itself is a beautiful old building of wood, with splendid carved pillars and narrow balconies under the wide eaves. Yet the house is almost dwarfed by the great barn with double doors that stands nearby! Behind the farm, beyond its orchards and pastures, runs a high forested ridge which, Emil tells us, is badly infested with wolves. The sight of that steep dark slope reminds me that we have not far to go. A chill goes through me at the thought.

The farmer is a big man with a prodigious black moustache, his wife a rotund, merry soul with ruddy cheeks and black hair. They welcomed us warmly and with much broken German and sign language. Their welcome for Emil and Elena was one of overwhelming friendliness, as if they were long-lost family! Dr Van Helsing explained that we shall require accommodation for two nights only. I think they would be happy for us to stay all summer, so hospitable are they! Basking in this rural life for a month or two would be pleasant, were I not so eager to see Quincey again.

Our hosts have seven children, almost grown to adulthood, three daughters and four sons, all as strong, simple and superstitious as their parents. Not that I would ever mock their superstitions! Emil seems more vivacious among them than I have observed him with his brother or with us, but Elena – though she is always smiling and deferential – seems ill at ease. Perhaps she prefers city life, but I sense that her father has given her no say in the matter. I will try to win her confidence tonight.

We are in a most pleasant room, simple and clean, with a view of apple and cherry trees and green pastures. I can hear birds singing and sheep bells tinkling. This all seems so cosy and pleasant, such a contrast to our last journey! We are being called down to dinner.

### Later

Jonathan is asleep in bed now but I am wide awake. At last I have had a good long talk with Elena! The family provided a lavish meal and we did it justice. Afterwards, Emil went for a stroll to seek vantage points from which to paint, and all our men went with him. The womenfolk were busy in the kitchen, so Elena and I were left alone by the fireplace in a tiny parlour with carved wooden tankards hanging on the walls, and many embroidered cushions scattered on the bench seats. She is a very handsome girl, with a sweet oval face, a rosy, brilliant complexion, dark smooth hair and brown eyes, and very dark, thick brows and lashes. She is slender but of no great height, so her form gives a pleasing impression of compactness and grace.

I did my best to put her at ease. Jonathan and I both know

what it is to work and serve others, so we have no airs and graces. I remarked on her excellent English. Her cheeks dimpled and her eyes shone as she replied, 'Madam Harker, my uncle André has always insisted that I be fluent in other languages. But my father is not so eager that I speak English. I hope you forgive my impoliteness, but that is why I have spoken to you so little. I wanted to!'

'But why would your father not wish you to speak English?'

She lowered her deep lids, her lashes making long black crescents against her cheeks. 'Oh, he does not like me to learn or know too much. He does not think that education should be for women.' She looked up and spoke with sudden passion. 'I feel there is so much you could teach me! We have so little time! If only I could come with you upon your journey tomorrow, we could talk all day!'

How I hated to refuse her! It oppresses me deeply to conceal the truth. To pretend that we are here for the sake of idle curiosity and amusement, when the true reason is so dire –! I refused her as gently as possible, and she took the refusal with serenity. But she is perceptive. She said hesitantly, in her beautifully accented English, 'Madam Harker, if you will forgive me so saying, you seem weary, and sad, as if a shadow lay on you.'

I answered, not untruthfully, 'I am missing my son.'

'Quincey,' she said, with a smile. 'Is that a usual English name?'

'It is more common in America,' I said. 'It was the name of a very dear American friend of ours, who died bravely.'

'I'm sorry. How old is your child?'

'He will be six in November.' I opened my locket and showed her the photograph of Quincey. I noticed that Elena's hands are quite large, the fingers long and well-shaped.

'Oh, he looks a beautiful, strong boy!'

'I wish he were stronger.' I told her how Quincey, since he was stricken by rheumatic fever at the age of two, has been weak and sickly. It shames me to admit it but tears came to my eyes. (Quincey needs my care, not my tears – and I will never cry for myself.) I think it was only the prospect of tomorrow's worrisome journey that so weighed on me. I mastered myself. 'He may not be strong in body, but his character and soul are the kindest that ever a child possessed.'

'I see it in his face. He has his mother's eyes,' Elena answered. 'Have you other children?'

Tears nearly came again! I explained that his birth was difficult and the doctors have told me I will almost certainly never conceive again. There, that is the first time I have ever written it. It was not so hard. Elena looked thoughtful, almost fierce in a strange way, and for some reason I found that far easier to bear than sympathy.

'But then you are free!' she whispered.

'In what way?' I said, startled. 'How can "freedom" from children be in any way fulfilling?'

'My father expects me to marry Miklos – that is, the young man that was at my uncle's house. A woman is born to serve her husband, then to serve her sons – but until then, I exist to serve my father. I try, but always he wants something different! He wants me married, yet he wants to keep me to himself. If I dare to speak to Miklos, he becomes furious, because we are not yet engaged! I do not know what I am to do to please him!'

She sounded distressed. 'Don't you love Miklos?' I said. 'You mustn't marry him if you have no feeling for him.'

'Oh, I like him well enough,' she said darkly. 'But only as a friend, a brother. I am not sure that I ever want to marry.'

I was shocked. 'But surely you must want children?'

'Oh, I am very fond of them,' she replied quickly. 'I would like a son, but without the rest . . .'

I laughed. 'My dear, you cannot have a son without a husband!'

'But is there no more to life than marriage? Nothing else

for me to do? Forgive me, I do not express myself well.'

'No, you do, very well,' I reassured her. 'But there is no greater fulfilment than motherhood. And look what rich lives these farmers have, living a simple life on the land. Sometimes I wish our own lives were so uncomplicated!'

'But I wish to travel, as you do, Madam Harker,' she said. Her face was very intent, the fire making two gold diamonds in her eyes. 'I admire you so much. I dream of being an English gentlewoman like you. When you are gone I shall try to be like you in everything! But in secret, only in my mind, otherwise my father –'

She stopped, and her face became fearful. I took her hand. 'You are a gentlewoman, Elena. You have all the womanly virtues; grace, kindness and dignity in what you are. I am sure your father could not be anything but proud of you.'

She almost crushed my hand between her own two, and her tears dripped on to our joined fingers. 'I want to go to England. I didn't know, until I met you. But now it is my dearest wish!'

The door opened and she pulled away quickly. Emil stood glowering at her, looking very fierce in the red firelight. He nodded to me, but said some gruff words to her. We rose, and Elena almost ran from the room with a muttered – and quite unnecessary – word of apology to me, and I came up to bed.

Enough now. Sleep is calling, and I must write to Quincey before I lie down beside Jonathan. I am so grateful to Elena for keeping my mind from tomorrow's journey!

### 23 July
It is over. What a day of wonder!

Lord Godalming and Dr Seward harnessed the horses at dawn. Mindful of our hosts' powerful beliefs and superstitions, we told no one our destination. We were in wonderful spirits, in the circumstances – perhaps because of them! The human spirit will always rally under duress. The sun was shining gently and the country looked so soft and green, filled with woods and fruit groves, it was hard to believe that such evil had ever been visited upon it – or, indeed, emanated from it.

But as the road climbed out of the valley, the landscape changed and we all grew quiet and sombre. Beech woods gave way to steep spruce forests which darkened the curving road through the foothills. The crags and peaks of the Carpathians towered around us in majestic, ever-changing perspectives against the sky. We passed deep narrow gorges, boulder-strewn rivers. I confess I felt a shiver, a echo of old fear and newborn excitement. Jonathan held my hand tight, but his gaze was far away. I see him remembering, at every stage of our journey, the thoughts and feelings of the past. Lord Godalming – climbing into the carriage as Dr Seward took over the reins – said as if to himself, 'I wonder why we are forcing ourselves through this.'

Van Helsing immediately clapped him on the shoulder and said, 'Courage, my friend! It is precisely to remove any trace of such doubt and fear that we make this pilgrimage!'

What a strange group of tourists we are.

As we reached the flat saddle of the pass, with the mountain walls close around us, I was suddenly aware how cold the air had turned. We had left summer behind and moved into the great, rolling atmosphere of the peaks. Although the sun shone, both air and light seemed thin, chill and ghostly. Dr Seward turned on to the neglected road that leads to Castle Dracula. He urged the horses on faster, and the carriage bounced on the rocky way. I hoped no mishap would befall us, no horse go lame or wheel come adrift, for I should hate to be stranded here, even believing the curse to be gone. Evil leaves its mark, I believe, at least in the atmosphere of a place. Perhaps as a reminder, a warning. I touched the little cross which I still wear, out of habit. And I thanked God that

I *could* touch it and not be burned; thanked Him for taking that curse from me.

As the road climbed through the wild mountains it seemed every bit as bleak and desolate as I remember, a journey of hours into the heart of a wasteland. We heard cataracts of water falling between the crags, strange birds calling from the wind-twisted trees. I thought I heard a wolf howl, although it may have been a dog on some isolated farm.

When we came in sight of the castle, Dr Seward reined in and we all got down while he unharnessed the horses to let them rest. Then we went a way on foot, our eyes fixed on the bleak wild battlements that rose above the deep precipice. Storm clouds were gathering behind it. I began to shiver and my heart beat strongly. Jonathan and I held each other's hands very tight. How pale his hair looked against the darkness of the rock. It turned white in shock when the vampire's curse was so nearly visited upon me, and has remained so ever since.

Van Helsing mopped the high dome of his forehead. I knew he was remembering his grisly work in the castle, his staking and laying to rest of the three female vampires within the old chapel. I am ever grateful to have been spared the horror of witnessing that terrible act of mercy – but how keenly I shared his feelings!

About a mile from the castle, we came to the place where both Dracula and brave Quincey Morris met their ends. We recognized the boulder on the slope above, where Dr Van Helsing and I had sheltered and watched our men pursuing the Szgany gypsies who were taking the monster back to his castle. There were some splinters of wood in the straggling grass at the sides of the road. I wondered if they were pieces of the cart or the box ... Most likely they were just fallen branches, blown from the trees and weathered by the winter.

In silence we climbed up to the boulder. I was quiet but my emotions ran deep, and all at once surged through me, making me dizzy. I felt the bite of coldness. A great cloud seemed to swirl around us, full of snow and a strange icy light. Through it – in my memory, yet so vividly that it might actually have been happening – I saw men riding hard through the snow.

I heard the thunder of hooves and wheels. There was the band of gypsy brigands, guiding the long cart with its ghastly cargo back towards Castle Dracula. I was shivering in the cruel blasts of wind. I saw the cart rolling and swaying under the weight of the earth-box. The mountains seemed stark and hard as iron, while the clouds thickened around us. The whole desolate kingdom was filled with the howling of wolves. Thick, swirling snow continuously blotted our view, but between flurries I saw Jonathan, Dr Seward, Lord Godalming and Mr Morris riding hard after the gypsies. All the action seemed condensed, vivid as the frigid sunlight that gleamed through the edges of the snow-clouds. I saw our men meet the Szgany in violent conflict, striving to reach the Count before sunset gave him back his unholy power. The sun was sinking fast, turning blood-red. The world trembled around me.

Then the lid of the earth box was flung back, and I saw the Count! His face was pallid as wax and corpse-like – but his eyes were open and blazed red! They stared straight at me through the chill mist and the sweeping snow, and the hellish glare of them stays with me now for ever.

Then the great knives of Jonathan and Quincey Morris came shearing down. Dracula's body crumbled to dust – but not before a look of peace had replaced the malevolence. I saw Quincey's blood run crimson on to the snow as he died, our brave friend, pointing to me with joy on his face. For the mark had left my forehead and the curse was over.

I came out of the vision with a shudder. None of the others seemed to notice; I suppose the whole thing must have been over in a few seconds. Had they, too, relived those moments?

I did not ask, for we were all alone with our thoughts. In reality the landscape was quiet, the only snow shining on far-off peaks, the sky darkest grey. Peaceful, but in a brooding, waiting way.

Suddenly the clouds rolled apart, and the sun fell down in golden veils. We all lifted up our eyes, and Jonathan said, 'Look!'

Castle Dracula stood against the sky, on a towering stump that appeared to rise unconnected from the earth and forest around it. I knew its twisted battlements, its bleak stones. But while the sky behind it was black, the castle itself glowed in the rays, as if it had turned to pure, beaten bronze!

Dr Van Helsing laughed, and clasped Jonathan's shoulder. 'It is so!' he exclaimed. 'The curse is gone. We lifted it, by God's grace, and it has not returned! Thank God!'

He led us in our little ritual; hymns, prayers, and the scattering of holy water. Then we turned for home.

I can write no more. I am exhausted, and Jonathan is already asleep. Our emotions are all too mixed and vivid to set down. Surely they need no more expression. Except to say that our main feeling is of gratitude, not elation. We feel no vaunting pride that we were the instruments of Dracula's downfall. We did what we must, that was all – for the sake of poor, beloved Lucy, and for all the other innocent victims who might have been. We did what we must.

### 25 July, evening

On the train back to Buda-Pesth; now we feel like true holiday-makers, carefree and merry! I felt sorry to leave Transylvania after all. Its ghosts laid to rest, the land seemed to take on a bloom of extraordinary beauty, and we came away laden with gifts from the farmers. Such good, generous people.

Elena spoke to me again last night and this morning as we took a last stroll around the farm. She was nervous of her father seeing her with me. He is a brusque, capricious man, and I can hardly blame her for desiring to keep his temper sweet.

Again she expressed to me her deep wish to travel and be educated. Poor girl, I wish there were something I could do to aid her! On reflection it does seem a waste that such a bright mind should be condemned to a life that she does not want. Is it a sin to be discontented with one's lot? I did not put this question to her, however, for I wished her to feel that I empathized, not that I condemned her.

I said, trying to cheer her, 'At least you have summer to look forward to in this beautiful place, which will give you time to make up your mind about Miklos. I would love to paint! You must find great satisfaction in your art, and companionship with your father through it.'

She lowered her head. 'Oh, Madam Harker, I do not paint.'

'But I thought –'

'My father is the artist,' she said, with a strange mix of humility and bitterness. 'I carry his paints and brushes and easel, I find him the most comfortable place to sit, I provide him with refreshment and praise – but I do not paint! He would never tolerate me aping his skill. He wouldn't abide it!'

While I am no supporter of the 'New Woman', I felt her sense of injustice very keenly. 'You mind very much, don't you? This is too bad! There is nothing unfeminine in sketching or painting in watercolours. Do you want me to speak to him?'

'No!' she cried, looking horrified. 'No, Madam Harker, it is so kind of you, but please do not. He would smile and nod at your suggestion, but when you are gone he would be furious with me! Anyway, it is not painting I care about. It is – what is the phrase? The principle. To travel, to write, to be free – they are what I crave. But all is impossible!'

When I wrote that Elena has little spirit, I was very wrong. She strikes me as being a creature of passionate ideals that have budded on a strange, dark vine.

'Well, the least I can do is help you to write,' I said.

Back in the farmhouse I gave her my English–Hungarian dictionary, a fresh notepad, pens and ink. They were all I had to offer. Elena was so overcome I thought she would fall down and kiss my feet! 'Oh, Madam Harker!' she said, tears rolling down her dimpled cheeks. 'I shall keep a journal, in –' she looked quickly through the dictionary – 'in emulation of you!'

I am glad I was able to make her so happy, with so small a gesture. But she remains uneasily in my thoughts. Was there truly nothing more I could have done for her? I suppose not. She was so unusual and charming that I cannot forget her. I have good friends, but none as close as dear Lucy was . . . and I shall never have a daughter. But with such a good husband and son as I have, I should be more than content with my lot.

### 30 July, Exeter

Home, to find that Quincey has had bronchitis! He is over the worst of it but very pale and wheezy. Alice Seward – Dr Seward could not have married a kinder, more sensible woman – has looked after him admirably, but still I was distressed and thought she should have called me home. Jonathan pointed out that even if she had, we could hardly have been home much sooner than we were.

I wish I were not so anxious a mother – but since I am, I shall keep my worries between myself and my journal, and not trouble Quincey or Jonathan with them! Both Dr Seward and Dr Van Helsing have examined the boy and say he will be well, and I am not to worry. Indeed, he had recovered enough to be bounced on Dr Van Helsing's knee!

We took out all the old papers, diaries and cuttings we

had assembled to record our encounter with Dracula. It was strange to read through them again. Far away, like a dream, yet painfully fresh as if it all happened yesterday! It did us good to talk it through. Jonathan says he will make a note of our recent pilgrimage (as Dr Van Helsing will insist on calling it) in order to round off the notes. Then we will feel that all is truly laid to rest.

Van Helsing made a confession afterwards. 'While we were in Buda-Pesth, I told my good friend André Kovacs about our experience. We talked long into the night. I need to talk of it and he – not like the sceptical fools who call themselves "scientist" – I knew would believe our story in every particular. Forgive my indiscretion, but the mingling of history and folklore is his interest also. He was disturbed and intrigued; he hears also many rumours over the years that come from the Carpathians and Castle Dracula. A place of which no mortal knows the truth, because no mortal dares to go there! But to hear the rumours are truth and not peasant imaginings – of this he is most happy and excited to learn!'

'Well, I am glad someone got some entertainment out of it,' Jonathan said drily.

In a few days our guests will depart – the Sewards and Lord Godalming to London, Dr Van Helsing to Amsterdam – and Jonathan and I shall return to our happy, comfortable existence. Jonathan will go back to work, and I shall have time to spend with our boy. I'll test his reading by asking him to read aloud the letters I sent, and then I shall tell him all about our trip.

Well, not *all*. One day, when he is of an age to understand, I will tell him the truth – but not yet. And by God's grace he will live to see such an age.

## 10 August

Last week after our return from Transylvania, I wrote a note to round off the collection of documents that make up our account of Dracula. I was in good spirits when I wrote it. I felt that it marked a closure to that time, a fresh, unstained beginning.

Now that our friends are gone, however, and the house is quiet, I feel a strange lethargy of spirit creeping upon me. I try not to think of the vision I had as we stood on the cold hillside beneath Castle Dracula, but it will not let me alone.

I felt that a tall shape was watching us; a solid black shadow, simply *watching* yet exuding such an intense, brooding malevolence that it pushed all the breath and reason out of me! Whichever way I looked, it was always behind and to one side of me – yet if I turned, there was never anything there.

I will say nothing to the others. They were all satisfied that the journey was beneficial. But I cannot rid myself of a persistent suspicion, like the most horrible insidious anxiety, that we were dreadfully mistaken to go there again. That it was the worst thing we could possibly have done.

# Chapter Two

4 August, Buda-Pesth

My dear Abraham,

It was so good to see you. Since your visit and our conversation, I have thought of nothing but the matters which we discussed – that is, your strange and wild tale of Count Dracula!

All my life I have studied tales from the 'horseshoe' of the Carpathians, that maelstrom of myth and superstition, tales of werewolves, vampires and the like. With my own eyes I have seen, in a Transylvanian village, the peasants rip the lid from a coffin buried a year and stake the corpse within – a corpse that looked fresh as life, and which screamed when it was pierced, issuing streams of fresh scarlet blood! Long have I tried to rationalize this as some natural phenomenon; unusual ground conditions that preserved the body, gas escaping, the blood a strange illusion created by my brain seeing what it feared to see, etc. – But now that you, a scientist as incredulous as myself, have found these matters to have a basis in fact, I find myself able, after all these years, to relax my cynicism. Suppose that such things can – through some wild combination, as you say, of natural, supernatural and diabolical forces – actually exist! And indeed, you and your friends have experienced it at first hand.

I had long heard rumours of a castle where the noble

family had died out, yet perhaps not altogether *died*. Now you say that these rumours were nothing less than the truth, veiled in whispers because no one dared to voice them aloud. I rejoice to hear that the curse is gone. However . . .

I write to tell you that your visit has inspired me to a project. The most intriguing of the matters we discussed you merely glanced upon, yet I feel it to be central. I refer to another place of myth and rumour, which has nonethless commanded my imagination. Friend Abraham, I have found mention of this place several times during my years of study, so to hear it mentioned again in connection with Dracula has fired my curiosity. I speak, of course, of the Scholomance.

Let me reiterate what we know of the Scholomance. First, that it was a 'school' or academy reputedly run by the Devil himself. Here he taught *in person* the arts of magic, the secrets of nature and the language of animals. Second, that he took only ten scholars at one time. At the end of the course of learning, nine scholars were released to exploit their dark arts in the outside world, while the tenth was kept by the Devil in payment. Third, that some members of the great Dracula family were reputed to have attended the school and there learned occult powers from the Evil One. Fourth, that Count Dracula himself may have learned his dark arts there. Lastly, that the Scholomance was supposed to lie somewhere above Hermannstadt, in the Carpathian mountains that divide Transylvania from Wallachia.

Whatever truth may lie behind the myth, it is my intention to discover it.

The initial expedition, I estimate, will take a month; two weeks to explore the mountains, a few days on either side for travel, preparation and rest. Miklos – my student and good friend, the nearest I will ever

23

have to a son – is coming with me. If we find anything of note, a more thorough expedition can then be mounted. I shall be back long before my brother and niece return from Transylvania, so there is no point in informing them of my plans.

I plan to keep a detailed journal in English for your benefit, so that when we meet again, you may immediately read of my adventure – if indeed I have anything to report. Wish me luck!

Your friend,
André Kovacs

PS Miklos wishes to marry Elena, but this will take place 'over my dead body', as the English say. She does not really want him; she blows hot and cold, according to my brother's whims, while *he* wishes some miracle would take place whereby she could give him grandsons without the intervention of a husband! I have to protect my dear Miklos from their machinations. Between them they would crush him.

– A. K.

## Elena Kovacs's Journal

### 25 July

I mean to keep a journal in imitation of our gracious English visitor, Madam Harker. She gave me the book, pens and ink. I will write very small, so that paper and ink shall last a long time – I could get none from Father without explaining why I need it. And I shall practise my poor English, to improve it – and so that my father may understand it less readily, should he ever find it.

I wish I need not write in secret, but I must. Father must never see this precious book. I know it would make him angry. And what might I record that must be concealed from his eyes? Simply the thoughts in my head, since I am not supposed to have any. Secrecy is sinful, but I will not dwell on that or I will never set down a word.

I have a little downstairs room to myself, which overlooks the rear farmyard. I can see the well, the side of the great barn and the orchards, and the pigs and poultry running about. Beyond the fruit trees, the forested ridge rises up as a great misty wall. It makes me feel lonely; I imagine jumping over the window-sill, running away and being lost on that ridge . . .

The farmer's daughters are as dear as sisters to me, but I am glad I do not have to share their room or I should never have a moment to myself. They are good girls but so simple, wanting nothing but to marry shepherds and breed more little shepherds. We have nothing in common. They could never understand me – why should they, when I do not understand myself?

I don't know what I shall write, in any case. I have spent so much time on this farm that nothing is new any more. Shall I write of turkeys and geese, the daily comings and goings of peasants, the long hours spent sitting at my father's feet while he paints on the slope of some pasture? Well, I may write about the visit of our English guests, at least.

I feel a strange yearning. Madam Harker did not create it, but she enflamed it. If she had not visited us, if she had not taken so kind an interest in me, surely this ache in my breast would not have stirred so fiercely! She brought the soul of England with her, with her beautiful sombre clothes and her lovely manners and fair complexion. She will never know what excitement she brought to my life . . . but now she is gone, how small my world seems. Not the physical world but the world with my father. I can *see* how vast and beautiful the world is, but he puts me in a little glass box.

Why do I feel this urge to defy him? Am I a changeling? If I were the dutiful daughter he wanted, I would not feel so afraid – so trapped!

God forgive me for such sentiments! There, that is why these words must be hidden from his eyes. I want so much from life, and here there seems to be so little!

I wish I knew where they went on their mysterious carriage journey. It made a change in all our guests, but most of all I noticed it in Madam Harker. Before she went to the Borgo Pass she was troubled, as if they brought some dark secret on their 'holiday'. Perhaps I imagine too much. But when they came back they were different, light of heart and laughing, as if they had found out something that pleased them. I don't mean they were (I must consult the dictionary...) frivolous. Madam Harker could never be frivolous or silly, as my father says women of foreign cities are. She was serene, glowing, and happier than before she left. Perhaps it was only that she is returning to her son.

The change in her mood made me feel strange. It made me ... frightened. Why? I did not realize until I wrote it. Oh, now I scare myself for no reason. How I hate the superstitions of this land! I hate them the more because I cannot dismiss them. They creep into the blood and become real. I wish I was like Madam Harker, brought up in a land free from beliefs that men change into wolves or that the dead can -- no, no more. I wish that I lived in a land of reason!

When Madam Harker first arrived, there was a shadow of sadness inside her. But when she and her party returned from their unexplained journey, the shadow had changed. It was still there, but outside her, so she was no longer aware of it. And it fell on me instead. By 'shadow' I mean a feeling, a mood ... some wisp of pain, fear and excitement mixed, but when I try to get hold of it, it vanishes between my hands. And then I forget it, and it appears again. Like something watching. This makes me shiver, I need my shawl. I did not begin this journal to frighten myself... or was the fear inside all the time, and writing only brings it out? There, I have learned something, but not the knowledge I thought I was seeking.

Father is calling me. My precious book, I must hide you!

### 30 July

I have been wondering about my mother. I barely remember her. She died of fever when I was a small child, my father says. This morning I was looking at the farmer's wife, her hands red-raw from endless washing, cooking, sewing, goat-milking, her face red-brown from the weather, and her daughters the same, and I wondered if my mother was like that! Or was she elegant like Madam Mina, intelligent and accomplished, with white hands and beautiful clothes? My father hates me to ask questions. I could ask Uncle André, when we meet again.

Father has been sketching the peasants at work in the fields. The pastures are lush but life is harsh here, especially in winter. The farmers see no beauty in the mountains, only that wolves may come down from the heights and kill sheep. My father is very taken up with this idea – the battle between man and nature – and pays me no attention, which gives me time to think. Shall I write poetry? I could become a great and famous Hungarian poetess!

I had a dream last night. It lingers with me, like a strange atmosphere that makes a silver mist over everything. Let me try to remember . . . I am in a dark place where all I can see is a thick white mist flowing very close to the ground. All is chill, with a smell of damp stone. A light shines inside this mist, throwing upwards a kind of radiance, against which stands a tall, thin, dark figure. This figure is all in black but it has no face. It is covered in a black shroud. This figure does nothing, it simply *is*. And I am filled with terror.

I can't say what so alarms me. *Just to know that such a thing exists.*

I frighten myself again, thinking of it! I could not wake up,

I struggled for breath. I thought to cry out and wake someone, but could not make a sound. At last I woke, suddenly, with a great effort, and found myself sitting up in bed. I felt an overwhelming urge to get up and look out of the window.

Moonlight flooded the farmyard, the orchard and the steep forested ridge beyond. But nothing stirred. I wonder why I feel so strange?

Now I know the value of this journal. Not to record the details of my life, which is dull, but to record my dreams and thoughts.

Oh, if I were a man, I could be a poet. I could go to Paris or London! If I married Miklos, would we travel? Would marrying make me more free, or less so? My father will never let me do anything alone!

### 2 August

Something dreadful is happening.

Let me set it down. I must know if writing will make it worse, or better.

Last night I could not sleep. Rather, I went in and out of dreaming. Not pleasant dreams, these, but a distressing, heavy state, in which I was too hot, and my head ached, and I could neither wake up nor fall fully asleep.

As I lay like this I heard a faint sound outside, the thin hard whine of some animal in distress. At first it seemed far away on the mountains, then as if it were right outside the window, then far away again. It was a horrible noise, which pained my nerves. I prayed for it to cease, yet I wanted to go out to whatever made the sound – to silence it, to comfort it, I do not know. This keening went on and on, near and far away. When I tried to get up and look outside, I could not move. This alarmed me greatly. I saw unpleasant things in this half-dream. The heavy white mist again, with red wisps swirling into it, like blood in water. I am trying to climb a dark mountain wall but I am struggling and slipping back;

it is too steep. I see some splintered timbers lying on a path, rotten and glistening with rain. These images make no sense, but each is terrifying and upsets me deeply. Even writing this down, I can make no more sense of it! And always that irritating bleat of pain!

I must have slept in the end, for I awoke at dawn and all was normal. But as we ate breakfast, a shepherd came to the kitchen door and told the farmer that a wolf had come down from the forests and taken a lamb!

Was that the sound I heard, that I thought was only in my nightmare? The lamb, bleating for help?

The men have gone out with guns to hunt the wolf. I hate to think of it being chased and shot, the poor wolf, which was only hunting to live. Must two animals die instead of one? My father would say this is sentiment. He would think me mad.

But the worst thing that happened was this. While he talked, the shepherd – a young, unappealing man with red cheeks and a long greasy moustache – kept staring at me. Perhaps he meant no harm, but I found his looks insolent, and they made me feel defenceless and somehow ashamed. If I could have left the room and forgotten it, it would not have mattered. But my father saw the looks, and got in a rage, and would have attacked the shepherd had not the farmer and his sons held him back! It was an ugly scene. When the shepherd had gone, amid raised voices, Father pushed me into my room and shouted at me that it was all my fault, I must have encouraged him, and I was nothing but a hindrance to Father's artistic career, and the sooner I am married and out of harm's way the better, and so on. Then he embraced me so hard my ribs were bruised, and said he could not bear me to marry, no man would ever take his Elena from him, and all this so rough and fierce that I found no comfort in it, only more pain.

I was left weeping. I still tremble now. Suddenly everything seems very dark and wretched and I wish I could leave, but I cannot. Where would I go?

There is a commotion outside. The men are home.

## 3 August

Father has been kinder today; or at least, he has kept me constantly busy, fetching and carrying, cleaning brushes. He commands me to sing folk-songs as he paints, then complains that my voice is weak and shaky. I wish I knew how to please him! Everything I do seems to disappoint him. If I had been a boy . . . Sometimes I wish I had never been born! I think he wishes it too!

They shot the wolf that took the lamb. The poor creature dragged itself off to die and no one can find it. I hate to think of any creature dying slowly in pain.

## 5 August

Last night as I lay in my bed I heard a wolf howling, a lonely, high keening that pierced the silence and brought me awake. It sounded uncanny, high at first, then falling and trailing mournfully away. The sound of it turned me cold. But I had to get out of bed and look.

Down in the yard, standing in the centre of a white splash of moonlight, there was a great silver wolf! He was beside the well, his ears almost on a level with its carved wooden roof. He was pale in the moonlight, but his eyes glowed red. He stared at me. I could hardly move for fear. This terror of wolves is very old and deep in the Transylvanian peasants – and in me, as if their fear has stirred and woken my own. Yet I opened the window wide, as if I were acting in my sleep.

The animal was there, looking up at me. We stared at each other. I felt a compulsion to climb out of the window and go to him. But he let out a faint keen, and suddenly the howling of dogs rose up from the village, from other farms. This was joined by the howling of wolves on the ridge, until the whole landscape was filled with their mournful keening. So disturbing was this sound that I drew back quickly and closed the window.

When I looked out again I saw the creature turning and slipping away into the shadows. But he went slowly, very lame, and I saw a dark splash like blood on his flank. My heart beat hard. This must be the wolf that was shot! It was wounded and in pain, I could not leave it! But it had gone, and I dared not go after it. All of this was very dreamlike. I lay down and slept until morning.

I tried to find the wolf in daylight but there was no sign of him. How far could he have gone, so sorely wounded? I have told no one. I don't know why. I feel it is my secret. I am afraid of the wolf, yet I want him to come again.

### 7 August
He came. I am fearful, but I must write of it.

Last night I was woken suddenly – not by any sound, but by an urge to look out of the window. I crept out of bed and looked, and the great pale wolf was there again.

He stood very still, his haunches bent under him, his eyes as scarlet as sunset. I was very afraid, but felt I must go to him. I undid the window and climbed over the sill, nearly tearing my nightdress. I had saved him a little piece of meat. I crouched down and held out the meat to see if he would come, and he did! He came limping to me and ate it out of my hand! Then he let me stroke him. I never dreamed I would dare to stroke such a fierce creature!

He put his big head on my knee and let me rub his soft ears. There was a big ragged hole in his haunch where the bullet went through. It looked as if it should have killed him! His eyes, which had seemed red before, were dark and filmy with weakness. He licked my hand as if to thank me, then he left.

I followed a little way through the orchard, hoping to find

his lair, but I lost him. Suddenly the trees seemed full of menace, and I looked around as if I'd woken from a trance. Something was watching me from the darkness; I couldn't see it, but I knew. I turned and ran back to the house, and soon I was in bed with the window shut, feeling safe but foolish.

I hope the creature will come again. I will keep food for him. If I don't feed him he may starve to death. Perhaps he cannot live anyway but I must try to help him.

No one must know, or they will kill him, and punish me.

### 9 August

All I can think of during the day is the wolf. While I am helping Father, I am only waiting for night to come. I am clumsy, I cannot pay attention. Father berates me but I don't hear.

The great wolf led me a little way into the trees tonight, and ate all the food I had saved. He was famished. I cleaned the edges of the wound as best I could with clean water, but it is very deep and not healing as it should. Something is wrong. He is too vigorous for an animal that must be dying. When he licked my hand, as if to say thank you, his tongue was cold. And before he left, his eyes again glowed scarlet, so bright I could not mistake it. I was frightened when I looked at his eyes. I felt dizzy, as if I would fall.

When I went to bed afterwards, I had a nightmare. It was real and vivid, but the events so wild and squeezed together I could make no sense of them.

I am lying in a box of earth, a big mouldering box like a coffin. Everything is moving violently around me, as if there is a cart beneath me, and I am afraid. No, not quite afraid, but urgent, angry and full of hatred. I see and feel, but cannot move. Now I see the sun dipping above me, red as blood. I smile. I know I can move once the sun sets. Then I will do something very terrible. (I shudder even now to remember that gloating anticipation.) I am about to do something violent and evil, yet I long to do it! Now I see two faces above me – pale, shadowed and colourless, with the cold crimson sky behind them, and snow blowing around them. I see two shining steel blades flashing towards me. I scream, my whole body jolts.

Then there is a deep, peaceful blackness.

This seems to go on for ever. I have no thoughts, no feelings, only a dull awareness. I know I am dead, but there is no Heaven or Hell waiting, not even purgatory . . . only this limbo. Nothingness.

(How horrible it seems, now I write it down! The faces, I recollect . . . One I did not know, but one was that of Madam Mina's husband, Jonathan Harker. I feel violent hatred for him as I write. What does this mean?)

After an indefinable length of this nothingness, I hear the fleeting murmur of a voice I know. A spirit brushes by me, like an angel! I stir. Something pulls at me and I open my eyes, but no one is there. Instead I see a stony road winding between the mountains, a thin bleak twilight lying on the cold stones. I see some greyish soil, like ash, lying in the cracks between the stones. The sight of this dust, for no reason I understand, fills me with despair and I want to roar with grief. But I have no throat with which to cry out!

Thank God, I woke then. I was hanging out of bed, shivering with the cold, and my chest aching from the position I had twisted into in my sleep. It's over. I said a prayer. I never, never want to have a dream like that again!

### 10 August

Prayers not answered. The nightmare again. The same, but it goes a little further this time.

As I stir from limbo, I see the angel who woke me. I hear her warm voice and see a fleeting form like a white ghost – and it is Madam Mina! Her presence is a hot, fragrant river.

33

I am a ghost while she is alive, mortal, full of blood and life
. . . and I long for her, I *must* touch her at any cost; she is as
vital to me as a mother to a child! But I can only observe. I
watch, coldly, the figures of her and her hated companions,
standing with their heads bowed. I don't know what they are
doing. The tableau of their heated, mortal, ageing forms fills
me with despair, as if I fall for ever into an abyss.

When I say 'I', I mean whoever I was in the dream – for
I was not myself. These visions and nightmares distress me
more than I can say.

## 13 August

Each night I stay as long as I dare with my friend the wolf,
because I do not want to go back to bed and have the dreams
again. But they always come eventually. I fight sleep as long
as I can, and my father says I look pale and tired, and berates
me for my lethargy. I think he has made up his mind I shall
marry Miklos now. He says my illness is because I am spoiled
and lazy, and I need a husband to keep me under control.
Unwell I am a burden to him, so he wants me to become
the responsibility of someone else. And again I disappoint
him!

I tell my friend about the dreams. That comforts me,
though I know he cannot understand. He lies with his heavy
body over my legs, and I stroke his fur as I tell him every
detail. His ears flicker as if he listens. When I look into his
glowing eyes he seems almost to speak to me. He seems more
real than my father, the farmer's family and the insolent
shepherd all put together!

I cannot wait for night to fall, and the shaggy white wolf
to stand under my window and call to me. I worry about
him. Although he eats the food I give him, he remains very
thin under his coat. He drags his hind leg and his wound
does not heal. He neither regains health nor loses it; he is
always the same, as if . . . as if he were dead, yet still walking.

I wish I hadn't had that thought! This room seems so tiny and ill-lit, while the world outside oppresses me with its wild, cruel darkness.

## 15 August

I think I have lost him. I am very afraid.

Last night he looked into my eyes and I felt him trying to tell me something. His eyes were like two great lamps, burning into my head. I had to look away, to push his head away, because I could not bear it. I couldn't understand. Then he began to snap and snarl at me. I cried out and ran away from him, through the trees and back to my room. He came after me! Surely he could have caught me easily. Just as I shut the window he jumped at the glass, making the whole frame shake. I yelped in fear! He stared at me through the glass, his lips drawn back and trembling. His long fangs shone and they looked so cruel and hard.

I was terrified he would burst through the glass. We stood eye to eye for a moment. Then he took his big paws off the sill and ran three-legged into the shadows of the trees.

I cannot believe he has changed and turned on me. What have I done wrong?

I did not sleep until the cold hour before dawn. But then I had another dream, the worst yet.

I see cold mountain slopes, a castle rearing above a precipice and folds of thick dark forest, as if I am a spectre wandering over a land I once loved, but which is now bleak and lifeless. I would weep if I had throat, mouth and eyes to cry with. All I ever loved has passed away to dust. All my loved ones are long gone. There is nothing but darkness to the end of the universe. Nowhere I can find rest.

As I describe the dream I cannot express the feeling of desolation with which it filled me. It is the most terrifying feeling I have ever known. This God-forsaken landscape is my own soul. I haunt the walls of the castle but I am exiled.

Someone woke me from oblivion, but she is gone and I cannot find her. Have no body in which to find her. I drift a long way over mountains . . .

I see a hairy wolf, dying at the foot of an oak tree with the glistening wound of a bullet in its haunch. I enter its body as its own spirit departs. Its corpse is mine and now I have a form in which to move. Now I can find someone to help me . . . One who has been touched by the same gentle spirit.

I can write no more. This is all I remember. The dream faded and as I try to recapture it I can only think how ridiculous it sounds.

I will steal a good piece of meat from the kitchen, in hopes of sweetening my friend. He eats most of my dinner and supper these days, while the farmer's wife frets that I grow thin. He thrives at my expense, then dares to snap at me!

### 16 August

He came back. He ate the meat, very slowly and lovingly, licking and tearing it into thin slivers. As if he knew the risk I had taken to steal it for him!

Then he came and licked my hands. The blood was still on his tongue and my hands became wet with it, but he went on working with his long tongue until all was clean. I am forgiven!

When I went to bed my dreams were as vivid as ever, and very unsettling. I dream that a tall old man is bending over my bed. There is a faint light behind him, but I cannot see his face. He is telling me something very important, whispering, whispering. (I cannot now remember a word but at the time it was vital.) He takes my hands; his own are hairy, like paws! He leans towards me and I think he will kiss me; instead he licks my throat with a long, rough tongue. I shudder from head to foot with revulsion . . . and yet I want it to continue. I have no will to stop him.

I paused in writing to say a prayer. It seems, as I look back at my journal, that all I have recorded are sick ravings. Am I ill? Surely these dreams are not healthy – will it call evil upon me, to write them down?

## 22 August

I can barely hold the pen to write. I am exhausted and my eyes cloud with pain.

Last night when I met the wolf he would not come to me, only looked over his shoulder and trotted away into the orchard. I followed. I know I should not have done so, but with him a strange condition of mind comes upon me; that I am conscious but bereft of my own will – or rather, my will is all to obey him. So I put on hide boots and a shawl and go with him. As we cross the pastures, my feet (even through the boots) become soaked. The sky is thick with stars and their soft light turns mountains and forest to an uncanny, shimmering realm. I look around fearfully as we go, yet with my friend I feel safe. He is so strange; sad and in need of my care, yet so strong – all that fierceness coiled up in his red eyes!

A spell is on me. We turn east along the base of the ridge, which leads us higher and higher along a slowly climbing deer track. There are spruce saplings around us. Then we cross a stream and enter the forest, passing a shepherd's hut as we climb the long valley. The slopes grow steeper. I am uneasy and out of breath. The ground between the great spruces is covered in thick black mould, full of fallen branches and trunks. Once I see two large shapes pass between the trees some distance away – bears. They watch us pass. My feet hurt, and I worry that we are going too far. I know I will not reach home again before dawn. But I cannot stop.

When dawn comes, we are deeper in the mountains than ever. We reach the top of a steep ridge just as the sun blazes on the silver limestone crags of the Carpathians. The chain of peaks rings us all around and they look as cold as snow. I am very tired now, cold and frightened. But whenever I falter, the wolf turns his bright eyes on me and forces me on. We are so far from anywhere!

Now we pass awesome narrow gorges and plunging waterfalls. I drink from streams, too tired to feel hungry. A mass of grey cloud comes down around us and soaks us in mist and rain. Animals watch us; wolves and foxes, lynx and wild pigs. They form a ring around us, as if the wolf draws them yet warns them away; as if he holds a magical power over them also.

The journey is confused and blurred. A mud path along a shadowy gorge, a grassy, open saddle with hazel groves, elders and blackberry bushes. We descend and climb a deep gulley, and the firs close in, very thick and dark around us. The wolf leads me out of the forest on to a rough track, the long white brush of his tail swaying.

There is a steep, thinly forested ridge on one side, a deep valley with a fierce river on the other, and a long silver line of mountains beyond. Far along this track, my companion halts. I sink down exhausted. I had my gaze on the ground, but as I look up I see a castle, a great, towering pile with broken battlements and ancient towers above a precipice. I catch my breath in terror. The Szekely farmers whisper of a castle from which evil has been visited upon them and their ancestors. No one speaks its name. But I know – with the deep dream-knowledge that my friend gives me – that this is that place.

The wolf leads me into the undergrowth below the track, and here I see the timbers of some great box that has been broken up and left to rot. He is directing me; I know what to do. Lifting lengths of timber aside I see a pile of earth that is darker than the brown mould on which it lies. Mingled with this substance are thick patches of a lighter dust, a sort of ash.

I spread out my shawl and with my bare hands I scoop the ash into it. It is damp, mould-scented, all laced with cobwebs. The wolf watches intently, panting, his tongue lolling over his long teeth. I cannot stop until all the dust is gathered. I make a bundle of my shawl. As I do so, he goes up on to the track and picks up something small and white between his teeth. Holding it delicately, like a cat carrying a kitten, he brings it to me.

It is a handkerchief, lacy and delicate, such as an English-woman would have. The initials 'W.H.' are embroidered on one corner. I use it to tie the top of the bundle. Then the wolf has me carry it to the courtyard of the castle.

The great gateway and the high frowning walls sway across my sight. I am terrified; ghosts and dead leaves blow about the courtyard, black passages yawn into crypts. Surely the stone towers will come tumbling down and bury me. My companion shows me a niche in which to hide the bundle. Then I run away down the long, hard path.

Of the journey home I remember little. My feet were sore, and I was delirious from exhaustion and lack of food. The wolf must have led me safely back to the farm; my strongest impression was of the force of his will, which seemed loyal, single-minded, yet wholly pitiless.

It was afternoon when I reached the farm. I looked around for my friend but he was gone. I had not eaten for two days, and I was all in filthy rags. The shock of my father and the farmers when they saw me! They had been searching for me! And I could not explain where I had been, or why, for I don't know!

Somewhere I stepped out of reality and entered a nightmare.

When I could not and would not explain, my father dragged me to my room, closed the door and beat me with his belt. I deserved it, I know. Now I am locked in the room alone, without food, writing my journal to keep me from crying with pain.

I can hear my father arguing furiously with the farmer and his wife through the door. Oh God, they are telling us to leave! They say that their youngest son saw me feeding a great white wolf by the well, that the shepherd saw me walking through the forest with my pale companion. They say I am a witch, in league with the Devil, I will bring a curse upon them if I stay!

Because of me, my father will lose his good friends and be unable to complete his paintings. He will never forgive me. Tomorrow, they say, we must go. Oh God, help me. Soon it will all be over.

# Chapter Three

***10 August***

I begin my record by noting that it is not only for my eyes, but for those of my good friend Abraham Van Helsing – assuming that I have anything of value to record! (If not, my friend, one of us shall consign it to the fire!) All there is to note so far is that Miklos and I have cheerfully endured a slow journey from Pesth to Hermannstadt, and that we have checked through our equipment; bedrolls, provisions, lamp and candles, and so on – the minimum we need to survive for two weeks.

It is strange to think that my brother and my dear niece are also somewhere within these mountains, albeit many miles to the east and north. I have heard nothing from them, but then did not expect to. They will come home, I dare say, as soon as the weather turns cooler. No doubt Emil's paintings will be admired for generations to come, while my dry studies are long consigned to a forgotten corner of some museum archive! Tonight we camp on a scrubby slope brightened by patches of dandelion and wood violet. Between the cultivated land and the mountains there is no hilliness – the mountains make a dramatic barrier beyond which it is easy to believe that a place such as the Scholomance, where Count Dracula learned his dark wisdom, exists – indeed, from which the Four Horsemen might come riding down to announce the Apocalypse.

### *11 August*

All day we have walked through the mountains, and the country, grows ever wilder and more magnificent around us. The weather is fine, making hot work of our walk, and we are both suffering blisters despite our stout boots. A minor annoyance. Nature in its raw state lends us vigour! Miklos and I imagine ourselves a pair of intrepid explorers, in search of some fabled land; and the grim nature of our goal seems to add fascination rather than fear to the expedition. When we make camp I must check our provisions. We have such tremendous appetites from walking, I fear I may have underestimated our need. There is no habitation for miles around.

I find our map to be vague, unhelpful and inaccurate. I am adding my own corrections and notes to it as we go. My compass and instinct prove to be better guides!

### *Evening*

Disappointment! Despite my careful researches as to the most likely location of the Scholomance – the region of Lake Hermannstadt – we have found nothing. All day we scoured the area for evidence; a man-made path, remains or foundations, the tell-tale patterning of the ground that might indicate a building once stood there.

I am being impatient, of course. I knew this search might take days, weeks, even months! I need only the tiniest seed of evidence to justify a bigger, more organized expedition. I am, of course, very much out on a limb. It is generally accepted that the place is a myth, simply a part of the rich folklore of this land. It is more than likely that there is nothing to find. I am prepared for that possibility.

There is also a chance, however, that the school lay near some other, unknown, lake, and that the two have become confused in folk memory . . .

## *12 August, morning*

The mountainscape in the dawn is breathtaking. Great peaks surge up through the mist, the lower slopes painted dark violet by shadow. Long tongues of forest run down into the valleys, but the naked rock of the peaks is drenched by the sun's first rays to the most wondrous hues of rose and silver. I wish I could have captured the moment before sunrise, when sky and mountains turned as ruby-red as blood.

We are very high up now, and seem to be beyond civilization, on the roof of the world. All along the way I have been looking for the smallest sign – and have asked Miklos to do the same – that human beings once passed this way. A horseshoe nail, a button! So far, nothing. Time now for a meagre breakfast, and onwards.

## *13 August*

Another fruitless day. We have climbed steep, rugged slopes, wound our way through thick forests until we are both exhausted and disorientated. My usually infallible sense of direction seems constantly to disagree with the compass! It will be restored by sleep. We are camped in the lee of a cliff, and it seems very dark tonight. The fire burns low and Miklos is in a deep sleep. The weather has turned cold and the howling of wolves sounds unutterably eerie. These mountains are so vast and wild, it would indeed be possible to wander in circles and never find our way home. It is all too easy, in a state of extreme tiredness, to allow all kinds of imaginings to intrude on the mind. No wonder superstitions take such a hold on the peasant brain. Away with these thoughts!

## *14 August*

We have cast the search wider and are making for a westerly chain of peaks that looks promising; great limestone obelisks towering from the forested steeps like a voivode's fortress. But the way is proving difficult. Our path has taken us down into a deep, narrow gorge and it is hard to find a route up the precipitous ridge of rock that rims the far side – especially with the weight of our knapsacks on our shoulders. We have attempted several deer tracks that look easy enough from below but are impassible, forcing us back to the gorge floor. The map is of no help. Miklos is tiring, but I cannot give up. I have a strong feeling that we *must* cross the ridge, that on the far side we will find nestling some extraordinary ancient edifice on which human eyes have not alighted for centuries! The more it defies us, the stronger the feeling grows.

I am worried about Miklos. His usual stoical good temper is failing him. He is very quiet. If I catch him unawares, I see an expression of extreme distress on his face, as if he were in pain or terror. When challenged he insists there is nothing wrong, but I fear the journey is proving too much for him. He may well have strained a muscle and be in pain, but it's the Devil's own job to make him admit it! I hear him muttering behind me as we walk. I cannot make out the words, except for, 'The dragon, the dragon.' I must confess it becomes very trying. But if I turn round and challenge him, he denies that he ever spoke.

## 15 August

We crossed the ridge today. Dear God, my hands are shaking so that I can barely hold the pen. I hope you are able to read it, my friend Abraham. No matter, I must set it all down.

At dawn we moved higher up the gorge and at last found a tortuous way over the great, frowning brow of rock. On the crest there was no more to see than a circle of fanged rocks cupping a sea of forest. Not the gleaming spires of the Scholomance, after all. Not that I actually expected to see a spectacle that I suspect exists only in legend, but I was disappointed, all the same. Still, there was such an air of mystery on the place that I was eager to descend. I turned to Miklos, only to see an expression of intense dread on his face. 'Must we go down there?' he said.

'But of course,' I replied. 'Miklos, whatever is wrong?'

'Nothing, sir.' His stoic look returned.

'You're exhausted. If you would prefer to camp here on the ridge and wait for me while I explore the valley, I will understand.'

'No, sir,' he said quickly. 'I cannot let you go into it alone!' And there was such fear in his voice it quite affected me for several minutes. Angered at myself as well as him, I led the way down the ridge in silence.

The dense spruce forest enveloped us. All was deathly quiet. Presently I saw a gleam between the tree-trunks, a glint of dark, glassy water. I hurried forward until we came out on to the bank of a small lake. I can hardly describe my emotions as we stood there. The water was darkest blue-green and although the lake was only a hundred feet in diameter it gave an impression of immeasurable depth. All around, the trees stood dense and silent, and beyond them the circle of jagged limestone. The air was thick with the scents of pine resin and stagnant water, motionless and brooding. The only movement was in the mist that drifted in sluggish layers over the obsidian surface; it seemed almost to writhe, as if sentient. I felt on the brink of revelation and terror.

'This must be the place!' I whispered, gripping Miklos's arm. I felt it necessary to keep my voice low, not to disturb anything. '*This* is the lake we sought, the Cauldron of the Dragon, and this is *Yadu Drakuluj*, the Devil's Abyss. We've found it. If the Scholomance exists at all, it is nearby!'

Miklos's eyes swung from side to side, as if he were terrified. I grew annoyed with him, I am ashamed to confess – especially in the light of what transpired. 'The peasants say that the lake goes to the earth's core, and a dragon sleeps at the bottom. If you throw in a stone you wake the dragon and cause a storm to shake the very world to its roots.' I picked up a stone and made to throw it in.

Miklos grabbed my wrist to stop me, crying, 'No!'

His voice echoed off the walls. His nervous state was so acute that I felt ashamed of my childish behaviour. 'Miklos,' I said, 'our expedition is almost over. I fear I've driven you too hard, for which I ask your forgiveness. Today we explore this valley, and whatever we discover, which may well be nothing, tomorrow we start for home.'

He nodded in relief. 'Forgive me, sir. I don't know what is wrong with me. I feel such a dread of this place . . .' He shook himself, and was again the brave, good-natured man I know.

All day we searched the valley and the slopes around it, finding not one scrap of evidence that a building of any kind had ever existed here. In the evening, as the dusk gathered and the first stars came out, we sat disconsolately on the bank of the lake. Miklos toyed with a large pebble he'd picked up. We were both tired and dispirited.

'Of course, the idea that there ever was a school run by the Devil is a fable,' I said, 'but there surely must have been something that gave rise to the fable. Behind all these myths and superstitions is a seed of truth.'

Miklos exclaimed with a savagery that startled me, 'But it is all so much nonsense! There's no Devil, no dragon! I won't let these phantoms terrify me!' And he flung the pebble into the lake.

The surface swallowed the missile with a *plop* so unnaturally deep and sonorous that it startled us both. Ripples spread out in perfect circles. It seemed to me that I heard a dull rumbling from a great distance. We looked at each other and laughed, very uneasy. 'Come, let us make our camp for the night,' I said.

As we were building a fire on the lake shore, it turned very dark and a chill wind sprang up. Then a great blaze of lightning split the sky. I looked up and saw thick greenish clouds rolling overhead, the lightning against them forking into scores of branches until the whole sky ran with white fire. A thunderbolt cracked deafeningly. We flung ourselves to the ground, our hands over our ears. Thus commenced the most violent storm I have ever witnessed.

Rain flowed down upon us in sheets. The thunder and lightning were continuous, confounding sight and hearing. The lake surface roiled. The ground shook and shuddered so violently that I believed we were experiencing an earth tremor in addition to the storm.

The fire hissed out. I began swiftly to gather up our equipment before it became utterly soaked. But as I was engaged in this task, Miklos leaped up and ran into the trees. Shouting at him to stop, I seized my knapsack – which contained food, candles, and this precious journal – dropped everything else, and ran after him.

Barely keeping him in sight, I pursued him to the valley's edge. As we came to the foot of the high ridge, lightning illuminated the black mouth of a cave. This was a feature we had missed in our search! 'The cave!' I shouted, although Miklos, evidently, was already heading for its shelter. But just before he gained the entrance, a flying branch, ripped free by the wind, caught him on the head, and he fell.

Reaching him, I found him semi-conscious and groaning. With the rain blowing wildly around us, I dragged him as best I could into the cave mouth to shelter. Here we remain for now.

Inside the cave is dry, but very musty and full of bats. The floor is thick with their droppings. We sit as close to the entrance as we can. I have made Miklos as comfortable as possible, but he drifts in and out of consciousness and I fear for him. We are so far from anywhere that there is no chance of finding help for him. He murmurs in his delirium of the Devil riding through the storm on a dragon to take us down to Hell, and although I am not a superstitious man, his mutterings fill me with the blackest dread.

I have a theory, for what it is worth, Abraham. Could it

be the nature of the storm itself – the thick, crackling heaviness of the clouds, static electricity or electromagnetic forces – that wreaks havoc with our brains and creates the effect, quite terrifying, that waves of pure evil are sweeping over us?

The shock of everything has quite undone my nerves. We have been here, trapped by the storm, for two hours now. Outside all is crashing thunder, fire and deluge. I watch the rain sheeting down against a flickering, greenish glow. I have lit a candle – the lamp was left outside, so the naked flame gutters madly – in order to fill in my journal; at least the writing of it has steadied me somewhat. Miklos is stirring.

### 16 August

Morning, and calmness, thank the Almighty! The storm only died out at dawn. Such a night. No sleep. Miklos is sitting up and eating breakfast, though he seems confused and winces at every movement as if he has a severe headache. He denies his pain, naturally, but I fear that he has a concussion. He needs a doctor. I can only pray he will be fit enough to make the journey home. I brought him into this and I feel responsible; if any harm befalls him I shall never forgive myself!

The storm has abated, but rain is pouring down again. I fear we are trapped here until it eases off.

### Later

Now do I mark this as a day of revelation or horror?

The rain went on and the trees shook in a wild wind off the mountains as we sheltered. (I still cannot understand how we failed to find this cave yesterday!) I dozed for a time, then awoke to find Miklos wandering off into the back of the cave. I followed, intending to make him come back and rest, but he shook me off, saying, 'No, no, he's here,' or something of that sort. Daylight revealed the cave as being much deeper than I'd realized. Curiosity got the better of me, despite my concern for Miklos's state of mind. I lit a fresh candle, slung

48

the knapsack on my shoulder – lest some wild animal come scavenging in the cave and eat both food and journal! – and went after him.

Much of the cave was thick, musty and disgusting with bat droppings. The creatures stirred over our heads, rustling, squeaking. Deeper in, the bat colony ceased and the rock floor was clear. Here the cave narrowed to a fissure, a mere corridor, but it wound on inside the massive ridge. Miklos felt his way along swiftly – at walking pace, but too fast for unknown terrain – seeming afraid. I, too, was deeply uneasy, but if I tried to make him slow down he became agitated.

We followed this passage for at least fifteen minutes. After that, however, I discovered that my pocket watch had stopped. Although I guess that we were moving in the direction of the greatest peak – that of the 'voivode's fortress' – my compass needle began to veer as irrationally as my own imaginings.

The candle guttered in a draught. The fissure ended at last in a small cavern of great beauty, forested with columns of stone. I admit, I was oppressed and wished for the open air – but Miklos, his face frozen with some inner compulsion, pulled me onwards. The cavern narrowed, then opened out – even now I can hardly overcome my disbelief – into a symmetrical, ten-sided chamber.

Lifting the candle, I saw mosaics on the walls and floor which could have been Roman, but all so thickly covered with black mould and cobwebs that it was hard to make out. The air was so stale I choked on it.

The chamber is approximately thirty feet wide and twenty high, with a domed ceiling – the ten sides converging to a central point. In the centre is a ten-sided marble block, perhaps an altar or dais. Webs lie as thick as fleece round its base, but carving can be seen on the sides; esoteric sigils that are echoed in the mosaics. Each of the walls has a plain marble bench; there is no other furniture.

'Ten benches, ten scholars,' I said. 'Never did it occur to

me that the Scholomance might not be a separate edifice, but part of the mountains themselves! Yes, of course, how better to conceal it?'

Almost wild with excitement, it took me a minute to notice that poor Miklos was panting for breath. I made him sit down and gave him some water from the flask. A look of quiet dismay came over his face and he sighed. 'Forgive my erratic behaviour, sir,' he said, sounding more his normal self. 'I've been prey to wild imaginings ever since we set out. Perhaps you should have brought Elena instead, she would have made a more level-headed companion.'

'Nonsense,' I said. 'Now we will sit and rest awhile, then conduct a very thorough scientific exploration. My friend, we are on the threshold of a discovery to rival that of the Egyptian tombs!'

Refreshed by a rest and a bite to eat, we set out to investigate the chamber . . . and now I know every inch of it. Oh Abraham, is there any point to recording this? Yes, be calm. We worked our way round, sweeping dust off the walls to reveal strange mosaics in intense deep colours. These represented stylized scenes of battles, hunts, saint-like figures preaching to mingled groups of humans and animals, all presented against a background of sigils so densely interwoven they confuse the eye and seem to move. These deserve scholarly interpretation, but at a primitive level they filled me with revulsion – as if they are a hellish inversion of biblical stories. I think it is the colours that give this effect. Somehow the shades conspire to produce a feeling of revulsion – deep coppery reds, dark purple streaked with bronze, thick greens slimed with silver, bluish-crimson – all give the impression of congealed blood . . .

But I wander from the point, which is that when we had worked our way all around, we could not find the archway by which we had entered. The ten sides of the chamber were seamless, as if the ingress had never existed. At first we couldn't believe it. We went around again and again. We argued about the position of the archway. (Our footprints had become so muddled as to tell us nothing.) But even supposing one of us were right, it is no longer there.

Now we sit on our bench, and once I finish writing all I have to say, madness will surely close in. Miklos is speechless, shaking with dread. He does not answer my attempts to comfort him.

We have twelve candles, which will last a few days at most. I should snuff out this one to conserve the supply, but I cannot bear to. The flame dances, so there is a draught from somewhere, but I cannot find its source. We will not suffocate, then - though that would be swifter and more merciful than starvation. In its dim glow, my eyes are constantly drawn to the base of the ten-sided marble block in the centre of the chamber. Its carved surface is also draped in thick webs. Sometimes this grey mass moves and bulges, as if huge spiders are moving underneath. At the base of the block, to the right from where we are sitting, these webs form a mass so thick and dense it seems to be a huge cocoon, the size of a man. My stomach recoils in disgust to think of what might be inside.

### Later

I fell asleep with the pen in my hand! I recall some vague, uneasy dream that by throwing the stone into the lake, we woke the dragon, caused the storm, opened the gate to the Scholomance . . . that we summoned the Devil himself.

Waking to darkness, I lit a fresh candle in a shameful panic, which has now abated a little. Miklos sleeps beside me, I will not wake him. My pocket watch works for a few minutes if I wind it, but is useless. Is it morning or night? I have searched again for a way out, but all is as before. By what freak of nature is this possible? In the circle of candle-light it seems we have stepped into the antechamber of hell. The Scholomance, the Devil's own school!

Oh God, the great cocoon

### Later

Must complete this, though my hand is crabbed by cold and the shuddering of my nerves. I am racked with grief and terror. This is my only hold on life.

I thought I imagined it, when I first saw the cocoon stirring. But I did not; I heard its fibres softly cracking. Something was rising out, some hideous grey thing with gaunt limbs. I dropped my pen in horror, rose to protect my companion and myself, only to fall dizzily on to the floor. The next that happened, I know not whether I saw or dreamed it. The thing that came out of the webs was a *man*, so ancient, grotesque and skeletal that he resembled a spider. Through a reddish veil of candle-light he came skittering towards us on all fours, papery and mummified. I tried to scream but could not. I saw the creature bending over Miklos. Then I lost consciousness.

When I came to myself – I know not how much later – several candles were burning. Who lit them, I dread to think. I looked around and saw that the cocoon was empty, a thin shell of dusty silk fibres, ripped open along its length. My next thought was for Miklos. He was sitting on the bench where I'd left him, his eyes open. I picked myself up off the floor and touched his arm. 'Miklos!' I said.

At my touch his body slid sideways and slumped along the bench. I searched feverishly for some sign of life but there was none.

My dear friend and companion, dead. He has been like a son to me. I would rather have given my own life ten times over than have dragged this dear, good man to his death! How am I to tell his parents – and Elena? How am I to bear it? I still cannot believe it. But there he lies.

I am exhausted from searching for the way out. I have hunted for hidden levers, secret doors, everything. Hopeless. But then, if the Devil exists, it is surely no great task for him to change the very structure of matter? Or at least to inflict the illusion of such a change upon us?

Whatever emerged from the webs and killed Miklos is in here with me somewhere. There is nowhere for it to have gone. Somewhere beyond my small circle of light, it waits.

Never in the world did I dream that a scientific expedition could come to this unthinkable end. Dear Abraham, if ever by a miracle this reaches you, beware the trap into which I have fallen – the arrogance of imagining we could toy with the Devil!

# Chapter Four

**23 August**
I am leaving the farm, but not as my father thinks. My decision is made and my heart beats so hard I turn faint. In secret I have packed a very few belongings in a small bag – to which I shall add my journal, when the time comes – and I wait.

I was meant to leave tomorrow with my father. We could not arrange a conveyance to Bistritz until then, and there have been bad scenes today. When I came out of my room, the family made the *mano pantea* at me, a hand sign against the evil eye, and my father grew furious with them and called them superstitious fools. The farmer, who can be very fearsome, with his long black moustache, grew even angrier. They would have come to blows, had the farmer's wife and daughters not intervened. They want us gone, and the atmosphere is very uneasy. I came back to my room, but my father followed and questioned me for hours about where I had gone for two days in my nightclothes, why was I seen with the wolf, and so on. He made me weep with fear, but I would not answer. Pride will not let me tell him even the little I know.

'Has some man dishonoured you? Some greasy shepherd, some gypsy?' he shouted at me. 'You have brought disgrace upon me! I should have known better than to trust you! Even Miklos will not have you now! What am I to do with you? What have I done to deserve so wild and disobedient a daughter?'

I felt a little sorry for him, for I cannot be the perfect daughter that he believes I should be. The fault is mine. But it cannot be helped.

At last he struck me across the face and left, locking me in. I am still trembling, exhausted from his questions and the injustice of them. But, strangely, I feel distant from all of it. No longer afraid of him, no longer distraught or ashamed – because I am going away. Father has lost me. Perhaps he has always feared this moment, and that is why he is so angry.

The door is locked, but I wait by the window for night to come.

All is quiet. A great silence lies on the world, as if it waits also.

He is coming! A long white shape in the darkness, speeding towards me. His eyes are two red stars. His great head rises up behind the glass, his tongue lolls over his long fangs, a strange blue-white mist shimmers all around him . . . and I must open the window, and go wherever he leads.

## 26 August

I have come a long way since I last wrote.

When I left the farm, I took a bag containing only a few garments, a little food I stole from the kitchen, and my precious gifts from Madam Mina – my journal, dictionary, pens and ink. My companion led me again towards the forest. We had gone only a few hundred yards across the pastures when my father came running after me in his nightclothes, shouting so furiously at me he was almost screaming. I froze in horror. So enraged was he that his face was dark with blood even in the dim milky moonlight. He must have been spying on my window from his own room!

He catches my arm and orders me back to the house. I pull away and refuse to go. At that, he strikes me so hard that my head reels and I find myself lying on the grass, with the stars and forested steeps whirling around me. As I lie there, I see my pale friend growling at my father. My father begins shouting at the wolf, trying to frighten him away. But the wolf puts his head back and howls; and suddenly, from every direction, huge, woolly, white sheepdogs come running, fiercer than wolves, barking and snarling, their ears down and lips drawn back to reveal ferocious teeth.

I see my father's expression turn to one of terror. These dogs are trained to kill. He turns and tries to run, but they leap at him, catching his arms and legs in their great jaws. One jumps at his face. He screams. I wish I could forget that sound, so raw, harsh and despairing! Part of me longs to help him but part of me wants only to watch, cold and passionless – and the cold part wins.

I see Father fall down among the long white backs of the dogs. They rip and tear at his flesh. I glimpse his face and throat, a mass of blood. He stops moving yet they go on worrying at him, tearing at his limbs.

Then my companion goes quietly between the marauding dogs. I am afraid they will attack him, too, for wolves are their great enemy. Instead they step aside to let him through, as if he were their pack leader. His tongue lolls out to lap blood from my father's throat.

I cover my eyes.

The next I know, my wolf is beside me again, urging me away with him into the trees. I see motes of light moving by the farm gate, lamps and torches. We hurry away, leaving the dogs to gnaw at my father's body . . . and although I am shocked, I feel only the faintest ache of grief, as if this had been meant to happen.

My friend leads me once more across the wild terrain towards the castle. The journey seems longer than before, if possible. I stumble after his wraith-like form along deer tracks and gorges, as if in a horrible dream. He must be a werewolf, I think, a man trapped in wolf's form . . . nothing is impossible.

Some hours into the next day, we reach the castle. In the

courtyard, with the stone walls and towers frowning down upon us, we recover the bundle of ash that I collected on our first journey from its hiding place. I carry it as he leads me along a narrow, arched passage to an ancient door of iron-clad wood. He indicates, with muzzle and paws, that I should open this door. A small wooden cross has been roughly nailed to it, and a whitish substance used to seal the crack between door and wall; the wolf growls with his head lowered and ears back to tell me most eloquently that this must be removed. The door is unlocked. I open it and pick the stuff away; it is a kind of putty, with other, papery, matter mixed in. I find a piece of fallen slate to scrape it away and to prise the cross from the door.

The putty has a smell of old, stale garlic. Someone has tried to seal the castle with wards against evil . . . to stop something going in, or coming out?

I discard the scraps and the cross at the far end of the passage, in a dank, mossy crevice where wall and flagstones meet. As soon as the door is clear, the wolf bounds over the threshold and into a low corridor. I feel intense tiredness creeping over me, and with it coldness and unease. I trust my friend, but this place feels bad. Ancient, full of loss and dark memories.

He leads me down into a deep, ruined chapel, where faint rays of daylight fall through the broken roof. The air is thick with the odours of mouldering earth, mixed with the charnel odour of decay, as if a thousand rats have died here. And I see rows of graves and great tombs. A crypt! All is still and heavy with dust, as if nothing has been disturbed for centuries. So desolate. My companion leaves me and slips between the tombs, jumping up to look inside some. He looks less like a living animal than ever; he is spectral, skeletal. A thin high whine issues from his throat, hurting my ears. I move like a sleepwalker through this death, this horror, until all of it overwhelms me and I sink down on the earth floor. All I want is to sleep. But the wolf takes my skirts between his front teeth and pulls at me. As I look up, I find myself beneath a great tomb with one word engraved upon it.

DRACULA

I cannot encompass how I feel. The name means nothing and yet is familiar; it produces in me a sense of breathtaking awe and terror, and this feeling is so vast it seems to pass outside me to take in all the ancient chapel, the steep walls of the castle, the precipice and beyond, all the dark, wolf-infested forest . . .

My companion will not let me rest. He snaps and snarls at me, until I get up, alarmed. In his jaws he brings an ugly brass urn from somewhere, a squat bowl with a lid, and directs me to put the ash from the shawl into it and keep it safe. Then he digs frantically at the earth, and instructs me to fill my shawl instead with loose soil. None of this makes sense. It only seems imperative that I do it. My hands are black with the malodorous stuff, and the bundle is so heavy that I can barely lift it. At last I collapse, weeping with exhaustion.

Then the wolf leads me, dragging my burdens, up a spiral stair into the body of the castle. I don't think I could remember the way back. He brings me to this room and leaves me, and here I remain. Where has he gone? Will he return? Now I am lying on a couch in a large apartment that I imagine was once light and pleasant with tapestries and rich furnishings; but now all is moth-eaten and draped with dusty webs. It is growing dark again. The waning moon rises. I ate all my food on the journey, so the only nourishment I have had is a bottle of wine I found, fifty years old and dark as blackberries. It was good, but has made me heavy-headed.

What will become of me? I will die of cold and hunger, but nothing seems to matter as I rest here in this dream-like haze.

I look across an expanse of flagstones shining in the moonlight. In front and to the side are vast latticed windows, the stone mullions as delicate as lace, the night sky and the forests below the precipice all silvered by this mystical light. The whole window expands in my vision, a great lacy veil of white and silver against which motes of dust glitter and dance. I feel hands stroking me. Soft voices laugh and sigh like glass bells.

'Sister,' they say. 'Sister, sweet sister.'

I am cold. So very cold.

### Morning

I must make this record quickly. My hands tremble and tears blur my eyes, but grief will pass and I must move on.

I fell asleep as I wrote, I think. Or as the waking dream took over, pen and journal fell to the floor. I remember shaking violently with coldness. The chill of the stones was seeping through my whole body. I wanted to touch the phantom hands of those women, to grasp them or to push them away, I know not which – but there was nothing there. I was alone with ghosts. I began to sob in fear.

Suddenly my friend was with me again! He climbed upon my couch and lay down beside me. His eyes were very bright, dazzling like the setting sun, and his tongue was warm as it rasped at my hands. (It always felt cold before.) I was too tired to think or to be afraid. As I slipped into a doze, I felt that he was actually lying on me, to keep me warm. I felt his tongue and teeth scraping gently at my throat. My whole body seemed to tingle and tighten with a strange breathless feeling – not unpleasant – and although my eyes came open I could not move. Then it seemed to me that the spectral wolf was actually a man, a tall figure in black with long pallid hands.

Yet this human figure is not upon me but very far away, and although he reaches out to me he cannot touch me. I remember a feeling of desolation, rage, the urge of the dead to clasp vivid red-blooded life. I see long, muddled visions of battles, armies, mountains, a strange cavern where flames leap from an abyss and turn the very walls to red and bronze. And again the two steel knives flashing down towards me. Death, limbo, Mina Harker's sweet presence passing me by, oblivious to my need. Longing, bitter anger, and then a thrust of will so firm and resolute it seems physically to pierce me. And all of this comes from the solitary pale figure in black. I am filled, as I was by the tomb, with dread and awe. At last, breathing heavily from the weight on my chest, I fall into deep, black sleep.

When I woke – half an hour ago – it was day again, I was once more shaking with cold and the wolf, my dear companion whom I have come to love, lay dead beside me.

I was grief-stricken to find him so. I wept bitterly, with my arms round his dear furry neck. But my tears stopped very suddenly as I heard a voice; heard it inside my head, not so much the words as the intent. What I understand from it is this.

The spirit that animated the wolf has passed, for a time at least, into *me*. Thus, it was never the wolf, the shell, that I loved, but the spirit inside. This is the soul – if soul is the right word, perhaps I mean will, or essence – of the tall man whom I do not yet know, but whom I will surely come to know. If I do not fail him!

He needs me. He tells me that it is all my responsibility now to help him be resurrected, reclothed in his own flesh. He has entrusted himself, body and soul, to me; so I am the only one now who can help him. I must not fail him. If I want to see him, to touch him in the flesh, I *cannot* fail him.

I feel that I have met the other half of myself, my shadow, my soulmate. I will do anything for him.

My father, Miklos, and Uncle André are nothing to me now. I leave my family and follow a rockier path, like a saint. He will be my guide. My Dark Companion.

### 1 September

At last I am able to write my journal again. I am at home in Buda-Pesth. My journey was terrible. I must have seemed a madwoman to the peasants who found me – walking alone in the mountains with a bag in my hand (the urn inside) and a shawl bundled heavily on my shoulder! I am certain I appeared a fright. I told them that I had been travelling with my father, but our carriage had an accident, and the rest of the party were killed by wolves, and I must reach Buda-Pesth urgently. They questioned me only a little, but helped me a great deal; fed me, cleaned me, gave me a suitcase of cracked leather in which to carry my burdens, and conveyed me to the nearest railway station.

Hunger and physical pain mean little to me, in any case. My Dark Companion is inside, urging me onwards. He is all that matters. How I am to do what must be done, I know not. I can only follow his guidance.

No one is here except the housekeeper, who tells me that Uncle André and Miklos have gone on some expedition and are not expected home for a week or two, at the least. It is no surprise. My uncle has always adored exploring. I am glad he is not here; it spares me the pain of telling him that his brother is dead. It helps me, also, that I do not have to make elaborate explanations for my actions.

There is a letter, unopened, from Abraham Van Helsing to my uncle. Uncle must have left before it arrived. I feel a strange urge to read it. I should resist . . . but what if it contains something important?

Now I must write no more, but make all ready for the journey.

## LETTER, ABRAHAM VAN HELSING TO ANDRÉ KOVACS
### (*Not received by him*)

Amsterdam, 28 August

My Dear André,

You will forgive me, I beg you, for the unconscionably long time it takes for me to answer your letter. My mind has been on other matters; dark sad matters, the clouds of which are only now beginning to move aside, leaving me to think of the outside (my friends, my work) rather than the inside (my sorrow).

My poor dear wife has died. It shames me to admit that my grief is more for her life than her death, but it is so. As you know she has been in the care of asylum nurses for many years; often she has not even known me. For a long time, I have been a widower in all but the physical thread of her life; now the thread is severed, it is to me less a great shock than a little sigh of relief. Yet still cause, you understand, for much recollection and regret.

But enough; it is over. I write to express my great interest at your archaeological expedition. However, a word of caution. We have learned, as you so rightly say, of the evil reality that lies behind folklore and myth. Dracula was real. Of course the Scholomance existed – or exists!

Whilst the Devil doubtless keeps it too well hidden for an innocent mortal to stumble upon, I do not doubt your ingenuity in overcoming such obstacles. As to the consequences, should you actually find it, have you considered what these might be?

My conclusion, should you seek my opinion – not that you are under any obligation to do so – is this. The Scholomance is best left well alone. Don't go!

I anticipate your report in due course. But if you are of a mind to listen to me for once, I entreat you once again. *Please don't go.*

Your friend,
Abraham Van Helsing.

Buda-Pesth, 1 September

My dear Madam Harker,

I write to you in the direst, most urgent of circumstances. Something terrible has befallen us. I hardly know how to write it. My poor dear father is dead -- dead, from a terrible accident. He went out alone at dusk to sketch – though I and the farmer warned him against it, for there are wild animals in the forests – and he was attacked, not by wolves, but by sheepdogs. They are trained to kill strangers near the sheep, as you know. He was so badly savaged that nothing could be done to save him. No doubt the farmer and the shepherds are as horrified and grief-stricken as I.

But I could not stay. I came straight home, only to find that my uncle André and Miklos have gone away. Little do they know what sad news awaits them on their return! The housekeeper will tell them, of course. As for me, I cannot stay here alone. I write to implore you, Madam Mina, for the sake of the deep regard in which I hold you, and the kindness you have shown me, to let me come and stay with you for a while. I ask something so presumptuous only in the direst necessity. I would be no trouble – indeed, would do anything to earn my keep! If it is impossible, I understand, but if it is in your power to look kindly upon my request I would be for ever grateful – you know not how grateful! I can write no more.

Yours ever,
Elena Kovacs.

## Letter, Mina Harker to Elena Kovacs

Exeter, 5 September

My dear Elena,

But of course you must come to us! My dear, you must feel distraught and very alone. We are all grieved and shocked by your news. It is a terrible reminder that we can never take the dominion of man over nature for granted, or think ourselves safe just because we are civilized, especially in such wild areas of the world as the Carpathians. We will let Professor Van Helsing know at once, for he is a great friend of your uncle and will wish to commiserate. I hope this blow will not come too hard upon him after the recent loss of his wife.

Now, will you let us know if we can do anything to assist in your journey? Whatever you need, be it documentation, railway timetables, the means to purchase tickets – anything, don't hesitate to ask. We have become quite expert in the business of travel! Once you arrive in England, you may take a train to Exeter or we can meet you in London. You have only to let us know.

There will be no need to 'earn your keep'; you will be our guest, of course, for as long as you wish. However, as you mention it, there is one matter in which you could help me greatly, as a friend. Quincey's nurse has left us to get married, and with his delicate health he needs constant attention. Alice Seward – Dr Seward's wife – has been helping us, but cannot do so for ever.

If you could be his companion, until a replacement is found – and knowing you, I feel certain that you and Quincey will be perfect friends – my debt would be to you, and not the other way round. Indeed, you would save my life!

Your friend,<br>
Mina Harker.

# Chapter Five

**_11 September_**
Elena has arrived. Jonathan and I went by train to London
to meet her, leaving Quincey in Alice Seward's care. I did
not want to leave him, for he has a chill, but seems somewhat
better now. Mary and I took trouble to make the largest
guest room very pleasant and welcoming, so Elena will be
comfortable. I am so glad to have her here, she will be such
a help and a good companion to both my son and myself –
indeed to all of us.

Her demeanour on arrival was very quiet; no doubt she
was tired from travelling and still shocked by the death of
her father, Emil. (We barely knew him, but it shames me
now to recall how I recorded in my diary that I did not like
him! How shallow such sentiments seem, when the object of
them cannot defend himself.) However, after a rest and a
good meal, she brightened and spoke briefly of her poor
father's death. She shed a few tears, but spoke so easily of
him that I have great hopes for her recovery.

As to his funeral, that was the only matter she seemed
unwilling to discuss. In the absence of her uncle, she has left
it in the hands of the Szekely farmers, or rather the Hungarian
authorities. This makes me fear that she has indeed fled, as
a means of avoiding the actuality of her father's death. But
she is young still, and has led so sheltered a life, that
I cannot blame her. On the contrary, she will find no
blame or judgement as our guest, but only our care and
love!

I told her that we, and Van Helsing, have had, so far, no luck in locating her uncle and Miklos. Van Helsing had a letter from Professor Kovacs, informing him that they had gone into the mountains near Hermannstadt. We can only wait until they return from their expedition – and meanwhile protect Elena from all anxiety.

After Elena had gone to bed, I sat in the parlour with Alice for a while, speaking of our guest. Alice will return to Dr Seward in a day or two, once Elena has recovered from her journey. 'I will be sorry to leave Quincey,' Alice told me, 'but it will be good to return home to my husband.'

'We are so grateful for your help,' I said. 'We will miss you, but it is unfair of us to have kept you away from home for so long.'

'I do hope Elena will be a help to you. She's little more than a child herself. There is something dark inside her . . . I think she has suffered a great deal. I can always come to you again, if you need me.'

Alice's words troubled me a little, for I trust her implicitly. I do so like her. I admit, we had reservations when, five years ago, Dr Seward first announced he was marrying her; a childless widow ten years older than himself, a comfortably built creature of a certain grace but no great beauty, and her hair already turning grey. But once we became acquainted, we were quickly won over. She is one of the kindest, wisest souls I have ever met. It was quite a strain at first, remembering never to mention Lucy's name in her presence. Once, Lucy's name did slip out, and I was mortified; but Alice took me aside, and said so sweetly, 'Mina, I know all about Lucy. I know that she was beautiful, which I am not, and that my dear John loved her, even though she was promised to another. And I know how she died, and that it broke his heart. Oh yes, John has told me everything. That is why he needs me; because he can tell me such things, and I will never be shocked or disbelieving.'

I was very startled by this, yet relieved that she knew our secret story of Dracula. It meant we could be open and trusting with her, and not have to watch every word. Alice smiled and went on, 'I know you must wonder why John is marrying me, and not a girl as young, pure and lovely as Lucy, especially when it would be easy for a handsome, accomplished doctor like him to make such a match. The reason is simple. He dares not love another Lucy, for fear that she would be taken from him as Lucy was.' There was no bitterness in her voice as she said this, only warm understanding. 'With me, he feels safe. He is a good, caring man, but he has his black moods when all that is bad in the world weighs upon him. He needs someone to protect him, someone who will never be torn away by another – be it rival or monster.'

That is Alice. Our rock! Proof that wisdom and good sense are far more valuable qualities in a wife than beauty – and all credit to Dr Seward for realizing it.

### *14 September*

Alice has gone home, and Elena is settling in beautifully. She is such a dear, helpful girl. Quincey adores her. He has roses in his cheeks and loves his new companion. She enlivens him when he is strong enough to play; when he is tired and peevish, she soothes him. It is a delight to see them together; Quincey, fair as an angel, his face rapt and intent on hers; Elena, neat and dark-haired, sitting with such demure grace as she reads to him. Her English is excellent; I have no fear of her leading Quincey into mistakes! Though once or twice I have heard *him* correct *her*, which made me smile.

I feel we will be soul mates. I have had no truly close woman friend since we lost Lucy. Elena is, naturally, very different from Lucy – who in life was a sweet, passionately animated soul. Elena is quiet and demure, with large, dark, watchful eyes. A little wary of being in a new country, with its different customs. But often a smile dimples her cheek, and there is such kindness and intelligence in her face. I truly feel as if I have known her all my life – perhaps in another lifetime! Almost without exchanging words I feel very close to her. There is surely a bond between us!

## 16 September
We have had the most delightful day.

Jonathan was at work, of course, but Elena and I took Quincey for a walk. I feared it would be too much for him but he marched along like a little soldier, and we went much further than we meant to. We are lucky to have the countryside within a few minutes' walk of our house. It was such a beautiful day, warm without being too hot, the sun gleaming on the meadows and edging the trees with soft golden light. The air was full of fluff and seeds, white gossamer! And late-summer flowers everywhere; roses in the gardens, wild flowers in the fields.

We stopped for a cream tea at a little cottage near the church, and had a long talk – the three of us – in the tea room. Quincey's talk is very grown-up for his age. (I suppose that is due to him having, of necessity, to be with adults rather than other children. I hope he does not feel too deprived, but we cannot risk him being exposed to every childhood illness.)

On the way back, Elena was very interested in the church and insisted on going inside the churchyard to read the gravestones. Parts of it are very overgrown with long grasses and cow parsley; so much life burgeoning among the lichen-covered stones. Indeed it is a bigger and more rambling place than I had realized, with long aisles that are invisible from the road and some remarkable tall gravestones with crosses and angels looking down. There are even sepulchres in hidden corners, monuments to the more influential families of the area. But these were overshadowed by dark yews and looked very dank and unkempt; I thought it would not be healthy for Quincey to explore them, and so suggested that we continue on our way. Strange, how Elena dragged her feet, as if she did not want to leave! I suppose she is thinking of her father.

She was not sombre as we walked back, however. On the contrary, she was flushed from the fresh air and positively glowing with health and good humour. I am glad. I hope she will not try too hard to resist the natural process of grief, then suffer for it.

Quincey did not want to be put down for his nap when we returned home, but Elena persuaded him. He was so well today – do I dare to hope he might shake off his ill-health and grow into a strong young man after all?

The evening, too, passed very pleasantly. After dinner, we sat under the rose arbour on the patio with Jonathan and enjoyed the evening sunshine. The garden is so lovely just now. How perfect everything seems at present!

As I was preparing for bed, Elena came into our dressing room – Jonathan was already in bed – and we sat in our nightclothes before the mirror and combed each other's hair, just as I used to do with Lucy. It made me feel like a girl again! We laughed and whispered as we stroked the long dark tresses of each other's hair. Hers is darker than mine, and very long – I had not realized how long, for she wears it quite severely in the day – and very thick and silky.

This was such a pleasant end to a perfect day.


## 22 September

I have had nothing to record for some days. How sweet life is when there is nothing worth writing about! Even now, I have only a dream to record. I shall keep it in its proper place by writing it down – rather than letting it grow to unnatural proportions in my imagination!

It has become quite a habit of mine and Elena's, to talk

in our nightclothes before we go to bed. Last night she seemed more than usually beautiful; there was a sparkle in her eyes and colour burning in her cheeks. As I brushed and stroked her wonderful hair, she caught my hands and said, 'Madam Mina! You will never know how much I owe to you – how much I will yet owe – to your goodness and kindness in letting me stay. I am so happy here. Here I am free, as I never was free with my father. I love Quincey so much. I love all of you.' And to my surprise, she put her arms around my neck and hugged me, planting fervent kisses on my cheeks and neck. While I was pleased and flattered by her affection, there was also something in it that disturbed me – almost repelled me, in some way. As gently as I could, so as not to make it seem I rejected her embrace, I held her hands and eased her away.

'And we feel the same,' I said. 'You have enriched our household beyond measure. Quincey could not ask for a better, more attentive companion. Indeed, we would like you to stay for as long as you possibly can. Permanently, if you wish, and if your uncle – who, I assume, is now your guardian – agrees. You will always have a home here.'

At this she wept, her tears falling upon my hands to sparkle there. Her complexion was brilliant – beautiful. She thanked me and thanked me.

Jonathan was already asleep when I lay down beside him. He has seemed terribly tired since we came back from our sojourn in the summer, so I did not disturb him. I lay awake for a while. Presently I began to feel that something invisible was buffeting the air around my head – like a bird or a great bat. This impression was so powerful that I fancied I could hear leathery wings beating. I sat up. This was not some strange form of headache. I could not say what it was, but when it did not stop I became alarmed.

In order not to disturb my husband, I went back into the dressing room, closed the door and lit a lamp. I sat down in front of the mirror. The strange flapping sensation went on. I looked at my own reflection; I looked quite ordinary, apart from a slight frown . . . but then I saw, through some malicious trick of the light, what seemed a trace of a burn on my forehead, the unholy mark of the vampire. With a gasp I shut my eyes. The feeling worsened and I became dizzy, as if I were spiralling down a dark vortex.

It felt – I can think of no other way to describe it – *it felt as if something were trying to gain entry to my mind.* As the intensity increased it was less a flapping than a steady pressure, a hand on my forehead. Hard fingertips with pointed nails. It seemed to me that the whole room was melting and running down around me like candle wax, while strange voices sighed and wailed in mournful disharmony. I felt . . . afraid, yes, but so caught up in these weird sensations that fear was the least of them. My sight darkened. I saw stars on the darkness. All these sensations wove around me, unpleasantly tight yet strangely sweet. I felt myself beginning to laugh. I could no longer see myself in the mirror, only darkness and two red stars . . .

It came to me suddenly that whatever the presence was, it had entered my soul, and I was no longer myself but something evil, utterly divorced from God's grace. The moment I had this thought I began to fight it! I said, 'No,' over and over again. With all my will I resisted this terrible entity, forcing it out. I prayed. I built a great golden wall in my mind, adorned with shining crosses, and so thrust the intruder back outside the walls, out of my soul!

Suddenly it was over. I felt the pressure leave me. There was a sighing flurry around me, as if something were whirling around me in frustrated rage. Then it flowed away from me, as mist might be sucked away by a draught. I came back to my senses, and all was quiet, as if nothing had happened.

I was very shaken, and went down to the pantry for a small glass of wine to steady myself. By the time I came upstairs again the whole experience was diminishing, and showing itself for what it was: a nightmare.

I went back to bed, and was not troubled again.

I cannot imagine what caused this strange phantasm. It was clearly something within my own mind, which is a little worrying. A bad dream, although I seemed to be awake – at least I thought I was! Perhaps I was in fact sleepwalking, while dreaming I was conscious? That must be it. I hope I am not starting to sleepwalk, as poor Lucy used to!

The memory of it is distressing, but will not trouble me as long as it does not happen again! Or if it does, at least I know I have the strength to fight it.

ELENA KOVACS'S JOURNAL

**25 September**
I am so happy here! I do not deserve the kindness the Harkers have shown to me. Truly I do not deserve it.

I have my own big, bright room with a sink in one corner, and I am allowed complete privacy. No one enters without my permission. I know they will not find and read my journal because they would not dream of abusing my privacy! This is a revelation to me. My father never showed me such courtesy.

The boy is a delight. I almost have what I desired; a son, without the tyranny of marriage! I love him so, I must remind myself he is Madam Mina's. Quincey is good-mannered and bright, yet too sickly to get into much mischief. Instead we play and talk quietly, and I lull him to sleep with stories when he is tired, which is often. Poor soul, I wish he were in better health. I feel an intense bond with him. That is, a bond between him, and me, and that other whose spirit travels with me . . .

I cannot allow myself to grow too fond of the family. I know that they did a great wrong to him who is my friend and my Dark Companion.

He has been urging me to find a suitable resting place. He is ruthless but never unfair; he knows that each step takes time, and he is patient. More patient than I!

The day Madam Mina took me to the graveyard of the little church, I knew we had found the perfect place. I could not appear too interested or explore too deeply, much as I desired to, lest she become suspicious. (I hope she has not – but why would she?) I hate the frailties of my mortal body – that I would be so easily prevented, were I found out! And I must not be, for he needs me. Weak as I am, while he is disembodied I am the stronger, like a mother trying to bring a child into being. His existence is in my hands.

The next night, long after everyone had gone to bed, I left the house. I was very afraid that someone would hear me and catch me, for every floorboard groaned at my passing. But I escaped through a back door, and I was alone in the night, with the burden of earth from the castle on my shoulder.

It takes me a long time to reach the graveyard, for I am lost. But an easy walk after my long treks over the Carpathians! At last I recognize the silhouette of the church. I walk down long avenues of graves, watched by angels with blank marble eyes, letting his will guide me.

There are three sepulchres, all neglected and overgrown; none befits him. I take a step towards the largest, but he turns me towards the smallest, the most obscure. I understand. It lies in a dark hollow, overshadowed by yew trees; a squat building of white marble, discoloured by centuries of weather and drifting leaves. The path that winds down to it is barren, but for the mould of many autumns. I walk down eight steps and push open a rusted gate. If it has ever been locked, the lock rotted long ago.

Inside, the smell of damp stone and fungus reminds me of English churches, of the chapel in the castle in Transylvania. Strange that I used to find this smell repellent. Now it seems

74

exciting, 'the odour of sanctity', or the scent of history coming to life.

I light the candle that I brought with me. I see tombs on every side, and one in the centre with a plain, flat marble lid. All is very plain, neglected and covered in cobwebs. The floor has a carpet of leaf-mould, leaves blown in year after year and never swept away. I reflect that he should have a magnificent setting, not this! A vaulting marble mausoleum with carved effigies; that would be more befitting! But he whispers, no matter. It suffices.

I perceive his will as my own instinct; that is, knowing what I must do without being told. Following it, I try to shift the lid on the central tomb. I cannot lift or push it; I almost cry with frustration. But then I find it will swivel, leaving just enough room to pull out the skeleton that lies within. It comes apart in my hands; I take it out bone by bone, piling it in a corner. I don't know or care who it was. In its place, I spread the rich earth from the castle.

Strange, now I think of it, that I feel no disgust at any of this. In fact I laugh as I work. It seems so right, so fulfilling, like gardening; preparing the soil for the seed.

When I have smoothed the earth as best I can, I heave the lid back into place and sink down beside the tomb for a little while to rest.

He rewards me with a vision.

I see a scene; a bedroom, a big bed draped in white, washed in moonlight. Jonathan Harker lies in a deep trance of sleep while Mina kneels up on the bed, her nightdress bleached by the moon, embracing . . . embracing *him*. My Dark Companion. He is a tall, pallid figure in black; his face dazzles me, I cannot recall it clearly. He holds her with such tenderness that I feel jealous. But she resists, so he has to hold her arms away. He parts her collar, speaking softly but sternly to her. When he bends his head to her throat, and I see them both stiffen, my own body convulses in empathy. It seems an age before it ends. He raises his head; the blood glistens red on his mouth and on her nightdress. He speaks.

*'And so you, like the others, would play your brains against mine. You would help these men to hunt me and frustrate me in my designs! You know now, and they know in part already, and will know in full before long, what it is to cross my path. They should have kept their energies closer to home. Whilst they played wits against me – against me who commanded nations, and intrigued for them, and fought for them, hundreds of years before they were born – I was countermining them. And you, their best beloved one, are now to me, flesh of my flesh; blood of my blood; kin of my kin; my bountiful wine press for a while; and shall later be my companion and my helper. You shall be avenged in turn; for not one of them but shall minister to your needs. But as yet you are to be punished for what you have done. You have aided in thwarting me; now you shall come to my call. When my brain says "Come!" to you, you shall cross land or sea to do my bidding; and to that end this!'*

Then he opens his shirt, and with a long sharp nail he opens a red wound in the flesh of his own chest. The blood flows out. *His* blood, which is now dust! And he takes Madam Mina's head and forces her mouth into the flow, so that the blood must run into her lips and down her throat, the hot-metal blood, like molten iron, liquid bronze to rage through her own veins. She must swallow it or suffocate.

She groans and trembles, blood on her mouth and on her splayed hands, as if the end of the world has come. Her menfolk come bursting into the room. My Dark Companion throws her down, and they force him back with their crosses, and he becomes mist.

The vision ends then. I rise, shake the dirt from my clothes, and make my way home.

I believe I know what the vision means, but I cannot write of it yet. All of this made me weep bitterly. With jealousy, grief, or longing, I do not know. He asks so much of me. Too much. But it must be done. I want . . .

I need no husband, no family to chain me. My father died for trying to imprison me. I follow a bright, burning path instead – the brightness of the moon and the burning of freedom, of passion. For this I will be reviled – but I cannot turn back.

## MINA HARKER'S JOURNAL

### 30 September

I have been unable to write until now. Quincey has been terribly ill. Pneumonia again. He is not out of danger yet. Elena has been wonderful.

How painful it is to see his sweat-dampened little face upon the pillow! Sometimes as pale as tallow, sometimes flushed with fever. How painful to hear such coughs racking his chest. I do not know how his heart and lungs have borne it.

We were almost prepared to lose him three days ago, but he has pulled back from the brink. He has such a fighting spirit inside him! I do not know how he has suffered so much illness and survived.

I believe his current bout of illness is my fault. That walk we took the other day – we went much too far. I overestimated Quincey's strength; he seemed so energetic, but children will always go on long after they should stop. It was my responsibility to say, 'Enough!' but I did not. This is the consequence! Jonathan, Elena and the doctor have all told me not to blame myself, but I cannot help it.

### 1 October

Quincey a little better. He is eating again, at least. Also played with his train upon the bed-cover for half an hour. Good. We are not out of the woods yet – will we ever be?

On another matter, it concerns us that we still have no word from Professor Kovacs. His expedition is obviously taking longer than he anticipated – I do hope nothing has gone wrong! We have all had enough worry lately. Jonathan and I know him only a little, but he seemed such a good man, and I know how hard Van Helsing and Elena would take his loss. Still, it has not come to that yet! He can only be grateful that we are taking care of his niece, however, for she has no one else.

# Chapter Six

**Date unknown**

I have no means of telling how much time has passed. My writing is so crabbed that I can barely read it myself. But record this I must, in the hope that even if not you, Abraham, someone, in some far distant time, might discover it.

I am still alive. For how much longer, I cannot tell. But of this I am sure; the Scholomance exists.

So my expedition has not been in vain. Even though I do not expect to survive, at least my death will have been in the pursuance of knowledge — with what sweet irony, since it was greed for knowledge that exiled Adam and Eve from Eden.

This is a labyrinth of mysteries that defies human understanding. I have merely set foot in the porch.

After my candles burned out, I spent what seemed an endless and hideous length of time in utter blackness. I knew that whatever had emerged from the webs and killed Miklos was somewhere in the darkness with me. I sat rigid, waiting for the faintest sound or the whisper of dry flesh against mine. I was aware that the creature might be a waking delusion, that it could have been the blow to the head that killed my friend – but it was the uncertainty that nearly unhinged me, the total loss of trust in my own senses.

When exhaustion overcame me, I drifted in and out of sleep. How long this phase lasted I do not know. At length I was woken by a blinding light.

I squinted against the brilliance, not knowing where I was. My head pounded, every inch of my body ached. At last my eyes began to adjust and I could see.

I was still on the floor of the chamber. But now the place was alight with candles! Miklos lay lifeless on the bench, where I had laid him out as best I could, that he might retain some dignity. His body was cold and waxen. An old man stood before me with a taper in his hand, his thin lips drawn back to show long sharp teeth. He had a cadaverous face, a long hooked nose and a bald pate with white hair flowing around it. The robe he wore was deep red and sewn with sigils like those on the marble block and the walls. These were all brief, dream-like impressions on my part. I was so caught up in horror that I could not even speak; a vile odour of decay and burning tallow choked me. When the old man spoke in the Magyar tongue, I heard his long teeth rattling in their sockets.

'My dear friend, my dear guest. Make use of you I must, but I will never misuse you. I have waited so long, my precious visitor. Welcome. Welcome.'

His face loomed closer and closer over me. I experienced the utmost revulsion and a desire to thrust him off, yet I could not resist. Then I felt a sudden intense cold that centred on my throat. I heard voices whispering all around me. This experience was unpleasant, yet there was something in it that I welcomed, as an exhausted traveller welcomes deep sleep.

When I woke again, I was lying on the floor with a jacket – Miklos's – pillowed under my head. The chamber was still alight with candles, but now there was a younger, pale-haired man sitting on the bench, his chin on his hands, looking down at me. He wore a red robe that seemed identical to the old man's; I mean that it seemed to be the very same garment. An odour of age and damp clung to it, and there were speckles of black mould between the gorgeous ropes of embroidery.

He had taken the rations from my knapsack and set them out, paltry as they were, as a sort of mock feast. Seeing the food, my hunger and thirst leaped ravenously. It must have been a day or two since I had eaten, though I have lost track of time.

'Eat,' the man said. 'Don't be afraid. My questions are pressing, but it would be ill-mannered of me to impose them on a guest who is starving.' So I did as he said. The effort of sitting up made me breathless.

Bizarre, it seemed, that I could sit upon the floor to break my fast while my friend lay dead nearby and this strange creature sat watching me, but my hunger overwhelmed all finer considerations. I was weak, and my neck pained me. Food, water and a few sips of brandy restored my strength somewhat. All the time I ate, the stranger watched me with a half smile on his lips. Out of courtesy – perhaps also out of the desire to find common ground, to make a frightful situation seem more normal – I offered him a share of my repast, but he declined. 'I have already partaken,' he said, with a strange, soundless laugh.

He was very thin, his wrists skeletal within the loose sleeves of his robe, his hair colourless, his age indeterminate. He was anything between thirty and fifty. He could have been the son of the old man I first saw. He could indeed have been the same man, at a younger age. And I, whether through the madness induced by captivity or some deep instinct, felt that this *was* the same man – grown younger by taking Miklos's life!

I noticed also a great axe leaning against the marble dais, an ancient thing with a pitted, curved blade that might have seen many a medieval battle. Had it been there all the time, hidden by the webs?

When I finished eating, and was packing what was left into my knapsack again, my companion asked, 'Who are you?'

I told him my name and title. My own voice sounded hoarse to my ears, lacking in any authority.

'I am called . . . Beherit,' he said. 'It is not my given name, but I am called it. Why have you come here?'

How difficult it is to communicate when one is in the dark, as it were – bereft of introduction, the mutual knowledge of status, position, purpose, etc., that oils the wheels of social intercourse! 'I am a scholar,' I began. 'My friend and I were engaged in an archaeological expedition . . .'

'You speak strangely,' he said. 'What were you seeking?' He sounded dangerously impatient, and I, being at his mercy, had no choice but to be honest.

'A fabled place known as the Scholomance. We sought evidence that an ancient establishment may once have existed that led to the myth. A secret order of alchemists, perhaps, or . . .'

He was laughing, a soft, inappropriate laughter that was almost feminine, yet sinister. 'And have you found it?'

'I believe so. Can you enlighten me?'

He didn't answer, but asked, 'What is the year?'

I told him. To my shock, he covered his face with his hands and let out a long, loud groan that made me tremble. Then he leaped up and stared at me. 'How is the world changed?' he demanded. 'Tell me!'

I was alarmed. 'Changed – since when?'

He pointed a bony finger at the cocoon. 'I have slumbered there for some four hundred years. Dreams come to me, but how do I know if they are true visions or illusions?'

'Much has changed,' I said, stammering. I began some garbled account of Wallachian, Turkish and Austro-Hungarian history, but I know not how much sense I made; calm again, he waved a hand to stop me.

'Nothing has changed,' he said idly. 'The same nations squabble over the same territories. How reassuring.'

'But the advances in science –'

He gave a quick, hard laugh. 'And where do you think that knowledge has come from? Leaked from here, I have no doubt. Why were you searching? Did you wish to apply? You are some four hundred years too late to join, I fear. The Scholomance has been long deserted.'

'So this is . . .' My scholarly spirit rallied, pushing fear aside. 'You mean that this truly is the place . . .'

'It was.' He sighed deeply, and I smelled a sweetish, metallic odour on his breath, like blood. By now I suspected, knew, what he was. 'And as you have found it, you must have been meant to find it. Which means . . .'

'What?'

'That the time has come for rebirth. The planets shift in their courses, the stars tremble, empires rise and fall, and our time comes once again.'

I said, 'My only concern now is to find a way out.' I looked at Miklos, my heart souring with grief. 'Though it is too late for my friend. Is it too much to ask that you help me . . . ?' I was going to say his name, but stopped myself, for I know that Beherit is the name of a devil.

'But my friend, you cannot leave me so soon,' he said smoothly. 'We are surely meant to help each other. Come, let me take you somewhere that you may rest more comfortably.'

He put out his hand and helped me up. My head span and I gasped for breath, in no condition to defend myself or flee from him. Once I was on my feet, he left me and went to stand over Miklos. He gazed tenderly, I would even say lovingly, on Miklos's face, and stroked the sunken cheeks in a way that nauseated me – almost gloatingly.

'They do not always rise again,' he said. 'The conditions must be precise. Three kisses. After all, how could they all come back? The Undead would spread like a rippling circle of plague, until there were no living left for us to prey on. Still, we had better be sure.'

Through a glaze of utter disbelief I watched Beherit take the battleaxe from where it leaned against the dais. In one swift arc he swung it down – I cried out but it was over even before I opened my mouth! – and the blade cleaved through Miklos's neck. The head rolled to the side and hit the floor. It lay there, discoloured, misshapen, a white bone gleaming in the purple ooze of the stump, candlelight shining like tears on the cheeks. I reeled away, sick, unable to comprehend what I'd seen.

Beherit came to me – having set the axe aside – and gave me plum brandy from my flask. 'Why, why?' I kept saying, but he gave no answer. He led me away – taking one of my candles, but leaving the rest behind – and I was so dizzy, so unmanned by horror, that I went meekly with him like a lamb. I could not look back at Miklos.

On the far side of the chamber, at a juncture of two walls, a narrow black aperture had appeared. I had not seen this although I had passed the spot a hundred times! It was an archway leading into a tunnel – but not the one by which we had entered.

'Why could I not find this before?' I gasped.

'Because you are not an Initiate,' he replied. 'You do not possess the key.'

I was being led deeper into my prison – but at the time I was only glad to leave the chamber and the ghastly body of my poor friend.

The tunnel was tiled with tiny mosaic pieces of deep ultramarine. A flight of steps led downwards, then opened into what resembled the courtyard of a Roman villa. There was a square pool in the centre, pillars and shadowy cloisters which hinted at rooms beyond. All was covered in, not by the sky, but by the roof of an immense cavern. Light fell through high embrasures, which resembled natural fissures in the rock. How glad I was to see natural daylight, faint and unobtainable as it was! Strange plants, like primitive, dark-loving ferns, grew profusely.

All was neglected, covered in dust and debris blown in from outside. But once it must have been a place of gleaming magnificence!

'Ah, too long deserted,' Beherit said softly. 'These were our living quarters.'

'But who built it?' I gasped.

'The students, of course. Have you never heard the Devil referred to as a geometrician, an architect? He, not God, gives this knowledge to men. God is too jealous to impart it.' What a strange mixture of contempt and irony filled Beherit's voice! And although I dreaded him, he also held me in a kind of fascination – as he holds my life or death in his hands.

Well, then he brought me here; a simple, spacious room off the cloister, where I sit and write these strange events in my journal. A couch with a padded seat and rolled arms makes a firm but welcome bed. He has left me alone for a time – where he has gone, I know not. I am afraid to sleep, but I must.

### Later

My sleep was undisturbed, though he has been back; I found the rest of my rations, water and brandy beside me. They will last some days . . . if Beherit lets me live that long. Only let him give me some answers before I die!

It was dark when I woke, but now a grey light has crept in. So another night has passed.

I have explored the courtyard and environs, but found no way out. This is a large, intricate villa, with other courtyards leading off this one and the most wonderful statues, tributes to the naked beauty of men and women, set beside formal pools. I almost lost myself among them, and only found my way back to this room with difficulty. So, I am still imprisoned. At least this place is less oppressive. There is somewhere to go, a sense that there *might* be a way out if I search long enough. This in itself lessens my urgent desire for escape.

(Note: The sanitary arrangements have a classical sophistication that puts our modern ones to shame! There is icy running water, and also a supply of scaldingly hot, sulphurous water, which indicates the presence of volcanic springs.)

As I am weak and constantly cold, I cannot walk for long without resting. So, a brief respite for food, then I will set forth again. But why should I return here? I can take my meagre belongings with me and rest where I will.

This is the most wondrous place, Abraham, whether created by the Devil's disciples or not. My fear has receded somewhat; after all, death is the worst that can happen to me. But to discover this lost citadel on my way – it would be a glorious manner in which to depart the world, if only I could make my discovery known . . .

### Later

Abraham, I have found the most extraordinary structure. A library, the like of which I could never have imagined. A scholar would give his soul to explore such a place! I can barely hold the pen in my excitement. How I wish Miklos were with me to share my discovery!

I have been in the library for hours and am now too tired to go elsewhere. I have no wish to leave, in any case! This is the most momentous and frustrating discovery of my life! It has taken me a good deal of time to be calm enough to write.

I have found three rooms so far. Each is a huge vault, simple in style, with tall, plain pillars and a gallery running round the walls at a height of about twenty feet. The books, manuscripts and scrolls arc shelved from floor to ceiling. The light, filtering through high windows, is very dim – just enough to read the clearer titles. I wish I had a lamp. The floor is filmed with dust, the air laden with the silence of ages. Statues stand on the broad marble floor. These are rooms that would grace any great university or museum!

There are works in Latin, Greek and Hebrew, some – I suspect – in older tongues and alphabets that I do not even recognize. Many of these appear fragile but well preserved; I would hesitate to touch them, even if I could. The translation of them would take teams of scholars a century! But, friend Abraham, I believe many of these to be copies of books lost in the destruction of the great ancient libraries. I have seen ancient histories, works of philosophy, apocrypha and gnostic tracts – this all found on the most superficial inspection!

This is such a treasure-house of knowledge that I tremble to contemplate it. But Abraham, this is also the most frustrating moment of my life. This is a chained library, a fascinating fact in itself; the books are chained to the shelves, so it should be possible to read them but not to take them away. However, the shelves are all closed in behind doors of thick, leaded glass. I have tried to open them; all are locked. I could weep. To have such glories at my fingertips, yet be unable to touch them – !

### Later, night

I fell asleep on a couch, only to be woken by a flare of lamplight swimming across the blackness. I opened my eyes and found Beherit leaning over me. His face was eldritch, all sharp planes and angles, washed with light from below. His hungry, cold smile filled me with terror.

'I could not find you,' he said. 'I might have known you would find your way in here, scholar! Now be still. You know what I need of you. I must have nourishment . . .'

He leaned down and down over me. I could not move, though I was in a paroxysm of fear. Instead I found myself loosening my shirt collar, as if to facilitate his vile intent. I saw the red tip of his tongue between his pale lips, heard his breathing grow heavier and more stertorous. A strange langour ran through me; the air seemed to gather and hold itself, vibrating as if a deep bell were sounding somewhere far off; I felt the tongue touch my neck, and the thin body pressing itself along mine.

I submitted, to my shame, no longer wanting to evade the embrace but welcoming it. Darkness sang in my head, drawing me down into an ocean that seemed at once sharply bitter and honey-sweet. I laughed breathlessly. How much easier it is to sink into the Devil's toils than to seek the narrow, thorny path to God!

The next time I opened my eyes – feeling that an hour or more had passed – Beherit had changed again. Now he is in the prime of youth, his flesh full and rosy. His hair – oh, his hair is a glory, a flow of rich pale gold falling past his shoulders to weave about his hips. A woman might sell her soul for such hair! And there is a light about him, almost a nimbus, a glow that seems to come from his whole body, his fair gleaming skin.

Such was the impression of beauty that I wanted to fall down in worship. He might have been a six-winged seraph; wings would have seemed a natural part of him.

When he saw that I was conscious, he gave me a tall beaker made of strange glass, dark blue with metallic hues caught in it. It contained red wine, which I drank greedily. Beherit sat beside me like a nurse, feeding me morsels of food. Then he began to question me again about the modern world; I cannot remember what he asked or how I replied, only his voice hissing on and on, and his hair gleaming in the light, and the sense of oppression and menace that lay upon me.

When I needed to relieve myself he insisted on accompanying me – where did he think I might run to? But it was as well he did, for on the way back I fainted. He helped me back to the library couch and sat on a chair beside me, watching me as a cat watches its prey.

Then he asked intently, 'What do you know of Dracula?'

This question shocked me so much that I did not know how to answer. 'Nothing.'

He had my journal in his hand, and waved it at me. 'I have read your scribblings. You know of him!'

I was strengthless; he was terrifying, with his hard white teeth shining. So I told him, Abraham, the story that you told me. If I did wrong, forgive me. I was – am – in thrall. As I spoke, Beherit interrupted with expressions of contempt that gave me the impression that he loathed Dracula. Yet when I came to the part where Dracula was destroyed, his reaction astonished me. He leapt up in a kind of panic, crying out, 'But Dracula cannot be dead! He cannot be!' He walked around the room, tearing at his hair and wringing his hands in the most startling demonstration of anguish. I was alarmed, and at a loss. Then he turned viciously upon me, his hand squeezing my throat.

'You lie!'

'I do not, I swear!' I cried in fear of my life. 'All I know is what my friends told me. Dracula fed upon their loved ones; they outwitted and destroyed him!'

I thought Beherit would kill me. Instead he let go and calmed himself with a sibilant, pensive breath. 'You tell what you believe to be the truth,' he said. 'I accept that. But I say again, Dracula cannot be dead. He was the most powerful student the Scholomance has ever seen. He would let nothing sever him from immortality. He must go on, in spirit, in a changed form. But dead? Impossible!'

I was almost too dizzy and exhausted to question him, but I forced myself. 'You knew him, then,' I said. 'He was here.'

'Yes. Of course he was here.' This said with a thin, mirthless irony.

'Then tell me, Beherit – tell me your story!'

'In time.' He smiled, but his eyes were calculating. 'Come, my friend, there is more to show you.'

I was barely able to stand. He supported me, but there was no question of my refusing to go. He tugged at a bookshelf and it opened like a door to reveal a corridor, barely high enough for us to walk upright. He went first, bearing a lamp; I followed, leaning on him, intrigued despite my misgivings.

This corridor wound deep into the mountain, now descending, now climbing, and its oppressive walls were wholly covered in mosaics of wondrous artistry but of lurid, disturbing images; sea monsters, hideous gaping fish, mermaids, leviathans, all portrayed with a lasciviousness of design and colour that sickened the very soul. These grew worse as we went, portraying mutilation and bestiality. Other tunnels led off the main one, and often we passed dark recesses in which the stink of alchemy still lingered. Shuddering, I wondered what experiments the Devil's students had conducted in these arcane laboratories. Once, the light from Beherit's lamp fleeted across the back of one such cave, and I caught a glimpse of jars in which pale shapes floated in greenish fluids.

With every step I sank deeper into a sort of loathing, a dread of what awaited me.

'Consider the Devil,' said my companion as we went. 'He it is who thwarts God's will by giving mankind the wisdom God did not mean us to have. God wishes us to be innocent and obedient. The Devil gives us knowledge and thereby the power to challenge God's will. Lucifer makes us disobedient, as he was disobedient – daring to challenge God for his throne! Can you not admire him a little, for his audacity? After all, it takes courage to question the arrogance of God.

'For that audacity he fell. Lucifer, the most beautiful of the seraphim, was cast into the darkness for daring to question God! Was he evil – or brave?'

I was in no state to make any comment on this dubious philosophy.

Beherit continued, 'Writings in the library tell us that God created man to replace the fallen archangels. They say Lucifer is jealous of God's love for mankind, of the attention He pays to them, and that is why Lucifer forever tries to subvert them to his own cause. But think; he does so not by tormenting them but by giving them great gifts. Knowledge and magic and science. All science has been called the work of the Devil at some time, mathematicians and astronomers burned at the stake! Who then are the fools? The Devil and his disciples – or God and his?

'A small matter, to sell your soul in return for such riches of wisdom, beauty, language, medicine, power. Truly it seemed a risk worth taking; ten scholars, only one to be taken by the Devil in payment, and each of us thinking, "It will not be me." '

I said nothing. The silence seemed full of a brooding, blood-red watchfulness; we passed through a series of ante-chambers, where the mosaic walls gleamed with dark hues of crimson. We were coming to a place of great significance, I knew, but I was unprepared for the tangible power of the place, the assault upon my abraded senses!

I can only describe the chamber to which Beherit brought me as a temple. It was perhaps fifty feet in diameter, ten-sided yet rounded in shape, like the inside of a sea urchin. As Beherit put down his lamp in the centre, I saw that every surface, even the floor, was fraught with feverish images; blood-stained angels, gorgeous demons, writhing monsters copulating with humans, scenes of battle and martyrdom among florid vegetation, all intertwined like some nightmare fable, and all in turbid hues of purple, bloody bronze, greenish copper. If ever colours could exude the very essence of corruption and degeneracy, these did! And they seemed to vibrate as if alive. Panic was rising within me.

On the far wall of the temple stood a great statue of a dragon. It was carved from black rock, monstrous but detailed in every gleaming scale, with huge amber eyes that shone from within. There was a door set between its forefeet, made of a translucent rock such as quartz with sigils carved into it. It seemed to me that a red glow came through the whiteness, edging the sigils with fire. The air was warm and thick with sulphur.

'Here generations of scholars have pledged themselves to Satan,' Beherit said softly. 'Nine to return to their lives and use their wisdom freely as they desired. One to give himself up to his Master's will.'

'Was Dracula the tenth?' I asked.

'He was. He bargained for immortality, as did the most adept of us, and he received it. But when it was time for the choosing, and he was chosen, he refused to submit. He would serve no one, not even Lucifer himself.'

I laughed; I could not help it. Beherit frowned at me. 'This amuses you?'

'Of course! You mean he rebelled against Lucifer as Lucifer rebelled against God?'

'He dared to defy the Devil, yes. We tried to force him – for if he were not taken, one of us would be in his place. In his frenzy, Dracula killed most of the other students and fled the school. I was the only one to survive. Even the powers of Hell could not hold Dracula. In rage, the Devil abandoned the Scholomance and vowed to teach no more.'

'It happened here, did it not?' I whispered in sudden, dreadful revelation. 'Dracula killed them here!'

Beherit let out the longest sigh, gazing at a golden mosaic star in the temple's apex. 'Yes. Here.'

'And . . . have you seen the Devil? What is he like?'

Beherit shrugged. 'Like a burning angel. Like a hideous horned dragon. Like you or me.'

'And you?' I whispered. '*Are* you . . . ?'

'Lucifer?' Beherit slipped an arm about my shoulders. 'That, my dear friend, I cannot tell you. But I need you.' His melodious voice lulled me. I wished him to go on talking to me, for however evil he is, he is the only companion I have. 'I am immortal but without blood I become languid. Four hundred years without blood left me as you saw, a dry shell. Your companion slaked my first, fierce thirst; I could not help but kill him. For that I ask your forgiveness. I was able to be gentler with you. You have given me back my youth and beauty, and I want to give you something in return. Immortality.'

'You wish to make me a vampire!' I said, shaken by violent disgust. 'No!'

'But if I don't, you'll die. Your body cannot support my appetites.'

'I would rather die!'

He spoke caressingly, his finger stroking my neck. 'And miss the library?'

I burned with longing to unlock those glass doors and draw down the chained books from their shelves, and he knew it! 'Why not just kill me? I am nothing to you!'

'On the contrary, I value you more highly than you know. I need you to make a journey for me; you cannot do that, dead. I want you to find Dracula.'

'I told you, he was destroyed!'

'And I tell you, he survived.' Beherit took my face between his hands. His expression was sad, full of suffering; not malign or gloating. 'He will return to life. He must. And I wish to prevent him ever coming to the Scholomance again.'

'But how would I find him?'

'Where your friends are, he will be. He will want revenge.'

These words chilled me so sharply, I began to forget my predicament. To think that you and your dear friends, Abraham, could be in danger again! 'Then I must warn them, but not Undead. Let me go! Why would Dracula wish to come to the Scholomance, in any case?'

'Because he left too hastily. One day he will realize that he lacks his full power, and he will return to lay claim to the vital secret. He was isolated too long in his castle to realize his full potential – but now he is in the wide world, he will think too much and remember. Imagine a vampire no longer tied to his native earth, fearless of any holy symbol or herb, whose powers in daylight may be as great as they are by night. Would he not be a creature to rival Satan himself?'

'You are jealous!'

'You are correct. However, it is in no one's interest that he comes back here and finds the secret of such power, is it?'

'What secret?' I said, confused.

Beherit went unexpectedly, intently, towards the door beneath the dragon. This gesture overwhelmed me with dread. I felt that something unspeakable lurked behind that weirdly glowing door and if he opened it I would be driven insane. I cried, 'No! No!'

He opened the door. I glimpsed . . . nothing to justify my abject terror, only a vast lightless cave, from which a sulphur-laden wind blew as if from an abyss. I heard water dripping into some unseen lake far below. Each drop was, I believed, the tolling of my own death-knell. I fell to the ground, screaming, 'No!'

The door slammed shut with an ear-splitting bang.

'All the powers of Hell,' came Beherit's voice. He was crawling towards me on his hands and knees, his teeth and eyes shining. 'Find Dracula for me, my love. Watch him. If he challenges you, warn him not to come here. Don't try to prevent him, or he will surely destroy you; only dissuade him.'

'Kill me, or let me go alive,' I begged, 'but not Undead!'

'But I am bound to kill you, for I need your blood. Therefore you can only help me Undead. But come to me willingly and I will give you . . .' He put his full lips to my ear. 'The keys to the library and all eternity to study there.'

I couldn't fight him any more.

He fed on me a third time, both of us on our knees in the

feverish womb of the temple. Demons came down from the walls and danced around us. Then he drew down the neck of his robe, pierced his own breast with a fingernail, and pulled my mouth to the wound. His blood ran into my mouth and I swallowed. 'Ah, now I know your thoughts. I know why you came. You did not lie. And you will not betray me.'

So now, dear Abraham, we know the price of my soul. A library.

### Later

I am waiting for death to come. We are back in the library, Beherit sitting cross-legged on the couch, I reclining against him, using what little strength remains to complete this account. I am sorry it is incomplete and makes so little sense. I am very tired now.

What lies beyond, I do not know. Elena, Emil, Miklos, Abraham, forgive me. My sight fades and I can no longer hold the pen. God hears no prayers from this place.

I asked Beherit a while ago why he could not make this journey to find Dracula himself. He replied, 'I cannot leave here. For me, Initiate or not, there is no way out.'

# Chapter Seven

*12 October*

I write this alone in my study, with the little white cat watching me. Puss is always a pleasant, quiet companion. I have taken to spending more time in here since Elena arrived. Not that I have any aversion to the girl, far from it; I am glad to see her lightening Mina's burden in caring for Quincey. But her arrival has coincided with a black mood falling upon me. I don't wish to dampen their spirits with my grim humour, nor to worry or affect Mina in any way. I will simply keep myself out of their way until I am more fit company.

I don't know what has caused it this time. Life at Hawkins & Harker has been no more troublesome than usual. Quincey, then; but concern for my son has never in the past precipitated such self-absorbed blackness as I feel. No, this is an old enemy. Each time I overcome it, I believe it gone for good, yet I should know by now that it will always spring back with renewed vigour.

I have often been prey to disturbing dreams and fancies, ever since I first went to Castle Dracula and there learned what horrors swarm beneath the civilized patina of our world. I was ill with brain fever for many weeks after I escaped. I don't expect the shadows of that ever to leave me. Yet I have reassured myself that they are only fancies – the natural, nervous reaction of my mind to extreme trauma, so Dr Seward says – and Mina is always there, of course, to comfort me with her kind, practical sensibilities. She has been my strength. Even when she so nearly fell prey to that foul monster, her spirit never faltered.

Sometimes, when darker moods come upon me, as now, one scene haunts me. To think that I lay unconscious while Dracula fed upon my wife beside me! I still cannot forgive myself, although Mina has told me often that I must. We all know that Dracula put some unholy sleep upon the servants and myself that night. But to think he forced her to drink from his veins – as if binding her in some unholy wedding, a marriage forged in Hell – and could only be detached from her by death!

How hard I have tried to blank that scene from my mind. Dr Seward, however, once suggested that the more strenuously I try to forget, the more fiercely and horribly it will linger.

I hate this mood, for it discolours everything. For example: I know that Elena is perfectly sweet and charming; Mina finds her so, and to all appearances she is perfect. But to me there seems something dark and sly about her – a sideways look from her eyes, a half-smile no one else sees. I do her a great injustice with these impressions, yet I cannot shake them off. She is a very handsome girl, it is true. I wonder if she must always wear her plain, buttoned-to-the-neck dresses like a governess? Perhaps Mina might take her to obtain a less severe garment, to wear for dinner or when we have guests.

I find myself watching Elena. I cannnot understand why it is that she fascinates yet in some way repels me. I watch for signs that she may not be the perfect nurse-companion for Quincey that Mina assumes. I see no evidence, have no basis whatsoever for these suspicions. I can only conclude they spring from my own disordered perceptions. As such, I must try to keep them in check.

### 14 October

Last night I fell asleep in my study while going over columns of figures. I dreamed that the lamp burned dim and I sat in my chair unable to move. Elena moved through the room like a ghost; I hadn't heard her enter. She seemed to glide along past the bookshelves and I could read the spines of the books *through* her! But the books had strange names and are none I possess. They had titles such as *Red Oyster, Violet Pearl; Prospero's Quill; Alchemy With Angels;* and other such nonsense. When she passed the mirror above the mantelpiece she had no reflection. Then she circled in the same fashion round and round my chair, her hair and dress like ebony, her face pale and glowing. She smiled. She reached out and stroked my hands and I heard her voice, faint yet icily musical as crystal, with her lovely accent. 'You are young and strong, Jonathan. There are kisses for us all.'

She leaned towards me and I was possessed by fear, revulsion and a strange excitement – an echo of that terrible time when the three women came to me in Castle Dracula. My mind rebelled but my body lay back in languor, waiting. As her burning lips touched my throat I awoke violently. I was, of course, alone. Then I felt dismally ashamed of myself. That I could equate Elena with those three lascivious female vampires who so nearly took me into their ranks!

I am truly mortified at the workings of my unconscious. Were I a Catholic I could unburden myself in the confessional; as it is, I could abide no clerical judgements upon my state of mind. I would rather entrust myself to science – for all the good that has done! The laudanum Dr Seward prescribed to help me sleep exaggerates rather than prevents the dreams. I am alone.

Why is this happening, when Elena is becoming such a valuable member of our otherwise harmonious household? What right have I to project my old fears – which by now should be long-dead and forgotten – upon her?

If I *am* going mad, I must do my utmost to keep my battle to myself, in order to protect my family, and to preserve us all from the stain. The next time I enter Dr Seward's house I wish it to be as his guest, not as his patient.

As I write this in the bedroom I can hear Mina and Elena through the closed door. They are in the dressing room, preparing for bed, letting down each other's hair and combing the long tresses. It is becoming quite a little ritual between them now. It soothes me to hear their laughter.

## 16 October

A peaceful day. My mind has been quiet and stays so, as long as I occupy myself with work. When I come home to Mina, her company also keeps me from the darkness. So far, she appears to suspect nothing. If only I can get through this trough – these episodes will come upon me all my life, I fear – and out upon the far side without troubling her, I will be content. She has trouble enough with Quincey. I am determined not to add to her burden!

## 17 October

I've had an intensely disquieting experience. Thank heaven for my long practice of recording such things in my diary! The journalistic habit makes for a degree of objectivity that I sorely need.

I was in my study, completing the accounts over which I fell asleep the other night, when I heard the cat miaowing outside. She was on the window-sill, pressing herself plaintively against the glass. I let her in and she sat for a while on the edge of my desk, watching me work. I cannot explain my feeling, for she was as quiet as ever, but she made me uneasy.

The desk lamp cast a long dark shadow behind her, and in this shadow I saw blue sparks dancing!

I dropped my pen, making an ink-blot on the ledger. I stared at the sparks, certain that my eyes were deceiving me. I could see these phantom motes – an eerie blue, like the flames I saw on St George's Eve night in Transylvania – nowhere else in the room, only in the cat's shadow.

The cat stared at me. Her reflective eyes changed from green to red, and a distinct, malevolent intelligence coalesced in them. Her ears went back, her mouth opened wide, so wide it seemed a gargoyle's leer, revealing her gums and thin sharp fangs. How she hissed! Such a harsh, fearsome noise that I could not believe it issued from her small body! Her usual hiss is a weak affair by comparison. That this affectionate small creature, our friend, could sit snarling at me like some demon from Hell horrified me.

I was about to shoo her away, but before I could move she launched herself at my head. Her claws and teeth pierced the skin of my forehead and skull. I cried out in pain and tried to throw her off, only to receive a savage clawing of my hands. I could not dislodge her! In panic I leapt out of my chair, shouting, and with a final effort took hold of the cat and flung her across the room. I am not proud of manhandling a dumb animal, but I had no choice. She collided with the mirror, scrambled along the mantelpiece dislodging several ornaments, and landed on her paws on the rug. With a yowl she fled through the open window.

I looked at myself in the mirror. My face was as white as my hair, with rivulets of blood branching across the paleness. But what struck me in restrospect was this; that as the cat struck the mirror, *she had no reflection.*

Mina and Mary came rushing in, exclaiming in concern as they saw my injuries. I explained that the cat had attacked me for no apparent reason. What I could not explain was the nervous state to which the incident had reduced me. I mean, the dread roused by the cat's strange behaviour, even before she pounced.

Later, Joseph – doing his usual rounds of the garden – found the animal cowering in the shrubs by the bird table. She was glad to be rescued, and after a dish of milk seemed quite her normal self again.

At least, that is what Mina tells me. I cannot bear the cat near me. They brought her in, while I was resting in the drawing room, to make friends – and although she was her affectionate, purring self again, my heart thundered and I broke into a clammy sweat at the sight of her. I had to ask them to take her out. I could not control or hide these reactions, so Mina is worried about me now. Precisely what I wished to avoid.

Mina says Puss must have got a fright before she came into the study, and that's why she behaved so oddly. I do not know. Once I caught Elena looking at me with exactly the same red eyes and mocking, malicious glance as the cat had – but a moment later the look was gone. I wish I could rid myself of these imaginings!

I will pray God to let me sleep and at least have a few hours' respite from the fevered whisperings of my brain.

MINA HARKER'S JOURNAL

**21 October**
Quincey continues to make good progress. He is listless and sleeps a lot, but the doctor says he is out of danger. I cannot stop worrying and praying. If anything happened to Quincey, I don't know what would become of me.

I am so glad to have Elena here, for I am anxious about Jonathan too. I fear he is working too hard. Since the incident with the cat – although the scratches he received are healing well – he has been preoccupied, pale and tired during the day but restless by night. I woke him from one wild dream, but he stared at me and claimed he could remember nothing! He says there is nothing wrong, but I know him. Poor dear, I hate to see him suffering so. I think he will not wish to talk to our own Dr Gough. So if he is not better soon, I will ask Dr Seward to come down from London. Oh, but he is busy, and cannot be at our beck and call.

We still have not discovered what made the cat behave as she did. She has exhibited no more wildness but has been as lovable as ever; indeed, I would not have believed she had such energy! I have to keep her away from Jonathan, however, for he cannot abide her at present. I hope he will not have a fever from her scratches. I must be careful with Quincey, also, though I would hate to forbid him to stroke his pet! He has little enough pleasure as it is.

As for myself, I am quite well. I am a little tired, for the strange dreams continue to haunt me. A heavy atmosphere hangs over the house, like a storm that will not break. We are all edgy. It is as if, although the sun shines and everything is serene, I feel a great shadow gathering and pressing on my back; and if only I turned round quickly enough, I would catch sight of an unutterable horror.

At least Elena helps to relieve these ridiculous but troublesome feelings! I suppose autumn is the season for thunderstorms. I blame all upon 'static electricity'.

### 23 October
Last night – I can barely bring myself to write of it, but I must, for honesty demands that even the most delicate of matters must and should be squarely faced. Anything I write here may serve to help my dear husband in the future – and should he ever read it, he will know that I think of him with the same deep regard and love as ever.

As for myself, I cannot answer. God shall be my judge.

Jonathan and I have always been as one in our belief that relations between married people should be restrained and decorous. Truly there is no place in a Christian marriage for lasciviousness in thought or behaviour. We have been in accord and very content in this belief.

Last night as we went to bed, Jonathan was very quiet, and there was a strange, almost wild look in his eyes. Usually I would have asked its cause, but for some reason I did not feel inclined to do so. There was an unnatural mood upon me, as well; a sultry closeness in the air, more of summer than autumn. The lamps burned low and red. I opened the window for some air but there was none, only a static thickness. I heard a dull rumble of thunder. The skies were all greenish and purple-black, lying low in thick masses, but they yielded no rain. The treetops and the church steeple glowed eerily. I saw a cloud of motes glittering by the window; they made me feel strange and dizzy, as if recalling me to some dark memory. I suppose they were only midges, but I closed the window against them anyway.

As I got into bed, Jonathan turned out the lamp and we lay in darkness. Usually he leaves it burning for a time while we talk about our day. I was uneasy. It was as if we were waiting for something. When my eyes grew used to the dark, I suddenly saw his face above me and his eyes burning down at me! I drew a breath. They did not look like his eyes! The irises were as crimson as blood, the pupils glowing scarlet even in the dark. A spell lay on me – for all I know, I imagined everything – so I did not try to evade him. His lips met mine in a kiss of incredible savagery and I - I found a fierceness rising inside me to match his.

I shall draw a veil over what followed. I am still shaken by the memory of the wildness that swept over us. Shamed, almost. For although we are married, it seemed to me that it was not Jonathan who . . . Oh God, I must stop. I did not mean to write so much. His eyes were red, his face gaunt. When I say it did not seem to be Jonathan, I mean that my darling was not himself. Nor was I; I have never known such savage feelings before and hope I never shall again! I burn at the thought. Oh, I hope he can forgive me for abandoning myself to such bestial passions!

### Later
I have taken a walk to the Cathedral and back, alone, to compose myself. With distance I can be more rational.

I believe that it was the oppressive weather that put us both in so strange a mood. That, combined with the stress

103

Jonathan is under. Perhaps we also have a touch of fever – that would account for the dreams that have disturbed me – and with the thundery weather, we were simply not ourselves. Dr Van Helsing himself has told us that certain eminent scientists, himself included, do not dismiss the effect of subtle electricities upon the human brain!

I shall talk to Jonathan of this later. I do hope he will feel like talking.

### 24 October

A sad, oppressive day. The storm will not break. Alas, I cannot persuade my husband to talk openly of what happened between us. His eyes are red-rimmed and distraught. He took my hand and said ardently, 'I will be well again soon, I promise. There is nothing to speak of; whatever we imagined last night was a dream which we must forget as it if never happened!'

'But my dear,' I said, 'there have never been forbidden matters between us, nor should there be!'

'Nothing happened,' he kept saying. He seemed quite angry, and he has never been angry with me before. He must have seen the look of distress in my face, for he suddenly buried his head on my breast and cried, 'Dear Mina! I am not a brute! I would not have hurt you for anything!'

'You didn't hurt me!' I replied fervently. Too fervently, perhaps, for he gave me a terrible look of suspicion. 'I was not myself, either,' I added quickly. 'It was the storm . . .'

Then an eerie change came over his face. All trouble passed from his expression and he smiled. 'It was not the storm,' he said, very soft, pressing my hand. Even his voice was unlike itself; deeper, and with the taint of an odd accent. 'You know, and your husband knows, what it is that you really desire.'

'Jonathan, what is it?' I said, quite disturbed. 'What do you mean?'

He recoiled, staring at me as if I had become disgusting to him. 'What did I say?'

'Do you not remember?'

'No,' he said. Then he leapt up and strode out of the room, exclaiming, 'No! No!' in such despair I almost wept to hear him. Oh, what am I to do?

### Later

After I had left Jonathan alone for a while, I went in to him again. He was calm but looking very frightened. I cannot bear to see him in such torment. 'Mina, all I remember of last night is . . . is wrestling with blackness, as if I had become some dull-minded beast that cared for nothing but its own vile impulses.' He began to weep. 'I fear I have done you some terrible harm.'

'No, you have not,' I reassured him again. 'No harm is done. Surely our love is strong enough to withstand these lapses in each other?'

'I don't know,' he said, pressing the heels of his hands to his forehead.

'And you do not remember . . . much?'

'Very little.'

'Then you must have had a fever,' I said, drawing his hands into mine and stroking his head. I breathed a sigh of relief that he might therefore have little recollection of my own uncontrolled response. 'And so had I.'

'Mina, forgive me.'

'My darling,' I said, 'there is nothing to forgive.'

He fell quiet then, but I fear . . . oh, what is the use of failing to articulate it? I fear that our trip to Transylvania was bad for him after all. That it woke memories, and perhaps a relapse of the brain fever that possessed him after his experience in Castle Dracula.

## 27 October

Something terrible is happening to me. I can deny it no more. Three nights in the past four this black beast, as I term it, has come upon me. It brings me out of sleep in the middle of the night, a fire raging in my brain, a black inferno. My ears fill with a sound like the beating of wings. I cannot think, cannot reason, can only succumb to blind impulse. I find myself forced by this dark raging to embrace Mina – to seize her, even tearing her nightdress in my eagerness to uncover her body – and not to desist until this grim, animal fire is sated.

Afterwards, I hate myself. I shrink with loathing from the horror that is my own body and soul. Yet I can never remember much; it is as if I see all through a thick veil, and am divorced from my own actions. I recall it with a kind of excitement, despite my loathing. I recall, also, that Mina never resists. I would expect her to draw away, to exclaim in shock, to bring me out of the trance and back to my true self with stern words. Yet she does not. She permits all that I – all that the beast does. She seems almost to encourage it, to participate in uncovering each other's nakedness, while her eyes turn liquid, languorous, glittering in the dark.

I found the marks of her nails upon my back this morning. They seem like the marks of Satan.

Mina and I have both been educated – by Church, family and society – in the true Christian belief that base impulses must be sublimated by the will. All our married lives, out of the love and intense respect I bear for my wife, I have adhered to that principle. I have troubled her as little as possible, and then as briefly as I may and with all tenderness, and only in the hope that Quincey might have a sibling.

For if these lusts are base in man, in woman they are an abomination. My wife is not wanton – God help me, I will not see her in that light!

There is only one explanation. That whatever malign spirit possesses me possesses Mina also; it is not we who couple like beasts, but some evil force using our bodies. Yet this line of reasoning also is madness – I am ill, not possessed! My thoughts whirl round and round in circles and I reach no answer.

I am afraid. What is happening to me? God, grant me an enemy I can see and fight with my hands! Anything but this!

One matter is decided. Until this fever leaves us, and is safely gone, Mina and I can no longer share a bed.

## MINA HARKER'S JOURNAL

### 29 October

I have today written to Van Helsing to tell him how worried I am about my husband. Jonathan, of course, did not want to trouble him, but this has gone on long enough and it is ridiculous to struggle on alone when we have such good friends who will help us at a moment's notice! Would we not do the same for them?

The past few days have been difficult. Jonathan insists on going to work, and apparently convinces everyone there that he is well, but once at home he falls into a dark mood and spends hours alone in his study. At night he is plagued by sweats and nightmares. I dearly want to be close to him, to soothe him, to show him that I am not afraid and will cleave to him through the worst of these attacks – but now he has banished himself to a guest-room, and will not even see me after he has retired.

Secretly, I am deeply unhappy about this. I am so lonely I have even considered asking Elena to share my bed instead – the very idea, it would be like returning to my girlhood with Lucy! How comforting it would be. Still, I sleep alone. Strange fancies swarm around me – some frightening and some pleasant – but I do not succumb. I do miss Jonathan, even – especially – that unknown, passionate Jonathan who embraced me in the depths of the night. When I think of those times it is with a kind of breathless wonder, not with any degree of revulsion.

But that is why he has left me. He is ashamed! And that has made me ashamed, too. But my only concern now is returning my poor dear husband to health.

Thank goodness Elena is unaffected by all of this!

### 30 October

A telegram arrived. Van Helsing will be here in three days' time! Soon all will be well.

ELENA KOVACS'S JOURNAL

### 30 October

It distresses me to see Mr and Mrs Harker, who have been such friends to me, suffering as they are. They think I do not know, but I notice many small signs. My Dark Companion is playing with them – with the cat, with Mr Harker. I have to remind myself how callously they destroyed him, then I smile, and know that their suffering is for a higher purpose: to give my love his revenge. And to help me give him back his earthly shape.

I must put aside my human concerns and fix my mind, my will, all my intentions, upon fulfilling him. I stroke the brass urn in which his ashes lie, and feel the subtle vibrations of his presence.

He is telling me that the time is drawing near, I must act quickly now. I am very afraid, my heart beats hard with anxiety, but I have thought of a way!

The child is very close to me now. The child will do our bidding.

# Chapter Eight

### 1 November

We are anticipating Van Helsing's visit with eagerness. The prospect of his presence is a great ray of sunlight dispersing our darkness. Jonathan and I are in better humour already. Dear Dr Van Helsing was always, in the dark days we endured, a steadying influence, the voice of sanity and wisdom piercing the chaos!

God forbid that black times should be falling on us again. But if they are, we shall face them with all the courage at our disposal. And learn the lesson that we can never relax our vigilance, never take the peaceful order of our lives for granted!

### 2 November

Well, I am going to be in poor form to greet our friend. A tiresome accident has sapped my strength and I have been unable to eat, which makes me all the more enervated.

Doubly tiresome, because it marred what was otherwise a perfect afternoon. It was Quincey's first day out of bed. Elena and I had lunch with him in the nursery, then we sat on the terrace to enjoy the sun. The weather was delightfully mild and the garden glorious, all wreathed in the lushness of autumn. The roses are still in bloom, red and apricot and white. Beyond the lawn, the sweet docile cows were nosing over the fence so Quincey naturally wished to pet them. The exertion made him wheeze quite badly. I was concerned for him, but Elena works wonders with the child; she is so calm, stroking his brow with her pale, firm hands. She has a wonderful quality of repose, despite her passionate nature.

We quieted Quincey by reading to him, and he soon recovered, sitting drowsy and happy on the bench between us in the golden light. When I finished the story, the dear boy wanted to bring me a rose as a reward. Elena quickly fetched cutters and a small brass bowl – in which, I suppose, she meant to place some blooms. Off Quincey trotted and cut a beautiful deep-red rose with a long stem. Bringing it to me, he climbed on my knee and insisted he must present the rose by placing the stem between my teeth, 'Like the Spanish ladies,' he said. He was so charming and so intent on this ritual that I complied. I opened my mouth to receive the rose, but instead of placing it between my teeth he laid it along my lower lip. Oh, I had not considered how long and sharp the thorns would be! I would have removed it but Quincey shut my lips with his fingers, saying, 'Hold the rose, Mama. You look so pretty.' Not wishing to spoil his game, I kept very still so the thorns would not wound me. 'So very beautiful,' he said.

But then, obviously not comprehending his action, his small fingers pressed tighter upon my mouth and I felt thorns pierce my inner lip and gums. I could not speak, but I made a muffled sound of pain. Realizing that he was hurting me, Quincey must have meant to relieve my pain as swiftly as possible.

He seized the head of the rose and tried to take it from my mouth by dragging it sideways across my lower lip. The tough thorns pierced me and ripped through the tender flesh. It felt like acid and fire; I cried out, my mouth falling open. The pain was so extreme it made me sob and cough; I could make no other sound. And the blood that poured from the wounds! I had no idea that the flesh of the lip could bleed so copiously. You would think some great artery ran through it! Quincey jumped off my knee – so shocked, I think, that he had no expression at all on his intent little face. He put his hand into the flow of blood, as if trying ineffectually to stop it. The next I knew, Elena was there, catching the blood in the brass bowl she'd brought out for the roses. (There was some dust or dirt crusted at the bottom; where she had obtained this appalling old object, I have no idea. From the garden shed, I imagine.) She held my head, tipping it forward so that the fast-flowing blood would collect in the bowl. I'm sure she was trying to help, but this was doing nothing to stop the bleeding. I, however, was too shaken to protest. I felt myself turning very faint and sick.

I fell into a swoon, and when I came round I was lying on the couch just inside the French window, with Elena and Dr Gough – whom, I found out later, Mary had called – leaning over me. He was holding a compress to my lip, and the bleeding had all but stopped. Mary was with Quincey, trying to reassure him. The pain was indescribable, all the more unpleasant for being in the mouth, and so bad I felt quite ill with it. Nevertheless I sat up and explained – as best I could, my speech being somewhat affected – that the whole thing had been an accident and Quincey was not to blame.

Then they let Quincey come to me and he was so mortified by what had happened he wept, poor lamb. His remorse distressed me far more than my own discomfort!

Well, that was yesterday. The physical shock has diminished. The doctor has given me tinctures for the pain, which he says will continue for some days before healing sets in. Who would believe that so trivial an injury could cause such prostration!

### 3 November

Dr Van Helsing is here. Although he has turned quite grey since his poor wife's death, and has a certain frailty about him, his vigorous spirit seems to bring our whole house to life! Quincey adores him.

He expressed great concern over my injury, but I explained

it was an accident. I do not wish to dwell upon it. Jonathan is the one in need of his expertise.

Over dinner (at which I was content to sip consommé and wine), Jonathan seemed more his normal self, and the evening was so pleasant that I did not want us to touch on our reasons for calling our friend at all. It was almost possible to believe that nothing had happened! But Van Helsing is too shrewd to let anything pass him by. After the meal, when Elena had gone to Quincey and the three of us were alone in the drawing room, he said, 'Now, my friends, we have endured too much together for this reticence. I know you would not call me so urgently without cause. You may speak frankly and freely. What troubles you?'

He said this with a charming but knowing smile. I was ready to begin, to spare my husband's feelings, but to my surprise Jonathan spoke first. 'I don't know where to start. We have no specific cause for concern, such as we had with Lucy. I have been suffering . . . dreams, nightmares, delusions. How foolish you must think us to drag you here for something so trivial!'

Jonathan paced about as he spoke, and his cheeks were pale. Van Helsing, watching him, replied gravely, 'On the contrary, a matter that so clearly distresses you cannot be trivial. And even if it is, so? It is still my dearest wish to aid you! What manner of dreams are these?'

'Horrible . . . oppressive.'

'I have been troubled too,' I said, almost forgetting the pain of my lip in my eagerness to speak. 'Though not as sorely as my husband. I fear that our second journey to Transylvania was unwise. It seems to have stirred bad memories.'

'But your memories were more fresh the first time,' said Van Helsing. 'Why not the bad dreams then? Why now?'

I said, 'I think it would save time if I showed you my journal.'

'Mine, too,' Jonathan said heavily. So we fetched our notebooks – we had not read each other's, so I don't know what his said – and waited patiently while Van Helsing read them. The recollection of certain events made me blush, but I suppose they were best disclosed. Van Helsing showed no sign of embarrassment as he read. In fact, at one or two points, he smiled! I was mortified, though naturally I hid it. I suppose he knows so much of life, nothing can shock him.

When he finished, Jonathan spoke more easily, as if relieved of the burden of explaining from the beginning.

'I have acted as a beast towards my wife,' he said in a raw, desperate tone. 'I have done something terrible, used her savagely. But why, I don't know, cannot remember. It is all through a thickness of dark glass, as if I were drugged, or fevered.'

I said quickly, 'I have told Jonathan many times, he has not hurt me. He did nothing that was . . . in any way unnatural between a married couple.'

Van Helsing looked so keenly at me that I blushed. 'It seems that you remember more than your husband, Madam Mina. Have you any theories?'

'Only as I wrote; a fever, the weather, the worry of Quincey's health . . .'

Van Helsing shook his head with a rather grim smile. 'You have seen enough of the supernatural to know that it exists as firm and solid as Nature; yet still you cling to the rational, the English explanation! But this is commendable. Dismiss the rational before you look to the irrational.'

'Well, what should we do?' Jonathan said angrily. 'Spend a week at the seaside to see if a holiday cures us? Quincey is not well enough to travel!' He sank down on to a chair. 'Forgive me, Professor. But I am at my wits' end. Mina doesn't deserve this.'

Van Helsing was contemplative. How wonderfully calm he is! 'You say you cannot remember certain matters. Is this blockage of your own making, one of denial, or something else? There is a way to find out, if you will permit me. I would like to hypnotize you, Jonathan.'

I saw my husband start back, his eyes so wild I thought he would dismiss the idea out of hand. But after a moment he lowered his head and sighed. 'Of course. Do what you must.'

Van Helsing hypnotized me often, when we were pursuing our enemy to his lair, and while Dracula's hold over me – his vile blood mingled with mine! – made a link between his mind and mine. The process holds no fear for me. But Jonathan was uneasy, even when Van Helsing had made him comfortable and made the usual passes in front of his eyes. Jonathan seemed to resist. But at last I saw him relax and sink back into the chair, seeming more peaceful than he has in days.

The atmosphere was thick and close; the deep brown of the walls and curtains a stifling barrier against the night, the gas lamps hot, dim globes. I have become too sensitive to such atmospheres; they afflict me constantly.

'I want you to think back, Jonathan,' Van Helsing began, soft and grave. 'You are safe, so the memory cannot hurt you. You are in bed beside Mina. You feel a strange impulse come upon you; all seems dark and unreal, as if you dream yet do not sleep.'

Jonathan frowned and uttered a moan.

'Tell me what is happening.'

'I hear . . . I hear the wings of bats all around me. I can hear voices sighing, but nothing is there! A black wind is whirling tighter and tighter around me . . . I cannot escape, I lie paralysed, not even wanting to resist. No! It's too late! He's inside me!'

These words sounded so forlornly eerie that I shivered. Van Helsing spoke soothingly. 'Who is inside you?'

'Dracula.'

As he spoke the name, the whole room seemed to jolt and

wheel around me. I think I knew that Jonathan was going to say it. Yet when he did, it came as a deep and violent shock, a wrenching of my whole being. I said nothing, lest I distract Van Helsing and ruin the hypnotism.

'How do you know it is him?'

'I simply *know*. I am him. He is me. I see Mina lying beside me, her face so beautiful beside me in the soft wash of moonlight through the curtain . . . Ah no, no. I cannot let him . . . but I cannot stop him! He must possess her. He laughs and I cannot stop him because he controls me.'

Van Helsing's face was impassive. 'Does he speak to you? Tell you anything?'

Jonathan paused. His eyes were closed but his face worked in a way that was terrible to see. 'He tells me nothing. He only possesses me . . . but I feel him mocking me. As if to say, "You think you have vanquished me but I can never die." And then Dracula uses my body to – to ravish my wife!'

I shuddered. Van Helsing said, quickly and calmly, 'And when it is over?'

'He leaves. I am myself again. Knowing I have committed a terrible sin. That we both have!' To my horror, Jonathan opened his eyes and pointed at me. 'She knows! She knows that it was Dracula who ravished her, not her husband! She knew and she did not fight. She allowed it!'

I rose to my feet and stood there, so shocked I could not move. Van Helsing gave me a swift glance and began to bring Jonathan out of the trance. 'You will wake now. There is nothing to fear. You feel at peace . . .'

Jonathan sat up suddenly, then leaned forward and dropped his face on to his hands, uttering a long-drawn-out groan. 'My God. My God,' he said.

'You remember what you said?' Van Helsing asked.

'I remember . . . everything.'

'Madam Mina, come. Sit down,' Van Helsing said gently. 'You keep the brandy . . . here? Sit, we shall all have a glass.'

He brought the brandy and three glasses from the side-board, and we sipped it in silence. Eventually Van Helsing said, 'Madam Mina, painful as the question is, delicate as it is, I must ask it. Did you know, or suspect, or even imagine, that your lover was not Jonathan – but Dracula?'

'I – I cannot answer. I am not sure.' I found, to my shock, that I could not in honesty give a clear, 'No.' The realization of this made me redden with shame, made Jonathan groan again and twist his head away. I said, trying to explain, as if I could, 'I felt that neither of us were ourselves. Outlandish as it sounds, I believe we were both entranced in some way.'

Van Helsing only nodded, but he looked graver than ever. 'And you, also, have felt that some evil force has tried to enter you, take over your spirit as it did your husband's? In your journal, you describe a sound of wings . . .'

'Well, yes. I have sensed such things, more than once. But I held myself steady, and prayed, until whatever it was that tried to enter me gave up and left me alone. And I put it down to nervous fancy. Professor, tell us the truth! Is this all in our imaginations? Or is it . . . something more?'

He held my hand. 'Little girl, I have not yet an answer. That you and Jonathan both have dreams and nightmares and bad feelings so alike – this might be no more than that you pick up each from the other, being so close. But I like it not. I like it not.'

Jonathan spoke up fiercely, 'Well, what if it isn't all in our minds? Now I can remember what happened, it seems utterly real! I was myself, yet somehow taken over by the Count's accursed spirit, as if he were directing my actions, laughing at me. I acted in a most beast-like, unforgivable way to my wife, before the fit was over! How am I to live with myself, not knowing why it is happening, or if it might happen again?'

I added, 'There has been a feeling of doom upon us, regardless of what we do to cheer ourselves.'

Van Helsing was quiet, thinking. Jonathan went on

hoarsely, 'Is it possible that these events are not in our minds at all? That Dracula's spirit – I won't call it a soul – has somehow survived, and come for vengeance?'

As he spoke the gas lights wavered. His words sent a shudder through me. I hoped desperately that Van Helsing would put our fears to rest, assuring us that it was all due to memory, some condition of the brain that might be corrected by scientific means. Instead, his noble face seemed to age five years with worry. 'I wish I could assure you once and for all that your fears are unfounded. But without proof, I cannot. Perhaps such a creature Undead remains Undead for ever, in some form. And yet I cannot forget the expression of peace on the monster's face as we delivered the final blows! Could such an expression be a deception, the precursor of a temporary sleep only, or knowledge that he dies not?'

'Professor, don't!' I said quickly.

He saw me tremble, and pressed his hand on mine. 'Forgive me, Madam Mina, I do not mean so to alarm you. I am thinking aloud. But you will see, I do not take your concerns lightly. You and your husband are not of fanciful disposition. And we would be fools not to consider even the possibilty of some supernatural attack upon you, though God forbid it should be so.'

'What shall we do?'

'To begin, there are simple protections that we know are effective. All members of the household must wear crosses. I shall have garlic sent from Amsterdam, as before, to seal all windows and entrances to the house. And wild rose to put upon the doors.'

As he spoke, I saw Jonathan's face working. Suddenly he jumped up and cried vehemently, 'No! I will not have all that – that paraphernalia in the house again! It makes superstitious fools and prisoners of us all. Is there any proof that it would be effective against an attack upon our minds?'

Van Helsing shook his head. 'No, but –'

'Then I won't allow it!' Calming down, he sat beside me, his head in his hands. 'No, Professor. None of that yet, I beg you. I do not want to believe that we have to go through all that sorrow again. The garlic and such might even summon the evil into some more substantial form.'

'How?' I gasped.

'By making it seem too real.'

Again a racking silence, as if our little world had been shaken by an earthquake.

'Perhaps Jonathan is right,' I said. 'What would we tell Elena, Quincey and the servants? I don't wish them to know anything about it!'

We were silent for a while. Van Helsing gave a heavy sigh. 'Very well, friend Jonathan. You are right, it has not come to that. For now, I ask only that you both continue to keep a record of all your dreams and moods, noting times of day or night. I watch over you. I study my books for some reference that may help. The question I ask is this: can a vampire have a ghost that haunts us? Or is it that our own minds turn against us – deceiving us that our memories are at peaceful rest, only to rear out of sleep like a fiery dragon when least we expect it?'

**Later**

Sleep will not come. My lip is swollen and pains me, my head aches from turning our conversation over and over in my mind.

Now that I am watching for something to happen, nothing does!

A while ago, I went to Jonathan's room. All I wanted was to slip my arms around him that we might comfort each other and thus find easeful rest. I went to his bedside and put my hand upon him, whispering, 'Jonathan?' But he started away from me. When he turned up the lamp, his eyes were fierce with dread. 'Keep away from me, Mina!' he said.

'Until I am free of him, you must not come near me!'

'But Jonathan,' I said, 'I am not afraid of you. I refuse to be afraid! I can't sleep. Let me comfort you.'

Then a look of such cold suspicion crossed his face that it makes me weep to recollect it. 'Did you come in here thinking to find *him*?'

The inference so horrified me that I gasped, and backed away. 'If you think that, I – I cannot stay until I am free of this stain of suspicion!'

As if stricken by what he'd said, he reached out to me. 'Mina – I am sorry – I –' But I fled the room, I could not bear any more. I feel so alone, I will see if Elena is awake.

Strange, Elena is not in her room! Nor was she in the kitchen, where I might have expected to meet a fellow non-sleeper. She may have been with Quincey – but as there was no light under his door, I did not wish to disturb him. Now I feel sleep coming at last, thank God. I will not fight it.

JONATHAN HARKER'S JOURNAL

*4 November*

Relations remain difficult between Mina and myself. After all these years without a cross word, never a moment of disharmony! I cannot believe it is happening – but I cannot forgive her, can barely bring myself to look at her.

It was not me to whom she submitted when those black fits came upon me, but to Dracula. She cannot, or will not, admit it, but I know the truth. We both know, and therefore we cannot speak openly, cannot even look each other in the eye. Of course we maintain the veneer of civility for the benefit of our guests – Elena suspects nothing – but Van Helsing is too shrewd to be fooled.

After breakfast he took me into the study and spoke fervently. 'My friend, I beg your forgiveness for bringing this trouble to you!'

'What do you mean?' I said, puzzled. 'The trouble is all ours; you are helping to alleviate it.'

'I mean that by hypnotizing you, I brought to the surface matters between yourself and Mina that were better left unsaid. But now they are said, they poison the love between you. Ah, this is all my fault! I would do anything to undo it!'

To this I could say nothing, for he was right. Not that I blame him in any way!

For who is to blame? Myself, for being so weak as to let Dracula's vile phantom inside me, or Mina, who resisted his attack on her mind yet welcomed his vicarious embrace? Oh God, dear God. Or is Dracula alone to blame? But how can we deny all responsibility? For every time we fail to resist evil, we collude with it.

Is it possible that Mina loved – loves – Dracula? How else could she welcome him so fervently into her arms? Or is it simply that I have gone mad?

How I despise myself for casting such vile stains upon my wife's character – she who has always been a perfect angel, to me and to everyone about us! But each time I look at her I remember her gleaming eyes, her parted lips, as if she had turned into one of those fiends from Castle Dracula.

I am sitting on the terrace as I write, trying to make sense of all this. Elena has come to sit beside me. She seems so serene. She says nothing yet her presence soothes me; as if, standing outside our trouble, she has the power to cleanse the taint from my soul . . . for a little while, at least.

MINA HARKER'S JOURNAL

### 4 November

Again I feel refreshed for a morning with Elena and Quincey, two innocents untouched by all this!

Van Helsing is talking of bringing Dr Seward and Lord Godalming here, but we have said no, not yet. We cannot ask them to fight an invisible enemy! Van Helsing is taking this so seriously, it alarms us more. It is a strain to carry on as normal, yet we must; it is our only hope, and of course our duty is to protect Quincey and others.

I am doing all in my power to ensure a happy day and a peaceful night; that is, keeping everyone busy, and praying at every spare moment!

## 5 November

All is quiet at last. I am exhausted but I must record what has happened, painful as it is.

Last night, an hour after I had gone to bed and still lay awake, I thought I heard sounds of disturbance from another room – Van Helsing's or Jonathan's, for it was a man's voice I could hear. It was hard to discern. It sounded as if he were arguing with himself, a sort of low growling punctuated by the occasional shout, and thumps, as if the furniture were being violently moved about. It was unspeakably chilling to hear these sounds, so faint I was not sure if I imagined them. I got up, put on a dressing-gown and went along the corridor.

The sound was coming from Van Helsing's room; I met Jonathan, approaching from the other direction. 'Perhaps he is ill,' I said. I was glad to see my husband, despite the barrier that has fallen between us.

Jonathan knocked but there was no answer. The sounds from inside the room were now distinct. Van Helsing was groaning, uttering staccato barks of pain, and there were muffled thumps as if he were throwing himself around the room. Urgently Jonathan tried the door, but found it locked. He knocked briskly, calling out, 'Professor, what's wrong? Let us in!'

At once the door shook, as if Van Helsing had thrown himself against it. He shouted gruffly, 'No! You cannot come in! Leave me, for your own safety!'

My sense of foreboding transfixed me. I took a step back,

but Jonathan didn't hesitate. He flung his shoulder to the door and the lock gave. The door burst inwards. Van Helsing, in his white night-robe, was standing a few feet away; his bed was in disarray, his reading table overturned and books scattered everywhere. The wall mirror lay broken on the carpet. But this was nothing to the chaos of his expression. His pale hair was on end, his face savage and wild, and his eyes so bloodshot the whites were near scarlet.

'Professor, what has happened?' said Jonathan.

He started forward, but Van Helsing put out his hands saying in a tortured, cracked tone, 'No, no, Jonathan, keep away! Take your wife away, don't come near, I beg you!'

I saw that he had a big knife in his right hand; the very bowie knife, I believe, that Quincey Morris used to slay Dracula. We both stood still a moment; I could find no power to speak or move. As we watched, Van Helsing, breathing fast and hard, turned the knife and began to force it towards his own left wrist. Sweat streamed down his high forehead.

Ignoring his warnings, Jonathan rushed to him. He tried to seize the arm that wielded the knife, crying, 'No! What the devil are you –'

Van Helsing's eyes blazed red and his lips drew back. Never did I dream that good wise face should show such savagery – but I never dreamed it of Jonathan, either. I cried out but neither man heeded me. Then Van Helsing turned the knife from himself and began to lash out at Jonathan instead. My husband put his arms up to defend himself. The blade came stabbing viciously at him and I held my breath as Van Helsing drove him around the room, slashing at him, his expression hideous.

'Fools!' he cried. 'Now you see that I have power over each one of you, and I have all eternity to torment you to your graves and beyond!'

He slashed the arms of Jonathan's nightshirt to rags. Red blood oozed through. Jonathan fell back on the bed, his arms across his face. He was crying out in agony. A great crimson weight of blood was gathering in his sleeve, dripping through the material on to the bedlinen. With a sob I rushed to him. Van Helsing, meanwhile, stumbled against the side of the bed and stopped, appearing to struggle violently within himself.

He gasped. He spoke strangled words of Dutch, which I could not discern. His face flickered – almost physically changed – between his own physiognomy and another that was evil but horribly familiar to me. He lifted the knife, turned it towards himself and to my astonishment began to force the point two-handed towards his own diaphragm. His struggle was terrible to witness. I wanted to stop him but could not move. His mouth was wide open and his red eyes held mine all the time, making me feel somehow embarrassed – exposed – almost violated, as if an appalling intimacy were passing between us.

The blade indented the folds of his nightshirt. A spreading stain of blood appeared. I shrank back, cradling Jonathan against me, because I was sure Van Helsing meant to kill himself – but as soon as he drew blood, he uttered a terrible cry and fell heavily on to the bed beside us. The knife clattered away. Van Helsing lay gasping and shuddering.

I cannot say how long we remained there; a few minutes only, though it seemed a frozen, ghastly tableau at the time. Then Van Helsing sat up and put his head in his large hands. He was weeping. 'My friends, it is worse, far worse than I could imagine. Your minds did not deceive you. Even dead, the vampire has a spirit that reaches through time to wreak vengeance. What are we to do?'

Some time later, after I had bound up both men's wounds and we had taken some wine to fortify ourselves, Van Helsing told us what had happened.

'I undressed for bed, then sat at the table to study my books. I was not sleepy so I intended to work into the early hours. But as I read I begin to feel strange; the lamp seems dim and I cannot focus on the words. I have a hallucination that the inside of my skull is a great, dark room, and that a voice is whispering in the darkness. I feel a fluttering like bats' wings, soft and intrusive, most unpleasant, but I cannot shake it off. And then I feel . . . I cannot describe it. I feel *him* come into this room, which is also my mind.'

'Dracula?' I asked. He nodded. 'Are you sure?'

'I know that malevolent will all too well!' Van Helsing said hoarsely. 'It could be no other. There is only one like him, with such an evil, primitive, arrogant spirit. He possessed me. I was still myself and yet I knew I was him –'

'Yes,' Jonathan put in. 'That's how it was with me!'

'Our two spirits immediately begin to war against each other. I fight to drive him out. He laughs at me. "Now you know the extent of my power," he says. "It is limitless. I can do worse than haunt you; I can control you. If I can order *your* actions, strongest of my enemies, how easily then can I possess those around you! Your good comrades, your sweet womenfolk I can make do anything. And you will never know where I am or who to trust!"' Van Helsing slumped. 'Well, I fight him with all my might. I must have seemed a madman, reeling around the room, shouting to myself – for the damage I cause, please forgive me – but I could not make him leave. Then it seemed to me that the only way to force him out was to harm my own body. I got the knife from among my belongings and that was when Jonathan entered. I begged you to stay away, knowing Dracula would try to harm you. He wanted to kill you, my friend!'

Shuddering, I leaned my head against my husband's. Van Helsing went on, 'I cannot begin to express my horror at what I was forced to do. I cannot ask you to forgive me. At last I knew that the only way to make him stop was to kill myself, to stake my own heart. That is what I tried to do. But the moment I pierced the skin, Dracula fled my body.' He was quiet for a moment, then groaned. '*Mijn God*, how are we to fight this? To banish him physically from the house was one thing – but to keep him from our very minds –! Must we destroy ourselves to destroy him?'

To see Van Helsing brought so low distressed me unutterably. I did my best to comfort and cheer the men, and they rallied, but my heart was not in it.

Jonathan's right arm is very badly injured. The knife has severed some nerves and tendons in his forearm, and he can barely move the hand. Van Helsing said it is possible the damage may never heal. He wept with remorse for having inflicted the injury, but Jonathan spoke stoically though he was white with shock. 'It was not you who did this, Professor. It was he, our enemy, Dracula.'

How extraordinary that Elena and Quincey should have slept through it! But what a mercy that they did!

### 6 November

Jonathan and Van Helsing are resting. We have had to tell Mary and the others that Jonathan slipped and cut his arm; I wish they would not fuss so! An atmosphere of oppression seems to lie on the whole house and nothing will dispel it. We look upon each other with suspicion, watching for the slightest sign of – what can I call it? Possession, infection. What a terrible feeling it is to trust no one, and not to be fully trusted! Surely, the last time, even in our deepest horror, we never lost faith in one another – even when I came so nearly into Dracula's power.

But I will write no more of it now. It may be over already, for all we know, a brief aberration of the spirit world. How pleasant it will be to spend the afternoon alone with Quincey and Elena. My task in reassuring them that all is normal will surely refresh my own spirit.

We are quite a houseful of invalids now! Elena is the only fit one among us!

Quincey is still the same, out of bed but listless and easily tired. Every time he succumbs to an illness, I fear it may be his last. Thank goodness Elena is so calm and happy! It steadies us all. Her eyes sparkle and her cheeks glow – almost as if she had a secret suitor, though I am certain she has not! I think it is simply her naturally sweet disposition shining through.

## Later

We have given in to Van Helsing's wishes, and summoned Dr Seward and Lord Godalming. Our little army will be together again (with, of course, the sad exception of Mr Morris). I feel saddened, yet somewhat reassured by this. We are no longer facing this alone, but with people who understand.

I have such a strange feeling today. It is as if the menace that plagued our dreams and minds is quite gone, yet . . . Oh, enough of trying to comprehend these moods!

## 7 November

They are here – without their wives, since we do not know what danger is to be faced. (For myself, I do not wish to be protected but to stand alongside them. It is no more than I have done in the past.) We sat around the dining room table as a sort of committee, as we have done before. Dr Seward looked very grim as we explained what had befallen us, almost as if he had expected this to happen. Lord Godalming seemed anxious and troubled, almost despairing; he cannot bear to be away from his dear wife and child, I know. I wondered if they would feel the same urgency of commitment as they felt before, without Lucy to unite us. But as soon as Van Helsing had finished, as one, without hesitation, we all began to remake our pledges. To stand by one another, and never to rest until the evil is prised out and destroyed! I must confess that tears were shed, and not just by myself.

As we all clasped hands, vowing loyalty, Jonathan suddenly looked up as if startled. There was nothing to see; he looked into space, as it were, and said something strange. 'He is gone. But he is coming!'

### 7 November

Madam Mina remarks how serene and well-tempered I am. If only she knew the truth! I am such a mixture of passions. Fear, triumph, excitement, and again, terror. Even now, alone in my room with a single candle burning, my heart races and my hands shake. No matter if my writing is unreadable, it is only for my eyes – and perhaps those of my beloved Dark Companion, who may then be doubly sure of my loyalty.

To take the blood from Madam Mina – that was a great obstacle. I could hardly lunge at her with a knife, and even if I had made to cut her accidentally with a paper knife, or prick her with a needle, I might have drawn only a drop of blood and failed to catch it. And such an 'accident' could never be repeated. Unless she was to think me *dangerously* clumsy!

I miss my love's spirit being folded up inside mine, like a child within me. When we arrived in England I felt him leave the sanctuary of my soul – although he returns often, of course. He has been among the family, and they know; I see the haunted light in their faces, the shadows in their eyes. I hear them cry out in the night. But they never speak of it. These are the English! In Hungary they would have hedged themselves about with herbs and garlic and every sign and incantation against the Devil! They are all fools.

I am jealous of Mina. Why must he need her so much? But I try to understand. I asked him how I was to take her blood but there came from him only a cold urge, do it, do it, as if he were testing my ingenuity. I was in despair until I thought of the rose.

When I thought of it I felt him respond, warming to me,

urging me on. (My mother cut her lip once and I remember how it bled . . . how strange I have that memory of her. But what a blessing!) So, the lip . . . but how to pierce it, how to catch the blood? Finally he gave me an answer. We would work together. He would control the child for a few minutes, and the child would do the deed.

Then, if it went wrong and I failed, it would be blamed on the boy anyway, so I would still have a chance to try another way. But all went well.

How Mina bled! The blood streamed from her mouth, bright and gleaming. I caught it in the base of the urn, where it ran down into the precious dust. How considerate of her to faint! Thus giving me the chance to conceal the bowl before I called for help.

I left the house that night with all black and silent. A chill mist floated about my feet and hung like rags in the bare trees. I carried the urn two miles to the churchyard and entered the sepulchre. Inside it was ice-cold and damp, the air dense with a miasma of stone and mould. The odours of wet earth and vegetation crept into our hiding place. The scent of new life. I turned aside the slab on top of the marble tomb. Over it lay a long black cassock that I stole from the church to clothe him. I tipped the ash and blood on to the sacred soil, hoping with all my heart that I have done everything correctly. Then I lit a candle, and sat down at the foot of the tomb to wait.

That night, and the following three, I kept a vigil in the darkest hours before dawn. Nothing stirred. I knew, from disturbances at the house, that my Dark Companion's spirit had not yet fused with his flesh; I began to fear that it never would, that I had done something terribly wrong.

But last night . . .

I watch the night sky through the bars of the mausoleum gate. The leaves of the yew tree are motionless. All is motionless . . . and I wait and wait, not daring to look into the tomb.

I dread to find nothing more than a mess of clotted ash and soil, but dread even more to see some spectral shape forming, or to hear a movement inside the coffin's stone walls . . . But mine is not to witness such mystery, only to keep the vigil.

I grow very cold, huddling there in the dark. A deep pall of despair falls on me, a misery so heavy and grey I wish to die. I can bear no more. I must look into the tomb, I must know . . . but I am falling into a deep sleep.

When I wake, a tall thin figure stands over me.

It is dark; the candle has gone out, but there is a chill clear glow to the sky, as of dawn's imminence. Against this glow, the figure is a silhouette, gaunt and dusty black. He is so still he might be carved of dark stone, one of the graveyard statues. I hold my breath, for I do not know if I dream.

He lifts a hand, and the gathering glow shines through the tips of his fingernails, making of them glistening, sharp crescents.

He reaches his hand to me and speaks in a voice of rusted iron, one word, 'Elena'

# Chapter Nine

He is standing between me and the light. His eyes glare scarlet into mine.

I touch his hand. For the first time in reality, I touch him. He grasps my hand in his; the palm is cold and rough with hair, the fingers powerful. They hold me like ropes as he pulls me to my feet. His nails almost pierce my skin.

I cannot see him clearly. My head comes barely to his shoulder; his form gives the impression of skeletal thinness and great age, yet of strength – a wiry, silvery strength. The shape of his skull in silhouette is magnificent, dawn making a nimbus of his white hair. He smells of earth – but so do I. It is a wild scent, wet and fungal, but at the same time wholesome as new growth.

Dear God, what have I done?

In my awe, I have no strength. His face is obscure but the twin fires of his eyes sear me. I would fall, but he holds me up with his sinewy hands.

He has put on the cassock I brought for him. It looks as natural upon him as feathers on an eagle; he could be an abbot, a man of untouchable spiritual authority. One of us must speak; I find my voice. 'Dearest companion of my soul, if there is any need of yours to which I have not attended, only tell me and it shall be done.'

His eyes become more tender. Long deep eyelids come down, the redness turns dark. 'Elena,' he says again. He speaks to me in Hungarian. 'You have given me back my existence. There is only one other need. Life.'

It is as if the whole world stops breathing; all is poised and fragile as ice. The darkness closes around me, the growing light blinds me.

He puts his arms about me and his chest presses hard against mine. So long I have dreamed of this embrace, yet now it comes I am so afraid I wish to escape. He holds me fast, so cold, so hard.

In spite of his strength there is something frail and papery about him, like a moth new-emerged from the cocoon. He puts his lips to my neck and I feel pressure at my throat. I am held to him by a circle of pain. I feel his tongue, his mouth sucking at me. My first instinct is to fight – then a dizzy sweetness pours through me, and I hang limp in his grasp, wanting to laugh through my agony. I come out of my body and see our two heads from above, his silver, mine dark. The fragile night throbs and explodes in thunder; I see trees thrashing, great mountains convulsing and falling. Then, with a racking spasm that seems the end of everything, I am in my body again.

And he is gone.

I see a thin layer of mist flowing through the gap under the lid of the tomb. Dawn pushes grey fingers through the bars. I am dizzy and gasping for breath; but as it passes, I dare to look into the tomb.

He lies inside. I see his face clearly! An eagle's visage, a nobleman. White hair flowing back from high temples, thickly curling eyebrows. I see the pink flush of my blood under his pale skin, my blood lying red on his lips under the great white eye-teeth. I am terrified yet I feel the surge of deep, unholy love; I am repelled and yet I want him to take me again and again until I expire in his arms.

He looks at me. I gasp, for it is as if a corpse looks up and speaks, with stiff lips, from a deep catalepsy.

'Faithful child,' he says. 'You serve me well, when all others conspire against me. I must rest now. Come to me again tonight, and we will talk of many matters. My beloved. Go home now and keep your silence.'

'Beloved,' he calls me!

I watch him for a while, but he does not speak again. I drag the heavy lid into place, so that he might rest in darkness. Then I go into the damp, foggy graveyard and hurry home, breathless and dizzy every step of the way.

O night, come quickly! How am I to get through this day?

### 8 November

The day passed easily enough. Mina remarked that I looked pale; I assured her that I am well, but once she was gone I pinched my cheeks and bit my lips to make myself rosy again. I must not arouse their suspicions!

Van Helsing and the other men, Dr Seward and Lord Godalming, are still here. I wish they would go; I know they are my Dark Companion's enemies, and are conspiring against him again! I grow angry with them, but then I laugh secretly, for I know they cannot win. There is much secretive talk behind closed doors, and at mealtimes the tension between them is so thick I might cut it to pieces with a cheesewire. Mr Harker looks haggard. I catch him gazing at me as if he guesses, though I know he cannot guess. I am tense, also, but for reasons they do not imagine.

I thought night would never come, but at last Quincey was put to bed, and I made an excuse to retire early. Then I had to wait for the household all to go to bed, lest someone should see me leaving!

By the time I reached the graveyard, I was no longer excited but trembling with terror. Why am I doing this, walking again and again into such danger for his sake? I pass between the avenue of gravestones and dark yews towards his tomb, but before I reach it a dark figure appears before me.

It is him. My heart fails. I almost cry out, but he catches

my arms and my breath stops in my throat. His form is so starkly black in the cassock. How fierce his face is, made more fearsome by the curling bushiness of his eyebrows, the long white moustache and the profusion of his long pale hair. I close my eyes, cannot look at him. I am faint with the conflict of desire – to escape him yet to be held captive.

'Look at me, Elena,' he says. His voice is stronger than before, rich and harsh and commanding. 'What do you see?'

'A handsome nobleman. One who was a great hero.'

'Do not flatter me. The truth!'

'You know I speak the truth!' My own spirit surprises me.

His lips lift beneath the moustache; it seems a smile, though a very bitter one. 'I have not seen my own face for more than four hundred years. No mirror can capture my image.' He draws me to an overgrown tomb and sits me beside him on the mottled stone. His frailty of the first night has gone, but I perceive a weakness in him, as if he were held by invisible chains to the graveyard. 'You will talk to me and tell me all you know of the world,' he says gently. 'I have walked upon it for four hundred years and more. Yet it has turned for seven years which passed as eternity compressed into a single moment for me. Now all is strange again.'

'Beloved companion, I thought you knew all there is to know. You have taught me so much!'

'And I have lost much. It could be, Elena, that you saw visions of matters that I have forgotten. Not all knowledge survives the grave. I have lain for so very long in one grave or another.'

We talk for hours. It is so bitter-sweet to lie in the arms of death and talk like lovers. I tell him how the wolf came to me and led me to the castle, the visions I saw. At everything I say, he nods, as if reassured. 'Yes . . . yes, I do remember.' And he tells me some of his own story; wild, rambling and so strange I cannot follow it all, but the core of it I understand. 'They destroyed me – the Harkers and the accursed Van

Helsing, who has made himself doctor of every discipline as though he would heal the very world of its sickness. Fool. Elena, my own land was frozen in the Middle Ages, drained of its vitality by war, a ghost of itself. I sought a new kingdom, to move among the whirl and rush of humanity in these great cities of the West . . . but they foiled me. And they did worse. They destroyed some I loved, who cannot return as I have. For that, they must be punished.'

He speaks simply, not vengefully. But such is his passion that I would give my life to help him. 'Van Helsing is a friend of my uncle. He is staying with the Harkers.'

'I know, Elena,' he answers. 'I have watched them through your eyes, through each other's eyes. I have entered their dreams and defiled them.' He smiles; it is almost a sneer, a hellish look of pleasure. 'Do they ever speak of me?'

'Not to me. They believe me to be utterly innocent, and they intend the child and myself to remain so. But now I know why they made the journey to Transylvania; to see again the place where they destroyed you! But among themselves, I am certain they speak of nothing else. They sent for the others, too, Seward and Godalming. They are very afraid.'

'Good. How sweet to see madness eating at them. They know I am among them. Jonathan yielded easily to me; Van Helsing drove me out; Mina I could not enter, but she is falling in another way. She is strong. I need her blood.'

'Is mine not enough?' I ask, jealous.

'It is the finest wine, beloved.' He touches my cheek; my skin tingles deliciously where his fingers pass. 'But my blood runs in Mina's veins. Until I taste it I cannot reclaim my full powers.' I fall quiet. I can't argue, yet still I hate it. I fear my jealousy will make him angry. Instead he stretches out his left hand above my lap.

'But how good it is to live again!' he says, flexing the fingers with their long, pointed nails. I take his hand between my own. 'You gave me this gift, beloved. To taste, to see through my own eyes, not those of others. To hear the music of the owl and the wolf, to touch skin. Your skin.' He leans closer to me, his mouth near my neck. I shiver. 'No earthly taste, no meat, no wine, no sweetmeat can ever compare to the taste of blood. No potion can mimic its vitality. Why do you tremble?'

'I am afraid of you,' I said.

'Then you are wise,' he replies, drawing away. 'But *they* are the ones who should fear me. You have nothing to fear – as long as you are loyal. Will your courage fail? You are a danger; you might give away my hiding-place to them.'

'No!'

'You chose to help me of your own free will, beloved child. You might as easily change your mind.'

'My choice is made!' I say fiercely. 'How dare you doubt me? I will never betray you!'

'Then you have only yourself to blame,' he murmurs, 'for whatever befalls. Do my bidding without question now, and later you will be rewarded richly.'

I bow my head, promising all. I am leaning against him; one of his arms is around me, the other moving to brush aside my hair and loosen the collar of my dress. My body turns limp with languor, my head falls back, and his teeth pierce my exposed throat. I come floating up out of my body, while the world spirals upon itself, full of stars and angelic voices singing in painful discord. The spiral tightens into a violent convulsion and I am flung back into my mortal body.

'Now leave me,' he says.

'Must I go?' I cling to him, but he holds me away.

'Yes, beloved. I have much to do; money, clothes, horses to acquire . . . There is no need for you to come here again. I will come to you. I am strong enough now.'

'To leave this place?'

'And to complete my revenge.'

I barely remember going home. At eight, Mary woke me only with difficulty. I must rest as much as possible, for the slightest exertion makes me breathless – but none of this matters. I am in a state of bliss.

I am not entranced or bewitched by him. When I began to help him, I chose that path – or it chose me. I know what he is, yet I knowingly brought him back. I am only the instrument of his rebirth, I know, but without me he could not have returned – any more than a child can be born without its mother. I serve him by choice, as he said.

He means to destroy the Harkers, I know that. They have been kind to me; I am fond of them in turn. I wish them no harm, I have no grudge against them as he has. Why then do I wish to aid him in their downfall?

Because they harmed *him*. Because he freed me from the shackles of my father, of marriage and society; I am now instead to him mother and daughter, wife and lover. Ours is the free exchange of true friends; I give him my aid, and he in time will give me the freedom that is everlasting life.

MINA HARKER'S JOURNAL

**8 November**
Life has been quiet, nothing more has happened. Indeed we have all sensed a relaxing of the atmosphere. Perhaps the haunting was only an aberration, perhaps it was dismissed by the power of our prayers – I know not. I wish only to forget it!

I must employ a nurse for Quincey. I think I have expected too much of Elena. She is meant to be our guest, after all. She has willingly taken constant and excellent care of the boy, but I fear it has overtired her, especially the worry of his illness. She seems very tired these past few days. I have told her to sleep in, if she feels the need.

Jonathan's arm is slow to heal. Dr Seward is very concerned about it. Poor Van Helsing is mortified by the injury, blaming himself though we all know it was not his fault. Again I have asked Jonathan to move back to our room, again he has refused.

## Later, night
I have had the most disturbing dream.

I dreamed that I woke in the night to find the room full of a thin, glowing white mist. A dark figure in silhouette leaned over me, with two livid red sparks for eyes. It was Count Dracula. I would have screamed in terror, had my throat not been paralysed. He did not touch me, however. He spoke, his accursed voice clear and lifelike, and exactly as I remember it.

'You know what I must have of you,' he said. 'I must have your life-blood. But this time you will give it of your own free will.'

'Why?' I said. It was the only word I could force out.

'God gave you a choice between good and evil. No act is evil unless it is undertaken by choice. Is it not so?'

'Some blame attached itself to me when you drank my blood and made me drink yours,' I cried, 'even though I did not collude. The stain did not leave me until you died!'

'Did you not collude? In your heart, at least?'

With that the dreadful figure vanished. I awoke properly then, thinking I saw a white mist vanishing through the cracks of the window. (I supposed it to be only a continuation of the dream, but I recall it vividly even now, as if I truly saw rather than imagined it.)

I sat up, very cold and upset. How I wished Jonathan were beside me! To my surprise – and relief, I must admit – at that moment there was a soft knock at my door, and Elena came in with a candle, all in white, her lovely hair loose on her shoulders.

'Mina, I cannot sleep. Please may I lie in your bed for a little while?'

'Oh, please do, dear,' I said, flinging the cover back for

her to climb in. 'I couldn't sleep either. Have you had a bad dream?'

'Not bad,' she said as she snuggled up beside me, 'but strange.'

'So have I. Let us comfort each other.'

It was a relief to have her there with me, such a gentle, comforting presence! She put her arms round my neck and hugged me so close that the satiny skeins of her hair covered my face, and almost deprived me of air. There seemed a strange smell in her hair; earthy, very nearly unpleasant, yet evocative of something I cannot call to mind.

'Mina, I feel so close to you,' she whispered. 'You have been such a friend to me, such a wonderful and loving friend!' And she planted kisses on my face and lips, becoming more and more fervent until I, growing alarmed, tried gently to push her away. For a few moments she resisted me, and I hardly knew what to do, for I did not want to be rough with her. Then, to my relief, she gave an exhausted sigh and fell asleep – wound so tightly around me that I could not move for fear of disturbing her. So I barely slept and met the morning tired and listless. Never mind.

What a strange girl she is. But I am glad that she has found such happiness with us, and trusts me enough to find comfort in me.

### 10 November
Our happiness is undone. All is recorded in Jonathan's journal. I can add no more.

JONATHAN HARKER'S JOURNAL

*(Dictated by him and entered by Abraham Van Helsing)*

### 10 November, evening
I have not written my journal for some days. My right hand is nearly useless so Van Helsing is writing at my dictation. Curse the fiend that inflicted this upon us!

We must record all that is happening, unbelievable and horrific as it is. Mina sits with us as we work, for I cannot bear to be alone. None of us can. God keep and protect us!

We had a few days of peace – a lull in the storm, as we now know. Tonight after dinner, Van Helsing, Seward, Godalming and I joined Elena and Mina for a pleasant game of cards. At about ten Elena excused herself, saying that she had a slight headache and would go to bed. Thank goodness she left us when she did!

The five of us sat talking pleasantly of happy times. At first all was well, but slowly we began to notice a change in the atmosphere, so imperceptible at first I could only put it down to my overwrought imagination. There was a chill in the air, a sighing sound, as of a gale blowing hard in the distance. We became tense, starting at the slightest sound, then looking worriedly at one another. A door banged upstairs. The fire flared, sending out a whirl of sparks, and at that the cat appeared from nowhere, raced across the room and stood against the flames, hissing, her back arched and her tail fluffed out.

This alarmed me more, for I had not realized Puss was in the room; I am nervous of her still, so Mina always shuts her out. I leaped up to open the door, meaning to shoo her away. But as I looked into the hall, the house felt wrong – as if the windows and doors were gaping open to the night, which came flowing cold and black into our home. This was an illusion, for I could see that all was closed and secure – yet the impression was so strong that I was for a few moments almost witless with terror. I saw my study door standing ajar. Something compelled me to go to it, to reassure myself that all was well and to close the door.

As I walked along the hall, I saw a dim light burning within the study. A sense of dread overwhelmed me; I caught a vile odour of earth mingled with blood, and this woke such terrible memories that my head reeled. My left hand trembled as I pushed open the door.

Sitting in my chair, at my desk, was a figure I dreaded to see – had thought I would never set eyes on again! I knew him instantly. I would know that accursed face anywhere, the aquiline nose and cold arrogance of the expression. Dracula.

If I had discovered the very Devil himself there I could not have been so utterly unmanned by horror. My knees buckled; I must have shouted, for Mina and the others came running; but those few seconds are blurred.

But to tell, objectively, what I saw: the man in my place was all in black, in an old-fashioned black coat buttoned to the throat. He was not quite as I remembered him, the first time I met him at the castle; the thick white hair, brushed back from his high temples, was now streaked with black. His brows were dark, though as heavy as before, almost beast-like in their profusion; his eyes dark, also, with no gleam of redness visible. He was clean-shaven. There was no moustache to obscure the voluptuous cruelty of his red mouth, or the long sharp teeth that rested on the lower lip. He was – as we had seen him once before – an old man turning younger.

The desk drawers and the safe were open, papers lying about on the floor, as if he had ransacked the place. He had before him on the desk a thick typescript, which I had caught him in the act of reading. I realized that it was our precious collection of documents relating our encounter with him.

He looked up very slowly and calmly after I cried out. By then, the others were coming into the doorway behind me; I tried to push Mina back. I heard Seward curse, Godalming give a gasp of despair. The Count rose to his feet. There was no violence in his demeanour, only the old-world courtesy that I remember from our first meetings, when I was still innocent of his nature!

After our initial outbursts, we were dumbstruck. Van Helsing crossed himself; at this the Count smiled, a smile that only the Devil could produce. He lifted his hands, palms turned outwards as if in a gesture of mollification or greeting. I saw the pale hairs on the palms, the sharp nails. A weight of ghastly memories fell on me and I would have collapsed, had Mina not held me up.

'Mrs Harker, bring your husband to a chair,' said the Count, coming from behind the desk. He held one hand towards us, the other towards the leather armchair by the fireplace, as if to guide us there. This seemed the most extraordinary parody of concern! 'He is unwell. I see from this that you remember me.'

I sank heavily into the chair, Mina sitting on the chair-arm beside me, the others standing erect as if to shield us. The Count stood no more than six feet from us, his face horribly pale against the midnight black of his clothes. Strange to say, in the midst of my shock, it was a relief to see him in the flesh; to know that our strange dreams and imaginings of late have had a concrete origin. That I am not mad, after all!

Dracula spoke mockingly. 'Why do you look upon me with such horror? You destroyed me, did you not? You have all the remedies against my kind at your disposal, Dr Van Helsing. Surely, then, you have no reason to fear me?'

'We destroyed you,' Van Helsing said gruffly, 'and we do not fear you.'

'I should think not, since you are four against one.'

'Five,' said Mina.

Dracula looked at her. I could have slain him for that look! 'Five. Sit down, then. Let us all sit down.'

'We prefer to stand,' said Godalming.

'As befits a hero,' said the Count. 'As you wish. You are good hosts and I have not forgotten how to be a gracious guest. Although I have had little practice of late, my memory is long.' Then he inclined his head to each of us in turn in a courteous greeting – or the mockery of one. 'Doctor Van

Helsing . . . Mr and Mrs Harker . . . Dr Seward . . . Lord Godalming.'

The Count's gaze met Mina's again; she stared back at him in such wide-eyed horror that my heart broke to see it. Fearing he was exerting some vile influence on her, I drew her head down on to my shoulder. The Count gave a soft laugh at this, as if my gesture was expected, but futile. I raged silently at him. I wondered if the poker might make a weapon with which to strike him through the heart, but I was powerless – whether through his influence or my own weakness, I couldn't say.

It was as if we were all paralysed, bound in our impotent circle by the chill blackness of his will. Mina, despite her terror, was perfectly composed; her spirit seems unbreakable. Van Helsing had a forceful but controlled passion about him. But the Count was wholly in command of the situation. 'I have not come to harm you – although I have every cause to desire vengeance.'

'Then why – what do you want of us?' Van Helsing said gruffly.

'I simply wish you to know that you have not destroyed me. That you cannot. My lust for life is greater than ever your desire to extinguish it could be.'

'No,' I answered, unable to contain my rage. 'It is more likely that you are so evil, even Hell itself rejected you!'

The Count laughed to himself, as if at some private joke. His mirth aroused my hopeless anger all the more.

Van Helsing asked, 'How *did* you cheat death? What did we do wrong?'

Another laugh. 'That is a puzzle to exercise your great mind, is it not?' The Count turned back to the desk and picked up the bundle of papers, brandishing it contemptuously. 'Is the answer in here, in this collection of rambling nonsense?'

'Put that down!' Mina cried. 'It is not for your eyes!'

Dracula appeared to mock her courage; he could never

appreciate the value of such qualities in anyone. 'There is nothing,' he said, addressing her in a low, ambiguous tone that repelled me, 'that is not for my eyes.' Mina looked away from him, blushing. How violently I hated him! I stirred, but felt Van Helsing's hand on my shoulder.

The Count went on, 'You have seen that I can enter your minds – yours, Mr Harker, even yours, Professor, though you fought me manfully. Even that of your little cat. Who then is safe from me? Your son?'

Mina went white. She leapt up, but Seward held her back.

'You have no defence against me,' said Dracula, 'for you do not know when or how I may next strike. You cannot escape my revenge. All your lives, I will be there.'

Van Helsing broke in passionately, 'Have we not suffered enough at your hands? We did nothing but good to you! We tried to bring peace to your restless soul, an end to your accursed existence. Surely you cannot wish such to continue? Even the Devil, they say, will repent and be redeemed at the end of time!'

'You term it "good" that you destroyed those I love?' The Count's sharp tone deepened my fear.

'The three hateful fiends in the castle?'

'Hateful to you,' Dracula said softly, a baleful gleam in his eyes, 'but not to me. Who are you to judge what is hateful? You know nothing of love.'

'That is not so. You are the one who put aside love, put aside the grace of Heaven, the day you chose to become Undead.'

The Count's expression became fierce; his red lips lifted over the dreadful teeth, his nostrils flared. 'Do you love life, Van Helsing?'

'Of course. It is God's creation.'

'You grow old, Professor. You grow weary of life and wish fondly for death. You will never know what it is to love life as I do – to love it so passionately that you are prepared even

143

to cheat death. To love it so deeply, indeed, that you cannot die – or cannot remain dead! What can you know of such passion? How then dare you judge me? Those three were not fiends to me. They cannot come back as I have. In my destruction you broke your own rules. Meditate upon your mistakes; you have time. Months, or weeks, or a lifetime of looking over your shoulder, watching and waiting for me to come again.' He shook the sheaf of papers. 'And I shall find much amusement in discovering what it is that you think you know of me.'

At that – taking all of us by surprise – Godalming seized the poker on which I had cast my own eye, and lunged at Dracula. The Count seized the shaft before it came within a foot of his body. Godalming cried out and released the handle; the poker fell, and singed the carpet, though it had been in its stand and not in the fire. At the same instant, Dracula threw our typescript into the air, and vanished. The pages scattered into a snowstorm. As they settled, we saw a layer of mist flowing out between the window and its frame.

Godalming was cradling the hand in which he had wielded the poker. Mina and I went to him; the moment Dracula disappeared, the nightmarish chill left the air and we could move freely again. 'Foolish, foolish,' Van Helsing murmured. 'You should not have let your passions get the better of you.'

'D'you think I don't know it?' Godalming grated.

'Were you burned?' Mina asked anxiously.

'The poker was cold when I seized it. But as he touched it, the handle turned red-hot! It is nothing, a slight burn.'

'I can't believe this is happening!' Mina exclaimed. 'Hurry, I must see that Quincey is unharmed. If ever Dracula harms him –'

We rushed into the hall and up the stairs. 'At least the enemy has shown himself!' I said as we went. 'Now we have a solid enemy to fight, instead of phantasms. It proves we are not mad!'

'But how did he get in?' said Van Helsing, hoarse and agitated.

'What?' I said. 'I don't know.'

'For he cannot enter a dwelling unless he is invited in by one of the inhabitants! So who? Who invited him to enter?'

# Chapter Ten

JONATHAN HARKER'S JOURNAL (*Continued*)

Mina was now so pale I feared for her, but she hushed us as we entered Quincey's room. We found the boy sleeping peacefully; nothing had been disturbed in the room, the windows were firmly shut and there was no sign of any injury upon him. He barely stirred as we examined him, keeping our voices low so that he should not be disturbed. He looked so innocent, with his fair hair dishevelled on the pillow, his round angelic face abandoned to sleep. The thought of any harm coming to him causes us unspeakable anguish!

As we left, Elena came out of her room, which is next to Quincey's. She was yawning, her hair loose, her face pale but for a rosy flush in her cheeks. 'What is wrong?' she asked.

What could we tell her? Nothing!

Mina guided her back to her room, saying, 'We thought we heard Quincey crying. It must have been the wind. The weather is so wild tonight, I was worried it might have disturbed him.'

The other men and I returned to the parlour. Van Helsing sat down and closed his eyes; I have never seen him look so weary. Soon Mina returned and said she had given Elena a cross and asked her to wear it at all times. 'She was puzzled and a little frightened. I told her I would explain, soon enough,' Mina sighed. 'We must tell her something!'

Van Helsing opened his eyes. I thought he had been resting – but of course, his mind was at work. 'We must tell her the truth,' he said.

'I dreamed of the Count last night,' said Mina. 'He

appeared in my room and told me that I must give him my blood of my own free will! Oh God, now I fear it was not a dream!'

Van Helsing was by her side in a moment, looking carefully at her throat. 'There are no marks upon you. You have no memory of him attacking you? No weakness?'

'None,' said Mina. 'I am sure he did not touch me.' Then she lowered her head, pressing her fingers to her forehead in anguish. I went to support her.

Van Helsing exclaimed, 'Ah, but now we have the advantage!'

'How so?' Mina asked.

'Our enemy is physical – therefore we can use physical means to keep him out! But of course we must explain to Elena the reason for this, and tell the boy some tale to lull his curiosity. Tomorrow we will set to work.'

I said with fervour, 'I wish Elena and Quincey were away from here. And Mina!'

Van Helsing shook his head. 'Impossible. They would not be safe. Without our protection they would be all the more vulnerable to Dracula. We must all stay here.'

(*Continued in Jonathan Harker's own hand.*) Van Helsing has called a halt, saying, 'Go to bed, my friends; I will keep watch. Dracula's purpose was to frighten us, which he has admirably achieved. I think he will not come back. But in case.'

Mina has gone to sleep with Quincey. But knowing I would not sleep, I am sitting up with Van Helsing.

So we pass the night in a state of siege. My right arm is still in a sling, but by wedging the pen between my fingers and bracing my wrist against the table, I can just manage to write legibly. It is very slow and laborious. Van Helsing says I should learn to use my left instead – the side of instinct and intuition, so he says, the irrational feminine side of ourselves – but I think he is putting up a joke on me. He will always find something to laugh at, even in the direst of circumstances. I am determined to use my right, the side of God and the masculine!

The wind gusts unceasingly round the walls; I hear voices in it, semi-human groans, the howling of dogs. The sound is enough to drive a man mad. Although we have turned up the gas lamps and lit two candelabras, there never seems enough light. I check on Mina and Quincey every hour, but they sleep soundly. At least they are at peace.

Now is the blackest hour before dawn rises in the windows. I feel sleep falling heavy on me at last, and Van Helsing is urging me to bed.

### 11 November, morning

Strangest, most horrible of dreams. I fell asleep, exhausted – it must have been four in the morning by then – and dreamed that a woman came into my room. I saw her leaning over me, her white nightdress shadowy grey in the darkness, her dark hair hanging heavy as snake's tails around her shoulders. It was Elena and yet it was someone else – Lucy? A fiend from Castle Dracula? I lay in that state between dream and consciousness, when one seems to be awake yet cannot move a muscle. She seemed to be all women; or rather, the archetypal dark woman, Eve, who sided with the serpent and dragged mankind into sin. I thought I had experienced enough terror for one night, but this woke new depths in me.

Elena – the woman who looked like Elena – bent lower and lower over me, and I saw her pink tongue moving over her deep red lips, making the lips shine. The tongue protruded further and further, sliding over the pearly teeth, longer and longer, and I saw that it was forked at the end like a snake's.

My whole being withered in dreadful anticipation as I waited for the two tips of the tongue to flicker on my neck. The skin tingled. My paralysed body stiffened and arched, wanting to escape yet wanting her to draw nearer – the two desires in exquisite conflict. She lay down upon me and I could not stop her; almost did not wish to stop her, to my shame. She spoke and it was Elena's voice. 'You do not want your wife,' she whispered, her voice a hiss that hurt my ears. 'You want me.'

With this, her jaw opened so wide that it seemed to unhinge. Two great fangs appeared, long and thin and curved as a snake's, as if they had unfolded from the roof of her mouth. A clear liquid dripped from them, and in the dream I knew it was poison. I tried to cry out; she lunged, and I felt a burning coldness in my throat, and my soul seemed to lurch right out of my body in a spasm that sent me falling down into greyness; drowning greyness, like the bottom of the ocean.

God, how horrible now I recall it! Why must I suffer such vile nightmares, in which apparitions come to me and tell me lies? I feel that I can never bear Mina near me again – that she is soiled and fallen, as are all women. No, I will not believe it! My love for Mina is pure – as is hers for me. Dracula is the one who wishes to sully it. He makes unclean all that he touches!

### Later

In the light of day, with a good breakfast inside me, I feel renewed. We are in better spirits. I told Mina of the dream, for I want there to be no secrets between us. She comforted me and assured me that it *was* only a dream. Thank God for her strength.

Van Helsing's plan is in motion. Initially he will protect the house by placing wild rose and crucifixes on all the doors and windows. He has also sent for garlic wreaths, which we know will prove a powerful deterrent to the vampire.

What a fool I was to refuse these safeguards when he first arrived!

Seward and Godalming will assist him, and begin the

search for Dracula's lair. Meanwhile, the Professor insists on my taking Mina, Quincey and Elena out for the day. I argued, but in the end was forced to agree. A day at the seaside (we shall take the train to the coast) will do us all good.

While Mina was getting ready to go out, I asked Van Helsing, 'But for how long shall we live in this state of siege? If anything happens to Mina or Quincey – or indeed to Elena, whom we love like a sister –'

He broke in, 'How long? Until we find the monster's lair and destroy both it and him.'

'And how shall we destroy him?'

'In the manner in which a vampire is destroyed!' Van Helsing answered irascibly. 'We pierce the heart and sever the head.'

'But we have done that once, and he came back!' I cried. 'Perhaps there is nothing that *can* destroy him – or else he is God's alone to destroy, at the end of time!'

Then I regretted my outburst, for Van Helsing's face went white and haggard. 'The truth is, Jonathan, I do not know. We use all the knowledge and experience at our disposal to outwit him – but until we find a new way, a certain way, I do not know!'

Now here is Mina in her coat and hat. I am glad to go. We shall have a pleasant day, and forget all this.

ELENA KOVACS'S JOURNAL

*11 November*
He came to the house last night, my Dark Companion. I stood at my window waiting for him, my breath clouding on the glass, until I saw his shadow. I threw the window wide; the night smelled of damp leaves and smoke, and he brought in the smell on his clothes. 'Welcome,' I said. 'Enter.'

He did not take my blood, only stroked my cheek and

gave me a single kiss on the lips. Then he softly opened my door and was gone. Without my invitation, he could not have come in. But I wish I could have been a witness to the scene that followed – to the horror of his enemies when they saw him in full, magnificent existence!

I write this quickly before we go out. Quincey is dressed and ready, sitting quietly on my knee as I write.

I am growing a little nervous. This morning, before breakfast, Van Helsing found me alone in the nursery. He said nothing of last night; the only sign that anything had happened were the shadows beneath his eyes, a deeper creasing of his flesh. He asked me if I was happy with the Harkers; I replied that I was.

'I have not had the chance to tell you, Miss Kovacs,' Van Helsing went on, 'how very sorry I was to hear of your father's death.'

I thanked him. I did not want to speak of it.

'And your Uncle André,' he persisted. 'You have still no news of his expedition?'

'None.'

He shook his head gravely. 'Nor I, though I contact his housekeeper weekly. The poor woman is very worried. She is concerned about you also; that you left so precipitously.'

He smiled as he spoke, and his questions were fatherly and friendly; but there was a keenness in his eyes that made me suspicious. 'There is no cause for her to be concerned. I am a grown woman.'

'Nevertheless, what happened in Transylvania must have caused you deep distress. The English way, to keep the lips tight upon grievous losses, is not my way. It is better to talk freely of such matters, is it not?'

His questions caused me discomfort. 'My father's death was an accident. I grieve in my own way. I thank you for your concern, but . . .'

'Transylvania . . . a land of great mystery and beauty –

and danger. A place where the supernatural is as common as the natural, where the barrier between our world and the spirit world is thinner than tissue.'

'Only to the peasant mind,' I said, sharp now. 'I am surprised at you, Professor.'

'Ah, but such strange beasts as werewolves and vampires cannot all be dismissed as superstitions. Such things may be as real as you or I. To refuse to believe in them is playing into the Devil's hands! But you are a good, church-going woman, of course, and have no cause to concern yourself with such matters.'

'No, and I do not.'

'Tell me, Miss Elena . . . have you ever walked in your sleep?'

'Not to my knowledge.' I gave him a hard look and turned away.

'You must forgive me,' he said, soft but determined. 'My questions seem impertinent, but are in an essential cause. It is not true, then, that the Szekely farmers, with whom you stayed, saw you walking in the orchard and fields at night, accompanied by a white wolf? That you vanished for two days at a time, yet could not say where you had been? Vanished again on the very night of your father's death?'

I was facing away from him as he spoke, otherwise he would have seen my face drain to white. How does he know these things? Has he written to the farmers, asking them about my behaviour? Perhaps he saw a tightening of my shoulders; but I composed myself at once and turned round, displaying all the innocent, wounded sorrow I could muster.

'There was a sick wolf, Professor. It had been shot but not killed, and I wanted to help it, out of pity. I – I tried to feed it. I know I should not have done so, that wolves are the farmers' enemies, but I felt so sorry for it! I went out to search for it, and got lost. My behaviour was foolish, I know, but I acted only out of compassion for a creature in pain. As for my father, I was so distraught at his death that I could not help but flee. I acted in haste because I was not in my right mind; I beg you, out of pity if not understanding, not to judge me too harshly. Whatever my reasons for acting as I did, they are mine alone to know. But tell me, what have I done to deserve someone, who professes himself a friend of my uncle and therefore of his niece, to spy upon me?' I wept; Van Helsing looked fittingly ashamed.

'Forgive me, Miss Elena. I ask these questions only out of concern for your welfare. I would not intrude upon your grief and privacy without good cause. You look pale; has your sleep been disturbed at all?'

'No, Professor! I have a slight cold, that is all.'

'But you will tell me at once if you experience . . . strange dreams, any feelings of illness? I ask only in order to help you. As a friend of your uncle, I ask you to trust me; you will keep your window firmly shut at all times, will you not? And invite no strangers into the house.'

I frowned. 'Of course – but why do you ask this?'

'I will explain in time, but for now I cannot. Only take me at my word. I wish you good-day and a most pleasant journey.' With that he inclined his head to me, and left.

I think I have allayed his doubts for now, but there is no question that he suspects me! I am so afraid he may guess – if he has not already. He is a very clever man; more clever than I realized. I must talk to my beloved – but how? We are to leave for this wretched day at the seaside at any moment. There is no possibility of seeing him before tonight. I must think of something, we must act swiftly.

Mina is calling. No time.

## *11 November, evening*

I can barely bring myself to record this. How much more of this nightmare can we endure? Is there any more the monster can do to us? The answer to that is yes, yes and yes. It has only just begun.

Seward and Godalming are with us in the parlour as we make this record. Mina is on the couch by the fire, sleeping; she does not wish to be alone in her room, for which I do not blame her.

Now I look back I can see that there were signs all day. All morning, on the train and at the coast, Elena doted constantly on Quincey, sometimes to the point of smothering him; she was forever kissing him, ruffling his hair, stroking his cheeks or picking him up. It was almost as if Elena were taking over the role of mother. Mina could barely come near him without Elena intervening, whisking him away to look at some new object of fascination to a small boy. Mina seemed not to mind, for she is too good and gracious ever to make a scene, but in her heart she must have been as discomforted as was I.

I did not like it. My dream of Elena hung on me, and it concerned me to see the woman who last night leaned over me with great snake fangs cossetting our boy. I dismissed the feeling, for it seemed so unfair to Elena. How I wish now that I had heeded it!

The sea was very wild, leaping and breaking on the cliffs in great fans of spray. The sky was wonderful, full of fast-moving clouds through which the sun blazed and faded at dizzying intervals; the cloud itself was many-layered, with bright, stately columns above and swift-flowing whorls of purple-grey below. The wind was so brisk it left us breath-less. On a normal day it would have been exhilarating, but in our state it seemed only to aggravate our raw nerves.

All morning I felt we should find some way to explain about our enemy to Elena, the better to protect her by being wholly honest, but Quincey was always with her and the opportunity did not arise. At last Mina whispered to me, 'Never mind, we will tell her when we reach home and Quincey is in bed.'

The thought of going home and facing another night like the last appalled me. I felt a deep depression creep over me, and wished dearly that we could simply step on a train, perhaps to London or Paris, and leave all this anguish behind – but what would be the use? I know that Dracula would hunt us to ground wherever we went!

Quincey, of course, grew tired by midday and after lunch was sleepy. Mina wanted to take him home, but I was reluctant to go back so early. So when Elena suggested – nay, insisted – that she take him home on an earlier train while Mina and I stayed a little longer by the sea, we agreed all too readily. How she has repaid our trust! But I am to blame, for I had noticed the strange looks she gave Mina, and I chose to ignore them! We waved Elena off with our boy, and then spent a few hours more strolling along the front before we gathered ourselves to face the journey home.

When we reached home in the evening, we assumed that Elena had taken Quincey to the nursery for a nap. We met Van Helsing and the others in the parlour, where they were studying some ancient tome; in response to our enquiry, they said that they had heard no one come in, and had assumed Elena was still with us. We found the nursery and Elena's room empty; we searched the house; we asked Mary if Elena had come in and gone out again; but it was soon apparent that Elena had not been home. Once she left us at the seaside, she vanished.

Mina collapsed; we helped her to an armchair, where she sat trembling. We were all too shocked to act at once. 'What if they have had an accident?' said Mina. 'Elena cannot have taken him on purpose. Perhaps she got on the wrong train by mistake, or alighted at the wrong station; she is a foreigner, after all! Quincey will be so overtired by now, he will be ill again!'

Here Van Helsing gave me a grave, knowing look that Mina did not see. It roused my deepest suspicions. Van Helsing will always think the worst, but he is usually right. (*And wishes he were not – Van H.*) I brought Mina a glass of brandy; we spoke of calling the police, but Van Helsing said heavily, 'Not yet. Listen to me first. I am reluctant to call into doubt the character of a young woman who may yet be quite innocent. But given the dire circumstance in which we find ourselves, I can no longer keep my doubts to myself.

'I have thought long and hard about this, but always I come to the same conclusion; it may have been Elena who invited Dracula into the house. Indeed, it must have been she! Your Elena, pretty and gracious as she is, although the niece of my good friend, never rings quite true to me. Think, we left her in Transylvania, there by the Borgo Pass, a few miles only from Dracula's castle. Then she comes to you so suddenly, her father mysteriously dead, her uncle vanished, yet so merry and serene in the face of these losses! When I write to the farmers, to enquire more of Emil's death, I receive at length a strange reply; that she was seen outside at night with a great pale wolf, that she once wandered from the farm and was gone for two days, yet could not explain her actions. After her father was killed, she was never seen again. They said that they believed her to be bewitched. Was this mere superstition on their part? They are peasants, yes, but you met them, and know them to be good, honest people.'

Mina protested, 'I cannot believe we could be so wrong about her! You must be mistaken!'

Van Helsing lifted his hand briefly and shook his head. 'I

have met Elena many times in the past, though I never know her well. But well enough to see that she is changed. There is a slyness in her that was not there before, a watchfulness. It may be yet that I do her a great injustice. I hope that I do; that this is all a misunderstanding and she may at any minute bring Quincey home with an innocent explanation. But we must be prepared for the worst.'

At this a memory came to me: that this morning, when I was left alone with Quincey for a few minutes, the boy said something strange. 'Papa, I read Elena's book this morning.'

'What book is that?' I had asked indulgently.

'The book she writes.' I still remember his pale, serious face as he spoke, the wind-reddened spots in his cheeks! 'Her diary, like the one Mama keeps. I sat on her knee and watched as she wrote. She wrote of a strange man coming into the house, and of Professor Van Helsing asking her about wolves and dreams. I read every word!'

'But she would write in Hungarian, Quincey.'

'No, Papa, she writes in English. I could not have read Hungarian,' he explained patiently. At the time I thought he was being fanciful, making up what he thought he had read. But in the light of what Van Helsing was saying – I leapt up, and repeated this conversation to the others.

Van Helsing groaned. 'It is true, I spoke to her this morning of such matters! I wanted to hear her story, to cast some light on my suspicions, in the hopes of laying them to rest! Instead – ah, my questions only upset her, and provoked her to take this action!'

'We don't know that,' said Mina, stroking his hand.

'Wait,' I said. I left the parlour and ran up to Elena's room. Improper as it was to pry in a lady's bedchamber in this way, I felt that Quincey's plight overruled other sensibilities.

How still and strange the room seemed; as if her presence lingered like a scent. I searched the writing-table first, but found only pens and ink there. There was a small gold cross on a chain lying on the carpet, as if it had been carelessly dropped; that was a sign, her contempt for Mina's gift. Then I went all around the room, looking in drawers, stirring her soft white garments in search of the diary. Finding nothing, I opened the wardrobe. As I carefully worked through the layers of dresses, shifts and nightdresses – thinking she might have left the book in a pocket – a fragrance wafted out. At first it was a delicious earthy warmth, but presently I caught a sour note mingled with it, which grew stronger and stronger. Seeking its source, I bent down, and in the base of the wardrobe I found an old shawl all bundled up. As I disturbed it, the stench became overwhelming. How familiar, how repellent was that odour of foul earth, mould and decay – for it was the odour of a vampire's grave.

In my revulsion, it was all I could do to touch the shawl again. As if I dealt with some monstrous spider, I snatched it and dropped it quickly aside. Underneath lay a book, like the notebooks Mina and I use.

I opened it at random and read a few pages. At once I knew that we had been betrayed. I could read no more – could only rush down and wordlessly give the journal to Van Helsing.

He assumed the burden of reading Elena's story aloud to us. The shame of reading a private journal doubled our misery, but it had to be done. We listened in grim silence as she described how Dracula came to her in the shape of a wolf; how he lured her to the Castle, made her collect his ashes and his native earth and bring them to England, carrying his spirit inside her. How gloatingly she writes of her triumph in stealing Mina's blood – no remorse for the pain she caused! How sickening to read of her vigil by the tomb, as if she were waiting for her lover to come, not this repellent fiend!

'Then I was right,' Van Helsing said heavily. 'My questions this morning prompted her to flee. I am so sorry, I can never ask your forgiveness.'

'But she may have planned to do it anyway,' said Seward, who looked as grim as I have ever seen him. 'She is clearly hand-in-glove with Dracula!'

'I cannot believe it!' said Mina, ashen and distraught. 'I can't believe we were so wrong about her! Dracula has bewitched her, she is not acting of her own will!'

'Alas, I fear she is,' Van Helsing responded. 'Every line of this ghastly account emphasizes her willing collusion. Dracula found the perfect ally; one who actively wanted to help him. He only gave her the means to plunge into the depravity she admits that she always, secretly desired.'

'But he must have found her though *us*,' Mina said hoarsely, clinging to my good hand. 'It was my presence that stirred him. My presence also that clung in some degree to Elena, thus drawing him to her! I gave her that book as a present when we left Transylvania . . .'

'Do not begin to blame yourself,' Van Helsing said quickly. 'The fault lies not in your gift. On the contrary, it has enabled us to find out the truth. And think; now we know the exact location of Dracula's hiding-place – and we know that this time, instead of fifty graves, he has only one! As for Elena, there is hope. She is still human, not vampire, and there is still the chance we may save her soul.'

***Later*** (*Continued in Jonathan Harker's own hand*)
Seward, Godalming and Van Helsing have gone out to hunt for Dracula's grave. Mina and I are still downstairs and fully dressed, exhausted as we are; neither of us can contemplate sleep. Mary has made a fuss over Quincey's disappearance; I wish she would not, since there is nothing she can do. We cannot tell the servants the truth about Dracula! The fewer who know, the better. We have sent them all away except Mary, and her I have told not to worry, that we are doing all we can, and that she must go to bed.

Meanwhile we sit here in silence, hoping that Elena may

bring the boy home. My nerves are raw; I keep feeling that something is outside the windows, scratching to get in. Once, in annoyance, I wrenched back the curtain and thought there was a face staring in at me; I almost screamed, but saw it was only some vague shape of foliage, caught in the light from the house.

Now Mina has gone to look for the cat. It may be Puss scratching the glass and watching us. Or Dracula watching through her eyes. No, I must stop.

When I look at Mina, I feel very distant from her. It is as if I do not know her any more. I cannot stop remembering how she welcomed the carnal depravity that Dracula brought to our bed. I love her still, but her goodness and suffering, like Elena's, seem a shell over a cankerous pit.

I would never cause pain or scandal by deserting her. We will keep up the appearance of marriage, of course. But I do not think we can live as man and wife ever again.

Why is she so long, finding the cat?

### 12 November

How bitterly I regret the sentiments expressed, a few lines above this – a lifetime ago. Regret them but still, to my shame, cannot take them back – more than ever now. Ah, God, where is this to end?

When I went to look for Mina, I heard her voice from the study, and what sounded like a man's voice, answering her. The very air turned icy as I approached the door in dread; I moved as if lead chains hung on me. As I opened the door I saw my wife standing beside the fireplace, her face etched with despair – and beside her, starkly black against the surroundings, stood Count Dracula.

'Jonathan,' Mina said, as if to both warn me and keep me from any rash action. The study window was open, the wild rose torn away and discarded.

'How did he get in?' I gasped.

160

'I let him in,' Mina said faintly. 'I had to.'

The Count inclined his head to me, in a hellish mockery of courtesy. 'Mr Harker, I ask only that you listen to me.' As always his presence was a frigid weight upon us. He stood beside Mina as if he were her husband, not I; while I could not move from the doorway. 'Van Helsing has tried once more to foil me; will he never learn?'

'Where is he?' I cried, but Dracula held up a hand to silence me. I thought my heart would explode with loathing.

'Your son and Elena have come to me. They are both mine. Elena has always been mine. I have been at work in your midst for longer than you realize.' He smiled.

'What have you done to our boy? You are the Devil!' I cried. I could barely speak for the violence of my emotions; Mina said not a word.

'He is unharmed. Elena is caring for him. Therefore you have nothing to fear, since you have so freely entrusted him to her care.'

'Where are they?'

'Mrs Harker alone is to know that. Not you. You will see the child again only if you prove obedient to me.'

'In what respect?'

Dracula spoke just as he had when first we negotiated the sale of Carfax Abbey; with the same easy manner, belied by the same saturnine cast of face. 'That Mrs Harker shall come with me, of her own free will. I will take her to the boy. You and your colleagues must not attempt to follow us; for if you do, or if your wife refuses to go with me, you will never see your son again. *Never.*'

Mina said, quick and soft, 'I must go with him, Jonathan. It is the only way.'

'No!' But all my fierce anguish was useless against this fiend; for if I raised a hand against him, it might result in Quincey's death! I watched helplessly as the Count gripped Mina's arm and began to pull her past the desk towards the window. She was physically helpless against him, but her eyes were calm, resigned, determined.

She said again, 'I must go to Quincey. Jonathan, forgive me.'

And I – I had no choice but to let them go!

I watched as Dracula helped her over the low sill of the window. They vanished into the garden; a few seconds later I heard horses' hooves, the creaking of a carriage and the snap of a whip. I rushed through the house and out of the front door to see a black caleche, drawn by two big liver chestnuts, sweeping briskly away down the road. They would be two miles away before I could hire a cab to follow – but if I did, God knew what Dracula might do to my son!

Oh God, Mina, Quincey, Van Helsing – it is all my fault that things have come to this desperate pass.

I went back into the house, too distressed to do anything but wander from room to room, sobbing like a child. I did not even care if a servant saw me in this unmanly state, but I managed at last to compose myself before Mary heard.

Hardly knowing what to do, I put on my overcoat and shoes and started towards the church. That was where Van Helsing and the others had gone, and I could not wait for them to come home. I was terrified for them now – for what if they had met Dracula there, and he had come to our house and taken Mina with their blood already on his hands?

# Chapter Eleven

It took me half an hour to reach the churchyard on foot. I had brought a lantern, for it was full dark. I wandered down long avenues of tombstones and statues, which towered over me and seemed to watch me with cold smiling eyes, whispering in Elena's soft voice, *Come to us, dwell with us in sweet death* . . . I called Van Helsing's name, but my voice was weak and hoarse.

My head spun with terror and exhaustion. I was lost and could not find my way; either to the tomb I sought, or to the gate. In all directions, crosses and angels loomed over me, speckled with lichen and moss, as if even they would be consumed by nature and sink back into the ground. My trouser legs grew wet from the long grass. I seemed to wade through a sea of grass and herbs and dying wild flowers, while all around me bodies were rising up from the graves, their eye sockets black and hollow in their skulls, their voices moaning, '*Come to us, come to us* . . .'

Long stems wound round my ankles and I lost my balance, falling heavily against a gravestone. I dropped the lantern but it did not go out; I scrabbled, with my good hand, to right it. As I did so, from the corner of my eye I saw a shadow rising up. My head jerked round; there was a man leaning over me! I could see nothing of him but a shock of wild grey hair. Yet as he leaned down towards me, the lamplight caught the side of his face as a starkly pallid plane and I seemed to know him. I could not call to mind who he was – only that he was familiar. It was not Dracula. But the mouth opened, and I saw a red tongue churning over thick, sharp white teeth which glistened horribly, and I heard the hissing breath, and I knew that *this was another vampire.*

I was out of my mind by now. By instinct I flung my left arm behind me to grip the gravestone – and at that the apparition stopped and drew back. I heard the hiss of indrawn breath through the ghastly teeth. It rose over me, its face showing a kind of anxiety before it was lost in shadow again, and then it turned and vanished into the gloom.

I am certain that this was no hallucination. All the rest may have been – but not this.

As I raised myself up, I saw that the gravestone at which I had clutched had the shape of a cross. A stone angel beside it seemed to have Mina's form; I felt that she had protected me, a guardian angel, but outside our circle of light the graves were bursting open, earth turning over in new-ploughed wounds, the fresh flowers withering, birds falling from the sky like hail.

I gave a long, involuntary cry of despair; I heard voices; three more figures reared above me, and I tried to scramble back against the grave, my heels skidding on the grass. My lantern sent their shadows looming like giants over graves and trees. Then a voice I knew said, 'Harker! How did you come here? It's me – John Seward!'

At this, my confusion subsided and I sat up, feeling foolish and shaken. Seward helped me to my feet and I saw my three friends, gaunt-faced in the eerie light – but on their feet. I cannot say unhurt, for when I looked at Van Helsing I saw blood trickling from an open wound on the peak of his high forehead.

'Professor – you are hurt –' My voice was hoarse and hardly coherent.

'It is nothing.' Van Helsing gripped my arm, looking concerned. 'But, Jonathan, what are you doing here? Why are you not with Mina! What has happened?'

I spoke with difficulty. My ribs ached, and I could not get my breath. 'Mina is gone. Dracula came and took her. He has Elena and Quincey, too. I believe he had Elena take Quincey as bait to capture Mina!'

Van Helsing uttered such a groan that I thought he would collapse. 'My God,' he cried in anguish. 'How foolish – how blind we have been, not to foresee this!'

I went on trying to explain, stammering and breathless, until Seward said, 'Enough, Jonathan. Tell us when we reach home, and you are calmer. Let us go back. Dracula is gone. There is nothing more we can do here.'

We made slow progress along the lanes that led back to the house, Lord Godalming supporting me while Seward assisted Van Helsing. How I longed to run! All the way I was constantly and horribly aware of something following us. It was as if a piece of grey shadow had detached itself and was running along behind the hedgerow. A stark white face with wild grey hair kept hovering in my imagination; a face that was tormenting in its familiarity. So overwhelming and ghastly was this impression that I could not express it. My head was turning about like an owl's, my skin prickling with terror. Godalming said, with a ghost of grim humour, 'Harker, if the Count is gone, there is no need to fear your own shadow.'

My tongue loosened; by now I must have sounded as mad as one of Seward's own patients. 'But I saw – in the graveyard – I saw another one. Not Dracula. Another vampire!'

'You must have been mistaken!' Van Helsing said sharply.

Godalming said nothing, but I felt the breath go out of him in a slow exhalation of dismay more vivid than words. No more. No more.

How empty the house seems without my wife and son! Like a deserted, haunted old pile. Van Helsing and I rested in the parlour as we talked, a sorry pair. Godalming sat in an armchair, his head on his hands. Seward paced about in barely contained fury. He is a good man, made cynical by witnessing too much of life's ugliness. 'What have we done, that this curse should afflict us again? What proof have we that Dracula will even take Mina to Quincey? He is a liar, a cunning devil!'

'Don't talk in that way, I can't bear it,' I said. 'I must believe that at least Mina and Quincey are together, or I shall go mad. If I am not mad already!'

Mary brought us supper, concerned but accepting my request that she ask no questions, all would be explained later; though I doubt that I shall ever be able to explain to her. Then Seward told us what had occured in the churchyard. All through this, I had the creeping feeling that something was watching us, a presence walking round and round the house, staring through the windows and scratching at the glass, at once hideous and pitiful.

'We explored, looking for the tomb that matched Elena's description. The place is a maze. We found it eventually, a ramshackle sepulchre along an overgrown path; over-shadowed by yew trees and the door rusting away. But as we entered we saw a tall man in black, leaning over a central tomb. It was Dracula. Our lamp sent a huge shadow against the far wall; the strangest shadow, like a kind of dull blue fire, full of sparks. We saw his face clearly; I'll never forget the expression of sneering, frustrated malevolence as he glanced up and saw us! His eyes were red as hell-fire. We had surprised him in the act of removing his native soil from the tomb, apparently, and scooping it into a big leather bag. I saw a human skeleton heaped in one corner – so it was true, he and Elena had desecrated this tomb and usurped the rightful occupant!'

Van Helsing added, 'And the whole place stinks of the odour that we know, the odour on the shawl in Elena's closet, and that which lingers on the Count himself, that smell of earth and death. I am too late to scatter in the pieces of Holy Wafer; Dracula is on his way to another hiding-place.'

Seward continued, 'We stood off for a moment; Dracula said something along the lines of, "You will die as you were born, Van Helsing; an interfering fool. Are you God? Then, until you see with my eyes, do not judge me! Again you think to thwart me, like sheep against a wolf, but again you are too late." First he flung the bag past us; we dodged aside as it landed in the doorway and skidded a little on the leaf-mould there. The next we knew, the Count jumped clean over the bier and came for us. I tried to protect Van Helsing; Dracula caught me around the throat with one of his broad hands and flung me against the back wall. His palm was ice-cold. I slid down and lay winded, but I could see his face blazing with demoniac fury as he seized Van Helsing. I saw Godalming thrusting a crucifix between them. Dracula gave a roar of anger and threw aside Van Helsing, who hit his head on the corner of the tomb. Then the Count seized Godalming's fist instead, and the metal crucifix that he was clutching in it began to glow red. Godalming refused to let go. Dracula snatched his hand away; the look of rage on his face was so terrible that I thought he would kill us all. You could see him struggling to resist the power of the cross. Then Van Helsing and I picked ourselves up off the ground and we each held up our own crosses against him. At that Dracula fled, seizing the bag of earth as he went.

'We had to rest until Van Helsing had recovered enough to go on. Then we searched the graveyard for a time – close to leaping out of our skins – in the suspicion that Dracula might still be lurking there. Now it's obvious he came straight here, of course. Then we heard you shouting, Jonathan. The rest you know.'

I asked, 'Did Dracula mean to kill you?'

'I think he means to,' Van Helsing said thoughtfully, 'but not so quickly. He makes great sport with us first.'

Godalming gave a faint groan. So far he had not said a word.

Seward asked, 'But what about this other vampire you mentioned, Harker?'

I explained what I thought I had seen. 'My mind was so full of imaginings. Perhaps I imagined that too. It seemed so real!' Even as I spoke, I still felt those desperate eyes upon me . . . I shuddered, but could not admit to such neurosis.

We poured ourselves some brandy, and were silent a few moments. Then Godalming began to stir, clenching and unclenching his hands upon his knees. I noticed a red mark on one palm, where the cross had burned him. 'It's no good,' he said suddenly, with a kind of dignified anguish that was very affecting. 'I can't go on, I can't stay. Forgive me; I never meant to let you down. It grieves me more than I can say to break my vow, to break up our brotherhood, but I must!'

Van Helsing stared at him; Seward looked angry. 'What are you saying?'

'That I cannot fight Dracula any more. It cost me too dear, losing Lucy, having to drive the stake through her heart with my own bare hands! I could never do it again. But that's what it would come to. For if I go after Dracula, make no mistake; he would come after my wife! And I cannot, will not place her and our child in such danger. I am going home to them now. I am going to take them abroad, as swiftly as possible, and out of danger.'

He was weeping now; I was close to it myself.

'Forgive me,' Godalming said again, 'for putting my own family before yours, Jonathan, but I must. I am not betraying you, but protecting them.'

'Of course I forgive you. You have no cause to ask.'

I had no hesitation in releasing him from his vows. Seward and Van Helsing looked stricken, even betrayed; but after a few minutes they, too, reluctantly took Godalming's hand. 'I understand,' the Professor said gruffly. 'Go then, and may God go with you.'

Godalming left swiftly, and with few words; there was no more to say. After he had gone we were more disconsolate than ever. I felt that our little band, which had once been so strong and vigorous, was now disintegrating – with age, tiredness, disillusion – while our enemy sprang renewed from the grave, ever reborn.

'You should both go to bed now,' said Seward. 'We can talk again tomorrow.'

I protested that I couldn't sleep, that I must go out in search of Mina at once, but Van Helsing said, 'John is right, there is nothing more we can do tonight. In this state our brains and bodies are of no use to Madam Mina. Nothing will help her better than our sleeping, and waking refreshed and alert.'

My sleep was poor, and fraught with nightmares. Nevertheless I feel refreshed, capable of setting pen to paper and even, to my surprise, in need of a good breakfast.

## 12 November, evening

A fruitless day.

We were up early, our spirits quite vigorous; our vigour springing from necessity rather than physical strength. I could see, however, that Van Helsing was pale and having to make an effort. Over breakfast Van Helsing, Seward and I again went through Elena's treacherous diary.

'How could she have taken us in?' I cried. To my shame, I wept – but I could not help it. To think of Mina and my son with that fiend is unbearable.

Van Helsing said, 'Elena is intelligent; she has a man's brain in that demure form. She says to herself, "Evil, be thou my good!" Well, she is unmasked, too late. All along she has fooled us. She came to us at Dracula's direction but how much at his direction, how much of her free will, I am not certain. Could she be again, in her heart, as sweet, good and pure as Mina, if she were only out of his power – or is she a demon from the pit of Hell?'

We talked of calling the police, but decided against it. They would not believe us, nor take us seriously; their questions might become awkward, and were more likely to hinder than help us. We must make enquiries of our own.

'It is tempting to rush into action, to expend our energy in useless ways only to satisfy ourselves that we sit not idle, but that is not the way,' said Van Helsing. 'We go slowly. First let us take stock of what we know of this monster.' The Professor began to seem his old, energetic self as he warmed to his subject. 'The vampire needs not blood to live, for he cannot die . . . but without it he becomes old and torpid. Blood gives him vigour; it makes him young, as we have seen. He must have it. He steals life at the expense of his victim – but it is more than energy he needs. He craves the warmth of the living, for he is jealous of them; he hates their freedom, their devotion to God. He must have power over them, to make them serve him instead; to be his jackals, as once he said to us. So strong is Dracula's desire to live that he even cheats death; cheats it twice, that we know of. But think; what did we do wrong in dispatching him? He says that he can come back, but Lucy and the three women we dispatched cannot. Why?'

Dr Seward gave a cry. 'Professor, did you not prescribe a specific method of dispatching the vampire? A wooden stake through the heart. But we didn't kill Dracula that way, we killed him with steel! We broke our own rules.'

Van Helsing nodded. 'Yes, John. I have thought upon this. It seemed to suffice at the time – but we cannot break the rules of the Undead, any more than they can. But there is more. Dracula made Madam Mina drink some of his blood, so that he would always have power over her, and his mind would command hers. That blood in her was some part of him still warm and living. Remember what we read in Elena's diary – how she stole Madam Mina's blood to bring Dracula back to life!'

Being reminded of this was horribly distressing. I tried to hide my pain, but felt Dr Seward's hand on my shoulder. Sometimes I think Van Helsing does not realize, in his eagerness to hunt down the truth, how blunt he is being.

'But I think this is not yet enough for him. When first he became Undead, he lost some mental agility; he is in many ways a child, learning by experiment. Now with his second rebirth it is the same. He is weak – strong against ordinary mortals, but still weak by his own standards. To regain his old strength, he must drink from Madam Mina's veins. That is why he has taken her.'

This brought me to the edge of collapse. Van Helsing patted my back. 'Friend Jonathan, be not too distressed. There is good news.'

'How so?' I cried.

'When the vampire was in the form of a spirit, he entered other bodies; Elena, the cat, you, myself. He tormented us, bringing dreams, imaginings, madness, even physical harm. But think; since he regained his corporeal form, he haunts us no more! His will is now trapped within his own body. He has greater strength, but less freedom. He cannot have both! It may be, in spirit, he could have driven us all mad – but his greed to take flesh again was too strong. So, physical, we can fight him.'

'We have to find him first,' I said.

'And who knows what new lessons he may have learned?' said Seward. 'Last time he brought fifty boxes of his native earth; this time, a mere shawl-full.'

'He learns to travel light,' said Van Helsing, chuckling. 'He must go at dawn to his place of rest; but what happens to him then if he go not? For we have seen him abroad in daylight. Say he sleeps from dawn until noon, then is able to wander about until dusk, but without his unnatural power to change shape?'

'But I have seen him in the morning, too,' I pointed out.

'Yet still I say, he must lie in his native earth, once each day, for a time, however brief . . .'

'Even if he didn't – say he could not reach it for some reason – I can't see that it would kill him,' I said.

'Not kill him . . . but cause him great distress, for that instinct of the Undead to lie in the grave is greater than ours to sleep and eat. It is sovereign. Therefore deprived of it he is lost, exposed, in a great storm of rage, of frustration . . .'

'A good deal more dangerous,' Seward said sourly.

'But more vulnerable! More apt to rash actions that may undo him.'

'Well, he seems to have taken the earth with him, so he must be going to make a new hiding-place somewhere. Wherever he has taken Mina and Quincey.'

'And we will take steps to find it. Jonathan, I do not think think harm will come to Mina and Quincey at once. He uses them to control us. Dead, they would be useful as hostages no more.'

I must be grateful for this blunt but honest nugget of hope.

By the end of breakfast, Van Helsing was pale again, and I was very concerned for him. At last we forced him to admit that he had a bad headache; the result of last night's blow to the head. Seward examined him, and sent him back to bed for the rest of the day. No use endangering his health when he needs time to recover. He would have been good for nothing today.

Seward and I spent the day making enquiries; I in Exeter, Seward further afield. So far, we have discovered the firm who hired a black caleche and pair to the Count, but no one who has seen or heard anything of it since.

## 13 November

Last night I experienced again the dreadful feeling that something was prowling, watching. This time Seward and Van Helsing felt it too; the Professor had risen from his sick bed in the evening, against Seward's advice, and was sitting with us in the parlour.

I hardly know how to describe the sensation. It was like wave upon wave of fear striking me. It was past midnight; we were all exhausted from searching, worrying, endlessly talking. It was too late and too dark to make any further progress, but the impossibility of acting only made us restless. Van Helsing loathes being ill. I fear we put too much unspoken pressure on him to recover, we are in such dire need of his wisdom.

We grew more and more uneasy. A strange sound began, first a ticking, then the beating of a far-off drum rising to a terrifying crescendo – the sound of someone beating violently at the front door! Then silence. As one we leapt up and went into the hall.

I took a walking-stick from the stand as a weapon. 'Slowly, now . . .' said Van Helsing. The door felt ice-cold as I touched it; I was certain, I know not how, that it was not Dracula there, but something worse – worse because it was unknown.

I opened the door. There on the threshold stood a gaunt man in a travel-worn suit that was plastered with loose soil, grass, even with dew and cobwebs. His face was salt-white, his hair a wild grey squall. It was the vampire I saw last night in the graveyard!

I recoiled. Seward's arm moved past my shoulder, rigidly presenting a large crucifix. The vampire drew back, and some quality of the gesture made me pity it. Yet it did not retreat. Instead it held out a leather-bound book and said, in a cracked voice, 'Abraham. Abraham.'

Van Helsing let out a gasp, terrible to hear. 'Oh, dear God and all the saints! André Kovacs?'

Yes, I recognized him then. Professor Kovacs, who had shown us such hospitality in Buda-Pesth, Elena's uncle. I still can't believe it – nor comprehend this tragedy!

'Invite me in, Abraham. I cannot come in without invitation, I have tried for days.'

'No.'

The apparition shook the book. His eyes were red-rimmed and staring. 'Then take my journal. I wrote it for you. It tells everything. I will wait here while you read it!'

Kovacs seemed rooted there. The scent of death and grief rose from him like an ice-vapour. At last, frowning and hesitant, Van Helsing reached out and took the book. Then he shut the door in the vampire's face.

We returned to the parlour, for it had turned so cold in the hall. We were all terribly aware of the creature outside the house as Van Helsing opened the journal and began to read it out loud. Seward and I attended in tense silence. The Professor began to shake his head, his high forehead creasing into deeper and deeper lines. 'He found the Scholomance . . . Ah, *mijn God*, poor Miklos dead!' And at the last, with feverish agitation, he flung the book down and pressed his hands to his temples in an expression of agony. 'Oh, my poor dear friend! Oh God, no! What more can we be asked to endure?'

Seward took the journal from him and we glanced through the entries. The change both in Kovacs's style and his handwriting was telling in itself; from bold and cheerful to frantic and demented.

Seward said, 'This demon, Beherit, is using him as some kind of . . . agent, spy against Dracula?'

'So it would seem,' Van Helsing said grimly.

'Then might we not also use him against Dracula?'

'What are you suggesting?' I cried. 'That creature, that piteous thing, is no longer our friend! It's not human! It should be destroyed, put out of its misery!'

'But John is right.' Van Helsing sighed. 'I cannot forget so easily that Kovacs was my friend, and must therefore give him the benefit of the doubt; that his love, also, has survived the grave. Would we not all do as much for each other? Come, then. Let us invite him over the threshold.'

It was an hour or more since we had shut the door upon the vampire. When we opened it again, Kovacs stood there as if he had not moved a muscle. When I, trembling and with constricted throat, extended a hand and said, 'Come in,' the vampire came to life and stepped quite graciously into the hall. There was no violence about him; only the cold radiance of death, and a sort of desperation.

He stood in the centre of the parlour, addressing Van Helsing as if Seward and I were not there. 'My dear friend, Abraham, when I wrote that last entry – when I sat at the very fissure of Hell with Beherit, and felt myself dying, I thought that I would never see the outside world again. All has changed since then. I look out from within the darkness, and understand. Can you forgive me, for what I have become?'

'As I am in no position to judge you – I must,' said Van Helsing. 'You wrote the last entry as you sat dying; now you are Undead. What became of you in between?'

Kovacs's face was so sad it seemed eerily beautiful. His words were horrific – yet I could say nothing to stop him, for they were also hypnotic. 'I came from Transylvania to England on foot, sleeping in the graves of suicides as I came. How long it has taken, I have no idea; all is different in the world of night. You cannot know, no one but the Undead can know, how sweet it is to hunt in the darkness like the owl and the wolf, to feel the blood of an unspoiled young boy spilling into your mouth, his blood mingling with yours, his holy life feeding the unholy . . . nor how bitter, how lonely, how comfortless. For I have nowhere to go, no connection

175

to this world, no living friend but would shun me with all the disgust the living pour upon my kind.

'I did die, there in the library with only a demon for company. A long time later – I know not how long – I opened my eyes again. I was alone. All was different. I saw, I heard, I felt, and yet I knew I was dead. Different laws work upon me now. I serve a different master.

'Much of my memory was gone; much of my human feeling erased. The urges that bubbled in my heart were animal ones – lust for blood – and deathly ones; jealousy of the living, cruelty, cold mirth at the futility of life. Beherit had left me. I chewed at my own hands in the need to pierce flesh and taste blood. Yes, picture it, my friend. Was I not pitiful? Would you not, had you been on hand, have dispatched me to true death without a single qualm?

'But when this activity yielded nothing, my journal caught my eye. I was like a child or a jackdaw, in my fascination. I picked it up and began to read.

'Oh, my friend, then knowledge came back to me! How much easier it would have been to remain child or animal in mind than to be given back the memories of who and what I was! How have I deserved this? I came into this through curiosity, not through deliberate evil. And yet, it was thus that mankind fell in the first place. Be warned, Van Helsing; our thirst for knowledge is against God's plan, for we are trying to become like God. Then we are cast out of Heaven and into the pit, as was Lucifer.

'Knowledge is the Devil's. There in the Scholomance he whispers, "I will teach you what God alone knows – but in punishment you will serve me for ever afterwards."

'I had not even the comfort of Miklos being with me in Undeath. How I wish Beherit had not struck off his head! What seemed a holy mercy at the time now seems a bereavement. But that is the selfishness of our condition – that I would rather he shared this ghastly existence than rested in holy peace!

'While I was alone I grew frantic, for the physical craving was intense, and I could find no way out. By the time Beherit returned, I was like a rabid wolf. I tried to attack him, but he only smiled and held me away. I railed at him, for letting me suffer this maddening thirst, for making me Undead.

' "Calm yourself," he said. "You shall be allowed to leave and satisfy your needs, if you only keep the bargain we made."

'I could not resist him. Repulsive though the idea must seem to you, he was so beautiful to me, despite the horror of what we are; so lusciously golden, with his shining hair and rosy flesh, that I loved him. That is the simple truth. Loathsome as Beherit is, I love him. He is damned, and so am I.

' "Find Dracula for me," he said. "I know he is not dead. Ensure that he never comes back to the Scholomance. If you succeed . . . you *will* be allowed back here, and the keys of the library will be yours." '

Seward said, 'It sounds a dubious enough bargain to me. How can you keep Dracula away, unless you shadow him for all eternity?'

'But I trust Beherit,' said the vampire. 'There must be a way. I do this to please Beherit, whom I love.'

There was something at once so childlike and so repellent in these words that I winced. Van Helsing said, 'Well, your Beherit is right. Dracula has returned. Jonathan saw you in the churchyard; you must have been only yards from the Count. Did you see or speak to him?'

'I watched him from a distance. He did not know I was there. If ever he sees me, confronts me . . . I can only hope that Beherit's instinct guides my actions.'

'Before Dracula destroys you? And did you know that he has kidnapped my son and my wife?' I exclaimed angrily, unable to contain my frustration any longer.

Kovacs showed no reaction, but said in the same melancholic tone, 'I will help you to find them, if I may.'

'He has Elena, too,' said Van Helsing. 'She is still alive – for how long, I dare not guess.'

'I know. I have seen her with him. I so wanted to speak to her, to ask how this happened . . .' Now a tear ran down his mournful face. I couldn't help remembering what a fine energetic man Kovacs had been, a bare few months ago!

'That, we can tell you,' Van Helsing said heavily. 'Ah, André, if only I had taken greater pains to warn you, to protect you! If only I'd never told you of Dracula or come near your family!'

'No, the fault is not yours,' Kovacs answered. 'We have much to talk about, Abraham. Do not think, that because I have become what I have become, that I feel no affection or responsibility towards my friends and kin. On the contrary, the Undead love the living with a passion you cannot imagine.'

# Chapter Twelve

*12 November*

I am writing this upon paper that the Count has allowed me;
I did not bring my notebook, indeed I brought nothing. But
he seems not to mind my writing. I fear it is only so that he
might read and mock it later – but still, write I must or go
mad! I work in shorthand, so it will be meaningless to him,
I hope.

When he took me from the house, I do not recall feeling
afraid – rather, my fear was all for my boy, and for poor
Jonathan. I was too shocked, I think, to feel anything, or to
pay attention to any emotion but my need to be reunited
with Quincey. The Count himself drove the caleche. He
drove all night at great speed towards London, stopping twice
to change horses, and to let me refresh myself. He knew that
I would not try to escape him at these times. At dawn we
came to an immense house, surrounded by a thick stone wall,
and I knew at once where we were. He has brought me to
Carfax Abbey!

Of course, to what other place could he flee? He bought
this estate through Jonathan's agency, and since his 'death'
it has not, as far as I am aware, been resold. How could it
be? We had no wish to notify anyone of the Count's demise.
Our only wish was to forget the matter and all connected
with it. So naturally, the Count still holds the deeds to Carfax!

The carriage passed through a huge rusted gate of oak
and iron, which the Count then padlocked behind us. The

high walls of the ground enclosed us in another world; a swamp-like, dripping world where the trees clumped together in dense thickets and there seemed no greenness whatsoever. All was grey in the dawn; the mournful hues of slate and stone, of graves. I glimpsed deep, dark ponds among the trees, a lake like polished pewter wreathed in mist. The feeling of a horrible, brooding spirit lay on the place – a thing not alive yet not dead.

The house itself has the look of a prison; an old fortress, rather, square and solid with high windows in the dark stone walls. Carfax – *Quatre Face*. My spirits, already worn down by anxiety and the journey, ebbed to their lowest.

When the Count helped me down from the carriage, it was with a strange mixture of courtesy and coldness. He seemed distant, a thing made of marble; so that although I physically shrank from him, my fear was less acute. I wished he would speak, but he did not. He and the caleche disappeared round the side of the house. Then the double door opened, and there was the treacherous Elena! She had a lantern in one hand; with the other, she beckoned me in. Her face looked no different; a pale oval with a pure, clear expression – but her hovering smile, which once seemed shy and mysterious, now struck me as malevolent.

I entered; we looked at each other; neither of us spoke.

She led me across a hall with a high, vaulted roof, up a flight of wide stone stairs, along a corridor and up a smaller, twisting staircase to a part of the house that felt cramped and ancient, with tiny windows. It made me very uneasy, and deeply distressed to think of poor Quincey being kept here!

She unlocked and opened a low door. It was small, but heavy and impenetrable, like the seal of a prison. I did not want to go through. I felt that I was being tricked, that Quincey was already dead. I felt as if I were walking into a tomb in which I was to be sealed, never to see the light of day again!

'Come, Mina,' said Elena. 'Quincey is waiting for you.'

With the deepest misgivings, I went through. She brought me to a locked door with a small aperture cut in it at eye level, and bade me look through. I saw a room with a fire burning in a big grate, warming the stone walls; and there I saw my son, playing on a rug before the fire, his blond hair shining in the firelight!

'Quincey!' I cried. 'Quincey, I am here!' He looked up, and came running to the door, calling, 'Mama! Mama!' How pallid his little face was, his eyes all bruised with tiredness. I tried to open the door, but it was solidly padlocked.

I turned furiously to Elena. 'Let me in!'

She only returned the same knowing, cat-like look. 'I cannot. You see that we did not lie to you; he is here, and he is safe. Look, he is not distressed. He trusts me.'

'Jonathan and I trusted *you*!' I retorted. I called gently to Quincey, 'Go back and play, dear. Mama will come to you soon.' He obeyed, seeming quite at ease. What a mercy that he is too young to realize his plight!

I turned to Elena. 'You know how delicate his health is,' I said. 'This will kill him!'

'I love him!' she replied fiercely. 'He will want for nothing here. Do you think I do not know how to look after the boy?'

As she turned away from me, I saw the marks of fangs upon her neck. I caught my breath. 'You will be allowed to see him, as long as you do the Count's bidding,' said Elena. 'Such favours must be earned.' Oh, the cruelty buried in the honey of her tone! How loathsome, the idea of making these implied bargains with the Devil! But what choice have I?

All at once my strength deserted me and my tears flowed. Elena lead me away, and although I despised her touch upon my arm I could not resist her.

She brought me up a spiral staircase to a room above Quincey's. This is the oldest part of the house, the keep. I am to be kept here; a large, irregularly shaped room with a four-poster bed, a cavernous fireplace with a group of chairs set before it, and an escritoire, at which I now sit and write. Between these are great areas of bare flags. The stone walls are thick, ancient, cold and dank; the fire, though hot, does nothing to dispel this impression. There are a few faded tapestries hung upon the walls, but they add no comfort; the figures in them look like ghosts. The windows have grilles across them. Very little light creeps through; all I can see is a small section of the grounds, with dark, twisted trees and part of the bleak outer wall. I have seen big dark dogs trotting through the undergrowth. The overall impression is one of intense gloom. I could imagine, if I do not keep myself in check, that my prison has become the whole world, that I will never see the sun again.

After Elena had brought me here, she left me for a while. I tried the door; it was locked, and I lack the strength to break it down. She returned some minutes later with tea, and a jug of water that she set behind a screen so that I might wash.

I said, 'I believed you to be my friend, Elena. It hardly seems fitting that you should now act as my maid. Does it not concern you that the Count has brought you to this?'

'I am still your friend, Mina,' she said coolly. 'It is as your friend that I tend to your needs, and to Quincey's. If I do not, you will both starve.'

'I would rather starve, than give one fragment of my soul to the Devil!'

She smiled, but there was anger in the look. What cause has she to be angry with me? She is still human ... but Dracula will make her a vampire, if he feeds upon her once or twice more. Then, oh God help us, dear Quincey ...

She withdrew. I drank my tea and tried to calm myself. I lay down and rested, but was woken, some hours later, by the terrible feeling that there was someone in the room with me. I sat up and saw, sitting at the writing desk, reading through a pile of papers, Count Dracula.

I caught my breath and got to my feet. He looked up. The cold glitter of his eyes exerted a physical force upon my heart; at once a convulsion of horror, and a desire to go towards him. Rather, a loss of will to resist. I said a silent prayer, and put my hand to the cross at my throat.

He said, 'You are rested, I hope, after an arduous journey. I will ask Elena to bring you some refreshment.'

'I am not hungry.'

'Nor thirsty?' he said, giving me a look at once hostile and gloating. I could see that he had not fed his vile thirst for some time; there were silver streaks in his hair once more. How terrible to see such malignancy in a face and form that otherwise would be noble! 'Why do you look upon me with such disgust?'

'You are keeping me prisoner!' I said angrily.

'You are not my prisoner,' he said.

'My door is locked!'

'Then I will ask Elena to leave it unlocked. But I think you will not wish to leave. You are not my hostage; your son is.'

I wanted to call him all the fiends in Christendom, but the words would not come. He would only have laughed. I tried instead to act as Jonathan and Van Helsing would expect, with dignity.

'Why? My son is innocent, he has never done a thing to harm you! If you have one mote of humanity left –'

'And I wish your son no harm. He was only the means to make you come to me willingly.'

'I did not come willingly.'

'You had a choice, therefore you exercised your will.'

'I had no choice!' I said fiercely.

He sat back, making a steeple of his coarse, sharp-nailed hands. 'But you do have a choice, and you must make it. No harm will come to your boy – but I will only let him go when you change your mind. Mrs Harker, I must have your blood.'

I turned away; a second later I felt him behind me, his hand falling heavily upon my shoulder. I was not entranced; would that I had been! The awareness that I was being touched by this Undead corpse, which rose again and again from a chill grave, paralysed me.

He said softly, 'You did not shudder so, the last time.'

'That is not true!'

He swept a hand at the papers on the desk. I recognized the transcript I had typed, of our first encounter with Dracula. He must have stolen it from Jonathan's study. 'Ah yes, in your old diaries you profess great revulsion, the natural loathing of a Christian woman for the touch of Satan. But were your true feelings contained therein – or were you not merely expressing the disgust that was expected of you, so as not to offend your husband and your companions?'

'No. How dare you!'

'Of the two of you,' he continued, leaning so close that I felt his cold breath upon my cheek, 'was not Lucy the more honest?'

'Lucy was pure in every way. How dare you mention her name! You only defiled her for a little while, until good men gave her spirit back to God!'

As I said this he released me, and moved away. I thought he would laugh at my defiance; instead I heard him sigh, as if my words made him weary. 'You must give me your blood, Mina. Give it freely. Even I have made mistakes, but I have learned. I will not take it by force.'

'Then you will not take it at all.'

Suddenly his arm swept down and sent the papers on the desk flying. He glared at me, eyes gleaming red. His sudden fury alarmed me. Scooping the scattered pages off the floor, he thrust them into the fire. 'This collation of lies and self-deception I consign to the flames, where it belongs!'

'We have other copies,' I said.

He turned to me with rage still smouldering in his hard, aquiline face. 'You will give in to me, beloved Mina.' Then he withdrew, kissing his hand to me as he went.

When he had gone, I rushed to the door and found that he had, indeed, left it unlocked. I ran down the spiral stair and looked through the door to Quincey's room. Quincey was on the bed, asleep; I could just see a twist of gold hair and the rise and fall of his chest. I did not want to disturb him, poor angel.

Even if I could find the padlock key and release him, how would we flee? We would not gain the outer walls before we were recaptured, or savaged by the dogs.

Wearily I returned to my room. Elena brought a tray of cold meats, cheese and salad, with bread and wine. I was in need of sustenance by now. She sat down and ate with me; we did not speak, but I caught her giving me sly glances under her long dark lashes.

When we had finished, she said, 'You must hate me.'

'I do not hate you, Elena,' I replied. 'Rather, I pity you.'

She bristled. 'You – pity me?'

'You have fallen under the spell of evil.'

'So, you think I am under a spell. You think that I cannot make my own choice, because I am too pure and good to do so? Mina, the menfolk are not here. We need not pretend to each other.'

'I don't know what you mean! Do you imagine Dracula cherishes you? He will kill you!'

'And I will live for ever, feeding on the living, never again afraid of the night. Is that so terrible?' She looked so serene and calculating, I was at a loss to reach her.

'You will be a corpse, driven by hunger. You will lose your soul, and never find rest. You will be barred for ever from Heaven.'

'Heaven sounds exceedingly dull to me,' said Elena.

With every word, she shocked me more. 'I am surprised

at you,' I said. 'When we first met, you spoke to me about your desire for freedom, your horror at the idea of marrying. And yet you have made yourself a slave of this monster, who is worse than the most tyrannical of husbands! What became of your ideals?'

Her face, for a moment, was fiery. 'I am not a slave! He is my companion. I aid him because, in time, he will make me free – free to love where and when I will, and never to be tied to one man, or to society or child-bearing and old age.'

'Only God can give eternal life!' I retorted. 'The Devil gives a parody of eternal life, because all he can do is ape God!'

'God is sterile,' she said. 'Parody at least has the virtue of being interesting. What is so commendable about your own ideals? You are expected to live without passion, in a world where nothing must ever be allowed to change. Nothing may ever be out of place, may it? And if it is, you and your kind turn your backs upon it, and pretend it does not exist, and drive it out with prayers and self-punishment! You are so afraid of anything that may threaten your cosy existence! You are as terrified of darkness as any Transylvanian peasant. What makes your narrow, frightened ideals so superior to the Count's noble ones? He embraces the darkness, he is one with wild animals, with storms and desires – with all that you fear. *He* is the one with the bravery to live as you dare not!'

I could say nothing to this. I sat stunned for a minute or so; she went to the window and looked out at the gloom. Already she seemed a part of it! I said desperately, 'Elena, it is not too late for you. You must have the key to Quincey's room. Help us escape. When Dracula has gone to his rest –'

'No,' she cut in. 'I want to help you, but not in that way.' Her skirts rustled on the flags like the hissing of snakes as she came towards me. To my astonishment, she embraced me. 'Come to us, Mina. Be one with us. We love you.'

186

She felt so warm, so sisterly and loving in my arms – but I controlled myself, and pushed her away. Elena gave me a burning look, and left.

After she had gone – once I had managed to steady myself – I opened the desk and found pens, ink and paper. So I sat down to write. At least this way I occupy myself and save myself from insanity.

### 13 November

Dracula came to me again last night.

He brought my supper and sat watching as I ate – and I was determined to eat, however little appetite I have, in order to keep my strength and wits about me. His demeanour was different, quiet and thoughtful where it had been aggressive. I was very afraid, but determined that he would not see it.

'Now we shall talk,' he said, leading me towards a chair by the fire. I noticed the mirror in its ornate frame above the mantelpiece as we approached; that it contained only my own reflection! I recalled how Jonathan had witnessed the same phenomenon at the castle, and how Dracula had destroyed the offending shaving mirror. But this time – presumably because the fact that I know the truth means he has nothing to hide – he only smiled demoniacally and paused there as if to draw my attention to the horror of it.

'Why do you suppose I have no reflection?' he asked.

'Because you have no soul.'

'But I feel passionately,' he protested. 'I feel loneliness. I experience love, anger, desire, ambition – how then can I have no soul?' He walked up to the mirror and pressed the point of one fingernail into the centre of the glass. 'If I am no more than a walking corpse, how is it that I can talk, and think, and remember? The looking-glass lies. It flatters and it deceives.'

I saw the pressure of his nail increasing. The glass bowed; I saw my own reflection distorting and sliding away. Then, as if the pressure became too great, the mirror cracked with a loud retort and shattered.

I recoiled in shock. Shards of glass spilled and broke on the floor at our feet. Dracula smiled. He bade me sit in a chair opposite his, as if nothing had happened, while the fire glittered in fragments on the floor between us.

I saw him look in contempt at the cross I wear, but he did not tell me to remove it. He asked, 'Do I disgust you?'

I said, as I had to Elena, 'No. I pity you.'

'Then pity me, if you must.' He gave a faint laugh, his lips drawing up over the great, sharp canine teeth. 'You know quite well, Mina, that under a guise of kindness that is the most offensive remark you can make to anyone. You are not so gentle, after all.'

'Not gentle at all, when I must fight for my child and husband.'

'I know your strength. That is why I need you. Women and men without spirit are of no use to me.'

'Is no one of any worth, then, who is not of use to *you*?'

'Why does this shock you, when you know what I am? How could it be otherwise?'

'You must have been different once.' I was trying, in desperation, to appeal to any humanity he might have left. 'When you were mortal.'

Now his smile was not cruel, but sad. 'But you know what I was, and have no doubt made your judgements. Ah, do not tell me that I am God's to judge. I have long ceased to have any interest in God's opinion – or in the Devil's. And I could tell you that all I did, I did in defence of my country and people; that it was necessary, in a fearsome world, to be the most fearsome thing in it. But I have no wish to justify myself, any more than you have to hear it.' As he went on talking I began to let go a little of the fear that had possessed me – at the same time knowing that the less I feared him, the more I might be sucked into the pit of evil and become part of it.

Nevertheless it seemed possible, and a great relief for my worn nerves, that I should suspend terror for a time.

'I view the past as if through a great wavering veil, a heat-haze rising from the field of conflict,' he went on, sounding weary. 'It was another man who lived through the blood and battles and heroism of those times. Not me. I cannot remember being other than I am. The days of war are long gone . . . and if they come again, as they surely will, it will be others who lead our armies into battle.' As he spoke, there seemed to be a great sighing space around him, aeons of solitude. 'Meanwhile, I go on, by my own choice. When I was in limbo, and when you passed me by and I felt your spirit touch mine, all I remembered was the pleasure of living.'

I recalled what I had read in Elena's journal; her experience of Dracula's dreadful solitude. It pulled at my heart. I cannot allow such sympathies to grow.

He went on, 'I had forgotten the terrible loneliness . . .'

'There is surely a cure for this loneliness,' I said sharply. 'To die at the appointed hour and go to your Maker!'

Dracula laughed, showing hard white teeth that made my stomach contract in anxiety. 'But I want life! I want dominion over life. Your Van Helsing destroyed not only me. He killed the three companions of my heart and they cannot come back.'

'The three women in the castle,' I said. 'Who were they?'

He spoke so softly I am not sure I heard him rightly. 'Daughter . . . sister . . . wife. Now they are gone.'

'But *when* were they gone? When Van Helsing destroyed them – or when you first made them Undead?'

He did not answer. I expected him to be angry, but he only looked thoughtful, and so grave, I began, again, to feel sympathy. I asked, 'Why can they not come back, as you have?'

'Van Helsing dispatched them more efficiently than he did

me . . . but there is far more to the matter than that. Through no fault of their own, they had not my knowledge or strength. They left no mortal walking the earth with their blood in her veins; no companion bonded in blood. They lacked my singular will, my appetite for life. I returned only through you, Mrs Harker, and for you. Do you not therefore bear some responsibility for my existence?'

I hated the way he tried to blame me, to draw me in, but in a sense it was no less than the truth. 'Perhaps. If it is so, I am as sinful as you.'

He smiled; his face, for a moment, was almost kind. I could see in it the mortal he once was, who presumably felt some tenderness at least for his family. 'No. You have far to go. But can you not be barred from Heaven as much for a small sin as a great one? Therefore it will make things no worse for you if you should go a little further. That is, to let wrong occur not by failing to hinder it, but by actively desiring it.'

'You know I cannot.'

'Can you not? Don't lie to yourself, Mina. A wrong, but for the greater good; your freedom to be with your son.'

'If I do as you ask, will you not only set us free, but leave us alone for ever?'

He paused. 'I cannot promise so much. This transaction is to allow you and Quincey to be together. To let you both go home unhindered – I may require more.'

'This is not fair!'

'It is all I can offer.'

'Why do you need me to consent?' I said angrily. 'Why not take me by force, as you did before?'

'I tell you again that I did not force you. You failed to hinder me, which was your subconscious consenting even while your conscious did not. You were yourself acutely aware of your "stain". I draw your attention again to your record, Mina: were not your spiritual agonies somewhat exaggerated for the benefit of your Christian fellows? But if, instead, you refuse to think yourself "stained", then who can make you ashamed?'

'That would be self-delusion!'

'I am talking about the free will necessary for transactions between good and evil.'

'Free will,' I said. 'Of course, the Devil can take only those who offer themselves willingly. If I consent, the power you gain from taking my blood is greatly enhanced. Is that the case?'

'It is so,' said Dracula.

'How *can* I consent?'

'Because I hold Quincey.'

'Then it is still coercion!'

'Not so, for it requires you to make a choice. Or, put another way, it enables you to make the choice while still telling yourself – and your husband and your almost-father, Van Helsing – that you were forced. I am cruel to be kind, Mina.'

'You are the Devil!' I cried.

'No. Nor do I serve him; I care nothing for him. But whatever I am, you know me, Mina. When my spirit entered Jonathan, you knew who it was that you welcomed into your bed. You knew that it was me and not your husband. Have you ever shown *him* such passion? I doubt it – nor he to you.'

I hung my head, blood rushing hotly into my face. He added, 'You are alive and I am Undead – yet which of us is it that knows how to live with all the passion of life?'

'You are jealous of the living!'

'Jealous . . . I do not think so. But I must be near them. I could not possess you, beloved; you were too strong. But I need your strength, your warmth. If you died in my embrace, and became Undead, all your arguments would vanish.'

'Yes, and that is where the deepest evil lies – that I would lose my conscience, and no longer care, and feed upon my own son!'

He leaned over and put his hand upon mine. It was warm from the fire. The worst thing was that I did not mind the touch! 'That is why I need you to choose, while you still know good from evil,' he said softly. 'When I was in Jonathan's form, you wanted me. We are husband and wife; you know this.'

'In a vile travesty of the Christian union. It has no weight in God's eyes!'

'Then there is only sin, in God's eyes. Give yourself to me, beloved, when the time comes. I must have your blood. Give it gladly, and you will be reunited with your son.'

It was as if he held a spell over me, so crystal clear that I could barely feel it – or was it that I truly was acting of my own volition? I cannot continue to blame him for my sins, when in truth they are mine alone.

I discovered that it is possible to step out of God's grace and into the darkness, not in glee or bitter rage, but with absolute calm and dignity. I met his eyes and said, 'Very well, I will deceive myself no longer. Let me see Quincey first, as a gesture of good faith.'

'But if I fulfil my part of the bargain first, you may change your mind.'

'I may,' I said, 'but will that not make it a true choice?'

Dracula has let me spend time with my son. Quincey is pale and has a chesty cough again, though he seems to be eating quite well. Poor lamb, this place will kill him if I do not get him away. I am desperate.

He said to me, 'Mama, is that man the strange man who came into Elena's room? I don't like him. The drinks he gives me are bitter. May we go home now?'

What could I tell him? I pretended it was a little holiday, but Quincey is too bright to be fooled. He knows something is very wrong – but at least, trusting Elena and me, he is not distressed.

What will happen to him, if one or both of us should die?

### 14 November, morning

What have I done? Turned my back upon God, and cast myself into the darkness.

I said good-night to Quincey, and came back to my own room for supper. As I prepared for bed, Elena came in and took the brush from my hand. I let her do what she would, and so she sat and brushed my hair as she used to. Her lovely face was flushed, her eyes glowing shyly, and she seemed all aglow with excitement, planting kisses upon my cheeks and lips. I did not want these attentions, and yet there seemed no use in stopping her. She brushed my hair until it shone like glass, smoothed my nightdress and tied the ribbons just so, for all the world as if she were a bridesmaid preparing the bride for the groom. When she undid the chain of my cross and took it away, I did not try to stop her, though it seemed my last connection to the light.

'This night is yours,' she said softly. 'But soon it will be mine.'

She left me with a kiss. I lay down to sleep but my eyes stayed wide open, watching the coppery glow of the embers. I knew what was going to happen. The two halves of me were warring – the light against the darkness. Should I sin willingly – even to save my son? Would it be better that he died, than that his mother gave herself to the Devil? I don't know, I don't know.

Soon I became aware of the long, dark figure of the Count standing over me. His face seemed to glow, candlelight lending his features an eerie luminescence. Like a proud, wild sculpture of some heathen king was his face, his eyes two red suns glaring down at me; each with a dark pool at the centre, and that blackness lit by strange stars. My breath was in the top of my lungs. I pushed back the covers of the bed and waited.

'Do you offer yourself to me willingly?' he whispered. His voice was throaty. One of his pallid hands came a little towards me, his fingers plucking at the air.

I said nothing. If I nodded, it was without conscious intention.

'Would you give yourself even if I told you that no harm will come to your son, that you and he are free to go?'

Oh, the cruellest thing he could have said! For his spell lay on me, the terrible spell of his kind, that I knew how damnable this was and yet still desired it; that I did not want to be shorn of my only justification! I should have said, 'Then let us go! I don't consent!' But I did not. Instead I answered softly, 'Do what you will.'

There is the sordid truth. He took every obstacle out of my path to the light, and still I chose evil! And he knew it. He smiled. His red lips lifted to show the great white teeth, and they shone as richly as ivory, and some wanton, voluptuous part of me – the part we struggle so wretchedly to vanquish – longed to feel them entering my flesh. He stood looking down at me a little while. His smouldering eyes warmed me, seeming to ignite all over me little fires that spread and ran together until my very blood was molten.

Then the hovering hand came closer and flowed over me. Not touching me, but following, an inch from my body, every contour of my throat, breast, waist, all the way to my ankles, and again upwards. My sinful feelings rose to a pitch of unbearable intensity. I craved the touch of that floating hand, I arched towards it, I stroked my own body in an effort to subdue my fever, but my own hands only inflamed me more. I could reason no longer. An agony of exquisite tension held me; I became blind to all considerations but that of releasing it, for I felt that I must either break it or die.

So it was I who pushed my restless flesh into Dracula's

hands, I who drew him down towards me. I write this as a confession, yet even as I write it, hating myself, hating my uncleanness, I still remember with tingling, unholy joy the breathless delight of it. I put my arms around his back. He embraced me, lying along me and over me, holding my face and looking into my eyes. He whispered, '*Mina* . . .'

I remembered those eyes shining from Jonathan's face. I remembered a time, seven years ago . . . We were not, after all, strangers to each other. There was something wondrous in that, a bond of flesh and spirit between us, of blood and this fierce fire which now drove my heartbeat, my breathing, the rushing of my veins. When he entered me, I welcomed the firmness of his lips upon my throat, the piercing hardness of his teeth.

The night and all the stars seemed to be whirling inside me. I felt my life going out of me from the wound and into him and I was glad, glad to nurture the devil who drank from my veins, who stroked my hair and held me in a spasm of passion as he drank. Oh, horrible. All came at once, the swoon and the knowledge of sin and the unholy consummation of it.

God help me, why did I fall? Not to save my son. Let me not deceive myself. I fell because the sweetly painful horror of it was nothing to the extremity, the agony of the pleasure.

# Chapter Thirteen

## Jonathan Harker's Journal

### *14 November, morning*

A breakthrough! Investigations fruitful at last. We found a carrier along the road to London who changed horses for a man answering to Dracula's description – then Seward telephoned his wife Alice and asked her to discover if there had been any activity at Carfax Abbey (which lies adjacent to Seward's house and asylum). Within two hours she had news. A carriage was seen going through the gates of Carfax, very early on the morning of the twelfth. The gates are now locked up, but smoke can be seen coming from the chimney!

We leave at any moment. Please God, let Mina and Quincey be still alive! But what does Dracula mean by making his lair in so obvious a place? Can he be that stupid, or is it, more likely, that he means to lure us there? Lacking any other clue, we have no choice but to chance the trap.

Kovacs is travelling with us. Dressed in a dark suit that I have lent him, with his hair combed, he looks human – as human as the Count once did to me, before I discovered what he is. His presence makes us deeply uneasy – but he offers no threat, and may be our only hope of infiltrating Carfax.

## Elena Kovacs's Journal

### *13 November, night*

I sit at the window with the child upon my knee. The room flickers with fire and lamplight; outside it is dark, a wet-black darkness. Dogs are howling, with the thin eerie sound of wolves, their voices rising one after another, twisting and falling in mournful dissonance. All over London, it seems, they howl. Quincey rests quietly against my breast; he knows that something strange is happening, yet he knows nothing at all. Guileless boy! How I love him – not for being a child, but for what he may become.

The singing of the dogs is sweet, but it cannot block my ears to other sounds. He is with her. I am jealous, I am jealous. I should not be. There is a place for us all in his family. But still.

A while ago Quincey said, 'Elena? What is it like to die?'

'I don't know, my lamb. Why do you ask?'

'Because I am so often ill, I am afraid I may die. That is, I don't mind for myself, I only mind for Mama, because it would make her sad. Am I going to die?'

'Everyone dies one day, Quincey,' I said soothingly. 'I expect it is just like falling asleep. But don't be afraid. The Count is a good man and he can work magic; he knows how to wake people up again, so they never die.'

'He wakes up dead people? I don't think I should like that. The bitter drink makes me sleepy. Does the Count mean to kill me? I don't mind. I am so very tired.'

Oh, Quincey.

Is it only in my own mind that I hear Mina and my Dark Companion sighing and murmuring together? It should be *me* in her place. My heart and mouth and loins yearn towards him . . . but I can do nothing, and so I sit here, and rock the boy, and dream.

I wonder if Dr Van Helsing, with his great brain, has yet worked out where we are? It cannot be so difficult. Let them come, it will make no difference!

And it should be me in *his* place, *my* lips upon Mina's throat.

He must take me to him soon. I have been patient, but I can wait no longer. Sometimes my eyes blur, and I cannot find my breath, and when I look in my mirror my reflection seems insubstantial, as if I am on the borderline between the light and the shadows. The light seems so dazzling, hostile and painful, but the shadows are soft and fluttery as wings and warm as a raven's breast . . . but still I live.

## *14 November*

When I took Mina her breakfast tray, I was surprised to find her up and dressed. She was at the desk, writing, but she propped herself there with her left arm as if to sit up were a great effort. She was pale and bloodless as wax, even her lips nearly white, with half-circles as blue as grapes impressed beneath her eyes. As she looked up at me with glassy eyes, she took a laboured breath, let it out, and took another as if she could not get enough air. Ah, I know these signs well enough.

I put down the tray and said, 'Here is your breakfast, my dear. You need your strength.'

Still she said nothing, but looked at me in voiceless appeal – a muted terror, mixed with an elation I understand only too well. I could not help but go to her. From behind I slipped my arms around her, and leaned down so that my head rested on her shoulder. I kissed her cheek; she shut her eyes, and her right hand came up to clasp my wrist. I tried to read what she was writing over her shoulder, but she cheated me; they were meaningless squiggles, her precious shorthand. But the wildness of the strokes – some so heavy the ink had run, others long, weak and tenuous – told me all.

I love her and I hate her.

'Soon we will all be together,' I whispered. 'A family.'

She shook her head weakly. 'Elena, I would like to see Quincey, if you please,' she said.

'Then eat your breakfast,' I said, withdrawing from her, 'and I will bring him to you.'

# MINA HARKER'S JOURNAL

*14 November, later*
I feel myself slipping, descending from grace into a dark place where I do not even recognize myself. I have looked back on my record of last night and think I should destroy it – yet my pangs of shame are dull, remote, and the revulsion I should feel is barely there at all. Instead the memories are dream-like; a kind of excitement, like the recollection, not of horror, but of a heart-warming delight. And that I feel so should appal me, yet it does not. I am too tired. Tired, and there is never enough air! I am so languid, I could have lain in bed all day, dreaming sweetly. (Would I have looked as sweet and rosy upon my pillow as Lucy once did, I wonder?) Instead I have forced myself to dress and write my journal, as a form of self-discipline, though it taxes me sorely to do so.

My memories are hazy now . . . but it seems to me that after he drank from my veins, he held me tenderly for a time. I did not resist this, for my mind was awhirl and I had no will to escape him. But I remember also that he pierced his breast with his nail, and that I sucked and swallowed the ruby of blood that oozed out . . . oh, God, did that happen also or did I dream it? Then I am more unclean than the first time, for this time he did not force me . . . But if I am unclean or ashamed, I cannot feel it. I feel . . . numbed, quite.

Elena has been and gone. She brought Quincey to me, and he seems content before the fire, drawing pictures. His cough is worse, but he does not wish to be in bed, and I will not force him if he is well enough to play. As long as he keeps warm . . . Oh, but how long must we be imprisoned here, how many more 'bargains' will the Count demand of me before he will let us alone?

Of course, he will never let us alone! The limits of these

bargains, he will extend to infinity, and he will renege upon
every one! What a fool I have been – but still, what else could
I have done?

### *Evening*

I am unsure of the time, for darkness draws in early. Elena
has taken Quincey to bed. They would not let him stay with
me all night. I am a little stronger, but I fear this solitude; it
can mean only that Dracula is coming to me again.

I sit and wait, shivering, for his firm step upon the stair. I
am afraid and yet my hand creeps of its own volition to
loosen my collar, to smooth my skin and push back my hair,
and I watch the firelight gleaming like molten gold upon my
arms, and I must keep wetting my dry lips with my tongue . . .

He has come and gone. How strange!

He entered quietly and placed his hand upon the scraps
of paper that serve as my diary, preventing me from writing.
He looked younger again; his hair was now all dark, very
thick and profuse, as were his black brows. His face, though
cruel, was smooth with the bloom of youth and blood. He
has been a very handsome man, once, very striking, with
great dark eyes. Is handsome even now.

'Always you must be recording every moment of your life,'
he said, as if amused. 'Elena has caught this habit from you,
also. It is a form of English neurosis, is it not, this desire for
truth, for order?'

'Perhaps,' I said. 'If it offends you, I will not do it. My
memory is very good.'

'Strong enough to survive death?'

At that, a hand of coldness went through me, touching my
heart. It was as if part of my mind suddenly awoke and said,
Look what danger you are in!

'Write as you will,' Dracula added. 'It means nothing to
me.'

'Nothing?' I said defiantly. 'By writing, last time, we outwitted you.'

'Piecing all together, like detectives,' he said, walking slowly around the room. His presence overwhelmed everything; how can I explain? The whole room seemed to be gathered and focused around him as if he were the centre of existence. I felt that if he left, all energy, passion and hope would vanish with him. But these are the seductive illusions with which the Devil ensnares us!

Jonathan, much as I love him, has never seemed to fill the room as the Count does. That is because true goodness is modest and does not draw attention to itself! Animal magnetism, Van Helsing would call it; that is what Dracula possesses. And it is as evil as it is seductive. I tried to fight it. The tension of his presence – the devil in me wishing he would touch me, the Christian part of me dreading his touch – was unbearable.

I spoke. 'We each kept our half of the bargain. How much more will you demand of me, before you set us free?'

He kept his back to me, and did not answer. I went on, 'I am asking, what must I do to make you leave us alone, once and for all? What ultimate, terrible thing will satisfy you? Tell me, and I'll do it!'

At that he laughed. 'You would, dear Mina. Anything at all to save your son. Murder your husband? Torture Elena with needles or watch her die slowly upon a stake? But you fear that nothing will satisfy me. Indeed, that I might keep you here for ever with false promises.'

He turned suddenly, and came so rapidly to where I sat that I started away. To my shock, he knelt down and gripped my hands. His are hairy, animal, and yet their texture, even their very hairiness, was soothing. 'There is something, beloved Mina. I cannot tell you yet, not until you give yourself willingly and freely to me.'

'Have I not done that?' I said bitterly.

'Not yet. You fight me, you fan the fire of your own despite constantly. If instead you would love me –'

I gasped. 'Now it is not enough that I let you wreak these foul designs upon my flesh – you want love? Never. I pity you but I will never love you.'

'You could. I think you do, a little. Stay with me.'

'What?'

'Stay with me for ever.'

How could I answer? I tried to pull away, but he pinned my wrists to my knee with one hand and rose, leaning over me, his other arm folding tight about my shoulders and his mouth clamping hard upon my neck.

I felt his hard teeth pierce me; I stiffened. Blackness rushed and whirled all through me, taking my mind with it, spinning through spasms of pain and unholy pleasure. But through this rush I heard sounds outside; indistinguishable snatches of human or animal cries.

Dracula let me go. He had not taken enough of my blood to weaken me. He stood up, and I saw the blood shining on his lips and teeth as he turned to look out of the window. He forgot me; his attention was on the ground below the keep.

I said quickly, 'If you do anything to harm my husband or our friends, you will have nothing of me, willing or otherwise. Nothing!'

The Count looked back at me for a moment, very grim. Then he went between the bars of the window and out through gap between casement and frame like mist. Shocked, I rushed to the window, and witnessed him walking, head first like a lizard, down the outside of the wall.

A chilly, sickening fear stirred within me and spread its tendrils through my whole being. I could see nothing in the gloom and tangled undergrowth, although it was not full dark. Only Dracula's black figure moving down into the swampy darkness. I heard dogs baying, louder and louder; I heard human shouts.

I ran down to try the outer door to the keep, but we are locked in.

No one has returned to tell me what is happening. But I feel the resonance of danger, like ghosts in the walls, and a dreadful sense of foreboding.

JONATHAN HARKER'S JOURNAL
*(Dictated by him and entered by Abraham Van Helsing)*

## *14 November, evening*

A day of hope and despair.

We found the gates of Carfax solidly locked, though there was indeed evidence of fresh carriage tracks passing along the drive. I had never thought to look on that great, brooding old house with its fortress walls again! A grey afternoon was thickening into the gloom of evening. Kovacs said, 'I can go in this way. But I can go no further into the house, without invitation, than the chapel.'

'Then we will meet you at the chapel,' said Van Helsing.

Kovacs turned sideways and passed through the join of the oak and iron gates, as if he had become as thin as paper. It reminded me of Godalming's description of Lucy, passing through the gap of a closed door to enter her tomb.

It was an easy enough matter to scale the walls of Carfax with the aid of a rope-ladder; not the first time we have had to do so, and I am all too familiar with the place. Van Helsing had armed us each with a wreath of garlic, a large cross wrought of silver, and other equipment for the disposal of vampires. But as we dropped down into the grounds, we heard the baying of a dog. It seemed far away; outside the walls, I thought at first, until it came rapidly closer, joined by the voices of its fellows.

Van Helsing passed Seward and I each a stake from his bag; these were all the weapons we had. Seward led us at a run into a thicket, and there we evaded the dogs for a time, doubling back and forth through thick bushes and thus keeping ahead of them. The dogs were dark shapes loping along behind the thick undergrowth as they tried to find a way through to us.

The thicket ended and we saw the door to the chapel vault, tucked into an obscure corner of the abbey walls. It was across a stretch of grass and down a flight of decaying stone steps. I saw Kovacs in the doorway, beckoning, but we had no chance of reaching him. The dogs had caught us.

We stood close, I gripping the stake in my left hand, cursing the uselessness of my right. The creatures came loping around us; six great German shepherd dogs, growling and barking ferociously. I was terrified, I confess. The leader leapt at Seward, clamping its jaw on his arm; Van Helsing lunged at the creature, stabbing it in the side. It let Seward go, gave a sort of twisting leap and went into a frenzy, snapping at its wounded side. Meanwhile I was trying to keep the others back with my own stake, but two of them seized it between their teeth and we wrestled; they growling viciously, I gasping and panic-stricken.

They had us trapped. If we ran, they would give chase and savage us. Van Helsing called urgently to us to keep as still as possible, but as he spoke, one leapt at him and sank its fangs into his thigh. Van Helsing cried out; then a harsh voice cut through the clamour.

'Back!'

Count Dracula was there; a starkly black figure against the mist-wreathed trees. Not even looking at the dogs, he held out a commanding hand to them, sweeping it in a half-circle to point at the ground near his heels. All slunk away with lowered ears to lie at the Count's feet. Shaming as it is to admit, I have never been so relieved to see him.

When I glanced again at the chapel door, Kovacs had vanished.

'Welcome, Dr Van Helsing, Dr Seward, Mr Harker,' said

Dracula. 'Forgive the attentions of my friends. Had you come in by the gate, you would have marked the presence of dangerous dogs and avoided putting yourselves so rashly in danger. You are not badly wounded, I trust?'

'A mere breakage of the skin,' Van Helsing answered as he pressed a hand to his thigh.

Seward said brusquely, 'We've come for Mrs Harker and her son. You must not prevent us taking her.'

'But I must, and I will. I have had much that I need of your wife, Mr Harker, but I will have more. I have an appetite for her company and the bountiful wine of her body. She is mine.'

His vile insolence! I would have attacked him, one-handed, regardless of the danger, had Seward not held me back! Dracula merely gave another mocking smile that enflamed my rage. He said, 'You were warned of the consequences if you tried to follow us. However, let us call a truce. Since you do not believe me, you may see Mina, and hear it from her own mouth. Do not attempt to trick me. These fetid garlands with which you have wreathed yourselves, besides looking ridiculous, will avail you not at all; although I cannot abide them, my friends – these cousins of the wolf – have no such qualms.'

'Keep your friends off, and we'll be peaceable,' Van Helsing said angrily.

'Wise. There is someone else in the house whom you will also wish to see, I believe. Come.'

Uneasy, we followed him. The dogs trotted alongside, a reminder that we were wholly in his power. He led us into the chapel where, last time, we had found his boxes of native earth and sterilized them with Holy Wafer.

We came cautiously into the darkness; my good hand was inside my jacket, clutching the cross in case it should be needed. The dogs came in with us and lay down in a loose circle around us, watching us with intent eyes and with their tongues lolling over their huge teeth. I dreaded to see Mina lying in a coffin, already lost to us, nothing left to do but drive the stake through her and deliver her soul from its torment.

Dracula vanished; all was silent, but for the panting of the dogs. We moved around restlessly, trapped and suspicious.

After a few minutes an inner door opened and two women came in; Mina holding Quincey in her arms, and Elena, both women with their hair loose on their shoulders. They were both as pale as ivory, their faces drawn and shadowed with the sickly look I know so well, God help me; the look of the vampire's fading victim. The Count followed them. How violently I hated him then! Yet some of the hate, the blame, seemed to attach itself to the women, too, unfair or not. They seemed to present a tableau of depraved collusion.

Mina gazed at me in astonishment. 'Jonathan!'

I held out a cross, trying to protect her. 'Mina, come with us. He can't stop us, if we stand firm.'

I started towards her, but the dogs growled until I had to let the cross fall. Seward pulled warningly at my arm. Even Mina held out a hand to keep me away. 'No, Jonathan, all of you. It's no good, you must go. Don't try again.'

'How can we not try!' Van Helsing exclaimed.

'Because of Quincey.' She curled a hand round the boy's fair head, as if to block his ears. 'You are putting his life in danger by coming here!'

'Is that the only reason?' I said, unable to control myself. 'Tell me there is no truth in his foul allegation, that you have fallen in thrall to this monster!'

Mina's chin rose, with a dignified grief that pierced me. 'Do you not know me, not trust me, after all we have endured?' she said softly. 'I can't leave. You must go, before you are killed. For our sake, mine and Quincey's.'

Dracula rested one hand on each of the women's shoulders, in triumphant possession. Our position was hopeless, yet it was impossible to give up; Seward and Van Helsing were both poised to seize some faint chance that might turn the tables.

At that moment, Kovacs appeared as if from nowhere. I didn't see where he came from, whether he rose from between the biers or re-formed from mist. But he stood like a spectre, saying nothing, only staring at Dracula from empty, weirdly innocent eyes.

Then he leapt at Dracula.

Everything was over very swiftly. Dracula gave a roar of anger. Evading the attack, his immediate action was to seize Mina and Quincey, thrust them into the nearest tomb and drag the stone lid in place over them – this with incredible strength, as Kovacs tried to attack him again. I bore witness in utter, horrified disbelief. Dracula did this, obviously, as the quickest way to prevent us making off with my wife and child! I heard Mina's muffled cries, heard Elena exclaim, 'Uncle!' The next moment, the Count seized Kovacs and thrust him violently against the crypt wall.

'What is this?' Dracula rasped in fury. 'What have you brought me? Betrayal!'

Up leapt the dogs, busy and ferocious. They closed in, driving us outside and all the way across the grounds to the wall. We reached our rope ladder in a breathless flurry of fear and defeat.

Dismounting from the wall on the far side, in my haste I fell and cracked a rib. We came back to Dr Seward's house, injured and in utter despair.

I cannot stop thinking of Mina, sealed in that tomb, wondering if she is there still. I am almost glad of the physical pain, to drive out that of my thoughts.

Van Helsing insists that this is not the end. We must go back, armed with guns against the dogs, and with a firmer strategy. We will get more men and storm the house, if necessary. But what is the use of it if, when we break in, we find Mina and Quincey dead? Why can we not admit that this is hopeless, that Dracula has won?

*(Only the battle, not the war. Courage! – Van H.)*

### *15 November*

I could not rest, knowing that Dracula was going to Mina again. I do not mind if he loves us equally; but I could not bear it if he loves her more!

While Quincey slept, I sat by the window and looked out at the grounds. I love this place. I suppose we cannot stay here for ever, but I wish we could. I love the dark trees; the gnarled oaks which are like old men, the yews with their thick, creased trunks. I love the winding stream and the mysterious pools that I stumble across when I walk through the undergrowth. Most of the trees and bushes are bare, and their grey twigs drip with rain. They look as if they have died or been poisoned, but I like that, for I have been poisoned too, and yet I live.

I love the high walls. They prevent the world coming near me, to make its demands upon me. Within them, I am free.

I was looking out in this reverie when I heard the dogs barking, saw the shapes of men running. This was no surprise; my Dark Companion and I knew Jonathan Harker would try a rescue. Presently my love came and told me to bring Mina down to the chapel. This to make them understand that Mina and I are with Dracula now.

But in the chapel a spectre appeared – even now I cannot believe what I saw!

He is tall, though not as tall as my beloved, and has a shock of silver hair. His hands are large and powerful. He looks idiotic at first, possessed. As he leaps towards us, his eyes become wild, ringed with white and netted with blood, long white eyeteeth gleaming in the open oblong of his mouth – but I know him.

Yet he is not as I remembered. He is mad. He is a vampire.

The horror of this realization makes all chaos. I scream, 'Uncle!'

The dogs drive out the intruders; Mina is safely sealed in a marble tomb. My uncle struggles against my Dark Companion, whose face is livid with fury, like a wolf snarling. I cry out to him to stop, but he ignores my entreaties.

'Who are you?' says Dracula.

'No one,' my uncle gasps. 'My name is André Kovacs. I found you, I came to you, only to put myself at your service, Count Dracula.'

His words sound unconvincing, even to me. My beloved shakes him, beginning to squeeze his throat. 'Why?'

'You are Dracula, Lord of the Undead. Whom else should I serve? Teach me; in return I give my loyalty –'

'You are lying,' Dracula says quietly. 'You attacked me, as if you would help Van Helsing and those others.'

'Please – in life he was a friend of mine – but –'

I see – having moved as close as I dare – Dracula's mouth open wide, the long teeth shining. My uncle's face changes, becoming aggressive, feral. He seems to transmute, shrinking, slipping out of Dracula's grasp. I cannot believe what I am seeing. Before my eyes, Uncle André changes into a wolf.

Dark-grey like a shadow, he slips under Dracula's arms and runs out into the grounds, away down a path through the thickly woven trees. A moment later, my Dark Companion, too, has changed. His wolf-form is bigger than my uncle's, and a brighter, silvery grey. I run after them, fighting between twigs and thorns and brambles, but cannot keep up. I lose them and, turning, see them passing me again on the far side of the thicket; a dim shadow and a bright one.

I want no harm to come to my uncle. But I cannot protect him against Dracula. I can only watch as they run, snapping and snarling, along the tortuous overgrown paths, the thick briars and brambles.

I lose sight of them. I run, trying to find them, until I have a stitch in my side, and my dress is wet from the dripping trees. When I come upon them again, on the bank of the deep, still lake, I see the lighter wolf bowl the darker one over, and pin it down, and close its jaw on its hairy throat. The darker one howls, surrendering.

They become human again. It is a kind of unfolding, the way a new-born animal unfolds itself; and it is a strange blurring from one state to the other, so that the eyes cannot quite capture it in the twilight.

I come closer, trembling, as Dracula lifts my uncle up by the throat and shakes him. Poor Uncle, he looks wild with fear. My love drags him, a prisoner, back into the dank black crypt. I follow. As we enter the chapel, Dracula says, 'Elena, bolt the door.'

I do so, and remain. It is so dark I can barely see, even though my eyes are attuned to darkness now. But I sense and hear the two vampires in the darkness, one tormenting the other, and I feel myself to be utterly alone with them, and with rats and blind insects and the bones of the dead.

'Now,' says Dracula, 'the truth.'

He has my uncle against a wall, his wrists pinned to the damp stonework with one hand, the other hand pressed to his throat. 'Who made you Undead, who sent you?'

My uncle breaks very quickly. Who can blame him, when my beloved's will is so hard to resist? Uncle was a good man, but I think he never had much strength. He was never good at keeping secrets, either. Too honest.

'I found the Scholomance. A vampire there, Beherit, he fed upon me, killed my companion, made me like this. And then he sent me to you.' Uncle says more, but this is the essence. It makes more sense to Dracula than to me; I think only of poor Miklos, dead. Poor Miklos. I did not love him, but still I feel sad.

'Beherit?' Dracula's voice is a dry whisper of disbelief. 'Why?'

'To serve you. To learn from you.'

'I think not.' He makes a movement; my uncle gives a gruff, soul-racked scream.

'He told me to keep you away from the Scholomance at all costs. There is something there that, should you find it, will make you too powerful.'

'What thing is this?'

'He said . . . the powers of Hell. He said, your soul.'

There is a brief, heavy silence. My uncle continues, 'He wishes you no harm, only that you keep away from him!'

'And he sent you,' Dracula says mockingly, 'you, a dry scholar, initiated two months into Undeath, fragile as a mayfly, to ensure that I never go back to the Scholomance? Four hundred years have made Beherit no less of a fool.'

Dracula thrusts my uncle away, so hard that he flies across the chapel, hits the wall and slides down. Then my Dark Companion goes to help Mina from the tomb where he trapped her for safe keeping; I hear her gasps of relief, of shuddering misery. He takes her away into the house. Damn them.

I run to where my uncle lies, groaning like a dying man; all hope, all spirit gone from him. I see that a piece of ornate metal with a cross at one end, part of some old chapel decoration, long since toppled from its place, has fallen against his hand; and the cross has burned its black image on to my uncle's pale flesh.

# Chapter Fourteen

I remain a long time with my uncle.

'Elena, dear Elena,' he says in a voice of cracked leather. 'Leave me. It is not safe for you to be with me.'

As he speaks I ease myself alongside him, amid the spilled earth and cobwebs. I do not care that my clothes are caked with the damp and grime of this place; I feel part of it. 'No, no,' I whisper. 'No danger. You are not alone, Uncle.'

'Elena,' he moans. 'If you do not leave me I will . . .'

'Do it,' I say, wrapping my arms around him and holding him close. 'I am not afraid.'

He turns his head away from me. 'No. Never! How did you come to this?'

'Uncle, how did *you*?'

As we tell each other our stories, the horror of what has happened to my uncle, the horror of everything, leaps into my brain with pitiless clarity, as if I have stepped outside myself, or been woken violently while sleepwalking. As I tell him about my father's death, tears roll down his face and his long teeth cut into his own lips, so that blood runs down with the tears. He looks grotesque, so plainly dead yet alive, so much the vampire that he has become, that my heart is broken. Yet I do not recoil from him. I have fallen in love with such horrors, with the transparent beauty of the unquiet dead.

He closes his eyes and tells me about the Scholomance, about Beherit, who, as dazzling as Lucifer, claimed and killed poor Miklos. All he tells me flares bright in my brain. I caress his head and draw his face into my neck; he protests, 'Do not, for I cannot stop myself!'

His attempt to hold me off is half-hearted. I slide my arms around his shoulders and hold him hard. He groans. I feel his eye-teeth lance my neck. We are locked together. More than uncle and niece. His hand comes to my cheek and I draw his forefinger into my mouth and bite it, sucking drops of blood from the tender, waxy tip.

Folklore tells us that those most in danger from vampires are the families of the deceased, for the Undead one's love survives the grave, and his thirst for the life of his best beloved will draw them with him into the grave.

I wish to die. I wish to be taken into Undeath now, for I have waited too long already, I fear my Dark Companion will never take me! But my uncle takes only a little blood from me. I could weep with my frustration.

'You must leave here now,' I tell him. 'Dracula will destroy you!'

'Then let him,' he sighs. 'I have nowhere to go. I cannot go back to Beherit; I have failed him utterly. I have no power to keep Dracula from the Scholomance! I wish you would go from me, Elena. I have lost those I loved; Emil, Miklos. Do not let me lose you also. Run away, back to the sunlight, before it is too late!'

'I care nothing for that!' I hold his shoulders. 'Take me into Undeath with you and you will never be alone!'

Anguish webs his face, turning lines to furrows. 'No. You do not know what you ask! I would not bring anyone into this darkness, least of all you, beloved Elena, sweetest, purest child.'

'I was never sweet. Never pure. If I seemed so it was all a façade, all for the benefit of my father and others who so arrogantly decide what a young woman must be. It was never me.'

'No!' he cries. 'Keep away!'

He thrusts me off with rigid arms; I rise, dizzy. I love him and pity him; I feel contempt for him, lying there broken. I say, 'Uncle, you should glory in this gift of immortality. You should carry yourself with pride and laughing arrogance. Yet all you can do is bemoan your fate! If you won't save yourself now, I can do nothing to help you.'

Leaving my uncle, I go in search of my Dark Companion. I am angry; I know he is with Mina, but I will not intrude upon them.

For a long time I wander alone through the great, dusty rooms of Carfax Abbey, feeling that some malign presence is watching me in every room. Am I becoming insane? I stop for breath on the half-landing of the great stone staircase in the hall. There, against the lattice of a tall, arched window, my beloved appears, as dark and still as the stone walls around us. I am startled.

'Why are you not with the child?' he asks in a harsh, thin tone.

I fear him again. 'The child was with his mother. What will you do with my uncle?'

'Do you care for him?'

'Yes.'

'More than you care for me?'

I feel defiant. 'No, but perhaps more than *you* care for *me*.'

His eyes narrow, reflecting red as a rat's eyes do. 'Do my attentions and my company not satisfy you?'

'If you hold Mina Harker in greater esteem than you do me, no, they do not.'

'This is childish,' he says wearily, and turns to put his foot on the next flight of stairs. 'Jealousy ill befits you, Elena.'

'Tell me!' I am fierce now. 'Would you make her Undead?'

'I would, if it pleases me to do so.'

'But not before me!' I run after him and catch the black

214

cloth of his sleeve. 'Take me first. Do it now. One more kiss –'

He pulls my hand away from his arm; my wrist turns numb at the pressure. 'There are marks upon your neck that I did not make. How great is your respect for me, that you give yourself to another, that you seek to order my actions? You will become Undead when I wish it – not when you demand it.'

'Please. Do it now! I hate being human, I want to walk in the darkness with you, your companion, not your – your maidservant!'

'Servant?' he says, turning and raising my wrist so that I am held stiffly away from him. 'Did you not serve me, at every turn, of your own free will? I called you to me; you were not forced to answer the call. Others would have done as well. Every action you have performed, for my benefit or your own, you have performed of your own volition.'

I am furious now; the pain makes me angrier. 'Are you telling me that you owe me nothing – after all I have done to aid you?'

'I am not yours to command, Elena,' he answers coldly. 'If I displease you, you have only yourself to blame.'

He releases me, begins to mount the stairs; I run after him and clutch at him. 'You cannot refuse me! Change me!'

He spins round, his face hellish with anger. I wait for a blow, though he has never struck me before. Instead he seizes me, and the pain in my throat is so exquisite, as knife-cuts are exquisite, that all the strength goes from me and I lean back like a dancer across his arm. I almost fall; he catches me and lets me down gently on to the half-landing.

We crouch there under the latticed window, Dracula holding my head to his chest and stroking my hair until it falls about my shoulders. 'Patience, Elena. You must continue in the light a little while longer. I need you to look after the child. Only do this for me now, and you will walk beside me in the darkness; it will not be long.'

His voice is tender. He tells me what he requires of me, and I promise to obey. I don't want it, I cannot bear to be parted from him although he says it will only be for a short time. But what else can I do? To seal the bond he pierces his breast with a fingernail, and I seal my mouth over the blood, and swallow. It is liquid gold, precious metal.

### MINA HARKER'S JOURNAL

## *15 November*

There is little time left, I am certain.

I spent some time at my window, listening to the hysterical barking of the dogs. I did not know what it meant, could see only the most tantalizingly vague movement of figures through the trees, and yet my heart turned over with fear. It must be Jonathan and our friends. And they were putting not only themselves in danger, but Quincey, too!

I ran down to Quincey's room; Elena let me in and I gathered the boy in my arms.

Some minutes later, Dracula came in and ordered us to go to the chapel with him. 'Make them understand,' he said with a callousness that chilled me, 'that their heroic attempt to rescue you is ill-conceived. If they try again, the child will die.'

How desperate and sorrowful were their faces – Jonathan's, Van Helsing's and Dr Seward's – and how it pained me to tell them, 'Go!'

Then something extraordinary happened. A man appeared from nowhere – that is, I didn't see where he came from – and attacked the Count. This man seemed familiar, although I could not place him; it was too dark to see clearly. He was gaunt, with thick silver-grey hair; I was unsure whether he was man or vampire! Dracula knocked him back.

The next I knew, Dracula was lifting Quincey and myself bodily and thrusting us into the darkness of a tomb.

I cried out to no avail. When the heavy marble lid slid into place above my head I was terrified. I struck the lid, shouting, but I could hear not a word from outside.

Quincey and I were cut off from all contact, in utter blackness. A dreadful terror overcame me; I hope I never experience its like again. All that kept me from screaming and beating my fists against the stone was my son. For his sake I must keep calm.

He must have noticed me trembling, however, and felt the pounding of my heart. Strangely – because he is so young, I assume – he didn't seem frightened at all. His little body was warm and relaxed against mine. I tried to frame some light-hearted phrase about this being only a game. He replied in an eerily calm tone, 'Don't worry, Mama. Don't be afraid. The darkness can't hurt you, while I am with you.'

I tried not to think of what it would be like to die here; to lie in the darkness, day after day, until we both slowly expired. Or to die and rise again without a soul, with only thirst for the blood of my loved ones to animate me . . . This seemed almost a comforting idea, soft and sweet as sleep . . .

After a passage of time that seemed unending, I heard the lid scraping back. Quincey had fallen asleep by then. Dracula helped us out; I was too shaken to express anger, relief, anything. He took Quincey in one arm and helped me with the other. I was weak with shock, but Dracula appeared forbidding, unassailable.

Jonathan and the others were gone. Dracula says they left without harm; I don't know whether to believe him or not. At least Quincey seems none the worse for his ordeal. We returned to my room – our prison cell, I should say, in the keep. I didn't see Elena. Dracula himself brought us tea and brandy to revive us. Quincey was soon sleeping peacefully on my bed with the abandonment of a child, his mouth open and his curled hands flung behind his head.

Then Dracula sat by me at the fireside. It took all my strength to regain my dignity and to keep hidden from him how afraid I had been. 'You must forgive me, Mrs Harker,' he said quite gently. 'I could not risk you being snatched away by your so-loyal husband and friends, nor risk you running away. You would have been in danger from the dogs.'

'The dogs!' I gasped. His gentleness seemed a mockery. 'You were protecting us from those savage hounds? You need not have been so solicitous.'

'Then I beg your pardon. But there may come a time when the tomb holds no such horrors for you.'

'No, for when I die I shall rest in peace.'

He smiled a little, and his eyes glittered. 'I fail to see why your menfolk can never take me at my word. I warn them not to follow; they follow, as if they can never let anything rest until they have proved themselves fools.'

'Were any of them harmed?'

'Not to my knowledge. They left the way they had come.'

'And the other man who was there?'

Dracula looked away from me, as if he were troubled, but trying to seem indifferent. 'He is of no importance. I will tell you all in time; not now.'

'But what if they try again? I know them; they won't just leave me here! Promise me you will not harm them! There is no need, surely!'

I wished I had not spoken. His dark, haughty eyes rested upon me, half mocking and half tender. 'I can make no such promise. If they do nothing foolish, they will be safe, but that seems unlikely. Or if . . . ah, what will you give me in return for such a promise, Mina?'

I felt myself blushing. 'You have had my blood. I have nothing else to offer.'

'Not true,' he said. 'There is still your soul, your love, your loyalty and company in this long twilight of loneliness. You know what I want.' A pang went through me.

'Me, to use against your enemies!'

'Ah, far more than that.'

'If you kill me,' I said, breathless, 'and I become like you, Van Helsing and the others will destroy me without hesitation, rather than let me fall to evil. Be assured that they will find me, and that you will lose me!'

'You are so eager to surrender to God, to martyrdom. Why not defy Him a little? If He loves sinners, I must be among His favourites.' The Count leaned forward and took my hands. His touch was light, yet I recoiled a little. 'Always you flinch when I come near you. Is this with fear or pleasure – perhaps fear *of* pleasure? You have no need to fear me, Mina. I have done my worst.'

'Truly, I am sure you have not. I want to go home. Let us go and I will ensure that Van Helsing and the others leave you in peace!'

'But will I leave *them* in peace?'

'I would have thought you too proud to sink to such vindictiveness. It seems ignoble.'

'I have never shown my enemies any mercy, beloved. I have always harried them to the very end. I am too old to change my habits.'

'Surely not.'

'Don't imagine you can change me.'

'I don't care to change you,' I retorted. 'My concern is to protect those I love. I have no concern for you whatsoever.'

'You lie charmingly. Even for the Devil himself, you feel some sorrow, some pity.'

'Then I confess. Of us all, I think you are the saddest.'

My defiance only made him smile. 'And you, Mina, cannot understand why you are so drawn to me. You know me better than you know your husband. He recoils from your passion, does he not, and speaks of madness and cure – but I accept all that you are, dark and light.'

Everything he said was true. Yes, I fear him, I despise him, but the fear and the despite are almost a habit, that I have to keep stoking up or else I forget to feel them. But this is the lulling influence of evil at work!

As we talked, I became aware of dogs barking and howling under the window. 'What's that?' I said, starting up.

'Nothing,' he said with a dismissive gesture. 'My helpers inform me of their presence, that is all. They remind us that no one may come in or go out without my authority.'

I made no reply, but my spirits dropped even lower. There was no hope of escape or deliverance. Dracula regarded me as if he knew what I was thinking.

'Mina, have you thought upon what I asked you?'

'I have. My answer is no.'

He sighed. 'As always you follow your morals, not your heart.'

'You are mistaken to think that they differ.'

'Very well, we will talk of something else.' He leaned towards me and spoke softly. 'Consider your son. He is a beautiful child, but sickly, is he not? His heart and lungs are weak. He could die at any time. A head cold could take him from you. You do not expect him to reach adulthood, do you? Deny it all you will, in your heart you do not expect him to live. Perhaps at twelve, or ten, or seven . . .'

By now tears were running uncontrollably down my face. His words undid me utterly. I managed to hold myself upright in my chair but I was racked by sobs.

'He need not die, Mina. I can give him immortality.'

'Make him –'

'Immortal, yes.'

'Undead!' I cried in horror.

'Whatever term you care to use, the point is this; what mother would not desire her son to live for ever? Or to outlive her, at the least. Mina, I have not touched a hair on his head; do you not trust me with him? I could almost love him like my own. Three kisses, so gentle he would not even feel them in his sweet sleep. Of themselves they would not kill him; I can be as delicate as I am brutal. But when his time comes – ah, then you need not mourn his death. For you know he will rise again, and come back to you, and be with you for ever. Your angelic, loving son.'

My brain is on fire. I cannot rest or sleep for the endless grinding of my thoughts. When Dracula left me, it was without touching me physically; he took no more blood from me, nor did he force me to drink his. But with his words about Quincey, he did something far worse.

I will not sell my soul for my own immortality. But for my son's – !

Oh dear, dear God, what have I done to be so tormented, so cursed?

### 16 November
Thank heaven for shorthand – I write at speed, and in inexpressible distress.

After Dracula had gone, and I had finished my diary, I lay down beside Quincey and stroked his golden hair. He stirred in his sleep; I promised him that we will soon go home. He murmured, 'But this is home, Mama. Elena says so.'

Now I curse the day I ever befriended her!

I fell asleep, and slept very deeply, almost as if I had been drugged – indeed, I am now almost certain that I was.

When I woke, it was well into morning, and Quincey had gone.

I ran down to his room; there was no sign of him or Elena, and the fire was dead in the grate, as if there had been no one there for hours. The door from the keep to the house was locked as always. I was frantic for a few hours, though I endeavoured to be as calm as I possibly could. I knew where the Count must be – unless he also had deserted me.

But at midday – a very foggy, grey day, with leaves dropping like brown rain from the trees – I heard the locks and bolts being drawn back. I ran down the stairs and was met half-way by Dracula. He looked so grim and angry that he quite unnerved me.

I told him I could not find Elena and Quincey. 'I heard nothing, my son was gone from my side when I woke!'

'They have left Carfax,' he said simply.

'Why?'

He took my wrist and led me back to my room. 'Elena has taken Quincey away, against my wishes,' he said, low and furious. 'She has defied me.'

I could not understand, and said as much. Dracula seemed as outraged as I was distressed. He answered, 'Yesterday she begged me to make her Undead. Her impatience angered me, and I refused. She is jealous of you, beloved. This is her revenge against us both.'

And it is worse than Dracula himself taking my son – for at least he has some authority, some integrity; he may be a devil, but he is at least a familiar one! Elena – who knows what is going on in her tormented mind? I put my hands upon his chest and implored him to help me find her.

'Of course,' he said. He was calm again, and so tender I was comforted. 'Mina, whatever else I may be, in this you can trust me. We will find her together. She went on foot; she cannot have gone far. Make ready to leave.'

As he went to the doorway, a thought occurred to me. 'But how did she get past the dogs?' The Count did not answer; he began to turn away but I became more insistent. 'Surely I would have heard a commotion, at least? They would not have let her pass in silence.'

'But I trained them to treat her as a friend,' he replied. 'That was my misjudgement.'

'What if Van Helsing and the others are watching the abbey? They might have seen her leave. They may see *us* leave, and follow.'

'The worse for them if they do,' he said harshly. 'But these are my concerns, not yours. Your presence will ensure that your foolish hero-husband and his accomplices keep their distance.'

I am still being used as hostage, I know, but my only care is to find Quincey. I can but pray that if Jonathan and the others follow us, they do nothing to endanger Quincey's life.

'And if Elena has taken a carriage, or a train? How are we to find her?'

Dracula answered, 'She cannot escape me, for my blood is in her, and wherever she goes, her brain cannot help but call to mine.'

## JONATHAN HARKER'S JOURNAL

### *16 November, evening*

I don't know if we have been heroes or lunatics today.

Seward has had a couple of men watching Carfax Abbey; they tell us there's been no activity, no coming or going, but whether they have been idle or unobservant, I do not know. Whatever the case, Dracula has outwitted us.

We made a second assault on Carfax this afternoon, armed with meat, clubs and a rifle against the dogs. As before the dogs attacked us, but this time we were ready; the meat provided only a temporary distraction, and Seward shot two dead before we gained the crypt door.

We knew the sound of gunfire – even muffled by the mist and thick stone walls of the abbey – must have been been heard inside. Our hope was that, as it was afternoon, Dracula would still be at his rest. Yet as we entered the crypt, the house had an eerily dead feeling – as if nothing were left there to hear us.

The crypt was as dark and odiferous as I recalled, the walls furry with grime. Now we had time to look around, I saw that the earth boxes, which he brought seven years ago from Castle Dracula, were still there, apparently undisturbed since we had last seen them there. I wondered, but did not voice the question (for it seemed sacrilegious), if the effect of the Holy Wafer were permanent, or if it faded as the Wafer dissolved into the soil? Whatever the case, Dracula seemed not to be using them.

The first tomb we opened was the one into which Dracula had forced Mina. It was empty.

We slowly explored the niches, pushing back lids and looking into tombs, finding only ancient skeletons. I remained terrified that we would find Mina in one. Or even Quincey, or Elena. So terrified that I was near to hysteria.

We did not find Mina, but suddenly Van Helsing let out a heart-rending shout. Seward and I rushed to him, and found him staring down at a male corpse, which lay wide-eyed in an open coffin on a dais. It was Kovacs. His skin was ruddy, the lips positively swollen with blood and indented by the tips of two sharp canine teeth. On whom had he fed his unholy appetite?

'Oh, *mijn God*, André!' Van Helsing cried. He beat his forehead with his fists; he sobbed in such a paroxysm of grief that Seward and I were powerless to help him. When he began to master himself, he said, 'It did not sink in until this moment, that this terrible thing has happened to my dear friend! When we spoke to him, it was possible to believe he was still human. But to see him like this – oh, God Almighty, what justice is it that so good a man should come to this?'

Then the corpse blinked. My heart beat violently, despite all the horrors I have seen – but God preserve me from ever becoming inured to them! The creature that had been André Kovacs turned his head to look at Van Helsing, and red tears ran down his face. That face was still noble and handsome, even in this unholy state. He reached out to Van Helsing. His movements were stiff and waxy, as he fought against the deep vampire sleep.

'Abraham,' he said, in a voice of rust. 'Ah, my friend, you came back to me.'

'Yes.'

'I have betrayed everyone. Forgive me.'

'You are forgiven.' Van Helsing spoke firmly, although tears were welling from his eyes, and he was already taking the stake and mallet from his canvas bag. Seward tried gently to remove them from him, for Van Helsing's hands were shaking; but Van Helsing said, 'No. As his dearest friend, it must be me who delivers him.'

He put the point to Kovacs's breastbone. I waited with beating heart for the end; for the fall of the mallet, the bursting of blood like some obscene red flower as the stake sank deep. And then the fiend gasping, arching its back as it writhed and convulsed, a foam of blood flying from its mouth. Then the silence, the look of peace. I was sweating, almost sick with waiting.

Just as Van Helsing lifted the mallet, Kovacs's hand came up and grabbed the stake. 'No!' he hissed in a deathly voice. 'Don't destroy me! The library –'

'Do it,' Seward said firmly. 'Don't falter.'

Too late. Van Helsing hesitated and lost his resolve. Stake and mallet tumbled from his grip. The corpse sat up in the coffin; I watched in frozen horror as Kovacs put his arms around Van Helsing's neck. Both were weeping. I felt tears of pity and horror. Then, from the side, I saw the vampire's mouth open, heard the hiss of breath as he lunged at Van Helsing's neck.

'No!' I cried. I brought my cross out of my jacket; in the gloom it shone with uncompromising brilliance. I thrust it at Kovacs's face and he shrank back, loosing his hold on his friend. Van Helsing staggered back, coughing and rubbing at his throat.

Meanwhile Seward grabbed the implements and stood ready to complete the task that Van Helsing had left unfinished.

'I am sorry,' the fiend breathed. 'I cannot master my nature.' Lying down again, he put out his hands to Seward and me, as if we were lights that dazzled and burned him. 'But I beg you, do not destroy me yet. Listen to me, I can help you. If you destroy me now you will never find your son and wife!'

'What do you mean?' I cried.

Seward held back. Van Helsing came right to the coffin lip, showing no fear of Kovacs. 'If there is anything left in you that recalls and treasures our friendship still, tell us all that you know.'

Kovacs's face was at once unnatural and beautiful, like an effigy, his voice deep as a grave, slow and cold as clay. I was held in a kind of fascinated horror as I listened. 'Dracula wanted you to destroy me. He knew you would come back. But you are too late. They have gone.'

'Gone – where?' All of this shocked me so much I felt that the whole world, not just myself, had turned mad.

'Dracula will have gone to the Scholomance. It is my fault. There is some great secret of power there that Beherit does not want him to have, but now, because I failed, he will find and claim it. Then no one, not even you, my friend Abraham, will prevail against him. And he had to take the others with him, for he cannot leave them alone to fall into the hands of others. As long as they are with him, he knows you cannot touch him.'

'You mean he's taken Quincey to Transylvania?' I cried. 'But it's almost winter! The cold will kill him!'

'When did they leave?' Van Helsing asked.

'Before midday, I think. Elena came to tell me. To say goodbye. Beloved niece . . .'

226

'Then we have time to catch them before they reach the coast!'

Seward said, 'But he'll use Mrs Harker and Quincey to keep us away.'

'But at some time, he must rest on his native earth,' Van Helsing said intently. 'Then we strike.'

'If we can find him!' I said. 'He left without detection.'

'That's why you must take me with you,' Kovacs said quietly. 'I know his destination is the Scholomance. Only I can guide you to it.'

'Why would you want to help us?' I asked bitterly. 'You are one of Dracula's kind now. Why should we trust you?'

'Because I must see Beherit again. Even if he destroys me, I can't die without seeing the library one last time. Ah, the library, Abraham . . .'

We did not leave Carfax without making a thorough search. But as Kovacs had said, they were gone. The door to the keep was unlocked, and in two of the chambers we found signs of recent habitation; the embers were still warm in the grates, and I plucked several of Quincey's gold hairs from the pillows of both beds. But the house was deserted, the caleche and horses gone from the stable.

When we returned to the crypt to talk to Kovacs once more, a weird fluttering of the air began. The whole, low vault of the chapel was coming alive, rustling, peeling off in sooty layers. The air was suddenly full of flying things; bats and huge moths. Disgust and panic gripped us as they swarmed around our heads. We struggled to beat them off, but more came, flapping around us, tangling in our hair.

Defeated, we turned and rushed out of the chapel, heads down and hands flailing wildly. Dracula's servants, the beasts of darkness, pay no heed to holy symbols!

Outside, the remaining dogs let us pass, but once we were beyond them, they leaped up and came growling after us until they had driven us off the premises. One bit me hard in my nerveless right arm; I barely realized it had happened until I saw the blood flowing. Seward beat the dog off with a club.

Disheartened, desperate and exhausted, we retired to Dr Seward's house. Alice Seward was there to meet us, and we have told her everything. She is like a mother to us, and unshockable.

As we sat over a hurried meal, Van Helsing said, 'Of course, it is obvious why Dracula wanted us to destroy Professor Kovacs!'

'Is it?' Seward said sourly.

'He wants no other male vampire, that might challenge his power. But the fact that Dracula did not do it himself, that he must have us do it – this means only one thing, that the vampire cannot destroy his own kind!'

'Or thinks he cannot, at least,' said Seward. 'The so-called Beherit seemed to have no difficulty in beheading Miklos.'

'Who had not yet become Undead. But that is a fascinating idea – a vampire who breaks free of the restrictions that nature and God have placed upon him! And this is the secret Dracula may discover, if we do not prevent him reaching the Scholomance!'

Van Helsing was animated – even excited. I said, 'I don't know what you find so amusing, professor.'

'The abstract idea. The ludicrousness of the natural and the supernatural. You know me by now, friend Jonathan – but I ask your forgiveness for my jocular tone, all the same. I cannot stop being fascinated by the unknown, however dire our situation.'

'But,' said Seward, thoughtfully, 'if a vampire can think, and reason, as Dracula clearly can, and feel regret, and self-knowledge, and concern for his living relatives, as Professor Kovacs obviously can – have we any right to destroy such a sentient being?'

'For pity's sake, don't start on this!' I cried. 'I shall go mad.'

Seward put his hand on mine. 'I'm sorry, Harker. At least we know Mina and Quincey are alive.'

'For how long?' I groaned.

Van Helsing said, 'Ah, friend Jonathan, do not lose heart! For I know what it is to lose a son in boyhood, and for this reason share keenly your sorrow. I too have lost wife and son and have nothing left but my work; therefore I am all the more determined that you shall not have cause to grieve as I have! For all that our brotherhood is diminished, shall not those of us who remain be closer, and more resolute than ever to go on to the bitter end? We have received another setback, but if I feel my resolve waver – then I have only to look on your sad face or to think of poor Madam Mina and the innocent child, and I am more determined than ever that the author of this misery must be destroyed, once and for eternity.'

Solemnly, the remaining three of us remade our promise; and my vow, even though I felt it to be hopeless, was heartfelt.

Well, I have all the time in the world to write this account – which I do, very slowly and laboriously, with my swollen right hand.

Van Helsing, Seward and Kovacs have gone after Dracula without me.

I find this unbearable, but there is no choice. I have only one good arm, yesterday's adventure has aggravated my damaged ribs, and to crown everything I have a fever. I protested, all the time they were making ready, but in the end I was forced to admit the truth. I am unfit to travel. I would only hold them back. I shall help Mina and Quincey more by remaining in Seward's house, under Alice Seward's maternal care.

How intolerable, to be so incapacitated! And every wound I have received, to body or mind, has been dealt by Dracula.

None of us are young men now. I am greatly concerned

for Van Helsing, in particular. For all his courage he is, truth be told, a tired and grief-stricken old man. Dracula has sucked the spirit from each and every one of us.

# Chapter Fifteen

*17 November*

I am certain that my decision to stay behind was for the best. My ribs are so bruised that I can stand only with difficulty. The bite I received from the dog is inflamed, and I shiver with fever; this in addition to the loss of use in my right hand! I am well enough to sit in a chair with a rug over my knees, like some ageing invalid – ah, but for heroic deeds, I am as useless as a girl-child.

Van Helsing has promised to keep us informed of their progress. As yet, we have heard nothing. He left us a bag containing the usual tools and wards against vampires, just in case we should need them, but I cannot bear to look upon them and have removed the bag to the other, empty guest-room.

I wish I could order my thoughts about Mina. In my heart I love her; I know she is still the good, pure woman I married; I would do anything to be the husband she deserves, to brave fire and flood to save her! I cannot bear my enforced idleness.

Yet in some cold, festering portion of my brain – which I cannot overcome, as if it were some ghastly sore planted by Dracula seven years ago – another Mina lives, and will not be erased. The fallen Mina, who welcomed Dracula's embraces, who went all too easily into the darkness with him.

Am I being quite unjust? Was there any manner in which she might have stood firm against him, refused his demand that she go with him? I don't see how. Yet I believe it would be almost better for our son to die, than for Mina to have surrendered her virtue – I mean the rich virtue of her whole, good being!

Alice Seward is looking after me. She is like a mother, so strong and good. She knows everything; I am glad she is not some innocent who must be shielded from harsh knowledge. I feel at ease with her. We can be gloom-ridden together!

She said, after Dr Seward had gone with Van Helsing, 'I fear I will lose my husband to Dracula even now; I mean, if not physically, that I will lose him to his obsession. He wants science, rationality. The irrational unhinges him.'

'But he works with the insane every day of his life, and has done so for years!' I protested.

'But that is *why* he works with them,' Alice answered. 'To understand them, to make sense of nonsense. He must go out and fight it, like St George against the dragon – out of fear as much as courage. The irrational never goes away. It comes back again and again, in different forms, to try the strong and the weak alike.'

I am sitting alone in the pleasant guest-room, which is cosy enough; yet certain companions seem all too close. That is, the chill of the night, the moans of the asylum inmates, and the howling of dogs from the grounds of Carfax Abbey.

### *19 November*

Last night, as I sat playing cards with Alice in the drawing room, we heard someone pounding at the front door. We both got up, startled. Then one of the maids came in looking worried, and said, 'A woman and child to see Mr Harker, ma'am. The woman seems indisposed.'

The visitors were shown up, and there in the doorway stood Elena, holding Quincey by the hand! I was so astonished that I could say and do nothing. Quincey looked sleepy and bewildered; seeing me, he cried, 'Papa!' and rushed to my arms!

As he left her side, Elena fell forward in a dead faint.

Quickly we took her upstairs to the unoccupied guest-room, revived her with smelling salts then gave her water and drops of brandy. While I sat with her, Alice took charge of Quincey, fed and bathed him and took him to her own room. (I can only hope that his childlike trust in Elena has shielded him from realizing the peril he was in.)

Elena had all the signs of Dracula's attentions: ragged, unwholesome-looking wounds in her neck, the rapid heart-beat and shallow breathing. Her flesh was tinged almost to pale yellow and drawn back against the bone, her teeth prominent under her taut lips. Her eyes were large and brilliant in lakes of purplish-black, the skin so thin the bones of the eye sockets could be seen through it. Her lids kept falling sleepily.

She looked very sick – near to death.

When we had revived her, she clutched at my arm and tried to haul herself up. 'Your friends,' she gasped, 'they are pursuing Dracula? Why not you?'

'I am injured,' I said. 'But I don't understand. How is it that you came here? Where is Mina? We were told that Dracula had taken you all away!'

She spoke with effort, between wheezing breaths. 'Dracula took only Mina with him. He told her I had run away with Quincey, that she must go with him to bring us back. Dracula lied to Mina, and I lied to my uncle.'

'But why?'

'It is my uncle's fault, for coming here and telling him about Beherit and the Scholomance. I wish Dracula had not gone! But he insisted he must go to the Scholomance at once. He needs Mina as his hostage; that is the only reason he took her, not that he truly wants her – not as he wants me. He lied about Quincey and me to ensure her co-operation. We would have slowed him down, you see; the boy would not have withstood the journey. So Dracula told me to hide with him in Carfax and remain there until he returned.'

'But we searched Carfax!'

She gave a smile which showed her long teeth horribly. 'You did not search well enough, Mr Harker. There are many hidden rooms into which you did not even glance.'

'But why have you come to us now?'

'Because I am dying,' she said, her voice fading. 'I feel myself growing weaker and weaker and I grow very afraid. I do not want to die and abandon Quincey to starve alone in that great, deserted house! Help me.'

I held her hand and wept. So Elena has still some human feelings left for us, after all! 'Of course we will help you. God has not deserted you! Thank you, bless you for bringing our son back to us!'

I went in to Alice, and found her putting Quincey to bed with hot cocoa. Strangely – and to my immense relief! – he seems well. I thought the damp of Carfax would have put a strain upon his lungs, yet he is alert and rosy-cheeked.

I took Alice aside, and asked if she had ever assisted in a blood transfusion.

'Of course. I have assisted my husband in many medical procedures.'

'I am going to give Elena a transfusion of my blood. We may save her life.'

She looked sternly at me. 'No, Jonathan. You are not strong enough.'

'I disagree.'

'Jonathan,' she said firmly, 'that dog bite you received is infected; do you want to risk passing that infection to our patient and poisoning her blood? Let me do it. I am large and strong, with blood to spare!'

I could not but admire Alice's courage. We attended Elena together. I gave Elena a draught of laudanum to drink, that she might sleep through the operation; Alice fetched her husband's transfusion equipment.

What an extraordinary picture we must have made in the warm light of the lamp and the fire. Alice sat by the bed, connected to Elena almost as a mother might be to her new-born; meanwhile I sat and stroked Elena's pallid, high forehead as the faintest flush suffused her cheeks. Poor dear girl! All she had done against us was forgotten; all I felt for her at this moment was the tenderest sympathy.

I felt a little uneasy, I must admit, performing this operation without the supervision of Seward or Van Helsing. Presently Alice began to look pale and listless, and we knew it was time to call a halt.

Now I have sent her to bed – she has Quincey in her room – while I sit up with Elena, and write in my journal in the hope of keeping myself awake. Elena looks so peaceful. Perhaps, now she is out of Dracula's grasp, she will turn away from evil and become the sweet, good woman she should be!

I wish we had word from Van Helsing. Are they still in England, or on their way to the continent by now? Will Dracula have gone by ship again? Is Mina utterly lost to us? My eyes cloud, and I cannot think clearly upon any of these questions.

### 20 November

I fell asleep where I sat, to my eternal shame. I remember only one thing more of the night; that as I was just beginning to doze, Elena's eyes opened and she spoke to me with heavy, laboured breaths. She said something of this kind, 'Take this, Jonathan. It is the remainder of my journal, the main body of which I left in Exeter; read it all, if you have not done so already. Then you will know my heart. I will write no more.'

She pulled some folded papers from her breast and thrust them into my hands. They were covered in her tiny writing. I put them aside and said, 'Hush. Go to sleep now.'

The next I knew, it was full daylight and Alice was shaking my arm. I was sitting up in the chair, aching all over and so stiff I could barely move; this the sum of my injuries and sleeping in so awkward a position. The morning sun pierced a gap in the curtains, widening to a veil of light as she drew them back; and this veil fell beautifully across Elena, who lay peacefully beneath the covers.

I leaned over her, and saw at once that she was dead.

Her eyes gleamed like slivers of dark glass under the half-open lids; her mouth hung slack as an old woman's, and her fingers were curled in pain. I started back with a cry; I could not, cannot believe that our treatment failed to save her! I was distraught but Alice's serene practicality calmed me somewhat.

She examined Elena for signs of life; finding none, she closed the girl's eyes, composed her body, and drew the sheet over her face with a sigh. 'Poor dear. Poor ill-used soul! Come, Mr Harker, come down to breakfast.'

'I cannot eat.'

'Then take some tea, at least. We can do nothing for her now.'

We said a prayer, and left the room.

Now I cannot avoid the suspicion that the blood transfusion in some way hastened her death, rather than delaying it. I did not say this to Alice, of course. I have no reason for my doubt, I am sure her blood was wholesome. But, oh God, what if, in trying to cure Elena, I have killed her?

### Later

This day has seemed endless. Pain pervades my whole body; I cannot separate physical ennervation from the gloom that lies over the house. One shades into the other. No news from Van Helsing. I am constantly aware of Elena's corpse lying in the closed room above us.

As darkness began to fall, I could no longer resist the compulsion to view the body. I crept into the room, and drew back the sheet . . .

Ah, God, her face! It was tilted slightly towards me and in death had taken on a fresh bloom of youth. Her cheeks and mouth were restored to their firm, flowing lines, her forehead was smooth. Her lips were slightly curved in mysterious amusement, and her hair lay thick and glossy upon the pillow. The full black crescents of her eyelashes, lying upon her cheeks, glittered as if tears were gathering between them. Her appearance of beauty, after all that had happened, flooded me with horror.

I screamed. What happened next is confused; I recall it as if through a black curtain. My only thought was that I must save us both from further evil. The bag of Van Helsing's, which I'd placed in this room to be out of my sight, lay on the floor against the dressing table. I opened the bag and took out a long wooden stake, sharpened to a lethal point. Gripping it as best I could in my left hand, I had the point poised over Elena's heart when Alice dashed in and grabbed hold of my arm.

'Jonathan, what are you doing?' she cried.

I struggled with her, to my shame – my only excuse being that I was half out of my mind. 'I must stake her through the heart! It's the only way to save her soul!'

Alice's grip was enough to keep my wavering hand from its task. I had thought she would understand the necessity; but when it came to the point, a surfeit of common sense overwhelmed the belief she had professed to hold in our experiences with the Undead.

'Stop it!' she said, as to a child. 'The body of this unfortunate young girl deserves to be treated with respect. How can you think to defile her? She is no vampire, she is dead, God rest her soul. In the name of mercy, Jonathan, leave her in peace!'

I let Alice take the stake from me. She replaced it in the bag, which she then closed firmly and removed from the room. Drained of my passion, I could see that from her point of view I was acting insanely. I had not the strength to resist her. I left Alice to replace the sheet over Elena's face, and to lock the door behind us.

'I will send for a doctor in the morning, then the undertaker,' she said more gently. 'Perhaps we will have word from my husband, too. Then all will seem better. You still have a fever, Jonathan; you should have a sleeping draught and an early night.'

Alone, I broke down and wept. Elena was so young! I can't stop thinking of her body, cold and stiff behind the locked door. I keep imagining her, warm and pliant as she was in life, when first she came to us; the way she used to sit with Quincey on her knee, her dark head bent over his golden one as she murmured to him. And then so waxen-beautiful in death, like an effigy, and the lamps burning around her deathbed, and her corpse stirring beneath the sheet.

### 21 November

When she came to me in the night, I thought I dreamed; that memories were invading my sleep, becoming real and walking around me like ghosts.

I heard her voice first. 'Jonathan, Jonathan.'

I opened my eyes and saw her drifting towards me, a soft white shape in muslin. As she leaned over me, her hair slid thick and lustrous over her shoulders and brushed my face. Her eyes shone, her complexion was of lilies and roses, so silken and dewy that I longed to touch her cheeks. I had left one lamp burning very low, and in its glow I saw the sheen of her full red lips. She ran the tip of her tongue over them and the sheen became a gloss.

Paralysis lay on me. I felt no shock, for it was as if I had known she would come – known since the first moment I met her. I was afraid, yes, but my terror seemed delicious. My longing for her was wicked and unashamed. I lay in blissful anticipation, waiting for those glistening lips to touch mine, for the hard white teeth to indent my neck.

Mina forgive me! I felt I had waited seven years for this . . .

Elena drew the covers away from my body and slid alongside me. Her body was not cold but hot like a furnace. With my good arm I held her to me and let her press her voluptuous mouth to mine. She arched her back, forcing her body against me all down its slender length. Her wantonness made my heart race. When her leg slid up and over mine I was lost, slithering down into a lascivious pit, all sense of right and wrong suspended.

The tip of one of her eye-teeth touched my tongue, so sharp it drew blood. At that she hissed and stiffened, drawing back like a snake. Then her head went down shudderingly to my neck, and two hard points touched the shivering skin of my throat. I felt her tongue churning against my flesh, unutterably thrilling, urging me to the brink of a raging delight. Then she bit down. The flesh broke. I gasped. I had never anticipated such pain, such intensity of sensation; no one could know or imagine until they themselves felt that infernal kiss! Agony and dizzy ecstasy swept me out of myself.

As she entered me I felt that we entered each other. I was being drawn down into a whirlpool, red and crimson and black all swirling together, faster and faster, until at last I dissolved into her, and she into me, and there was red fire, and then blissful peace.

All the time I knew that this sin would condemn me to hell – and it will, for I cannot repent of it. If she came again to me now I would still . . .

When it was over, she lay with her arms about me for the longest time, and I did not want her to leave.

She whispered that she loved me. 'This is love, Jonathan, not the pale shadow of it that you share with Mina. Do you wonder that she and I fell so easily to Dracula? Do you still think her an angel, and me a devil? Well, we are the same. She fell to him with a thousand protestations of virtue and reluctance and shame; I did so with honesty. That is the only difference between us.'

I wanted to protest that she was wrong, there is such a quality as virtue, but I could find no words or strength to say so. She went on whispering against my cheek, 'What misery it is, that one man and one woman may know only each other. I may love Dracula, and many other men and women, and lie with them like this and drink their heart's blood, but I will never love you any the less for it. Bury me close to your dwelling, that I may come to you again.'

The stirring of protest grew stronger. I took a deep, quick breath. I was enmeshed. What use to get Mina and Quincey home, unhurt, and to continue our lives, when this fiend would only come again and again to draw us into the dark? For I could not destroy her. I was hers. As fallen as Lucifer.

'Let me tell you what it is like,' said Elena. 'Where did I write to, in my little journal? To the place where Dracula kisses me upon the stairs under the lattice window, the third and last time? And then he is kind again, and tells me his plan, and I agree to it all – for he promised me eternal life. Behold, he has kept the promise! But at the time, I think I have been cheated.

'When Dracula has gone I go to the chapel. I feel my heart labouring from the loss of blood, the breath swift and shallow in my lungs . . . and I cannot understand why I am still alive. My limbs tingle and pain shoots through me. How much more, then, must it hurt actually to die? I recall a great groan of despair issuing from my throat, my whole body shaking with the force of it. Tears blind me and I curse silently at fate, or God, or the vigour of my own body – whatever has cheated me of immortality!

'The thin light of dawn reaches into the chapel, and in it I see my Uncle André lying in an open tomb. His hands are folded on his breast, his eyes open but sightless, his lips ruddy with my blood. But he does not look content in his catalepsy. His face is strained into an expression of distress so ghastly that I recoil from it. I tell him the lie, that Dracula is taking us away. His eyes come open and he grips me with stone-cold hands. "Don't go, Elena, don't go," he says.

' "You must leave too, in secret," I tell him. But he says, no, he must wait for Abraham to come again. I answer, "Abraham Van Helsing will kill you!" But my uncle will not listen and so I leave. I weep. I fear I will never see him again. So unfair that Uncle André has the gift of immortality and hates it – while I long for it yet am still trapped in that weak, living form!

'Alone in a little, secret chamber with Quincey, in the top of the keep, I feel death coming upon me at last. Ah, so painful, Jonathan, like suffocation. There is no air, and your limbs burn with needles, and your heart flutters like that of a mouse. My sight darkens. I panic; I imagine myself dead, and not rising again, and poor Quincey crying over my body. Too piteous. I never wished him harm; I love him like my own.

'I hardly recall coming here. I have some vague image of Alice Seward sitting by me, and her blood passing into me, and I thinking, this is a great irony; she who would look on me with loathing if I took her blood in the manner of a vampire, gives it this way quite willingly! At first I am dismayed, to be drawn back from death's brink. Later I feel my veins on fire, as if her blood were warring against mine, and killing me. And I am glad!

'The pain is not in death, dear Jonathan; it is all in life. The blackness that claims me is sweet. When I open my eyes I feel that several centuries have passed. But my pain is gone, and the darkness has opened up its sweet secrets to me, as I knew it would. I don't even mind that Dracula is gone now. I don't need him any more. I have what I want. Freedom. The warm blood of the living.'

She rose over me again. It was too easy to melt into her carnal warmth again, too hard to resist.

I don't know what alerted Alice. I must have cried out in my unspeakable joy. Of a sudden the door opened, there was a flood of lamplight into the room – and in came Alice in her nightclothes, with the large wooden crucifix that Van Helsing had left us held boldly at arm's length. She resembled a Valkyrie!

'Leave him, foul demon!' Alice shouted. 'Begone, in the name of God! Begone!'

Elena rose on her knees, facing Alice, her hair tangled and blood smeared around her mouth. Seeing the cross, she uttered a horrible shriek; a mix of frustration and pure terror. The transformation of her face was ghastly. The sweet softness of her expression contorted to demonic white fury, reminding me starkly, horrifically of what I had done, the nature of the thing I had allowed into my bed – into my wife's place! I groaned, but could not move.

Elena confronted Alice, her face writhing. But the power of the cross was too much and she began slowly to retreat from it, sliding off the far edge of the bed and backing up to the wall – the gap in between being no more than four feet wide. Now I saw that Alice had in her left hand the wooden stake that earlier she'd prevented me from using!

Elena was uttering terrible snarls that would have given the bravest man pause, yet Alice seemed aflame with wrath and courage. Although the bed stood between them, she would not be hindered. Indeed, I would not have believed a woman of her size and years could move with such agility – for Alice simply went leaping and running straight across the bed, near crushing my legs as she passed.

As she alighted on the other side, Alice dropped the cross, took the stake in both hands, and ran it through Elena's breast. Blood surged out, staining both their nightdresses. I was too late to look away; would that I had, for now that horrible sight is with me for ever! The vampire uttered a hideous scream, not loud, more a sort of anguished expiry of breath; then she simply froze where she stood, hands gripping the shaft that protruded from her body. All malevolence passed from her face, which became smooth and peaceful. Her eyes fell shut. She was dead; upright, pinned, but dead.

Alice stepped back and sat heavily on the bed, as if shaken by what she had done. I began to tremble violently in shock and a tumult of feelings I could not comprehend. Elena, poor Elena!

I don't recall what Alice and I said to each other; I think we were both too shocked to speak. In the silence I heard, from the part of the house that forms the asylum, Dr Seward's patients shouting and howling as eerily as wolves – as if they understood more than the sane ever could.

Then Alice roused herself and turned at once to practical matters, as is her sensible nature. Now there could be no summoning of doctor or undertaker. We couldn't leave the body of Elena in the house, especially since Dr Seward was not present to write a certificate of death. So Alice and I had no choice but to carry the body back to Carfax. Indeed, Alice did the greater part of this grisly work, for I was faint, ennervated, and barely in my right mind. Her courage, I must note not least for her husband's appreciation, was astonishing! She seemed a veritable Amazon, quailing not once as she hefted the corpse and bore it across the asylum grounds and into those of Carfax. The Count left the gates unfastened when he fled. How gloomy and ill-favoured the night seemed, the abbey so deathly quiet among the gnarled trees and deep dark ponds. But the dogs, at least, did not trouble us. They have deserted, now their master is not there to feed them.

We brought poor Elena to the crypt, laid her in a coffin, and pushed garlic into her mouth. I could not bear to do more; I mean, to behead her, nor to suggest that Alice did so. We said a prayer. Looking down upon Elena's form now rent by the stake, the hideous blood stain beneath the sweet repose of her face, mad grief overcame me at last. I collapsed, weeping; I remember little more, but I know that Alice – good, brave soul! – somehow got me home and helped me to bed. There she gave me a draught which restored me somewhat.

She said, 'Forgive me, Jonathan, for keeping you from an action that might have prevented this! I was too much a sceptic. I believed all my husband and Van Helsing's stories as gospel, yet when it came to the reality, I could *not* accept it. It seemed wrong to violate a corpse. I don't know why I woke tonight; the inmates were restless and there were strange sounds, strange cold breezes sighing round me, and such an odd glow, as if there were spirits in the room. And you know I am not a fanciful woman! So I got up and looked in Elena's room. I had to unlock it – but the body was gone! Then I heard you give such an anguished cry. I acted by instinct on what Van Helsing told me, that the Undead abhor the sign of the cross, and I armed myself with the stake. When I saw that creature upon you, I did what I knew must be done to save you and put that poor creature from its evil misery. Oh, forgive me for ever doubting you!'

### 26 November

So, Elena is at rest. Alice Seward, like a fiery angel at the gates of Eden, has delivered us. I should be grateful for it, yet I cannot stop thinking of Elena's dark hair brushing me and her sweet voice whispering . . .

Each day, Quincey asks, 'Papa, where is Elena?' Not, 'Where is Mama?' Once he said another strange thing. 'The tall man was not cruel to me. But he used to give me a bitter medicine to drink. I did not like it.'

Dear God, was Dracula trying to poison Quincey? I can't

see how, for the boy is the healthiest I have ever seen him. He appears to have suffered no ill-effects from his imprisonment, and there are no signs of the vampire upon him. Yet whenever he is not engaged in some boyish activity, he will always sit looking fixedly out of a window, as if willing Elena to come back.

Now when I think of Mina, I know that I have forgiven her at last. How arrogant I was to consider my dear wife in any way stained or unacceptable to me! More than forgiven, for I am in no position to withhold or dispense absolution. If she has fallen then so have I, and in just the same way, and although convention teaches that it is worse for her than for me, I cannot in my soul believe that. In God's eyes our sins are identical. I understand her. So as we are both sinners, we can surely live together in tenderness, where before there was only condemnation and distrust?

I have given up trying to write with my leaden right hand and am learning to use my left – the feminine, intuitive side, as Van Helsing would have it. Dear Mina, shall I ever see you again – or has understanding come too late? I shall tell her all of this, if God will only grant me the chance! So far from deigning to bestow my compassion upon her, I shall only offer myself up contritely to receive hers.

So here I sit alone in the drawing room, thinking constantly of Mina and praying for her safe deliverance. Yet when my thoughts stray, as often they do, Elena's image haunts me, the demure companion, the wild, blood-dappled temptress; and her image becomes mixed up with Mina's, so that I cannot tell them apart; and often I start up from writing or reflection, feeling as vividly as life Elena's soft voice in my ear and her cool gentle hand upon my arm.

28 November, Vienna

My dear Jonathan,

News at last. We discovered, through much painstaking investigation, that Dracula has this time chanced the train across Europe – so much more swiftly to reach his destination! Loaded on to the Vienna – Buda-Pesth train has been one large box, accompanied by an Englishwoman of Madam Mina's description. No mention of Elena and child, however. We are now, we estimate, approximately half a day behind them.

Kovacs travels parallel to us, as it were, rather than with us. My supposition is that he travels as wolf, and finds the unhallowed graves he needs for rest along the way. Rivers may only be crossed at the slack of tide, you understand. But the restrictions that delay us delay Dracula also!

He seeks the Scholomance, I hardly need add, precisely for the purpose of finding a way to rid himself of these limitations.

I hope you are on the way to recovery in Alice Seward's tender care. Keep up your courage, my friend!

Yours,
Abraham Van Helsing

# Chapter Sixteen

*30 November*
It is a long time since I have felt able to bring this journal up to date. We are in Sighisoara for one night; tomorrow we go on to Hermannstadt. I am in a little hotel room with crooked walls and ivy hanging over the windows, the foliage crusted with light snow; the Count . . . but let me record all as I remember it.

I was in a state of bewilderment when we left Carfax. I could not believe that Elena had fled with my son, could not comprehend her reasoning. Something seemed wrong, but Dracula assured me it was so, and I had no choice but to put my faith in him. He said, 'She believes that I have broken faith with her, therefore she is fleeing to another, who, she thinks, will confer immortality upon her. Her uncle has given her this idea. She is on her way to the Scholomance.'

'How can you be certain of it?' I asked.

'When my blood was in you, and yours in me,' he said, looking intently at me – even, I might say, with a kind of brooding affection – 'were we not linked? When I returned to Castle Dracula, you knew, at every stage of my journey, where I was. Is it not so? That was how your menfolk followed and destroyed me. Well, it is the same. I know where Elena is bound.'

'Then why can you not call her back?' I exclaimed. 'Surely your will is stronger than hers?'

He paused, then gave a strange reply. 'Sometimes the Devil's call is stronger.'

I am so afraid for Quincey. It is almost winter, and the Transylvanian climate is bitter. His delicate constitution will never bear it! Still, I must focus all my will on finding him alive, or else I shall go mad.

We went in the caleche to Dover, and thence by boat and train towards Transylvania. Since Dracula cannot travel without his native earth, a great box must be conveyed with us. I acted as solitary guard to the box in which he lies, on the long train journey across the continent, supervising the transfer of the box from one train to the next at every stage of the journey. I was surprised at my own resourcefulness in this, using all my wiles and authority as an English 'lady' to sweeten recalcitrant foreign guards along the way.

Sometimes the Count would be at rest in the box. Then I would wonder how easy it might be to prise open the lid, to gaze upon his waxen, aquiline face, and then to plunge some sharp implement through his heart. I thought of it constantly. But I could not do it. Alone, I would have no hope of finding Elena. More than that; I have grown used to him, seen every shade of his temperament; his tenderness and nobility, as well as his brutality. I feel, however wrongly, that the world would be a lesser place without him.

And then I remember the evil he has wreaked upon us, and I despair.

As the train rattled through the darkness, and I sat in the guard's van watching over this strange cargo, a white mist would spill from under the lid, and the Count would stand before me; a pillar of obsidian, his white face fierce as an eagle's, his eyes agleam like rubies. And each time I would experience the same *frisson* of fear and longing.

Often he would be gone from the train for hours. I imagined him racing as a wolf through the night; perhaps waiting by a bridge for the slack tide that would allow him to cross the river, then gliding as a bat through the chittering darkness to rejoin the train.

248

I have grown used to the odour of Castle Dracula's earth upon him; there is a comforting quality to it, a dry spiciness and something of autumn and woodsmoke. He has not taken my blood a third time. There are silver streaks in the darkness of his hair once more. It seems to me that he does not absolutely *need* blood, for he is immortal anyway; rather, he takes it for vigour and power. And even, or – God have mercy on me! – above all, for the carnal pleasure of it.

I had a great shock on the stretch from Buda-Pesth to Klausenburgh. I was sitting as usual in the dinginess of the guard's van, quite comfortable upon some sacks of fleece. It was morning, but the motion of the train lulled me towards sleep, for I was by now worn down from the constant travelling and the ever-deepening cold. Of a sudden I woke from my doze, roused violently by a fierce sense of alarm. Two men were coming along the swaying, creaking carriage, making their way between the stacked boxes and chests. Their faces were haggard with strain, horrible to behold.

I almost did not recognize them as Van Helsing and Dr Seward! I started up, amazed; mirroring my shock, they rushed to my side. 'Come away, Madam Mina,' Van Helsing said urgently. 'You are safe now.'

'But how have you found me?' I cried, utterly dumbfounded.

Van Helsing responded with a grim smile; grim, I knew with great regret, at least in part because my demeanour on greeting them had been one of dismay, not joy. That must have convinced them that Dracula was turning me against my own . . . but I found myself unable to dispel this impression. He said, 'Have you forgotten what detectives Dracula forced us to become? An Englishwoman travelling alone with a great chest does not pass unnoticed. Our greatest struggle has been to close the gap of time between us; it has taken us all the miles between Dover and the plains of Transylvania to do so.'

'Oh, Professor,' I said, ashamed. I could imagine their desperate journey! 'Where is Jonathan?'

'His health would not let him travel, but he is in Mrs Seward's care. Is the Count . . . ?' Van Helsing looked at the box; I nodded. 'Then we will dispose of him at once.'

He was already reaching into his case for the wooden stake and other paraphernalia; I felt quite sick to see it.

'No,' I said quickly. Panic-stricken, I spoke with a good deal of force. I had to make them understand! 'No, I cannot come with you, nor can I let you harm him.'

'In heaven's name, why not?' Dr Seward cried.

Van Helsing said, low but firm, 'This time we make no mistake. We dispatch him with wood, not metal; we force garlic into the mouth.' Then with his black humour, 'Think, even should he come back *again* in seven years – we need only a few days, a few moments to free you and Elena and Quincey from him!'

He held my hands, but I pulled away. 'No. Elena and Quincey are not with us! Don't you understand? Surely you know!'

They shook their heads, frowning. 'Kovacs told us that Dracula took you all.'

'Then he was wrong. Elena quarrelled with Dracula and she ran away. She took my son with her. We are following them! Only Dracula can find her, so if you destroy him, we may never see Quincey alive!'

Van Helsing turned away, pressing his fists to his temples in silent despair. Seward said furiously, 'So he frustrates us again!'

'Please go,' I said. 'I am in no danger. But I don't know what Dracula may do if he knows you have caught up with us. For my sake, please go!'

'Leave you with this monster? Impossible!' said Van Helsing.

'But you must,' I persisted, growing desperate. 'If we are to have any hope of seeing Quincey again, you must!'

At last they saw that I was right, that they had no choice. Their faces working with frustration and grief, they began to withdraw. But before he went, Van Helsing clasped my hands and said warmly, 'Little girl, we will not desert you. We shall follow at a distance; and although you may never see us, be assured that we are not far away. You have endured much, but the end cannot be long in coming.'

He gave me a gold cross to wear around my neck. I did not tell him that I could not bear the sight of it; the metal felt scorching hot upon my flesh, which confirmed all that I feared. As soon as they were gone, I threw it away.

So, Jonathan is safe in the care of Alice Seward. That is one less matter to worry about, at least.

Today we came to Sighisoara. It is a citadel on a hill, with high, tightly clustered roofs reminiscent of a Dürer engraving. The walls have a red-roofed turret at every turn. I feel, as I always do in Transylvania, that I have stepped back into the Middle Ages. The air is biting, but everywhere is the frost-coated evidence of summer's abundance; tangles of leafless creeper and vine, bare linden trees.

I climbed alone up the rocky massif on which the town is built, past a jumble of ancient houses towards the squat-towered *Bergkirche*, until I found the tiny hotel to which Dracula had directed me. I am to have a night of rest – with, I hope, good hot peasant food to drive the chill from my bones. The Count has engaged some Szgany gypsies to take us on to Hermannstadt. His native earth is now in their care, but I am glad I did not have to stay with those villainous-looking brigands.

At the hotel I was received with great warmth and intense curiosity. I had to reserve a room for 'Mr and Mrs Harker' and invent some story about my husband being 'delayed'. The Count will never show his face. The superstitions of these people seem primitive, yet serve them well; I believe that they would recognize him for what he is at once. (The Szgany recognize him also, but are too ungodly to care. They have their own morals, I suppose; to them he is *boyar* and protector.)

I don't know how far or near Van Helsing and Dr Seward are from us now. I have not seen them since the incident on the train. I cannot believe they are far away; I know that they would never give up, whatever I might say to put them off. In one way it is comforting to think that they are close by, alarming to think that I might be altogether alone; yet in another, I fear desperately for them.

I have no fear for myself any more. Only for my dear friends, and Quincey.

***Later***
Dracula has been to me.

I saw his face through the frosted panes of my little window, framed by ivy and a cold, bluish mist. Then he was inside the room; a forbidding, powerful figure who yet held me to him as a wolf might hold a tiny cub. His sharp fingernails pricked my neck and my waist.

'Don't be troubled, Mina,' he said. 'Soon there will be nothing in the world to trouble you.'

If he meant I would soon be Undead – I did not ask. Then all the shame of my collusion with evil descended on my soul, and I spoke with sudden misery.

'Jonathan will never take me back now. I will lose my son and be an outcast!'

'For what reason?'

'All I've done, and allowed – don't imagine that my husband does not know! He knows everything. Any Christian husband would shun his wife for what I have done.'

Dracula sneered. 'And you wish to return to these *bourgeois* rules of your so-compassionate society? I care nothing for their petty values! You think me a monster? Yet I am the one who will never condemn or desert you. I will welcome you always, though you go from me and suck the blood of all your beloved men, of thousands of men throughout the rest of time. You may be more easily rid of your husband, Mina, than you ever will of me. Don't mourn the loss of him. Jonathan will be yours in the end, as will Quincey.'

I closed my eyes. How could I answer?

'Have you made your decision? Do you wish to watch Quincey die, or to see him live for ever?'

'Just to see him again, alive – that is all I ask!'

## *1 December*

We have arrived at Hermannstadt.

The gypsies conveyed us along the broad valley of the Tirnave river in their creaking wagons. None spoke to me; they are the least courteous men I have ever met, and very intimidating with their swarthy looks and great black moustaches. I am more afraid of them than of the Count! I occupied myself by observing the scenery; the tiered fields and the leafless poplars, charming villages with low, red-roofed houses. Most have a fortified Saxon church at the centre. But all this medieval charm only reminded me how far I am from home and family.

I can and I will remain strong.

This room is a little larger, but even more eccentrically proportioned than the last. There is a lot of dark wood, and a good fire in the grate; I feel warm, for once. The door gives on to a vine-covered courtyard with stairs and galleries, but from the window I have a fine view of the town. Below me are narrow, cobbled streets with gabled houses, some with baroque fronts on their crooked medieval shells. Raising my eyes I see the spires and domes of churches, and a long, tearing pang of guilt goes through me; but then, far beyond, there is the sudden blue wall of the mountains. That is where our destination lies. Dear Quincey; can he still be alive in that high, cold wilderness?

It seems strange that Dracula would let Elena reach the Scholomance; I thought he would have overtaken her by now! He has his reasons, I dare say. I must trust him. Ruthless as he is to those who cross him, he has a certain integrity . . . a nobility.

### Later

Now I am destroyed. I must pray, if God has not entirely forsaken me. Oh God, dear Lord, let this all be lies!

Dracula came to me again. This time he did not seem tender but hard; like a man carved of marble yet animated by an inner fire that I have never seen matched in any mortal man. He held me tight and forced me down on to the bed, pinning my wrists so that I could not struggle even if I had wanted to. Oh, the curse of his kind – that I did not want to resist him – was very strong upon me! I could only gasp, holding myself rigid, as his silken lips moved over my face and down the shivering skin of my throat. Then he bit down – and for a long time I came quite out of myself, and all was breath, and heartbeat, and delicious dizziness; all sensation, not thought. If he is as much beast as man, he is turning me into a beast also; a creature of flesh, not spirit. And for such lusts, utterly damned.

When these fires ebbed away and I came back to myself, he still held me down, though more gently now. He had taken only a very, very little blood from me, I could tell, not even enough to make me faint.

'You remember,' he said, 'this – seven years ago.'

'That you violated me while my husband lay sleeping beside us?'

'If you would term it so. I would call it consummation. But you have seen, now, how delicate I can be . . . as with you, so with a child. Your son, Mina . . .'

'Stop,' I said. Tears came painfully to my eyes. 'Don't talk to me of Quincey, I beg you. I cannot make such a decision.'

'You cannot decide, then, that he should *not* become immortal?'

'You are tormenting me. If you wish to prove that I can no longer renounce the Devil, have you not already done so? Quincey is also Jonathan's. He would never agree to such an abomination!'

Dracula smiled at me; a strange smile that was part tender, part malignant. 'Surely it is a decision only a mother could make. Yet you would consult his father?'

'I would not countenance even mentioning such an obscene notion.'

'But if his father was willing, more than willing, to let his son live for ever?'

'To *exist* for ever,' I said. 'No . . .' But still the idea of Quincey living for ever was so seductive, I could not let it go. And Dracula knew it.

'After that time I refreshed myself from your veins, while Jonathan lay asleep – how many months passed before Quincey was born?'

I could not understand why he asked this. I paused to recall. 'Thirteen.'

'It is said that the Devil's get take thirteen months to come to term.'

He let me go, and stood beside the bed, looking down at me with a hellish expression of – what? A sort of possessiveness, mixed with triumph. 'Ask yourself, then, who is truly the father of your son?'

His words struck such horror into my heart that I could

255

not breathe. Even now I can barely write the words. I tremble and my tears fall on to the paper. How could he, even he, be so cruel as to suggest such horror, such blasphemy? Many thoughts ran through my head, like a rosary of torments, but I could only whisper at the last, 'Fiend, *fiend* . . .'

The Count laughed. His face, for all its harsh angles, became reflective, even tender. 'Such insults fall so easily from your lips. Does it not strike you as ungracious, Mina, to speak so disparagingly of a man who may be your child's father? For Quincey's sake, at the least, you should accord me the respect and affection due to one who considers himself your devoted husband.'

I could not speak. I closed my eyes and lay motionless as he stroked my hair. 'Tomorrow we go into the mountains. You will need the warmest clothes, thick furs and food enough to last a few days. I will make all ready for you. You will soon be reunited with your son, my beloved, I promise.' Then he added with sudden passion, 'What does God care for you, that he would take your son away? Come with me and he will never know death. Only the Undead can truly appreciate life in all its warmth and richness. Only the Undead.'

When I looked up again he was gone, and there was only a thin mist swirling outside the window, and a sudden icy draught. I stoked the fire and am sitting over it even now, shivering and forcing myself to set down these words. I feel that I am going mad. Dracula must be lying, tormenting me – but how can I ever be sure there is not some grain of truth in his hideous implication?

### 3 December?
I am unsure of the date; I am losing track of time. We left Hermannstadt yesterday, and the Szgany brought us towards the mountains until the way became impassable for the wagon. Since then we have made our way on foot.

Dracula led me through silent pinewoods and stretches of

high pasture. It was growing intensely cold; frost glittered upon the branches and the forest floor crunched beneath our feet. As we emerged from the trees on to a broad saddle of grass, a bitter wind cut into us. I flinched; the Count only looked up at the sky. In the moonlight every grass blade was crusted and quivering in the wind, a field of fragile pennants.

As Dracula watched the horizon, clouds began to bank along the mountains and surge towards us. They came so fast, forming out of thin air as they came, that I knew this was unnatural. It was as if he summoned the clouds himself! Soon they clotted thick and low in the sky, obscuring the moon. Darkness folded in, yet I could still see my way, for the clouds and the landscape had a curious luminosity.

He took my arm. As we went on, light veils of snow began to dance across our path. We must have appeared a pair of spectres in the snowy wilderness.

The mountains rose steep and black before us. The sight of them filled me with dismay, for I was shivering and exhausted. At last I said, 'I need to rest. I cannot climb the mountains tonight!'

'Then I will find you somewhere to rest, and I will go on alone,' Dracula said simply.

Strange, how at some moments he can show such effortless courtesy. That both kindness and cruelty should come so instinctively to him, as to a child!

Presently we came to a sloping spur of grass, with the forest running down steep on either side. Near the highest point of the spur was a low wooden building with a steep, overhanging roof. A cart track led us to it, and through a wattle gate in an arched gateway. It was a church. Not a fortified Saxon church but one of the picturesque Orthodox ones that are less common in this region. The spire rose like an arrow against the snow-laden sky; around us, gravestones, walnut trees and waist-high grass were quickly turning white. The reflective paleness of the snow made it increasingly easy to see, and as we came close to the church I saw that it had a galleried porch with great carved posts, long low walls of massive planks which were curved at the apse like the stern of a ship. It made me think of the ark. A refuge to keep me safe from the storm?

Dracula stopped before he reached the porch but held out a hand, ushering me towards it. I saw, beneath the tiny windows, memorial crosses nailed, and pale outlines where older ones had fallen away. I wondered if he could enter a church, or only a chapel where his native earth lay?

I hesitated, with the flakes swirling into my face, the wind biting my cheeks. I did not want him to leave me. He leaned down and kissed me, full on the mouth; then he said, his voice stern as the snow, 'I know not how long I will be gone; in the Scholomance I can rest without my native earth, so I need not return to the Szgany. But I will come back to you as soon as I may – if not with Quincey, with news of him. By then you must have made your choice.'

With that, he stepped away from me, and almost immediately vanished into the swaying curtain of snow, which was growing heavier by the minute. Quickly I entered the church.

Near the altar I found matches and candles, and I lit three – no more, although it hardly seemed possible that anyone would pass the church and see the glow. With the benefit of light, I found there was a stove to the left of the nave, and a good supply of dry wood in a basket beside it. The lighting of this kept me occupied for some time. At last the fire took and I was able to warm myself.

I ate some bread, cheese and sausage, rationing myself, though I had a tremendous hunger from all the walking. Then I settled down in my furs – resting on the floor by the stove, with my back against a wall – and tried to forget my bodily discomforts in prayer.

But I could not pray. God has surely abandoned me, and will never take me back until I repent – but how can I, when Quincey's life is in the scales?

I must make my choice tonight. Oh, impossible, cruel choice!

Opening my eyes again, I noticed the paintings. Every wall was covered with frescoes! There were saints and martyrs looking down upon me, Moses with the stone tablets, Elijah in a chariot drawn by winged horses, Jacob's ladder, a beast with seven heads and the angel of the apocalypse with a face like the sun. They were peasant paintings, naïve and with crooked perspectives, but their very awkwardness gave them an eerie power. They had been clouded by centuries of candlesmoke, and stared at me through the waxy layers as if through a dim veil of time. Tiers of icons glimmered on the decorated screen that separated the nave from the sanctuary. The mingling of candleglow with the snowlight that now filled the windows created the most unearthly effect. The saints watched me with pitying, terrible eyes. And there, arrayed above the screen – the iconostasis – was the Last Judgement; the sinners being cast down into the flames of Hell!

I covered my head, but I could not hide myself from their eyes.

If I am to be damned and suffer eternal torment, I tasted it that night, which seemed to last for ever. Despite the fire I ached to the bones with cold, but this was nothing to my spiritual anguish. I drifted in and out of sleep, but in both states my mind clamoured with terrible images. I heard the screams of the sinners as they fell, cast out for ever from grace. I fell with them, while the angels watched without pity.

It should have been easy, should it not, to choose good above evil; to let my son die at the appointed time – and not try to cheat death or God's will for the sake of my own selfish longings! But still I could not decide.

If Quincey is Dracula's son, do I love him any the less? No, and a thousand times no. There exists no revelation under heaven that could make Quincey less sweet and dear to me.

I kept seeing the noble, harshly carved planes of Dracula's face, his proud eyes gleaming beneath the bushy profusion of his eyebrows; seeing the sadness in his eyes; feeling his lips upon mine; hearing his words, so grave and persuasive. *'What does God care for you, that he would take your son away? Come with me and he will never know death. Only the Undead can truly appreciate life, in all its warmth and richness. Only the Undead.'*

I woke before dawn, to that singular drear bleakness when one's spirits are at the lowest ebb and all breathes with desolation. Embers in the stove glowed coldly red. My candles still burned, but I felt the church trembling from the force of the blizzard outside. The rising and falling moan of the wind sounded deathly. The snow was much worse; I could see it whirling across the windows, against the dim unnatural glow of snowfall. I was so cold now I could not move, could not even shiver.

Then the door of the church burst open. I sat up, very stiff and slow, my body not responding to the alarm of my mind. Snow whirled in on a blast of wind; and through the swirling flakes, as if carried in by them, came two human figures. I knew them – and this time was glad to see them! I called out, 'Dr Seward!' and the next I knew he was kneeling beside me. His face was blue with cold.

'Mina!' he cried, his lips stiff and frozen. 'Van Helsing, I have found her! Oh, thank God. We saw a light in the windows, and came to see what caused it, in the hope – oh, Mina, how are you? How long have you been here? Where is *he*?'

'He has gone after Elena to the Scholomance,' I said, and my lips, also, would barely work. Van Helsing came quickly to me and gave me a sip of plum brandy from his flask. He felt my pulse, looked into my eyes, carefully examined my neck. Meanwhile Dr Seward fed more wood into the stove.

'I am well,' I protested. 'Only chilled.'

'Then you will need all your strength, Madam Mina,' Van Helsing said gravely. The tip of his nose was bright red, like a cherry. 'We have a way to go before we find warmth . . . Why are you smiling?'

'Your nose, Professor!'

He laughed, but it was a grim sound. 'Then make mock of me all you will. Little girl, I would give much to see you smile again, for any reason!'

At that I turned my face away, and could not speak.

They asked if I had seen Elena; I answered that I had not. Van Helsing said, 'Wherever she has gone, I can only pray that she has taken Quincey somewhere safe and warm! Madam Mina, if you can walk, we should go. We must prevent Dracula reaching the Scholomance. Doubtless it is impossible now that we should overtake him, but we must try.'

I got up, summoning what energy I could – for that of a mother trying to rescue her child is never quite exhausted. But when we put our heads outside the door, the blizzard was wilder than ever. Snow filled the sky and lay thickly on the ground, muffling every discernible feature. The world was a white nothingness.

'Dracula has conjured this weather to trap us,' I said. 'We can't follow him but neither can we escape the church!'

As I spoke, a third figure loomed grey through the clotted snow, frightening me so much that I clung to Van Helsing's arm. It came closer, almost to the porch. Its face and hair were crusted with snow, as if it did not feel the cold; the face was white as ice, the lips red, and I knew that this was a vampire – the one I had seen at Carfax Abbey! And I recognized him, and almost cried out.

'Don't be afraid, Mrs Harker,' said this apparition. 'My only wish is to help you. For the esteem in which we held each other in life, I implore you to trust me. I would never harm you or my friends.'

Van Helsing patted my shoulder. 'Kovacs has come with us, to help us find the Scholomance. Without him, we have no chance.'

'No chance, I fear, in this blizzard!' I said.

'Mrs Harker is right,' Dr Seward added. 'Until this dies down, we would be foolish to wander out in it.'

But Kovacs raised a pale hand and beckoned to us. As he did so, I saw other shapes moving behind him which I could not discern through the swirling snow. They were not human.

He said, 'These powers are new to me. If only I had had time to grow adept before Beherit sent me to find Dracula! But come. I will guide you as best I can.'

Through the veils of whiteness I heard deep, animal growls. The moment was so eerie that I could not find my breath. I managed to say, 'Professor Kovacs, I fear there are bears outside.'

Kovacs inclined his head to me. 'Indeed, Mrs Harker. I called them. They will make a path for us.'

I understood, then, that he commanded these beasts as I had seen Dracula command wolves and rats. We made our way – I leaning on Van Helsing's arm and Dr Seward bearing a lamp – down the treacherous drift that had covered the porch steps, and forged into the snowstorm.

The downfall of snow made the air less biting. Five great bears went ahead of us, moving ponderously, with snow crusting in thick ropes on their fur and the steam of their breath clouding from their muzzles. Around us stood great, sculpted drifts of snow, uncannily beautiful; but only the path the bears trod down made it possible for us to walk. Thus we progressed; the animals leading, Professor Kovacs following, with Van Helsing and I in the middle and Dr Seward bringing up the rear. Kovacs looked every inch the gentleman explorer he had been – and was still, I suppose, as Dracula, despite everything, is still the nobleman.

How long the journey took, I cannot now recall. Two days, I believe, although the sameness of it all makes the memory seem both interminable and condensed into a few hours. Van Helsing kept us alert by explaining Professor Kovacs's story as we went. The story might have made me weep, had I had any energy to spare for tears; as it was, it only filled me with deeper dread for Quincey's fate, and with horror of this creature called Beherit.

We took frequent but brief rests to sleep and eat, so that we did not become too cold. When I slept I would dream that I was still walking, but now seeing through Dracula's eyes the same intersecting slopes and lofty forests, the same pyramidal peaks linked by narrow ridges. But now the mountains enclosed me like extensions of my own self, as if this domain were completely mine to command. I was outside humanity but part of earth and nature. Wild animals howled at my passing and answered my unspoken commands. Behind me, billows of snow clouded my footsteps and confounded my enemies; in front, the way was clear and glittering. Even the weather shaped itself to my will. Yet in the dream I – Dracula – had no sense of Elena's presence, no feeling that she was ahead of me, drawing me on. She was absent. It was something darker that drew me.

We were all but dead on our feet when Kovacs at last led us over a ridge – an exhausting climb and descent – and into a small, deep valley. There were tall spruces, through which I glimpsed a snow-covered lake, and around us a circle of jagged, white peaks. I was immediately aware of an atmosphere; a brooding consciousness. An icy wind howled. We were not welcome, I was certain of that. Drifts of snow came whipping at us off the ridge, and we heard the rumbling of an avalanche beginning high above.

Dr Seward gave a warning shout. Van Helsing gripped my arm, just as I saw the bears running away and vanishing between the trees. (I can only hope they escaped and were not buried.) Calling us to follow, Kovacs began to run. We ran after him, gaining the mouth of a cave just as a huge weight of snow broke and slithered down to block the entrance.

In the light of Dr Seward's lamp, we stood in astonished silence. All changed in a few seconds from wild wind and snow to enclosed darkness; and our panic, which at least contained the healthy will to survive, turned to a creeping horror, like that, I imagine, of being buried alive.

Van Helsing was almost purple with exertion, but gruffly dismissed my expressions of concern. The cave in which we stood was musty, and I sensed a soft rustling in the darkness above our heads. 'Now we are trapped,' I said, with a great effort to contain my dread. 'We shall have to dig our way out.'

'No,' said Kovacs. 'This is our destination; the way into the Scholomance.'

I did not want to go. I felt such foreboding I would rather have braved snow, bears, any danger of nature than this. But I swallowed my fear and made no protest.

We turned; we took a few steps deeper into the cave; then it seemed that my very dread surged into a blaze of light which was golden and yet soul-sickening, like the fires of Hell. Through it I glimpsed a figure, tall and bright-haired, almost beautiful except that this was a corrupt beauty, florid, red-dabbled and caked with blood. Grinning horribly, it reached for me. The light vanished, Dr Seward's lamp was extinguished. I heard Dr Van Helsing cry out. Then, in pitch black-ness, I felt hands close on my shoulders, and I fell, and knew no more.

# Chapter Seventeen

When I came back to consciousness, I found myself lying on a couch in a dimly lit room. My head ached; my first thought was of Quincey. I tried to sit up, and then I saw two shadowy figures looking down at me, and my heart throbbed painfully in fear.

The room was plain and sparely furnished, with mosaic walls that put me in mind of a Roman villa. I had a profound sense of being underground, buried. The window had no glass but a sort of honeycomb grille, through which a bluish glow silhouetted the two tall figures who gazed down upon me.

One was Professor Kovacs. He looked white and grizzled with ice, like the corpse of a man who had expired in the snowstorm yet still walked. A smell of damp rose from his clothes, and from my own, for the air here was warm.

The other man, the stranger: it was he who struck the deepest dread into my soul. He might have stepped from a portrait of an Elizabethan alchemist, dressed in a long blood-red robe that hung heavy with embroidery and dull jewels. His hair was golden, his face pure and luminous – reminding me, painfully, of Quincey – yet no one could have perceived him as angelic! His beauty contained all the corruption, laughing cruelty and foul appetites of the damned. I felt coldness, the certainty of death, the unbearable knowledge that I might die without ever knowing what became of Quincey! My soul failed, and I cursed the folly that had led me to discard all holy defences against his kind. His kind? Or mine, also?

I rose to a sitting position, much as it pained me, and he spoke, bowing with apparent courtesy. 'Madam Mina, I bid you welcome to the Scholomance. Do not be afraid; you are safe. I am Beherit. Your journey has been long and arduous, and you deserve all the hospitality I may provide. You will wish to rest and eat . . .'

Now I stood, despite my dizziness. 'Where are my companions?'

'Safe, as are you, Madam Mina. You may see them, in time.'

He seemed to know everything. The next question I could hardly bear to ask, but I must. 'Is my son here? A fair boy with a dark-haired Hungarian woman?'

Beherit paused, a smile playing on his red lips. 'He may be here. You may be allowed to see him, if your conduct pleases me.'

At this I almost fainted. Kovacs caught me, helped me to sit down and held a glass of water to my lips. So I am to be this demon's puppet, as I was the Count's!

'And Dracula?' I asked, my voice trembling.

'Ah, yes, Dracula is here.' As Beherit spoke, Kovacs moved back to his side and both watched me with the same luminous, unearthly stare. 'André has served me well.'

Now I was confused, and angry despite my fear. 'But I understood Professor Kovacs was meant to warn Dracula *against* coming here! He has failed you, surely.'

Beherit answered, 'But what surer way to draw Dracula here than to whet his curiosity, to rouse his war-like and defiant spirit by forbidding him to come? So far from failing me, my dear friend André has fulfilled my plan beautifully!'

Beherit's next action I could hardly believe. He bent to Kovacs and kissed him full on the lips, just as a man would kiss a woman – and Kovacs allowed the kiss, nay, returned it! Now I know for certain that I am in the Devil's realm, where all of nature is turned upside down!

'Will you wish also to see Dracula?' Beherit asked, still caressing Kovacs.

I was unsure how the question might be meant to trap me. 'I – I don't know.'

'Well, all shall be known in time,' he said enigmatically. With that, he and Kovacs bowed to me and left. I ran to the door after them, but found it locked; worse, there was no visible handle or keyhole. My head throbbed and spun from the exertion. Through the window I could see a courtyard, deserted and ghostly; no sign of my companions. When I called, there was no answer. Above the buildings, there was an indistinct darkness; no snow, but an echoey vault like the inside of a great cave. A hollow mountain. The Scholomance.

There is an inner door – an archway concealed by a screen – which leads only to a little room, all marble, with a bath and privy. I say 'only' but this is remarkable; running water, hot and cold! Is such sophistication, such extraordinary architecture, achieved by necromancy? My practical mind will not accept it. I would rather recall the Roman influence upon this land. Yet the mosaic frieze along the white walls – showing, as far as I can tell, scholarly scenes of teachers and students – seems a parody of Roman art; the colours are so darkly succulent as to be repulsive and even the figures seem full of malign insinuation.

Understanding that I am a prisoner, I refreshed myself, then mastered my situation as I always do; by bringing my journal up to date.

### Later

Kovacs has paid me a visit, alone.

I slept for a while and was woken, again, by a presence in the room. I heard a voice say, 'Madam Harker, do not be startled. I have brought you some food.'

For a moment I thought it was Van Helsing! But with a weary mixture of dread and disappointment, I recognized

268

Kovacs, who was setting a tray down on a small marble table. I asked, 'Professor, is Quincey here? Have you seen him? For the sake of our friendship in life, please help me!'

'I cannot help you.'

'Where is Count Dracula? Why doesn't he come to me?'

'Please, Madam Harker. I don't know.' Kovacs came and sat beside me on the couch. He looked at me and then I saw all the horror of his fate in his eyes, in his hangdog white face. Such despair! He said, 'I came back to Beherit in terror, believing I had failed him, but where I expected punishment I found joyful gratitude. Now I have all I desire. Beherit and the library. Yet how hollow it seems to go on without human love from now until Judgement Day!'

His voice was cracked and dry, as if it issued from a corpse! I wanted to show him compassion but I recoiled, unable to help myself. Then his hands shot out and seized my shoulders, like winter twigs, and I felt his breath fall cold upon my neck, and I heard the churning of his tongue over his great sharp teeth.

'In God's name!' I whispered, 'Don't!'

He flung himself away from me with a groan. I fell back on to my elbows, panting for breath. I saw Kovacs by the door, his gnarled hands dangling by his sides and his countenance suffused with shame. 'I should be destroyed. But the library . . . for that I will survive. Nothing matters but the library!'

'Not even my son?' I cried, but the door opened and shut quickly, and I was alone. I dried my tears as swiftly as I might, for my becoming prostrate with grief will aid no one.

Then I ate the meal, which consisted of paprika chicken, potatoes and hot spiced wine. How this was produced I don't know, unless the Szgany serve Beherit as they serve Dracula. I was too hungry to decline the meal, and I tried not to think of the consequences, in fairy tales, of eating 'goblin food'.

Now I feel restored in body, but in mind – ! These monsters are all around me. How, after seeing the evil in Beherit's eyes, the despair in Kovacs's, can I even contemplate Quincey becoming one of them?

Or myself. When it so nearly happened to me the first time, Jonathan said he would rather come with me into that unknown country than let me go into it alone – and no more could I let Quincey enter Undeath without me! I have such fond thoughts of Jonathan now. He seems as wholesome and good as milk against these bloody, brimstone spirits that have stained me!

Yet Jonathan would disown me now, and quite within his rights. My son is not his son. But if he could forgive me, and I him, and if we could accept each other, our faults and sins and all . . .

### Later – 5 December?

Now all is dark, and the end surely not far off. I have time, I hope, to finish this account, if any ever discover it. I have only a few sheets of paper left and I am almost too exhausted to write, but let me record what has happened in order. The lamp will last a little while yet, I pray.

As I was writing my last entry, Beherit came to my room and to my astonishment held open the door, beckoning me to go outside with him. 'Come,' he said, with a passable show of friendliness. 'Walk with me. I would talk to you.'

I did not trust him, but what was the use of refusing? So I went, tucking the sheaf of paper that contains my journal inside my dress but leaving my heavy furs behind. Outside – strangely I remember little of our surroundings, Beherit's voice had such a lulling effect upon me. I recall a dull white courtyard, tumbling ferns, and then dark caverns with an underwater glow glimmering on the walls, shining now and then on a startling mosaic of dragon or serpent. 'You must not fear me,' Beherit said. 'My quarrel is not with you, and my need to restrict your movements only for your own safety. The Scholomance is greater in size than a castle, with many dangers.'

'Then I am free to go?'

'Yes, but how could you go, *sans* friends and child, into that blizzard?'

'Of course, I can go nowhere! But I must know where my companions are.' He ignored my question. I grew outraged. 'Are you a courteous man, Beherit?'

'Naturally.'

'Then do me the courtesy of telling me the truth! I have no power over you, I cannot use this knowledge to harm you. If you ever had one ounce of compassion within you, you would understand my natural feelings as a mother and friend.'

'But try to understand me,' Beherit said. Here I recall we were walking upwards through a sinuous tunnel whose walls were decorated with fantastic and obscene images; even their visceral hues were shocking. The air became steamy and oddly lukewarm. 'Someone cheated me. Someone failed to pay the Devil his due, for which omission I have been held hostage for four hundred years and more, and may be held for ever if the debt is not paid. Dracula must be made to pay.'

I understood, yet in another way felt I did *not* understand. 'You mean he must give himself to the Devil, then you will be free to roam the world?'

'Yes, my dear Madam Harker, as in the Bible; a tooth for a tooth and so on.'

And I could feel the Devil's presence very close; a dragging down of the spirit, a heartlessness, a hollow glee without joy, which sickened me to the very stomach. To think of Beherit at liberty in the world! 'But you insist the Count is here!' I said. 'Isn't that enough to buy your liberty?'

'Not enough,' Beherit said quietly. 'What is he to you?'

I gasped at the impudence of the question. 'That is none of your concern. Sir, you are most impolite.'

'And you are easily offended, madam, for a woman who

271

demands frankness. Yet you didn't answer as I expected, "He is a monster, I wish him dead." You love him, then.'

'That is an extraordinary assumption,' I said. I felt blood rushing to my cheeks. 'There is no love here, nothing but greed for knowledge and power. Dracula was unfortunate to fall among such as you.'

'Unfortunate? I beg you, don't make him a victim of this. Don't you know how powerful, how ruthless he is?'

'But I have seen a nobler side to his nature, of which you cannot conceive. There is no such side to you!' I don't know how I dared speak so provokingly to a vampire who had corrupted Professor Kovacs and murdered his friend Miklos. I forgot myself.

Beherit said, 'But I had brothers to surpass, a father to prove wrong . . .', and I caught just a glimpse of the human he had once been. All humanity worn away by a surfeit of arcane knowledge and centuries of bitter imprisonment. 'You feel some tenderness, at least, for Dracula.'

'Very well, yes, I do. Christian pity.'

At this he gave a smile of such sneering contempt that I blushed. 'The object of your pity arrived less than a day before your party, Madam Mina. I regret to say that we fought and that Dracula fled and locked himself in a section of the library, denying me access. Unless I can persuade him to come out . . .'

His tone was quite soft, not dangerous, or so I thought. But suddenly Beherit stopped and pulled me to face him. Then I saw the fierce rage swimming in his eyes, almost a madness, and I was terrified – not entirely for myself. I saw his sharp ivory wolf-teeth.

'Please, unhand me! There is nothing I can do!'

'You can persuade him to come out.'

'So that you can destroy him?'

Beherit released me. 'I cannot and will not destroy him,' he sighed. 'Believe me. I cannot physically harm him. He is as strong as me, if not stronger. I wish only to talk to him.'

Oh, I so wanted to see Dracula, but I was sure I was being tricked! We walked in silence, and the eerie corridors began to oppress me unbearably. I was aware that if he abandoned me I would be utterly lost! I saw an even stranger glow ahead, a reddish light that cast an unutterable spell of dread over me, and I felt an inrush of foul air; not icy, but unpleasantly warm and sulphur-scented.

The passage gave into a series of antechambers all surfaced in mosaics as richly red as poppies, and then into a great chamber worked with such an obscenity of colour and design that I could not endure it. The bestial scenes, the intensity of the oily purples and dripping, subterranean greens revolted me, and yet I felt that if I looked on them too long I would be quite mesmerized – corrupted! Kovacs described this place. I can add nothing, for I have seen images no Christian woman should see.

Beherit took me towards the grotesque, obsidian dragon statue, and between its great claws to the door Kovacs so dreaded. I felt no great fear, only mixed fascination and anxiety. The door was translucent white with darkness behind it. Beherit opened it and led me through.

We came out upon a long ledge of rock that ran high above a gloomy chasm. Disorientated, I clung to his arm in shock. Beyond the ledge on which we stood soared a cavern so vast I could see neither the far side nor the roof. The air was damp, and somewhat rank; draughts moved sluggishly through the darkness. By instinct I wanted to cling back against the wall, but Beherit drew me forwards to the very edge.

I gasped. The slippery ledge on which we stood was the lip of a cliff that fell a hundred feet sheer towards an underground lake! One thing gave me the courage to remain there; that there was a great protective gate or fence running along the lip, like the black, spaced railings of a graveyard. To left and

273

right it ran, and upwards, vanishing into darkness. Resting a hand on one of these railings, I looked into the void.

I saw the same faint light that shines everywhere reflected off the lake far below, and a different light coming from beneath the lake, as if from an underwater fissure that looked fathomless. Deep in the abyss there was a globe of dull bronze light, like . . . oh, dear God, like a great baleful eye under the water!

'What is it?' I said.

As my words died, I saw a roiling under the surface, as if the glowing sphere were rippling and rising. A great bubble surged upwards. I watched in alarm, as if some hellish monster were about to unleash itself upon the world. The bubble breached the surface in a plume of steam and spray; nothing more, but the stench of brimstone that drifted up made me cough. Little flames danced on the water for a moment, then all turned to coldest, darkest blue. But the eye was still there in the fissure. All of this filled me, not with clear terror, but with darkest unease.

'The Cauldron of the Dragon,' Beherit said with a soft laugh in his voice. 'The lake in the valley passes under the roots of the mountain and surfaces again here; a dual lake, of darkness and light. The Cauldron in which all things are made and destroyed. We name it also the Gate. And then again, *Yadu Drakuluj.*'

'Why did you wish me to see it?'

'I am showing you my domain, like a good host. But we were speaking of Dracula . . .' I said nothing. Beherit took my hand and kissed it, an intimacy I did not want or invite; looking into my eyes he said, in a soft malicious tone like the very Devil, 'Your child, Madam Mina. If you wish to see him again you will answer me. Does Dracula love you?'

'I won't answer!' I cried, pulling free. 'Your question is obscene. You are a liar. This is a place of lies, and a cap over the very mouth of Hell! Sir, if my Quincey is here, I must insist that you take me to him at once!'

I cursed my outburst, for I hated to show my weakness to this creature. I felt suddenly desperate to flee from him, from this madness; I took a few steps away, but Beherit did not move or speak. I stopped where I was, leaning on a railing. I had an overwhelming sense that I stood on the threshold of a vast graveyard, where ghosts and vampires moaned, and the black-clad figure of the Grim Reaper walked slowly towards me . . .

There came voices, at first afar, then close at hand; a lamp shone in my eyes so brightly that for a moment I could not see. Then Van Helsing's face appeared through the glare! 'Madam Mina! Kovacs brought us to you – thank God!'

I saw Dr Seward just behind him. Both men were panting for breath, as if their search for me had been long and arduous. Seward was brandishing a cross at Beherit, who withdrew slowly and with an expression of contempt, until I could not see him in the shadows. I saw Kovacs in the temple doorway, more than ever as pale as a walking corpse.

They clutched my hands, Seward and Van Helsing, but I could not respond to their expressions of concern. 'I am well,' I said. 'No, I have not seen Quincey or Elena – or Dracula.'

'Nor have we,' said Seward.

We talked rapidly, I relating my experience, then Seward giving his own account: 'We blundered about in the dark for a long time – I could not relight my lamp – until we found ourselves in the ten-sided chamber of which Kovacs wrote. It was only then that I got the lamp lit, by which time you and Kovacs had long vanished. We were trapped there for many hours. The experience came close to unmanning me, I must confess. The body of poor Miklos was still there. The severed head . . . I'm a doctor, I have cut up my fair share of cadavers – but still this made me almost sick to see and smell it! Van Helsing saved us; after much exertion he found a secret mechanism that caused a door, a quite invisible door, to open. As we explored, Kovacs found us, and we made him bring us to you. Kovacs has betrayed us; he was only ever acting for Beherit! I don't know what loyalty we expected of a vampire.'

I hardly knew what to say to them. These men who are so dear to me seemed to be strangers! 'You must be exhausted,' I said. 'I have at least had rest and food.'

Van Helsing waved his hand impatiently, as if bodily needs could not matter less. His face was wrought with strain, yet his eyes still gleamed with the look of wonder I knew so well. 'But what a place is this! The Devil's or not – a structure of the most extraordinary engineering. Weighted doors, magnets, subtle mechanisms; heat from some underground fire, technology the Romans possessed but which we have lost; science in advance of our own! What tragedy that we come here in such circumstances and not as discoverers!'

Beherit said contemptuously from the shadows, 'To seek knowledge of the Devil, whom you profess to despise?'

Kovacs added, 'You accuse me of betrayal, yet it is in my nature to betray the living. But look at the library, my friends, before you condemn me. Millions of books believed lost, burned, destroyed. A complete perfect copy of the Dead Sea Scrolls. Treasures you can't guess at.' I saw a glint of temptation in Van Helsing's eye. 'Why is your scholarship godly and ours evil?'

'I am tempted to ask the same question,' said Beherit, 'but I will not.' He came into the lamplight; Seward lifted the cross again. Revulsion flickered on Beherit's face but he said, 'Please, put down your holy weapon. I am not your enemy. We all wish Dracula destroyed, do we not? Therefore let us call a truce and help each other.'

I saw my two companions exchanging cautious looks. But

I was horrified. I said, 'No! Professor, don't listen to him! You cannot take his side against Dracula. Can't you see that Beherit is even worse?'

'But Madam Mina, our priority, our only hope of saving Quincey, is to destroy the Count, that monster!'

Van Helsing looked keenly at me; I could see he was already lost! Corrupted, like Kovacs! Some strand within me, stretched beyond tolerance, now broke, and I turned away and went running along the rock, holding up my skirts around my ankles, the cliff edge and the tall railings to my right, the cave wall on my left.

This wall curved in front of me, but there was a fissure within it, a short tunnel into which I ran, thinking to hide but finding only a dead end. I know not what I meant to achieve with this flight. I acted in desperation, that is all I know.

I heard the others coming after me. Then a light flooded from the blank end of the tunnel and a voice said, 'Mina!'

A hand seized mine, pulling me through a doorway into a small well-lit room. A door slid shut behind me; glancing around, I saw there was only a bookshelf where I had entered. And before me stood Dracula!

His hair had gone almost white again, but with stark black streaks; the effect against his austere black clothes was startling and handsome. His face, ageless, with its bushy brows and strong nose and the deep-coloured lips lifting over the great white teeth . . . he looked serious, tender, yet monstrous, like some infinitely wise yet utterly depraved necromancer . . . and yet I forgave him this. He held my hands; he embraced me. I think I wept.

'Can Beherit come in here?' I asked.

'No, the doors are locked. Has he harmed you? I never meant to place you in danger! It would have been wiser if you had travelled with me, or stayed in the church . . .'

'He hasn't harmed me,' I said. 'He only asked questions

about you, which I refused to answer. I am so tired. I want my son and I want to go home.'

'Come, sit with me,' said Dracula. 'You are safe here. I have so missed your company, Mina.'

This was part of the library that I had blundered into; a small, octagonal reading room, with a pattern resembling the points of a compass on the floor, and a cupola above, painted blue-black with silver stars. The walls were lined with shelves, but all the books were shut up behind heavy leaded glass. The whole room was in white and black marble, and windowless; the light came from candles and an antique lamp.

We sat at a round marble-inlaid table in the centre. One large volume lay open upon it; I glimpsed rows of arcane symbols and medieval etchings of demons before Dracula closed it and pushed it aside. Sorcery.

We began to speak, like long-lost friends, of all that had befallen us since we parted. Dracula sat very still and upright as he spoke, one hand resting on the table. 'When I arrived, Beherit attacked me, which was no more than I had expected; I shut myself in here, not because I fear him, which I do not, but so that he would leave me in peace with the books.'

'Are the books all that concern you?' I said, sharp with fear. 'What about Quincey and Elena? You have said not one word about them. Are they here? If not, I can only think that they have died in the snow! But you must know!'

'Ah, Mina.' He was shaking his head, pressing my hands between his own. 'I have led you amiss, I fear. Higher considerations have required me to be less than truthful; for that, I beg your pardon. They are not here, but I assure you they are not dead.'

A mingled wave of anger and confusion swept through me. 'Then where – ?'

'Quincey and Elena never left England. They are quite

safe at Carfax. You will be reunited with your son as soon as you go home; in that, I did not lie.'

My emotions at this news – I cannot even begin to express their intensity! I trembled, I all but swooned. At first I was so relieved I could have fallen on him in gratitude; the next moment I was ablaze with fury. 'You lied to me! You lied, to bring me here! Why?'

He appeared unmoved by my passion. 'Because I wanted you to share in this, Mina. Forget Beherit, he is a mere caretaker; I speak of this glorious knowledge.'

'No. More likely I was a mere shield, to keep your enemies at a distance! I stopped them destroying you, because I thought Quincey –!'

Dracula nodded; shamelessly, I thought, although there was no mockery in his demeanour. He seemed weary and thoughtful, as if he carried the weight of history on his shoulders. 'Your presence has been strategic, Mina; I would not deny that. But I have made you my helper now solely in order to make you my beloved companion in the future.'

'And what of Elena? You seem to think nothing of discarding those who have been useful!'

A red gleam came into his eyes. 'You are unjust. Elena will be with us too. She has served me and loved me well. We are not bound by the narrow laws of your petty society, that I may take only one bride or you one husband. And I have been without a family for too long. Your Van Helsing destroyed the last of those dear to me.'

He sounded so sorrowful that I could only with immense difficulty feel anything but compassion for him. And this is how he wears me down, exciting not evil in me but my tenderest passions! Even knowing consciously, with wide-open eyes, that this is the Devil's work – I still cannot turn aside!

I asked, 'Have you found what you hoped to find here?'

'Such a process cannot be realized in a day. It may take

279

years, but time is on my side. If Beherit tries to hinder me, he will suffer. He tricked me, of course – or so he thinks.'

'In what way?'

The Count gave a cruel smile that showed his teeth in all their sensual sharpness. 'He knew that if poor Kovacs said to me, "Do not under any circumstances go to the Scholomance," I would immediately wish to come here. Although I saw the deceit for what it was, it made me stop and reflect. Beherit is and ever was, you see, an unholy fool. There *is* knowledge here.'

'Which no Christian should possess!'

'And since I am no Christian; I believe there could be, in truth, a remedy in the Scholomance for all the restrictions that have plagued my immortal existence.'

'So you came here with no thought of redemption, only of increasing your evil powers.'

'Don't think you can redeem me,' Dracula said fiercely. 'Accept what I am, for I will never change. Yet believe this; I spurn the Devil! Kovacs sold his soul for access to undreamed-of wisdom – as did I. But I refused to pay. Therein lay my crime. I was the tenth scholar, chosen by the Devil to be taken in payment for the rest – but I have been warrior, warlord and *boyar*, and I bow down to no one, not even to Satan himself. I refused to give myself up; I killed those who tried to force me. Beherit was the only one left alive – Undead, rather – and he has spent hundreds of years in my place, waiting for me to return. Now he learns that it has done him no good.'

All of this he said quite calmly. I asked, 'Then you don't serve the Devil?'

'I care nothing for him or for God!'

'But if you don't serve God you *must* aid the Devil. And you still fear God, or you would not flinch from holy symbols!'

'Do leave aside your theology, Mina. Your reasoning may be correct. But Beherit is right, I left here too soon, before I armed myself with the arcane secrets that would free me from all such constraints.'

Now I sensed a trace of desperation in Dracula that I had never marked before. 'Beherit means to harm you. I think he is afraid of you, and jealous.'

'He can neither harm nor command me, and he knows it. I ask only that he let me alone to conduct certain studies and experiments. You should stay, Mina; you would be more than comfortable here, and I will protect you from his foolishness. Is there not the slightest curiosity in you about this forbidden knowledge? No taint of Eve? Women were taken as students here. Lucifer, they say, has an especial fondness for women . . .'

'Were you really tutored by the Devil himself?' I whispered. 'What did he . . . look like?'

'Like Beherit. Like each student's reflection; he stole our reflections, indeed. Like an exquisite black-haired woman. A horned snail. A little golden child . . .' I could not tell if he were serious or mocking. He went on, 'We can send for Quincey and Elena as soon as the weather is more clement.'

I turned quite hollow inside, and could not speak. Beherit seemed nothing now; Count Dracula was the only lord of this domain. He gripped my hand more tightly, saying, 'Well? Quincey will join us, will he not? You must have made your decision.'

And I had, although I did not realize it until that moment. The Count might kill me where I stood for making my answer, but that was better than being toyed with and tormented over my poor son's soul.

'Yes,' I said firmly. 'I have made my decision. If Quincey's days are meant to be short, God's will be done. I would rather nurse a broken heart the rest of my days than think that I had condemned a child's soul – and who knows how many others through him – to eternal damnation!'

Dracula flung my hand from him, and rose so abruptly

his chair flew back and hit the floor with a bang. His eyes blazed. The white brows knotted above the hard lines of his face, and his wolf-teeth showed in all their terrible bestiality. He seized me by the shoulder, lifting me so that I hung from his broad hand, gasping with the pain. And the pale infernal light that glared from his face! I feared for my life – and yet it was that very hellish light that told me I had made the right decision. I could never be a part of this. Even if it cost me my life!

He shook me. 'How dare you defy me!' He gathered me to him and I felt his lips and teeth on my throat; I thought that was the end. Yet I felt his mouth relax, and move over my jaw and cheek to rest in my hair. Dracula wept.

I believe I ceased to resist him then. I allowed his embrace, even returned it, my shoulders softening and my head falling back. Holding me, he spoke softly and desperately. 'Mina, I love you. I have a powerful will to live, yes, but that will is all for you. If you reject me – what then is left?'

I could not answer. There was nothing I could say. I had no words of comfort; how can such an awesome being be comforted? Tears fell from my eyes. I can't express the pain I felt – feel. For I so wanted to tell him . . . but I could not. Because of Quincey, because I cannot give us both up to damnation.

Presently he put me away from him and spoke, very grave and sad. 'Ah Mina, I cannot complain at your determination. It was your very strength that drew me to you.'

He kissed my hand and bowed his head to me, as if acknowledging the end of a contest. 'Quincey will live,' he said, his tone soul-weary. 'He will grow out of his childhood weakness and thrive.'

'How can you know that?'

'We studied all arts here; medicine as well as alchemy, necromancy, weaponry and the command of nature. I gave him, while he was in my care, certain mixtures to strengthen his constitution. But you will see for yourself.' He turned away.

I knew then that everything had changed. That when he gave his word to accept my refusal, he meant it! But to realize this was more than astonishing. To think that Count Dracula would, at my bidding, cease to haunt me, cease to persuade or seduce my good intentions to bad – I felt as if some great prop had been jerked away from under my very being, leaving me in a heap upon the earth.

I had won my liberty, and now was not at all sure I wanted it. Do not judge, you who read this, that women are weak, unless you, also, have had to make the decision that I made!

The Count looked up into the starred cupola. 'The sun rises outside. I would rest awhile. If you wish to leave me, as no doubt you will . . .' He showed me levers, in two of the eight walls, that would open the concealed doors. 'But keep vigil over me, Mina, for old times' sake.' He lay down at one side of the room, hands folded over his chest, as if the room itself were his sepulchre; and while he lies as if dead, I sit at the table and write.

I have sat alone here now for hours. What will befall me when the sun – although here the night is eternal – sets again in the outside world? I dread to think. I can imagine no future. I cannot imagine myself ever holding Quincey in my arms again.

What will become of me now? There is nothing left. Never in my life have I felt so cold and desolate as I do now; the candles burn low, the lamp begins to fail. Now this journal is more to me than the friend and the discipline it has been; it is my only lifeline, the veritable thread of my sanity! And even this is fading. There is no more paper. If I am still here when Dracula rises I know I will become Undead . . . I must leave but I dare not; I dread what lies outside, while here at least is a devil I know – all too well. Shadows walk around me, and I hear voices whispering, and Beherit's footsteps coming closer, and the protective walls rent like veils. Oh, heaven help me! Farewell, Quincey. Farewell, all.

## JOHN SEWARD'S MEMORANDUM

I must finish this account, much as it pains me, for Mrs Harker cannot.

We were distraught when she vanished; the more so when Beherit told us that the secret door through which she had passed led to the library room in which Dracula had ensconced himself! But Beherit calmed us. 'Dracula will not harm her, of that I am sure. Have you not seen evidence of it? He has been long enough in her company to take her life a dozen times over, yet she is still human, still alive. Think, we have them trapped. We will use this time to plan our campaign. Our greatest problem is to unlock the doors; I do not know how it is to be done.'

Van Helsing said, 'But might you not enter the room in a changed form, as mist?'

'You fail to understand, some laws of our existence are suspended within the Scholomance. We can rest without our native earth, but we cannot change our forms. Such tricks, you see, impress humans but would be an insult to our Master. The doors are not flimsy barriers of wood; they are thick, impenetrable, held shut by subtle mechanisms that cannot be forced . . .'

I said, 'And if we do gain access and surprise them?'

'Do as I say, but do not question me,' said Beherit. I was more doubtful than Van Helsing, but made no protest – would that I had! 'Yes, I am of the Devil's party and you of God's, but this I swear; my only desire is to make Dracula pay his debt. I wish no harm to the rest of you. Aid me now and you will be allowed to leave safely, you will never hear a word of me again. God strike me down if I lie!'

And we were so desperate to destroy Dracula and free

Mina from his foul influence, and to find the poor little boy, if he lived still, that we agreed. I still do not know, for all my agonizing, what else we could have done!

Beherit had Kovacs take us to a chamber, and left us there to eat and rest. Presently Beherit returned. He made no explanation of his business, but his face was agleam with a malevolent joy that made my soul revolt. I surmised that he had found some way, distasteful as it is, of spying upon Dracula and Mrs Harker! He said only, 'Now I know all that I need to know. Dracula sleeps.'

'Then we must rescue Mrs Harker without delay!' I said.

'The doors will take time . . .'

'We do not need to force them,' Van Helsing broke in excitedly. 'Madam Mina, forgive my indelicacy, will be prompted by her human needs to leave the room eventually. We have only to wait!'

'You are a clever man, Professor,' Beherit replied with a languid air. 'You would have made such a scholar . . . But we must plan carefully, for the moment we take Mina, Dracula will wake, be it day or night. Now no harm will befall your Mina, I promise. We require her only to lure Dracula out . . .'

So we made our plans. I lost all sense of time and felt buried alive, trapped in eternal night, wretched and anxious. But Van Helsing, poring over plans of the library with Beherit, unravelling the secrets of the Scholomance's bizarre structure, was in his very element. Ah, he was not to know that Beherit's promise was worthless!

There were two doors into the reading room where Dracula had so arrogantly ensconced himself. One led out upon the cliff above the underground lake; the other led into the main body of the library. This was where Kovacs and I waited, I with an implement somewhat resembling a crowbar in hand, sharp at one end and hooked at the other. The door itself had panelling of polished white marble, engraved with a pattern that disturbed the eye, compelling it endlessly along sinister mazes to nowhere. How I grew to loathe it! The mysterious library behind us lay in gloom, and I felt imprisoned in an underground purgatory, the victim of some hellish joke.

The waiting was long and arduous, but at length I heard a soft noise. The door drew back, and a sliver of candle-light appeared. For a moment I saw Mrs Harker's face in the gap, white and thin as a ghost's! At once I forced my crowbar across the jamb, and hooked the door's edge, so that she could neither open nor close it. Mrs Harker struggled briefly with the door; then she paused, staring straight at us through the gap. The look of terror that suffused her face! It must have been the sight of Kovacs that so alarmed her. She withdrew; I could not see what she was doing. I allowed her a few seconds – as we'd agreed – before I pushed open the heavy door.

As we entered, we were just in time to see a section of the wall to our left swinging inwards, and the hem of Mrs Harker's skirts flaring out around her booted ankle as she fled. I knew Van Helsing and Beherit were waiting for her, out upon the rock ledge. All had gone to plan. I saw Dracula lying in his death-sleep on the marble floor . . . Then his eyes opened and he rose; going from death to violent animation in an instant! I caught one glimpse of his furious, pallid face, before he strode out after Mina.

The moment he'd gone I hurried after him across the room, through the second door and down the short tunnel that led into the cavern. Kovacs followed me, bringing the hooked pole; a useful weapon, I thought.

As we reached the ledge I heard Mrs Harker scream! No sign of the Count; the next I knew, there was a roar of rage *behind* me, and Dracula seized me and flung me up against the railings that guarded the cliff edge.

The pain and shock were so great they all but blinded me. The Count's face almost touched mine, distorted and horrific with fury, like some beast-demon. I thought my end had come. But then there came a shout from further along the ledge.

'Dracula!'

The Count looked round. With a snarl, he lifted me off the rails and flung me down hard upon the rock.

I was stunned for a few seconds, and could see no more than colours upon the darkness. I came back to myself to find Van Helsing leaning over me. 'My friend, can you get up?' he said, grave and urgent. 'Beherit promised safety for Madam Mina once we had lured Dracula from his hiding-place – not this! I caught her but she was taken from my arms. *Ah, mijn God.* Let me help you, Jack . . .'

Through this I could hear the Count speaking furiously in the deep, commanding voice that few can resist. I could not tell what he was saying, only that his fury was directed at Beherit.

As I got to my feet, I saw the cause of Dracula's rage and Van Helsing's distress. A short distance from us, no more than thirty feet, I saw Beherit with Mrs Harker in his arms. She seemed paralysed, as if he held her with hypnosis or with pure terror. She was bent back across his arm, her neck exposed and gleaming in the faint luminosity; I could see the movement of her throat as she panted for breath.

Beherit was holding out his palm against Dracula, who stood facing him just beyond arm's reach, a towering figure in black. 'I will not loose her,' said Beherit. 'And if you come one step closer I will tear out her throat! Now move back. Back!'

Dracula complied – one could not say *obeyed* of such a man – edging a little way towards Van Helsing and myself, where we stood supporting each other. I could not see what had become of Kovacs. Then Beherit began a chant – an incantation – I know not how to describe the hideous syllables that came surging from his mouth!

The Count shouted, 'No!', followed by furious words in Hungarian – yet even his powerful voice began to be drowned by Beherit's.

Louder and louder Beherit roared, until I was forced to put my hands over my ears. Even that would not block out the chanting. The horror of it was not the physical volume but the unutterable sense of evil that the words stirred, a sense of gathering doom and horrors beyond human comprehension. In desperation I drew out my wooden cross, only for it to slip from my fingers and go tumbling through the railings and down towards the lake far below.

Staring at the water, I shook Van Helsing's arm in astonishment. All over the surface, little flames were dancing! As we watched, we saw an orange globe, deep in an underwater fissure, glowing brighter and brighter. The surface began to churn. Light ran across it in veils and skeins of palest yellow; this seemed uncommonly beautiful at first, but as the pattern became wilder, the glow redder, the beauty seemed to sicken into something unspeakably grotesque. Gusts of heat and choking sulphur came sweeping up to us and the cavern walls flushed red. Beherit's fair hair streamed back in the foul updraught.

The lake was turning to fire!

Beherit was doing this, waking the dragon that guarded the very gates of Hell. The air shook with the force of the incantation; the mountain itself began to tremble under our feet. Dracula went on commanding him to stop, but he could do nothing, for Beherit held Mina . . . and I realized then that Dracula, even Dracula was not wholly evil, for Beherit was the one who cared nothing for her life. Mina – she would excuse this familiarity, I know, being no less than a sister to me – Mina had been right when she warned us against him. Every time we disregard her judgement it leads to disaster!

'Behold!' Beherit shouted suddenly.

The whole lake was burning. It was not a fire upon the surface of the water; rather the water itself had turned to flame, while great columns of light and of molten droplets came roaring up from the depthless chasm. I glimpsed a boiling pit, redness seething through a black crust. The noise was of a great furnace roaring. My face was scorched.

A screeching noise behind us made us look round. I saw, in the baleful reflected glow, Kovacs in a recess of rock, grappling a great black wheel that was wrought with suns, moons and planets in shining metals. As he turned it, a terrible sound roared out; the scream of metal against rock, of chains rattling and huge cogs grinding. The railings that guarded the edge of the cliff were rising into the air, catching flashes of light as they rose above our heads into the darkness.

I seized Van Helsing and we drew each other away from the lip. We had been leaning on those rails! Now there was nothing to keep us from the drop. We withdrew, but Beherit remained on the very edge, with Mina in his arms.

'Look,' said Beherit, his voice suddenly quiet yet very clear. 'Be still a moment and look on this wonder. Few can say they have looked into the very mouth of Hell. This is the Gate, as Dracula knows full well. This is where our Master dwells. Once opened, the Gate cannot be closed again without sacrifice. This is the Cauldron of the Dragon for whom your family the Draculas were named – and named well! *Yadu Drakuluj* – the Devil's Abyss!'

The Count's face was livid, its hard lines painted with red fire from below. 'Let Mina go. Let all of them go. This quarrel is between you and I alone, Beherit.'

'True,' said the demon. 'But I won't release them until your debt is paid, for you are treacherous, Dracula. My whole existence has been mortgaged to your folly. Pay the Devil his due. You know what is required!'

Their forms were outlined by wildly leaping fire, Beherit red and gold, Dracula stark black, his white hands and face stained with scarlet. He said, 'I am not at your command. The Devil himself does not command me, and you are only his lapdog. I say again, let her go.'

'But I know that you love her,' said Beherit, sneering.

'She is nothing to me,' Dracula answered. 'Mere refreshment.'

'Liar.'

So saying, Beherit gripped Mina in both hands and held her out over the drop! She came to life, struggling and gasping in breathless horror; becoming as suddenly motionless when she realized that her struggles made it more likely that she would fall. She was coughing, her eyes streaming from the stench. Van Helsing's face worked with impotent fear and he cried out in protest, to no effect. I grew afraid for him, his face was so ill-coloured.

Dracula roared, 'Beherit!' He made an abortive lunge, stopping dead as stone when the demon gave Mina a threatening shake. She made not a sound, but her face was ashen.

Beherit said, 'Either you throw yourself into the Abyss, Count Dracula, and give yourself up to our sovereign – or I cast your beloved into the fire!'

I had never seen Dracula so racked with despair. He took a step towards Beherit, who stepped neatly away. 'Thrust me in and she goes with me,' Beherit said. 'What choice have you? I heard the words you spoke to her in your grief. She rejected you, and you answered that without her love, you have no reason to continue. From this death there is no return. You know I would throw her to Hell without a second thought. I have no mercy.'

Dracula's face was hideous with anguish. He seemed to age as I watched him! In the pause that followed, I felt a growling undernote, as if the roots of the mountain were trembling. I was almost faint with dread. How could we be sure that Dracula would *not* destroy Mina to save himself? For Beherit to gamble with her life in this way was an atrocity, never part of our plan!

When Dracula spoke his voice was hoarse and hollow as death, 'And what guarantee will you give me that if I do throw myself through the Gate, she will live?'

'My promise, that is all. Here stand her dear friends, her champions. Once you are gone from between us, I will hand her back to them. I have no interest in causing her death for its own sake. You must believe me. For if you don't, she *will* die.'

Dracula stared at Mina. She raised her head and stared back at him, her face pallid with terror and appeal. 'No,' she said, to my shock. 'Don't do it, not for my sake.'

'Count Dracula, you must!' Van Helsing broke in harshly. 'For her, and for all the sorrow you have caused!'

Dracula pointed a shaking finger at Van Helsing. 'I curse you!' he said. 'May you know how it feels to die as my beloved women died, pierced to the very heart! I curse you!'

'Your life,' said Beherit, dangling Mina over the boiling chasm, 'or hers.'

Dracula became very still and dignified. He gave Van Helsing and me a hard, cold glare. 'I charge you to hold Beherit to his word. May you save Mina or share my fate! My will to live has been taken from me – but remember this, that I put her life, her priceless blood, above my own!'

Then he looked at Mina, and his eyes became tender, his demeanour gentle. So noble and dignified he seemed in that moment, the knowledge that such a man had devoted his life to evil seemed an insupportable tragedy. Mina gazed back at him, her mouth open and tears flowing down her face. In the reflected light the moisture shone like fire. Ah, I would have done anything to shield her from such suffering!

'Mina,' said Dracula, 'all my desire for life was contained in you, in your blood and flesh and soul. And you have rejected me. You are a crueller lover than ever I was! Since one of us must die, let the remaining life be yours. Much as I have loved my existence, I love yours more. Remember: I do this so that your son may not be deprived of his mother's tender love! Farewell, Mina. Take care of the child.'

And with those words, Dracula stepped to the very edge and leapt.

An ear-splitting cry of anguish rang off the walls. 'No!'

It was Mina who cried out. The agony of grief and loss in her voice rent me to the core. It will haunt me for ever; I might have expected to hear no more and no less for the death of her very son! '*No, no!*'

Dracula's form plummeted towards the flames, black against the red, his clothes fluttering in the fierce updraught. He broke the glowing crust and was gone. But then the Abyss began to roil and heave, and the heat came boiling upwards so strongly that I feared we would all perish.

Beherit was laughing. He set Mina down rather carelessly, as if he were not so much eager to keep his promise as no longer interested in her. Van Helsing and I started towards Mina. At first she appeared dazed, tear-streaked. She turned a little, saw us coming, but did not fly to our arms. Then, a change! I had never seen her face so resolute, so absolutely pure in its intent – as if Dracula's death had redeemed her, his sacrifice transforming her from fallen soul to fierce saint.

Above us, the fence was descending as Kovacs turned the wheel.

As it fell, Mina turned again to Beherit. With his arms raised in exultation, he was paying her no heed. She ran at him and with her little hands gave him a quick, strong push. Beherit slipped. His face dropped in horror. He fell.

He went curving, tumbling down the drop, and the fire swallowed him in a great gout of molten gold droplets.

I screamed, for Mina, too, lost her footing and was slipping towards the edge! Then the railings came down with a great clang, the Gates of Hell indeed, and she slid against them and came to rest on the very lip.

I reached her first, leaving Van Helsing behind. Mina clung to me, shuddering with spent emotion. As I helped her up, she gasped and said, 'Oh, Dr Van Helsing is ill!'

I saw the Professor, my dear friend, leaning against the railings a few feet from us. He was clutching his chest, his face was grey with pain; yet he was waving his free hand at the shadows, trying to tell us something – trying to warn us, as I realized too late! 'Seward – ah, the pain, my heart –' and all this time the fires went on churning, the mountain rumbling ever more violently.

Through it came an indistinct, half-human sound, a sort of keening. Had I only understood what it was, could I have prevented – ?

As Van Helsing extended his hand helplessly to me, the keening I could not identify rose to a full-pitched, ghastly, deep scream and Kovacs came rushing towards Mina, brandishing a length of metal like a spear. It was the implement I had used to jam the door, now held with the sharp end aimed at Mina's heart. I have never heard such a cry of animal grief! *'Beherit! You killed Beherit!'*

I was paralysed, too slow to pull Mina away. Instead, it was Van Helsing who flung himself in front of her! I stared in unutterable horror as Kovacs drove the spear-tip into Van Helsing's chest; only then did I wrench Mina backwards, just barely in time, for the sharp point came right through his body and would have pierced her too! As we got clear, Kovacs bore Van Helsing down and pinned him to the rock.

Our poor, dear friend! Mina hid her face in my shoulder but, God help me, I shall never forget the look on his face! Kovacs glared at us, his unhuman face ghastly and flecked with red foam. I thought he would attack Mina again. I was ready for him. Instead he seemed to have a change of heart, as if some unbearable despair overcame him. With a hoarse groan he turned away, forced his way through two of the railings and leapt, flailing, after his evil companions into the maw of flame.

Through my tears I saw blood forming a great stain across Van Helsing's chest and dripping on to the floor. I could see he was dead, with that shocked expression frozen on his noble features. I believe I fell on him, weeping, pleading with him to rise again; it was Mina who pulled me away and brought me back to my senses. 'Come, John, please, we must go. There's nothing you can do for him. Come on!'

As I looked up, it seemed the whole fiery lake was on the point of exploding. Burning fountains of magma erupted. I saw a great shape rising from the Abyss, a ghostly, wavering form of bronze light with staring red orbs for eyes. The orbs fixed us, glowing and swirling with the rage of Lucifer; for a moment I was convinced its great head was snaking down to consume us!

With a cry, I dragged Mina away.

Both sobbing, we ran. It seemed the whole mountain was quaking with the rage of Hell and Heaven. There was a deafening crack. Mina cried, 'Look!'

And I saw, ahead of us, a blade of light falling through the rock wall on to the ledge; faint and greyish, but clear and pure as water in contrast. The upheaval of Hell, whether in rage or unholy joy at receiving its own, had forced open a crack in the mountainside.

Whether God opened that fissure to rescue us, or Satan to expel us, I know not. It was enough to be free; to breathe the icy, fresh air in place of that sulphurous stench! As we came stumbling over a mass of rock and out on to a snow-covered slope, we saw that a dozen fissures had opened at the base of the mountain, and that molten lava was flowing out to melt the snow to steam. We ran, with the ground bucking and trembling beneath us, until we could run no more; and then we stopped and looked back at the barren peaks against a dead grey sky, as the last tremors subsided, and wondered if Satan had only been waiting for Dracula to return before he woke the Dragon in the lake and destroyed the Scholomance.

I said, hoarse and broken, 'Quincey . . .'

It was then that Mina told me of Dracula's lie. And all for a lie we came here. We thought of Van Helsing, and wept, and she held my head on her breast as if I were a child. When I looked up again, the clouds had broken, and the moon shone brilliantly, washing the snow-veiled mountains in the most glorious white light; and Mina and I raised our eyes to this splendour and shared, in the midst of our sorrow, a moment of divine peace.

For Abraham Van Helsing, there are no words. He died as he lived: a hero.

# Epilogue

I returned to Hermannstadt in the spring, when the snow-line had retreated and the weather was clement enough to allow a comfortable expedition. I retraced our steps precisely; every detail of it was engraved upon my mind. I used compass and maps; I knew the shapes and angles of the peaks against the skyline; there was no mistaking the gorge and the ridge beyond which the Scholomance lay.

And yet I could not find it.

On the far side of the ridge, the valley I remembered, with its circle of fanged rocks and its deep green lake, was not there. I found only a plain slope dropping into a spruce forest. I searched and searched; I went in circles, I tried from every angle.

There was no valley, no lake, no cave.

The Scholomance, it seemed, had ceased to exist. Or perhaps it is that the Devil has sealed the entrance against us. He opened it for a while, for his own purposes – and when payment was exacted, he slammed the great rocky jaws shut against all intruders.

We should be glad of that, I suppose. God forbid that they should ever open again, spill forth their vile contents or draw more souls – whether innocent or corrupt – into their maw!

I did what little I could for our friend Abraham, my dearest friend and teacher; that is, I placed flowers for him on the ridge, and there said a prayer for his immortal soul. He would be glad to see, at least, how happily and passionately attached are Jonathan and Mina, how well Quincey thrives; to know

297

that his lifelong crusade against the darkness did not come to nothing.

Many days after the terrible events in the Scholomance, when Mina showed me the journal she had kept upon writing paper during her captivity and asked me to complete her account, she made confessions of such trusting intimacy, such as may be made only between patient and doctor or the dearest of friends, that I could not help but be moved.

'I shall never keep a journal again,' she told me with gentle sadness, 'for it would only remind me of those terrible times. Jonathan and I already have too much to remind us, in our own memories and in each other.'

I had thought, after all that had befallen – not Dracula's evil alone, but Elena's – that there could never be peace between them again. Somehow, in my awkward way, I said as much. I thought Mina would be offended, but she only smiled sweetly and replied, 'Did you think we could never forgive each other, Jonathan and I? But as he says, our sins are just the same! It is true our union is not as peaceful as once it was, that we must often comfort each other's nightmares or brood upon our own failings; but neither is it as staid and proper as once it was. For we find in each other at least a little of the wild darkness that lived in Dracula and in Elena. I do not believe that an understanding which yields such joy can possibly be wholly evil. Do you, Dr Seward? And Quincey – Quincey is Jonathan's. We must all believe it.'

It is not for me to condemn them, and indeed, I do not. Nor would Van Helsing, I know, for none of us have been above temptation, not even he.

# Note

What am I to make of this account, which my mother has shown to me on my twenty-first birthday while I am on leave?

She said that she wanted me to know the truth now, while she and Papa are alive to answer my questions – rather than for me to discover these accounts among their papers after their deaths. But I cannot bring myself to ask questions of them, nor even to mention it.

My life has been so happy until today, secure in the tender understanding that has always existed between my parents. But to discover that their intimacy sprang from – from this!

Memories stir now that I had thought long lost. I had forgotten Elena; forgotten my incarceration at Carfax, or rather dismissed everything as some disordered product of my many childhood fevers. Even forgotten, or transformed into some ogre of nightmares, Count Dracula himself.

But now I begin to remember. Once flung open, the casket lid cannot be closed.

Is it possible that I had two fathers – one a saint, one a devil? From which do I take my spirit?

Ah yes, now I remember Elena. Her soft dark hair, her lovely accent, the warmth of her breasts and thighs as she held me upon her knee and stroked my hair with her long, warm fingers. And one day she was no longer there. She vanished into the night.

I cannot believe she is dead.

I have seen death, and it is brought by bullets and shells, not by vampires or wooden stakes or by fiery chasms that are gateways to the realms of the damned.

I must find her again, when this war is over. I must find

Castle Dracula. I will never know who I am until I see their faces again; two pale and dark phantoms, who haunt me yet dissolve whenever I reach out to touch them. I cannot rest until I find the Scholomance itself, and there discover what became of my other father, my dark father, Dracula, the Undead.

– Quincey A. J. J. A. Harker

LaVergne, TN USA
13 June 2010
185878LV00001B/2/P